B

All That Belongs

Also by Dora Dueck from Turnstone Press

What You Get at Home

All That Belongs

Dora Dueck

TURNSTONE PRESS

Turnstone Press
Artspace Building
206-100 Arthur Street
Winnipeg, MB
R3B 1H3 Canada
www.TurnstonePress.com

Turnstone Press gratefully acknowledges the assistance of the Canada Council for the Arts, the Manitoba Arts Council, the Government of Canada through the Canada Book Fund, and the Province of Manitoba through the Book Publishing Tax Credit and the Book Publisher Marketing Assistance Program.

Cover art: *Gertrude* by Agatha Fast.

Printed and bound in Canada. by Friesens.

Library and Archives Canada Cataloguing in Publication

Title: All that belongs / Dora Dueck.
Names: Dueck, Dora, author.
Identifiers: Canadiana (print) 20190150823 | Canadiana (ebook)
    20190150831 | ISBN 9780888016812 (softcover) | ISBN 9780888016829
    (EPUB) | ISBN 9780888016836 (Kindle) | ISBN 9780888016843 (PDF)
Classification: LCC PS8557.U2813 A79 2019 | DDC C813/.54—dc23

MANITOBA ARTS COUNCIL
CONSEIL DES ARTS DU MANITOBA

Canada Council   Conseil des arts
for the Arts   du Canada

Funded by the Government of Canada
Financé par le gouvernement du Canada | Canadä

Manitoba

for
my seven siblings
and
my longtime friend
Eunice Toews Sloan

All That Belongs

Prologue

This is how it started, that year of my preoccupation with the dead.

On my last day of work at the regional archives, just hours before my colleagues whisked me away to my retirement dinner, a couple from Australia stopped in with a request. I was hanging about the reception area with nothing to do—my desk was empty, files cleared—so I greeted them and helped them find the evidence of a second cousin they believed had lived and died in Winnipeg. Not that it matters one way or the other, they said, but since we're travelling through Canada anyway.

They were delighted with what I discovered: a mention in the archives finding aid, a short article about the cousin's appointment to a contractor's firm, the death notice. They told me they'd heard he was a scoundrel and they clapped their hands and laughed, as if this paucity of information confirmed their suspicions. The

Australian woman was small and bony in appearance, clad in a flowing black garment, caftan style, rather too big for her, but she bubbled with eagerness and warmth and this swelled into the dress. I was drawn to her.

After the search, the woman and I discussed genealogy. I asked her how far back she could trace and she said, To the first fleet of them. To the first shipment of convicts.

Your forebears were convicts? I'd completely forgotten in that moment how Australia came to be populated with Europeans.

Oh yes, yes, convicts. There was a lilt in her voice. She said convict as easily as she'd said scoundrel. It may have been for something horridly horrible, she went on, maybe slaying the master or a neighbour. Or as trivial as stealing a rabbit from a rich man's woods.

Her husband, who'd been distracted by files unrelated to the second cousin, lifted his head and chipped in with a bit of a speech. There was a patient of Carl Jung's, he said, who feared to accept things in his life lest they overpower him. But his fear turned out not to be true. As he learned to be receptive to all that belonged to him, good and bad, light and night continuously alternating, his world came alive.

The woman touched his arm. Jung, Jung, she said, as if this was his name. Yes, she told me, Jung and his patient were right. This credo has served us well. She took her husband's hand and began to guide him out, the hem of her dress undulating around her legs like a wave goodbye.

She stopped, called back, You've probably got something in your family too! A little embarrassment! Family trees are rarely reassuring!

I smiled and gestured indecisively and they carried on through the exit. I felt a sensation of judgment rising and pressing against my heart. It felt like the vague heaviness that used to oppress me during evangelistic meetings in my childhood church, an

inchoate insistence to which I always responded with fresh avow-
als of surrender to God. My past seemed unremarkable but I was
ashamed of it nevertheless. My odd Uncle Must. The whole lot of
it, in fact, everything he dragged in his wake, everything in my
chronology, the choke and pother of my earlier self, the losses, my
brother, that slight souring at the edge of every bite. Uncle—yes,
and everything! Circumstance and disappointment, permeating
like yeast.

My assistant Joan was heading my way. She looked plump and
superficial after the tiny woman in black so I pretended I didn't
see her and strode to the window. I stood stiffly and stared out as
if not to be disturbed. I was caught up in the couple's words, in
the personal history that weighted me—suddenly, unexpectedly.
The boulevard trees were almost bare, autumn light between their
branches weak and disconsolate, as if aching for green. That man
and that woman, they'd caught me off guard. As if, released from
these archives, I ought to be ready for my own.

Outside, two boys rolled by on their skateboards, their shouts
like ribbons daring me to grab and hold. So young, I thought. So
young and wonderful! Then they disappeared around the corner.

Had I harboured shame for too long? Been too fearful—of
overpowerment?

You're an archivist, for pity's sake, Jim had remarked to me
once, you ought to be at home with your past. We were at a summer gathering of his family and he and his brothers got each other
going about their childhood, scooping up mutual antics like min-
nows, the pail sluicing over, their voices sounding ever wilder and
happier, reminiscences like tin and clang to me and everyone else
in the family who was sidelined by their hoots of conversation.
Later I chided him. Maybe enough of the boyhood, I said. He'd
tensed and frowned. I saw the lines alongside his nose. Shallow
cracks I hadn't noticed before. I wanted to stroke those runnels
of skin, ponder where the years had gone, but I couldn't risk

touching him after he'd put me on the defensive. I said, I've never had the nerve to consider my past that fascinating. Not like some.

I'd paused, calmed myself, continued, Honestly Jim, for pity's sake indeed, I'm not a rememberer.

And he'd waited too, then said, I don't believe you for a second. But his voice had been fond and it was fine between us again.

Now I heard my colleague Lucy, noisy as she neared. Let's go, let's go! she cried. I told Jute that you and I are leaving early today. He's so busy writing his flowery director's speech about you he couldn't refuse!

I chuckled and turned. Jim slid out of mind, the Australians too. The street outside was empty now, the flow of traffic elsewhere, and perhaps the clouds had blown on, for in my final glance the air seemed radiant. A strange excitement for remembrance, for welcome to all that belonged, stirred in me, nudged against my habitual resistance. It moved in me like the slip of water over stones. I was aware of it moving and rising. And it moved and it moved in me that entire evening, a murmur like arousal, through the feasting, toasts, and many anecdotes of a wonderful dinner in my honour.

1.

That year, I say, with the dead. A year in the school calendar sense, from fall to early summer, because Jim was a teacher and we always visualized time by his schedule. A year of changes colliding. We'd moved some months earlier, my retirement—taken early and ratcheted high with expectations of bliss—came next, and then I'd opened to the past, put my hand on the latch as it were and pushed, that small woman in black fluttering about my head like an annunciating angel. I wanted to open, and I did, but it was nerve-wracking too, because of course my Uncle Must loomed first.

Not Dad. As far as Dad and I were concerned, he rested in peace. And Mom—well, she was still alive that year, so very present tense. But my uncle was past, a man I'd been ashamed of, a man I'd wished to ignore.

And my brother was past as well, insufficiently grieved, and he loomed next.

That year, conscientiously, I remembered them. Though I had no idea, starting out, what this would unearth.

I looked back at them, and I looked at myself looking or not looking. I suppose, in truth, I was mainly looking at myself. I was navigating a new stage of life and it seemed imperative to settle the sway of where I'd travelled before.

Why do you call him that? my school friends would ask. I had an idea but wasn't absolutely sure so I answered that I didn't know. I said his real name was Gerhard but we were used to Uncle Must. I said he came from Russia, as if that would explain the weirdness of things. My friends were mostly Mennonites so their roots also dug in there; they would nod. His English name, I would say, was George. Then I would change the subject.

But now I remembered that supper, me eleven or twelve, all of us around the large oval table in the kitchen, Dad at the head and my uncle just around the curve from him, when the topic of his name came up. Uncle was a bachelor. He lived in a tiny house across the road and ate his evening meals with us. He and my dad had both rolled the sleeves of their blue farm shirts up over their elbows as if they were twins. They'd splashed water on their faces and hair and their caps were off so the tan lines showed across their foreheads. It was hot and Mom, heaping our meal into serving bowls at the stove, glistened in the heat. She was cheerful, though. Cooking made her cheerful.

We had a guest with us: a salesman. He was young and enthusiastic and neatly dressed, his hair sculpted into a stiff mound at the top of his head. Next to Dad and my uncle, his skin looked pale, as if he'd put it on that morning. He clasped and unclasped his hands, then rested them on the table. He acted as if he owned the place but since he was company, he would be excused. I was wearing my coral blouse and what we used to call pedal pushers. Like capris. They were brown. I thought I looked rather nice. Nifty, I thought, fingering the rickrack around my collar.

Earlier, the salesman and Uncle had been hidden away in the living room, examining books and record album sets and packets of pictures and what-not-all. We children weren't permitted in for even a look. Mom said if anything was purchased, our uncle would do the purchasing and it would just look greedy, wouldn't it, us hovering there with our big beggar eyes?

My uncle bought us books. Materials, as our mother said, of educational and moral usefulness for children. He bought the piano as well, especially for me, because I'd shown signs of musical giftedness. It was a regular parlour piano and I was glad for it, and for the books, but I wondered why Uncle Must could afford them when my father couldn't. They farmed together, didn't they?

I was the one who was dispatched to let him know of the salesman's arrival. I found him in the barn. The message seemed to distress him, as if shovelling manure out of a trough was too precious to interrupt. But the salesman had asked for him specifically—George Riediger—and in a jolly manner too, waving a postcard from him as if they were pen pals. You sent him a card, I said. I named the salesman's company.

Oh yes. Yes. His expression altered, turned resolute. He rested the shovel against a post and set off for the house in his strange swift gait, swinging his arms widely as if to help his legs by propelling his body forward. I tried to keep up. The salesman had already been let into the house to set up his wares. I lolled about the kitchen until Mom made me sweep the floor but I took a long slow time with it, concentrating on the tones of appeal and approval I heard in the salesman's fervent voice behind the door. I loved to read and was sure I would want everything he had on offer.

Eventually there was more approval than appeal in what I heard and then Uncle emerged and rushed back to the barn. He looked resigned and satisfied and I felt vindicated for disturbing his work. The salesman packed up slowly and seemed satisfied too. Lugging his cases through the kitchen, he discovered one thing after another to discuss with my mother and finally she invited him to stay for supper. Which explained his presence at our table that day.

Grace was barely said when the salesman announced—looking from me to Darrell and back again—that a volume of the biographies of good characters and famous people would arrive for us every month in the mail. And every month a book of nature stories too, all of this thanks to our uncle. The salesman listed people and subjects we would learn about: inspiring folk like Johnny Appleseed and Helen Keller, animals like tigers and walruses, matters such as volcanoes and condensation. And so on and so on. His lips were wide and white. I'd never seen anyone's lips move as much as his did while he spoke. I might be scolded for it later but they riveted me. His sentences seemed to pile up and stay above his head, like people's words in comic strips. When he finished explaining the books, filling his plate as he went, he ordered me and Darrell to thank our uncle, and it was actually a relief, the chance to move my lips to speak as well, and out it came from the two of us and our younger sister Lorena too, a ragtag chorus of Thank you Uncle Must.

Uncle was busy eating, however, and seemed unaware of what we'd said.

Our children are rather precocious, I'm afraid, Mom told the salesman. He smiled. I repeated *precocious* in my head so I could look it up in my school dictionary later. It sounded positive, but maybe not.

The salesman directed further commentary to our uncle, as if he knew better than we did that Uncle Must was paying attention, even though it was clear that he wasn't. Between every bite the young man's colourless lips formed descriptions of the products he displayed throughout the whole province of Alberta. He said that everything his company did was designed for the educational advancement of families like ours. He said that people snapped his products up. They were amazed at the possibilities. He said *nowadays* a lot and when he reached the end of his lists of books and albums, he began again. He must have thought that since our uncle George Riediger paid for the books, he was the main man in the house, and all the while Dad was eating and smiled at the salesman now and then and seemed relaxed, like he was glad he could stay out of it.

I'd overheard Mom once say that Uncle Must was shy at the best of times but he might as well be absent for all he pitched in, talking-wise, at meals. This was true. He ate in peck-like bites with the self-absorbed manner of someone eating alone, swabbing steadily at his mouth with a napkin as if grateful for this one companion. He and my father and guests got cloth napkins at their places. For the rest of us, Mom kept a wet dishcloth beside her plate that she handed to the child whose chin or mouth required it. Sometimes she just reached over and wiped the offending face herself. Which I abhorred.

That day, besides quiet, my uncle looked morose. He was more than inattentive, I decided; he was weary of the salesman's chatter and the repetition of his name, George this and George that, and the way the salesman's lips pushed out to fondle it. Not that Uncle Must was looking, but he surely heard the Georges bunching up. Maybe he was thinking that since he'd agreed to the monthly volumes, he hardly needed to be flattered again. By then I was tiring of the salesman myself and beginning to sympathize with my uncle's bad manners.

Lorena's voice, child-high and innocent, interrupted the flow. He says George! she cried, pointing a chubby finger first at the salesman and then at our uncle. He's not George! He's Uncle Must!

Lorena was four and sounded smart for her age. I wanted to

laugh. Maybe we all did. I dared not look around. There was an uncertain silence until my mother passed the gravy to the salesman for his second helping of potatoes and then she told him, in a rush it seemed to me, that the children—referring to Darrell and me—couldn't pronounce our uncle's name when we were young so he became our Uncle Must. And that was how it stayed. She told him that the two oldest—again meaning Darrell and me—were only thirteen months apart. When we were little, she said, we two did everything together, even learning to talk.

Darrell grinned and set down his fork. It meant he had something to say. I went along with you to his house, he told Mom. You had a loaf of bread for him. Uncle said he was eating already. And you said, That's not food, that's mush. So all the way back, across the road and up the lane, I repeated it like a song, my Uncle-Mush, my Uncle–Mush.

Mom said, It was cornmeal. Porridge. He was having cornmeal for lunch.

Darrell picked up his fork but laid it down again without taking a bite and once more he had the look of speechmaking about him, that junior high, smarty-pants attitude he was beginning to show. The words became his name, he said. Mush became Must. This is what happens to words and languages over time. They change. They get corrupted. Mush to Must.

Darrell emphasized the final consonant.

Corrupted! The salesman punched this out as if in awe, as if he'd discovered Darrell was no commonplace boy but a prince. Now here's a young man, George, he said, who would benefit from that large-volume dictionary I showed you. You'll remember that it comes as a bonus when you buy the encyclopedia.

Someday my brother would fancy himself a poet, but on this day I was sure he had concocted a tale as tall and ridiculous as the Paul Bunyan stories we were reading in school, even if Mom had supported his explanation with her reference to cornmeal. I might be younger than Darrell by thirteen months, but I was just as smart. *Must* originated with me!

Although the salesman had snatched up Darrell's word, he seemed disinterested in Uncle's alternate name. He was marvelling over Mom's fried chicken. Delicious, delectable, flavourful, he said, as if compliments were *his* linguistic specialty. And the vegetables in white sauce, quite wonderful. While the compliments marched out of him he was sneaking glances at the apple pie biding its time on the counter. I seized my opportunity when he reached for the last piece of chicken.

No, I declared, I was playing in the barn and then I saw him. He was walking around in the pig pen—

Mom jumped in. The used-to-be pig pen? She believed children should be allowed to talk at the table, to improve their conversational skills. It was the current approach and she concurred completely. Better than how she and Dad were raised: permitted to be seen, not heard.

I felt uneasy that the subject of my upcoming speech was seated at the table but on I went. There were no pigs in it then, I said, and it wasn't messy either, and he—he was walking from one corner to the other! Diagonally, I said, so the salesman would know I was capable of bigger words too and would also benefit from the large-volume dictionary that came as a bonus with the encyclopedia. I felt disapproval in the air but my story was up like a kite and I had to let it fly. I could still see the beat-down posture of my uncle's head, the black wool hat in his hands, his body whipping with each corner's turn as if struck. I'd come upon him unawares and he hadn't noticed me standing in the opening of the pen. I was scared at first, then quiet as a stone.

I could feel the scene. (Feeling was *my* specialty.) The walls of the enclosure high and prison-like, the barn dim but sunlight sliding through slits, a-float with motes of dust, assuring me that all would be well in spite of the beating and repeating voice within.

I'd grasped my smallness on the threshold of the pen, the mistake of me so near, but I was sure of my safety in those peaceful lines of light.

I looked boldly at the salesman. Every time he turned, I said, he shouted I must! I must! I must! So I called him Uncle Must. Then Darrell did too. And all of us did. Everyone!

I wanted to add that nothing about the word was corrupted but realized I'd said enough.

I glanced at my uncle, who'd raised his head. Injury crossed his face, swift as a gopher peeking out of its hole and diving down again.

Oh, that look! His startled eyes met mine for a moment, something vulnerable in them, weak, previously strange, severe, distant, even passionate, but never susceptible to me before. My thoughts in response were perplexed and defensive. Didn't everyone know—especially Uncle Must—that it was me, not Darrell, who gave him his name? And why would it bother him? Didn't he know he was peculiar? *I* knew he was peculiar—not stupid, and obviously richer than my father, but certainly peculiar—and since *I* knew, he must know it too. Didn't adults know the things about themselves that were clearly known by others? Had he thought his mutterings in the pig pen a secret when we'd been calling him Uncle Must for what seemed like eternity by now?

In the turmoil of my confusion I loathed him for the first time in memory. His face ruddy and intense as if flushed to exhaustion! Those brows! Thick as fence posts. And my loathing confused me too, for if peculiar, he'd also preached on occasion, and wasn't he on a church committee or something? Peculiar and religious weren't incompatible, it seemed, so what right did I have to loathe? I worried what the salesman would think of our family when he drove off, what he would think of my uncle. Of me. I was sick and tired of his taffy-pulling mouth, and the books had been purchased and would soon be coming monthly in the mail, but I wanted him to think I was smart. And cute. Me in my coral blouse with rickrack and my brown pedal pushers!

A tiny mountain of potatoes streaked with gravy sat suspended on Uncle's fork between his plate and his mouth. It seemed to bother him. He twitched slightly and pulled it toward himself and then his mouth opened and once more his focus was downward to his eating and he might as well be gone for all that he was there.

Darrell muttered disdainfully in my ear. I must what? Must what?

Dad cleared his throat. Darrell and Catherine, he said, enough! The modern, participatory methods had their limits and apparently we'd reached them. For the rest of the meal the conversation would exist in the adult realm and my brother and I wouldn't be able to argue it out. He glared at me and I returned the glare and so it ended in a tie. But yes: *must what?* Darrell had poked a question at me I'd never considered. To me, the force of my uncle's exclamations in the pen were their very meaning, the *must* self-evident. Just that he must, whatever.

2.

I told Jim over dinner one evening that I'd been thinking about my uncle and I could tell he was pleased by this and the back-and-forth that ensued. We'd decided to retire more or less simultaneously, which he'd proceeded to do in June and I'd proceeded to do just recently, in September, but then the school board persuaded him to fill a contract position for a year. He would teach music as before, but fill gaps in a number of schools. Sure, I'd agreed to it—it was obvious how thrilled he was—but now I was on my own for something we'd planned to accomplish together and I resented it. At least a little. And I suppose he felt responsible. The signs of my developing curiosity, a possible new focus, must have encouraged him.

At any rate, we sat over our fish and potatoes and salad that evening and attempted between the two of us to figure out when we'd last considered Uncle Must in any kind of sustained way. We realized it was fifteen years ago, around the time of his bizarre, mysterious death—when he drowned, disappeared, or whatever it was that did him in. And, of course, around the time of the memorial service my parents hosted in their living room, when I tried my best for their sakes to lament his passing.

Mom had answered the door that Saturday and it frightened her, she told me later, two policemen on the doorstep, asking to enter and was her husband home. It was the weekend, so yes he was, and they came in and took seats, and she was going nearly crazy, she said, wondering what they wanted, after everything she'd been through already. By which she meant what she'd been through with my brother. When they finally got down to business, the men informed her and Dad that Dad's brother George Riediger was missing, probably dead. Drowned, they presumed, on the basis of the overturned canoe and the life jacket with his name on it, which he'd clearly neglected to wear. A red life jacket, tattered and stained with oil. They found it lapping at the shore, and his ancient blue pickup parked on the service road leading to the lake. Not a lake that people went to much, the policemen said. So after they left, Mom had called me with the news, and she told me how they came inside, those two pleasant constables, how they accepted her offer of coffee and baking, how they praised her cinnamon buns. Fresh out of the oven. She was glad she'd had something warm and yummy to serve. They sat down with her and Dad, grateful for the seats and her offer of coffee and food— they must have smelled the cinnamon—and maybe it was coffee break anyway and then they went over it, the evidence at their disposal. They weren't in a hurry. The situation had been investigated, could be investigated further if required, but foul play was not suspected. Nor did they expect to recover the body. Not with the partially iced-up water and other factors like the lake having an under-surface tow.

They came on behalf of a northern detachment, my mother

said, the one responsible for the Gilly Lake area where Uncle lived at the time. Though it wasn't Gilly Lake he drowned in but a smaller lake maybe fifteen minutes away. They were sympathetic, comforting in an official sort of way. Mom said she and Dad had decided they wouldn't provide others with details, except to say he was dead. If pushed they would say, Looks like he drowned, and then clam up.

My mother always worried what people would think.

Uncle died the year before my folks moved into the city, so the call from Marble to me in Winnipeg was long distance and every silent second would be sure to distress her, but I'd asked her to hold on. Jim had been vacuuming in the bedroom and the whine of it suddenly seemed intolerable. I didn't say the reason, just interrupted her. Said, Hold on, please. If I'd told Mom my husband was vacuuming, her disapproval would have dived at me through the line like a swallow. In her world, men never vacuumed. What would be the point?

While I hurried to the bedroom, emotion welled up inside me. I was actually afraid I would burst into tears. But I didn't, I held them back, and after that it was like the emotion had been sealed off. I unplugged the machine and muttered to my slave-husband doing the carpet that it was Mom on the phone with news. I'll tell you later, I said.

When I was back at the call with Mom, she continued from where she'd been forced to stop. She spoke more quickly now, as if afraid I would put her on hold again. She informed me that she and Dad wouldn't tell me and my sister Lorena much more than the basics either. We all had to accept the policemen's report. They couldn't go searching—they were hours from the lake.

Then she asked, Do you remember that Miller woman? Who took over his house back in Tilia?

Of course.

Did you know that she lives up there? In Gilly Lake?

I could imagine my mother, phone held tightly to her ear with one hand and the other lifting or pointing or swirling about. She couldn't speak without her hands. The motions would be small and tidy though. And she would be standing. Telephone talk was a duty, not something to get comfortable about. I guess they're not suspicious, she said, but that doesn't mean I can't think my own thoughts.

I knew a tug-of-war was going on inside her, between a longing to elaborate and some warning Dad had probably given her to keep her opinions to herself. She couldn't help herself though, she had to say it. She had to say that she and Dad knew Uncle Must gave money to that woman—that Miller woman. Not much, no, there was actually very little money left. But still, police people look through papers and bank accounts when they investigate a death. They'd searched for the next-of-kin information right off the bat and Dad was pained by the fact that it took them a while to discover him. Pained to hear that his name wasn't plainly in sight, after their closeness as brothers. There were only the two of them.

She paused, and then she backtracked, as I'd expected she would. Dad won't want me telling you this, she said, about that Sharon Miller. You won't say anything, will you, Catherine? The policemen explained everything and the woman's been cleared. Both of us believe them.

She paused again, then said, Well, he helped *us* too. Financially, I mean. I should have mentioned that. He didn't need very much for himself.

I think we can trust the police to know what they're doing, I told her. An accident's an accident.

Then, a month later, when it seemed certain there wouldn't be a body, my parents held a service in their house. They couldn't bring themselves to use the church. Not with the lack of resolution they felt. A dozen mourners sat awkwardly on the brown country-style sofa and armchairs and the straight-backed dining chairs hauled into the room: Mom and Dad, four of their friends, several step-cousins, the minister of their congregation, and me and my sister. Lorena had come to Marble the day before to help our parents, even though she was too young when Uncle Must lived with us to have much of a connection with him.

Not like you, Catherine, she said.

We didn't have a connection!

Well, you knew him at least.

This irritated me but it wasn't the time to lecture her on the semantics of knowing and not knowing and connecting and not connecting.

I'd driven down the morning of. Jim was in the States that week, on tour with his school choir and band. He was conductor and teacher-chaperone and couldn't rearrange the commitment just because an uncle had died and Mom and Dad decided it was time to have a memorial, not even checking to see if it suited.

Mom had purchased white flowers and greens from a local shop and arranged them in her best vase. She'd done a lovely job of it; the roses were plump and beautiful, the carnations perfectly fresh and delicate. The flowers served as a focal point for the circle of guests. We made small talk about them until it was time to begin. Then we circulated three photos Mom had rummaged up—Uncle Must as young, middle-aged, older. The minister had never met the deceased but seemed a kind young man and did his inexperienced best. He read from the Gospel of John, the story of Mary and Martha and the raising of Lazarus. He made some remarks on *Jesus wept*. He said a prayer. Afterward, there was coffee and dainty sandwiches and a great variety of sweets.

I reminded Jim now that he'd called me from Chicago the evening of the service.

Jim complimented the fish and Yes, he said, he vaguely recollected the call.

The fish is pickerel, I told him unnecessarily. I added that I rather enjoyed cooking since ending my career. Cooking, I said, makes me cheerful, just like Mom. Though the cheer could have been a cover for what she felt was thwarted in her. Maybe it's that for me as well.

Jim raised his eyebrows but didn't react further and we went on to reminisce about the fact that I'd talked at length during that call between Marble and Chicago about my four-hour trip to my parents' home. I said I'd enjoyed the drive alone. Fog in the morning, not thick enough to be a problem, more like dust in the air. Towns along the highway in their usual sleepy condition. Traffic sparse. The pea-green tones of the landscape because spring was on the way.

He'd asked about the service. Ah yes, the service. The service was rather generic, I said. Probably disappointing for the folks. And I'd been seated across from that painting! The reproduction, that is. Wilderness lake, no people in sight, just water and trees. Nature in a tranquil pose as sold by lower-end furniture stores. Meant to inspire, or pacify perhaps. But all I saw again and again as my eyes drifted to it, frequently, as if lured, was the northern lake where Uncle met his end. As if my parents had prophetically purchased a picture of his grave. I kept seeing him spread-eagled on the bottom, his eyes wide open, like wide, wide—

Catherine, Jim had interrupted. To caution me.

Well it appalls me, I'd replied, a man of eighty-six setting out in a canoe.

Maybe, he said. Maybe not.

It's not a mystery and even if it is, we're not about to solve it.

It *is* a mystery but don't worry, Catherine, I'm not about to get involved. Your side.

My side of the family. Right. Thanks a lot, Jim.

Then I'd asked about the tour, whether the kids were behaving, and he mentioned a couple of things, but not much. It was the day of the memorial and he must have thought we ought to spend our conversational capital on the deceased; he returned to that. But I hadn't come up with much to say about Uncle. He'd been too large in my childhood, in my youth, and then, as it were, we both left home. I certainly never missed him. He'd seemed old for a very long time and now he was over.

I followed the river trail to the Legislative building, climbed the stairs to the sidewalk, crossed the bridge into Osborne Village. I was on my way to meet former colleague Lucy for coffee. She'd just retired from the Archives herself, abruptly and unexpectedly. We'd already talked about it by phone but I wanted to hear everything again: what prompted her decision and how it went down with Daniel Jute and the rest of them at the centre. I knew we would spend the entire time discussing our late place of work and looked forward to this; I think we were both nostalgic about it already.

While walking, however, I thought about my uncle. It was the day after Jim and I had recovered—exhaustively, it seemed to me—memories of his death and the subsequent service. Now, however, I searched beyond what we'd revived over our pickerel dinner. I recalled that the last time I'd seen Uncle was three or four years prior to his disappearance, during an Easter weekend when Jim and I visited my parents. Stooped and lean he'd been, a wobble of bones. Otherwise as formless as a ghost. I couldn't recall anything he said, if indeed he spoke. I'd made no effort to engage with him. By that point, he could be pitied.

There was a lily in the house, for the season, and I remembered how the evening fragrance from the waxy, open blooms spun like gossamer toward us while Jim and I chatted with my parents, Uncle Must out of sight in the main floor guest room like an infant tucked in early. I remembered how happy Dad was that entire weekend. When he stepped outside to meet us his enthusiasm seemed disproportionate, his hellos too loud. He was wearing the green checkered flannel shirt we'd given him for Christmas. Was it us and that shirt? Then I saw Uncle's truck in the driveway and realized it was his brother's arrival, not ours, that accounted for my father's energetic joy. This had deflated me.

I remembered Mom's festive spread: ham slathered in raisin sauce, fruit soup loaded with cherries, her unbeatable potato salad, her Easter bread. Uncle Must would have relished my mother's cooking too, after so many years away from it, though it would have taken more than a weekend to fatten him up. He was thin. A decrepit old man who could easily tumble out of a canoe and never find his way through ice slush to the surface. An old man who would lie stunned at the bottom of a lake, eyes permanently open to register indignation or fluster.

I remembered further back, to the leaflets. When he lived with us. I was sixteen, maybe seventeen. I never glanced his way in those years, did I? Too irritated, wary, mortified, couldn't-care-less. But too quickly cowed and affected. Leaflets like those paper bombs dropped out of airplanes, propaganda in the modern wars, information for welfare of civilians, or to threaten, disturb morale, prepare them for surrender. Well, not exactly leaflets, but the same idea. Pieces of paper he wrote on and left by my plate or slid into a school book or even handed me directly. They'd seemed quaint at first, mildly bewildering but easy to ignore, Mom tut-tutting, You know he means well. They said *Be ye kind* or *Love one another*, bits of advice I'd memorized years ago in Sunday school.

They got longer and more explicit. *She that liveth in pleasure is dead while she liveth* after I spent the day giggling around Tilia with my friends and he happened to drive by. *Chaste conversation coupled with fear* after some similar flippancy somewhere or other, and *foolish and unlearned questions avoid* out of nowhere, and *not with braided hair, or gold, or pearls, or costly array* when I sported some new accessory. Words like a rain-sogged ceiling sagging ever lower, me bending underneath. Half-goaded into guilt. As if in fact he'd received divine orders to let me know. But I wasn't a difficult teen! I might be proud, maybe self-satisfied, maybe goofy sometimes, but I wasn't extreme. Good grief, it was a sleepy, sheltered town in Alberta I lived my teen years in, not Toronto or San Francisco!

I'd assumed Darrell received some leaflet admonitions too, but then I discovered he didn't, and when they got more pointed, when they were no longer fragments of text but *your skirt is too short* and *silence becomes you* and all of them in the most elegant handwriting, like hoary oracles in ink, I found myself crying bitterly in front of my mother—I'm trying, Mom, I wailed, I'm trying to be good—and she said, as she always did to console me, You know he means it well, but that one time she hugged me and let me weep and she registered alarm, as if the crying had finally resolved her on behalf of her daughter, and after that the messages stopped. So she or Dad must have talked to him.

Newly retired, I bought myself an expensive notebook. A Moleskine in red. It made me happy—the look and feel of it, the brand—but I wasn't sure what I wanted to do with it.

Not for me, growing up, those little five-year diaries with miniscule flaps and locks and keys, their four or five lines per day, which my girlfriends kept. We all got diaries like that for Christmas one year and when I opened mine I acted excited. But I couldn't bear to write in it. It reminded me of a tiny suitcase for trinkets. Word trinkets. I found my own way to be special. To be myself. Only extraordinary days, I decided, written on foolscap and stapled and folded and kept in a box. An extraordinary day could take reams and reams of paper, it could wander backward and forward into other days from the perching point of any moment. An extraordinary day might be a day in which something important or interesting happened, but any day in which I felt the urge to write would qualify. I felt my very thoughts contained the tincture of the extraordinary, that was the point, and extraordinary, too, the act of writing them out.

Later, in that sneering, casual manner most of us treat our even slightly-younger selves, I burned the pages along with the other detritus of the Big House when my family moved provinces, from Alberta to Manitoba. I'd re-read them and was dismayed at their ramble and gush. I hadn't kept a diary or journal of any kind since.

I sat at the dining table with my lovely new book and slipped its elastic band on and off. The balcony door was ajar. I had the time and this beautiful book and ordinary things might be extraordinary still but I was scared to entrust myself to paper lest I crumble, before I knew it, into silliness again. I listened; again and again I glanced outside. Felt pleased with the place we lived. Fort Street, sixteenth floor and facing east. The building's lower levels with their copious pillars, lions, and statues of heroes and maidens were irksome, yes—pretentious—but *Old World charm and castle motif, etc., etc.* had nothing whatsoever to do with my compact and well-decorated rooms and I certainly had not tired of the view: the bustle of the train station and the Forks beneath me in the foreground, St. Boniface across the river, Transcona a shimmer in the distance. The very notion of *view* suggested perspective. Possibility. After selling our little house in East Kildonan and moving up here, I finally had a view of my own. I caught myself humming sometimes, surveying it. A love hum to Winnipeg.

It gave me a sense of security too. High, but like a cave. And an agreeable sense of transience, being renters. Not even once had I regretted the apartment. Even if Jim wasn't completely convinced.

As if he ever spent much time in it.

I heard the traffic far below and it sounded like wind. Those two pleasant constables told my parents there'd been no wind the day that Uncle went missing. No wind at the lake when he (probably) drowned. I couldn't recall why this mattered.

But wind. My childhood was full of wind and mostly I loved

it. Wind the size of a cup, the size of a barrel, whirlwinds twisting up dust on field or road. Look, look! my friends and I would yell like the Dick and Jane of our school readers as the dervishes went mad. Mild chinook winds from the Rockies like mischief, melting the snow. Pouring in through the air holes at the bottom of the storm window one evening when I fancied the aroma of something tropical—coconut or pineapple—which made me wonder how far chinook winds travelled to reach Alberta. How far from wherever they began, to this, our farm two miles from Tilia at the edge of the prairies? To our house, splendid on its rise like a monument, over a landscape that sloshed and tipped like water in a bowl? Pretty land—rolling land, it was called, as if the foothills were alive and tumbling merrily around our Tilia, the village nearest us, though we usually simply called it Town.

One Saturday morning, we bundled up and set off down the lane. It was a curving-down lane lined with poplars. The whole family was together and I thought we were leaving for an adventure. Maybe like Christiana and her band in *Little Pilgrim's Progress*, which Mom was reading to Darrell and me. Off to the Wicket Gate and the Celestial City beyond it and any number of escapades enroute. But halfway down the lane Dad told me we were going to Uncle's to plant a hedge. That's all it was. From the two-storey farmhouse we called the Big House down to his house, the room-and-a-half shack that hunched across the road. He had a solitary poplar on his yard, like a castoff from our row of trees. Otherwise the ground was bare. The road between our place and his was no major thoroughfare, but he must have felt exposed to passing local traffic. He'd decided he needed a hedge.

He burst out to meet us and then he and Dad began to spade out holes in a line along one side of the house, along the front, and in a curve beside the driveway to the stoop that served as his porch. Mom handed Darrell and me each an old serving spoon. We lifted out the caragana seedlings Uncle had started in a cold frame and carried them into the holes, one at a time. We pushed the spaded-out earth back around each plant to hold it firm. It was a slow and boring operation. It seemed too difficult for me. It bothered me that Darrell was industrious instead of grousing but I clenched my jaw and kept quiet, though peeps of my whining must have escaped.

Mom walked around with Lorena in her arms and supervised the two of us. Lorena was a baby, just a few months old. She was wrapped in a soft white blanket. She was a precious child to us because I was eight years old and this is how long it had taken Mom to have another baby, when she'd been wanting one all that time. Mom's hair was tucked behind a black and tan patterned scarf made of some kind of shiny fabric. Before we set out from the Big House, she'd pulled another scarf from a hook in the entrance and handed the baby over to Dad for *half a minute* in order to wrap the scarf around my head. She tied it with a large bow at my throat and giggled, as if we were matching Audrey Hepburns. The gesture had misled me about the morning, especially now that she walked around instead of helping, just opening and closing the slit of the baby's blanket to let in a bit of air and the warmth of her voice. She bobbed at the baby like a crow poking at a patch of shrinking snow, and in between she looked up and prodded me and my brother on to the next seedling, the next hole.

The wind was chilly, a continual sting. It tore Mom's voice into shreds. She was inconsistent, too faint or too shrill. She repeated herself. She told us how to lift the seedlings out of the starter soil and into our spoons, how to carry, hold, protect the roots. Soon my mittens were caked with earth and stiffening into cardboard. I took them off. My bare hands cramped in the cold and dirt. I hated the choking sensation of soil against my skin and under my nails. The earth I pushed around the seedlings was hard and lumpy. Spiteful. My mother seemed to think it was easy. She said to loosen the dirt, break the lumps with our fingers. And all she had to do was coo at Lorena and command us. When I pushed the scarf off my head, Mom said I shouldn't, I'd be sorry, and she was right. My hair turned into slapping streamers in the wind. I asked to change places but Mom said no, the baby was fussy. She said we were doing an excellent job. She promised to mix up a batch of sugar cookies when we got back to the house. She said Dad would help us with the planting once the holes were measured and dug. She said we were nearly done.

It seemed to take forever and when we were finished, the row of stalks with their tiny leaves looked pathetic.

Uncle Must constantly moved among us, deliberate and persevering. Since it was his hedge he seemed to like it, small and ugly as it was. When done with his digging he followed us along the row with a pail and dipper and watered the seedlings. He put the dipper close to each plant so the wind wouldn't tear the water away. He sometimes adjusted a stalk, or pressed the earth more tightly.

Then, that sensation of suddenly seeing someone—a person familiar, known—as if a total stranger, which had not happened to me before and has never happened since. That jolt of otherness, that doubling which cannot be consciously produced. The impression was unforgettable. I was done my work and had plunked down on the ground while waiting for something better to happen, like going back to the Big House, for instance. I was twisting the old spoon between my fingers when I glanced up to see a man in front of me, a tall, thin man dressed for labour, dark navy work pants and boots and a jacket and cap, dark hair sticking out, his features dark as well and looking as strong as metal, though not unusual otherwise in a physical way. What I perceived in the man, however, young though I was, was an aura of concentration and longing so fevered it struck me as a warning. I couldn't have articulated it then, but I would have stepped aside to give him wider berth if he'd been coming toward me, and the most surprising reason came into my head. He's petrified, I thought. He's scared. His head tipped imploringly upward, as if he saw something or someone in the sky. I didn't dare a peek, though, to see if it were true.

The man moved forward and then he was merely our usual Uncle Must, methodically watering twigs. I felt cranky again. Dad was using his spade like a bolster and informing us that the plantings were Siberian pea shrub, though people called them caragana. I heard *Siberian* and expected my father to wander into the story of our long-ago and faraway relatives, the ones who were banished to Siberia because they didn't get out of Russia in time like he and his brother did when they were young. Dad told stories like that to make us grateful.

I wasn't grateful that morning. Why were we helping my uncle when it was *his* job to help *us*? Didn't he show up at our house at breakfast each day, like a servant, before he and my father went off together to do whatever farmers did? I envied my mother and baby sister, snuggling as if fused together. What paradise a mother's power and affection seemed to me! I felt I'd never been cuddled and consoled as Lorena was, even though Mom told me more than once that I'd been a beautiful baby and smiling all the time. I sat there and I watched and I counted off the pairs: Mom and her baby Lorena, Dad and his firstborn Darrell. Which left me and Uncle Must.

How unjust it was. And the wind that day, so vicious.

3.

If I was going to look back and face all that was mine, if I was going to be receptive in hopes of a better position on things, I would have to enlist the help of my mother—Edna Riediger—while she had some memory left. So there I was, striding past the front desk of Maplebend Seniors Home—the receptionist giving me a sharp glance to make sure I was elder-friendly—and down the long hallway with its gentle blues and beiges and sunshine streaming in through windows that faced the street, my boot heels clack-clacking past an old man shuffling behind his walker, past a grim circle of semi-slumped residents in their wheelchairs in the recreation room. My steps always quickened the moment I entered the Home. I would find myself as brisk and conscious of my competence as Florence Nightingale with her succor and lamp. Far from old myself, I insisted, and ready to do my duty: *honour your (father and) mother.*

Goodness' sakes, I thought then, I'm retired, so what's the rush? I slowed dramatically. I turned into Mom's corridor, strolled down it like an evening in Paris. Took in the sights. A laundry cart, a lift apparatus, a *Caution: Wet Floor* sandwich sign, people motionless in chairs or beds, their names in framed boxes outside their rooms, along with a keepsake or photo of themselves. Usually at a younger age. *This is how I used to be* standing in for *this is me*.

My mother sat in her wheelchair in her room, reading the paper. She squealed when she saw me as if I'd been absent for months. Her hands flew up and the sheets of newsprint slithered apart and drifted and settled around her chair. Her smile quivered at the edges, like a pulse. She was deeply lined and jowly, her skin had zero elasticity left, but that dazzling smile, like a flower blooming in gravel! Her best feature.

I stepped over the sheets of paper and leaned in to kiss her cheek. She smelled like curdled milk and, on closer view, I saw her teeth and gum lines were clogged with food.

Catherine, she said, he fell like a cork!

Who fell like a cork?

My husband Jake. Your father.

Oh, okay. I figured you were talking about something in the news.

Cork was light and would bounce, and I'd always imagined my father's death—tumbling from a ladder while cleaning the second storey eaves, which he'd no business doing alone—as thudding and mordant. Like a tree biting and wounding other trees as it fell.

I crouched to retrieve the newspaper, ordered and folded the pages.

I've been waiting and waiting, my mother said.

I'm here the same time as always.

I've been sitting here for ages. Since breakfast.

Same time as always, Mom. Morning visits now, since I ended my job.

I've waited for ages.

Honestly, what I needed at that exact moment was for a Maplebend aide to pop into the room and assure me that Edna Riediger was sharp as a whistle. Which she generally might have been, yes, just the beginning of dementia, the head nurse had advised me and Lorena. Very early, she'd said, speaking matter-of-factly, as if dementia wasn't the gargoyle of a word for her that it was for me. Talking like it was a cold sore that would soon clear up, as cold sores do.

Early and mild, I reminded myself. And speaking of whistle—Dad was the whistler. He'd whistled while he worked, which had always seemed to me, as a child, a splendidly hopeful way of existing in the world. Uncle Must never whistled, though I heard him singing now and then, under his breath, a baleful monotone, pious and pessimistic. A hymn, I assumed, German most likely, text and tune like stumbling along in a sorrowful ditch. Like a soundtrack to the *Martyrs Mirror*, that chronicle of early Anabaptist suffering with its graphic illustrations of burnings, beheadings, live burials, and drownings displayed on the parlour table at my aunt and uncle's in Idaho—Mom's family—because *that* uncle came from the Swiss branch of the Mennonites, unlike Dad's, which traced back through Russia and Prussia, and before that, probably to the Netherlands. For the Swiss branch, the tome of martyrs' suffering was second only to the Bible. I spent hours with it one summer while we holidayed with the Idaho relatives.

My mother didn't whistle and the only time she sang was during church services they held at Maplebend. But *sharp as a whistle* some staff would announce in front of my Edna Riediger, voices elevated though her hearing was good. A matter of comparison, I supposed, many at the facility lost to Alzheimer's and other diseases. Mom landed there because of osteoarthritis, and the broken left leg, then hip, for which she had emergency surgery, nothing healing as well as was hoped. Mobility issues, in health-care-speak.

Issues! As if she were a bulging dossier of movement variables awaiting a thesis.

The tremors in her hands were also getting worse.

We conversed a while, disjointedly, then set off on a walk along the Maplebend hallways. Down my streets, Mom said. She could still maneuver her wheelchair but she let me push her. We exchanged words—or confusion—with other residents and hellos with passing staff, studied announcements and the latest obituaries at the bulletin board, returned the folded newspaper. The sections she'd grabbed today were four days old. It can't be helped, she said, there's a man who always gets the daily paper first, he hides it behind his back so no one can find it.

I halted at the birdcage. I liked the budgies but Mom told me she didn't and reached for her wheels to get moving again. The birds chirped fretfully behind us as if the antipathy were mutual.

We reached the formal sitting room: drapes-drawn dim and quiet, stiff blue and rose sofas, fireplace, piano, and shelves of Reader's Digest Condensed Books, every book the same height for the decorative effect of an old manor library. Barely settled, I began. What was it with Uncle Must? I asked. I mean …

Mom registered the question. Her expression seemed sly at first, then disapproving. She made that clucking noise she'd perfected over the decades. I think you could drop that name by now, she said. He's gone and you're a grown woman.

The rebuke unexpectedly heartened me, like an antiseptic swipe that would keep me and my uncle germ-free in subsequent encounters. It's what I'm used to, I said. But what in the world was wrong with him? I mean, was he just off-beat or inhibited or something, or was there a name for it? Obsessive-compulsive? Some years there, I was just so bothered. Though you probably didn't realize. I barely realized myself. What comes back to you, Mom?

About what?

Uncle Must.

Who cares about Uncle Must?

Was this a wee spot of dementia or just Mom's routine stubbornness?

Oh I don't know, I said. I reached for something inconsequential. For example, I said, I remember how Dad always said, Good morning, Brother, when Uncle Must came in the house. Like he was comfortable with him.

Well of course he was. They were brothers.

But I don't recall Dad using his name. He said Brother, and that sounded strange to me. But kind of special too. But Uncle said, Good morning, Jake. He always said Jake.

Well, every morning for breakfast, when the hens were laying, your father ate four eggs. He liked them soft and runny.

My mother rooted about in the crocheted bag she always kept on her person, as if a woman's need for a purse, once developed, was absolute. Have I ever told you how we met, she asked, how we nearly didn't marry?

Yes, Mom, you certainly have. You don't have to tell me again.

In fact, we kids must have heard it once a year at least, like an anniversary ritual our parents tag-teamed through: how Edna showed up in Tilia, Alberta from Idaho because her sister lived there at the time, how she spotted Jake Riediger, or he spotted her—he'd left his father's home in Manitoba to farm with his brother who lived in the area—and just like that they were attracted, so he claimed in front of us—he the handsome immigrant boy from Russia and she the lovely, spirited American. He'd noticed her smile. Irresistible, he told us, though it was her he meant to tease. Mom would say she couldn't remember what she'd noticed first. She was nineteen to his twenty-six when they married; she blamed her relative youthfulness for her hazy recollection of the finer details of their romance. But she'd had her reservations too, and if Dad was relaxed in the telling and Mom coquettish, the reason tumbled out.

She was speaking of it now, in a non-sequential jumble. I knew it all, how Dad unrolled his dreams to Edna as any beau will: he and his brother farming grain and other crops with chickens and a cow or two besides, for fresh cream and butter and milk, and the surplus to sell for cash. He wanted a cow because he was fond of cottage cheese *vrenike*, cream gravies, noodles. Dad was fond of these dishes and Mom could giggle about it later but in Mennonite custom—in *Jake's* version of Mennonite custom at least—milking was a woman's job, and blissful young Edna, while she rallied to dreams of a farm with a garden and chickens, and certainly cooking and canning and sewing, had never learned to milk. She was a town girl and proud of it. Leaning her head against some hairy hide, some bovine beast, touching and pulling on teats! Brave young Edna, eager to be a submissive wife, couldn't visualize any circumstance whatsoever that would make her stoop to milking. If marrying involved milking, the relationship was over. Thus her Jake found himself wedged betwixt and between. He was a considerate man, never controlling, but in the context of the time and the marriage norms of his community, the condition she'd placed on him was a formidable one. Did he want to begin on a footing like that, with her refusing to do something expected of her? What would it lead to next? But he couldn't see himself milking either; it would not look right.

Of course, it all worked out, like true romances should, the remaining details vague though they included him sharing his heart and predicament with his older brother. And lo and behold, when Jake approached Edna next with a formal proposal of marriage, it included a promise from his brother—yes, our Uncle Must—that *he* would milk the cow. He'd milked a few times in Russia and knew what to do. And he didn't mind what people might say. And he knew of someone with a cow for sale.

I interrupted my mother's ramble. I remember the end, I said. Uncle saved the day.

He wanted better cooking. Enough to milk. He thought Jake should have me. He wanted Jake close. He liked me.

But who cares about Uncle Must? she said. She lifted a hand as if to sweep him away and pulled a packet of greeting cards out of her bag. It was clear to me at that moment—and I felt I could see it all the way back—that Mom was ashamed of him too.

My mother's birthday was six months past but she opened the cards as if they'd just arrived. She read the verses and inscriptions, explained who the senders were. I knew the people, the cards. We'd done this before.

Yours is the best, she said. *You* read it.

A pink card covered with flowers and sparkles. I read, Happy birthday to a terrific mother. We're so thankful to have you in our lives. Love, Jim and Catherine. I handed the card back to her. She gave it a pat. Such good children, she said. But isn't it time for you to play the piano?

I played two short Bach pieces by memory, then opened the worn hymnal on the piano. Mom liked to hear me play. She liked the hymns, and she mouthed the words. She liked it when people stuck their heads around the door to see who was playing. My daughter, she would call. She'd never relinquished her opinion that I was a musical genius, even though I'm only a passable pianist. I sometimes joshed with Jim that I'd practiced all those hours as a kid just to get his attention at college. By now, playing once a week in the seniors' home sufficed.

Three songs in and it was time to quit and wheel Mom to the dining room. Our visit always ended at lunch. I tied the towel-sized bib—termed *apron* here, for respect—around her neck, squeezed her shoulders, bent to say goodbye. It wasn't that bad, she whispered. But it wasn't easy, you know. I called him George, when I called him. I grew up in Idaho. I grew up English. That's all I spoke, growing up.

I stayed bent to my mother and quickly inserted another round of my questions. What was it, actually? Wrong with him, I mean. Did you like him?

I was too late. A kitchen aide approached with a serving cart covered in bowls of thick tomato soup and Mom's attention was diverted by the bowl that was lowered in front of her. She blinked her eyes for a prayer and blew on her soup.

They probably don't serve it hot enough to burn, I told her. She blew again and the spoon, held tightly in her right hand, the steadier one, plunged in. The young woman serving the soup exchanged glances with me. All they really have is eating, she said, her tone confiding. I was tempted to reply that she probably liked eating as well, but I gave her a charitable half-smile instead and walked to the nursing station to register a request that the staff help my mother with flossing and brushing her teeth.

One of the older aides was at the desk. It used to be we could put their teeth in a cup with some fizz, she said, and they'd freshen overnight. More and more now, residents have their own teeth.

It seemed a poor excuse, original teeth as an imposition, but I nodded. Increasingly better dental care, I said. Still, it would be nice—to have what they've managed to keep, I mean, at its cleanest and brightest. Mom was always vain about her teeth. I'd like her to be assisted.

You're talking about Edna Riediger?

Yes. My mother.

Edna doesn't want our help. Says she'll brush them herself. She knows her mind.

She can hold the brush but she misses parts, I said. Her hands shake. As you know. So I'm asking for staff to assist her, even if she claims otherwise.

Well if we're talking about Edna, I'm sorry, but you need to know she's awfully difficult at times. In terms of her oral procedures. But yes, of course, we'll keep trying.

I thanked her, fuming inside. My sense of failure frightened me back to the dining room. Was my mother in danger? No, but her crackers certainly were; they were about to scatter into her coffee instead of her soup. I guided the trembling hand over her bowl.

She was absorbed in her eating. All four women at the table were absorbed in their eating. I decided to stay a while longer, superfluous though I would be. I said No thanks to an attendant's offer of coffee or a plate of lunch, simply stayed, because I finally had time. Stayed, watching her, this woman, my mother, *please not big-time dementia or Alzheimer's please, please, not big-time dementia or Alzheimer's* looping through my brain like a chant while I held a napkin at the ready, snagged dribbles of tomato soup, brushed away bits of sandwich lettuce and crumbs. The sight of this woman, the one of the four of them who was mine in particular, was beautiful and depressing.

I rested my fingers on my mother's arm. Perhaps she thought the touch was staff. She liked to greet staff but considered them— when they helped her—pesky, like the budgies. Beneath her. She acted oblivious. Then dessert—a dish of jiggly caramel pudding— was served and she swivelled her head. Her face opened into another food-clogged but marvellous smile.

Why Catherine, she said, how delightful that you've come! Is it you who's been wiping after me all this lunch?

That'd be me.

Why bless you, Daughter. Bless you for the sandwich and the soup. Bless you for your service to my chin.

We laughed together, and it seemed a relief, as if we'd been arguing and finally reached a truce.

He was such a soaker, she said, the way he carried on.

Who?

Your Uncle Must! Who else have we been talking about all this time? She shook her head as if I were a child and not paying attention.

Right, I said, though I didn't know what she was talking about. Such a soaker.

Driving home that day from North Kildonan, through East Kildonan, on through Elmwood, the juxtaposed shabbiness and affluence along Henderson Highway depressed me. Illogically, it seemed a dilemma for which I might also be responsible, besides my mother's teeth and remembering Uncle Must. The buildings were a mishmash of exhausted stores and fine brick churches, tiny box-houses sharing a neighbourhood with large riverside homes. The day was warm, exceptionally warm for October, but I was inside the car and what I perceived of nature could have been a poster for Bleak: bare trees, branches a welter of veins and capillaries, clots of stubborn brown foliage, sky overcast and pale. The dearth of colour felt curiously thick; like glue.

I reached the Disraeli Bridge and knew that if I asked my mother too many questions about my uncle, she would think I was siding with my deceased father against her and her beloved and also deceased only son Darrell. For me, every fleeting recollection of Dad was simplicity itself—just a wish that he was alive. Missing him. A flit of tender gratitude. And Darrell? He was a numbness in me too labyrinthine to pursue. So I hadn't. But my mother owned the absence of them both in an irrational competition she imagined between herself and her late husband Jake, still believing he'd failed to mourn his son as much as he'd mourned his brother. As if grief could be mathematically proportioned. I miss my Jake, she would say. And then go on, But I was bereft about Darrell and Jake never seemed as hurt as me. Not like he was about his brother, that George of his, who was old and drowned!

I miss him too, I always responded, meaning Dad. But it's not true, Mom, I would argue. It's not true that Dad grieved Darrell any less. He was bereft like you.

And, I would add, more loudly, their deaths were years apart.

40

She couldn't be persuaded.

I crossed the bridge, the river wide and lazy below, for my favourite view of the Winnipeg skyline. A modest skyline, miles more modest than Vancouver's or Toronto's. A small clump of skyscrapers like a prairie oasis. Good enough, though. Something resolute in it. And I was nearly home now to my own sweeping view, the prospect of a walk, and a lunch more appealing than Maplebend's tomato soup and caramel pudding.

I walked south over the bridges by our apartment, then east. Meandered along the river behind the St. Boniface Hospital. I pressed my hands around some trees, considered the temperaments of bark. I stopped at the Grey Nuns memorial and squinted back at our high-rise block, visible through a gap in the trees, a grid of windows and balconies like distant shelves for knickknacks. I located our home in the rows—there, *mine*—and when I noticed the personal possessive I justified myself: I have the apartment, *he* has his work, his contract position in the school division's musical education department. *Second verse, same as the first.* They liked having him there. Jim Reimer the motivator, problem solver, amazing conductor.

I yearned for him. I couldn't solve retirement. Of course not, it was barely begun, my pie chart of volunteering, walking, reading books I'd never had time for, trying recipes I'd never had the energy for. Jim no more or less present than he'd ever been, he and his thick, soft patch of chest hair, nearly white, more hair there than on his head, he said when I stroked at it. He and his amiable decency. But two days in a row, straight to choir rehearsals after work, back when I was asleep, gone in the morning before I woke. It was *my* time that had altered, yawned apart. *My* time not at ease yet within my days.

This morning he'd left me some bouncy lines on a notepad on the kitchen counter. Hey Babe, got milk? We're out! Have a good day! XO Jim.

Well, ha ha ha. He only called me Babe when he felt guilty about working too hard, about letting me down. His work like a badge he wore to flash busy-ness and prestige while my badge had been surrendered. I didn't miss work and I'd started volunteering at the thrift store one day a week, even though a few shifts in I already knew what a cliché this choice had been for me: the place brightly lit and brimming with positivity, money raised for a good cause, the other volunteers *so* darn friendly, but every time I entered, the same apprehension hitting me like a bad smell (though it actually smelled amazingly fresh—maybe they piped essence of vanilla or pine through the vents), because everything here had had a previous life and what was the point of it now, reduced to this partiality, to the efforts of someone pretending it never belonged to anyone else, making up their own story for it. If I was going to be involved with old, left-behind objects I could have stayed at my job, I groused to myself; the documents we processed and protected from decay had the integrity of their historical description at least, they weren't piles of discards that tumbled from cardboard boxes and garbage bags onto the sorting tables and provoked annoyance at people who dropped off stuffed animals with eyes missing or their innards depleted, pants with broken zippers, dishes with cracks and chips, the sole survivors of sets. One slow hour last shift, I counted mismatched glasses for sale in the store and there were 138 of them.

I wouldn't quit yet, I would give it a run. And surely—eventually—I would get my retirement mix into shape. And I was okay on my own—of course I was; I was a modern, confident woman—and sure, I'd said, take the contract year, why not, but it was crazy, this yearning, this waiting. Like wandering in some kind of desert. Like watching. Sentry-stance: attentive, slightly anxious, nerve ends elevated until every rustle in the metaphorical bush seemed a sign of some possibility going unfulfilled while we were apart. I couldn't define it beyond waiting: waiting for something new, something undiscovered we'd planned to discover together. Oh, I knew what I had to do, what I wanted to do alone; the sensation of my last day at work, the invitation for remembrance had not yet abated, but I felt the loneliness of it, how it produced at the same time a weakening of self-assurance. I would have to persist with the belief that a pilgrimage into the past could be a re-set, that rehearsing shame could lessen it. Persist, even if retrospection was inherently disorderly. Even though I might feel my feelings too much.

The good thing about both yearning and remembering was that not much of it happened on the surface. Control could be maintained. I had—still have—a tremendous capacity for calmness on the surface. As well as a tremendous capacity for effervescence when required. Honed because that's what short women do, all that looking up.

You come on too strong with your analysis and needs, Jim had said to me once. Years and years ago, but as certain lines in marriage will, it nailed itself into my brain. It makes me pull away, he'd said.

But I learned from it. Learned to step back so he was compelled to step forward.

I walked on, and on, around the Cathedral and beyond, then looped back toward the apartment. I was no stricken princess needing rescue by a prince. My waiting was plainer, less innocent than that. Not like waiting two years to marry him after we met. Me and my mad crush on Lars Thiessen at the beginning of college but knowing as early as the fall retreat at Camp Chipewyan that I wanted Jim, beginning to yearn then too, but biding my time, finally convincing myself Lars and I were theatrically unsuitable. That morning at Chipewyan in the Whiteshell, in the dark but instantly wide awake, recollecting where I was—in a log cabin, in the autumn ochre and russet around a boreal forest lake, eight of us in the room and the air perverse by then—pulling on my clothes, slipping outside. The darkness weakening before the dawn, the activity area beyond the cabins strewn with reminders of the evening before: scattered benches and picnic tables and chairs, left-behind jackets and sweaters in heaps, damp with dew. Thrilled to be away from home, glad to be at college, but homesick too. Moving along the trail past the lodge, wishing I could move backward in time, or stop at least until I was sure of myself. Birds full-throated around me whose names I didn't know, whose calls I couldn't identify. I grasped how flimsy I was, how unprepared to exist in the world, and this on account of my illiteracy about species, flora and fauna, the nouns of Nature, the specific, hard categories of things. I was an adjective person, a person *affected by*. I knew *pretty, beautiful, graceful, gorgeous*, these common words and their opposites, and if I ever took up residence in *Roget's Thesaurus of Words and Phrases*, the only place I would be fully resonant was Personal Affections. This seemed pitiful, a far too narrow tenement.

A band of fog lay doe-like on the lake. I climbed a rise in the opposite direction to catch what I could of the sunrise. Pale layers of rose, white, and blue, the white thick like butter icing and the blue so delicate it was barely there. The layers shifted and merged at the edges, pink yielded to mauve and pearl. The sun appeared. I turned and looked back in the direction I'd come. The easterly wooden wall of the lodge was bleached nearly white under the light and the lake was golden, for the fog had slipped away. I saw a figure on the beach. Someone playing guitar. It was Jim. I could tell from his big hair and the bright tangerine-coloured shirt—probably with the twill weave checkered pants he'd worn the day before. Jim, I thought, was someone who would know his flora and fauna, someone who had concrete resources. And I could help him with his wardrobe. I walked toward the lake but the ground levelled and banked to a ridge before it descended steeply to sand and I couldn't see him anymore. I could hear him though, playing and

singing, the mystery birds twittering too. "Morning Has Broken."
Clear, perfectly pitched, a slight vibrato like the waver of the lake.
I didn't think he'd seen me. I loved that song and now I'd fallen
in love with his voice. It was a voice you could listen to for a long
time without ever tiring of it.

I emerged from my reverie to find myself back at the front
doors of our high-rise. I went up and cooked butter chicken with
rice and made a spinach and strawberry salad and Jim came home
and we ate and caught up. He told me how things were going in
his classes, about the progress he was making, incremental as it
might be. Jim turned kids on to music, that was the sum of it, and
he showed teachers how to accomplish the same in their bands
and choirs. He delighted in his work but he always came home
tired. He tried his best though to keep up the conversational
steam through dinner. I didn't have much to say about my day,
so he listed the Christmas pieces he'd picked for the adult choir
he conducted on the side and ditto for what the choir he sang in
was going to perform at their holiday concert. One of the pieces
overlapped. Which was a help, he said. He'd been recruited for
several other one-off Christmas musical events and he'd agreed
to them all.

It's going to be busy, Catherine, he said. I'm terribly sorry. He
pushed his glasses tight to his nose and peered at me.

Well, I said, if it keeps you from hanging around the 7-Eleven
and getting into trouble, it will definitely be worth it.

Jim doesn't appreciate snarkiness but he smiled. Funny, he
said. He pushed—for no good reason—at his glasses again.

I once told you I'm no rememberer, I said. But I've taken it up.
Keeping my inner archivist up to snuff.

He took this at face value and thought it was great. He liked
my reversal, my surge of interest. When he passed me the pickles,
he actually praised the retirement *fulfillment* he'd noticed in me.

He was sincere, I couldn't doubt it, but it was simply too much.

I bit into a pickle, concentrated on its tartness to keep from countering with a petty remark.

The pickle wasn't tart enough. I said, But when I get really bored, I generally head over to the local convenience store myself and do a bit of shoplifting.

Jim jerked in alarm.

Kidding! Kidding! I cried.

I know I'm too busy, Catherine, he said.

But later, we sat on the sofa with our evening mugs of decaf coffee and we clicked the television on and watched the rescue of a group of Chilean miners, more than two months underground, and I felt close to him, and he to me I think, sharing the suspense of it. Good news for a change, he muttered even before we knew whether the risky scheme to get the buried men out would succeed. We held hands while the seven-year-old son of the man selected for the first attempt sobbed near the shaft where his father would rise. We held on tightly until that first miner stepped out of the capsule alive. Then we went to bed, and snuggled some more which turned into sex, which was terrific, and then Jim fell asleep but I wasn't tired and since I didn't have to work the next day I returned to the living room and watched two more miners rise to the surface.

4.

Jim's sheet music occupied three drawers of the filing cabinet in our apartment den and our joint records were squished in the fourth and bottom drawer. In a slender folder labelled Riediger Stuff—Riediger being my maiden name—I found the draft of an attempt in my early teens to draw a family tree. It seemed remarkable that the page had escaped every garbage barrel fire of my youth.

My name was large at the top. Catherine Riediger. Second child of Jake and Edna (Toews) Riediger, born January 12, 1950. Beneath my name, my brother Darrell, then alive and since deceased, and sister Lorena. Their birthdates. Under that clump of information, Katharina Riediger, my great-grandmother on my father's side, because I was named for her.

Zeal oozed from my long-ago script, and it amused me now, the swirled letters, the *i*'s dotted with circles. I'd needed help for my project and Dad reluctantly agreed. He'd lowered himself onto the brown nylon chesterfield beside me, as if unconvinced it would hold him, me at attention with this very piece of paper and a pencil in what I imagined was a journalist's pose, angled slightly forward, both feet on the floor. Eyes probably as relentless as searchlights. I remembered that when I crossed my legs, he crossed his. The rest of the family was in the kitchen, a patter beyond us like rain, Mom shadowing past the doorway. She thought my idea frivolous. She had very little use for history, beyond the days of the Bible. You know the names of your parents and grandparents, she said. What more do you need?

I replied that I wanted it down so it would last. She responded with an impatient cluck.

It didn't occur to me at that time to trace my mother's line. The drama in the world of my origins adhered to Dad's roots in Russia across the sea, and drama attracted me. Dad was acting wary, though, and I didn't understand why. As if there was something subversive in genealogy. Dad, Dad, I said, soothing and cajoling. Dad, I said, all I want is the facts for a family tree.

Well, he said, I don't know very far back but I'll do my best and tell you what I can. He still seemed nervous and I guessed it was on account of his being a farmer while I was a lover-of-school kind of person; he wouldn't want to seem incapable.

I wrote down the bits he told me, put three exclamation marks after Katharina Riediger when Dad reminded me I was named after her. No particular reason, he said, it was in the family and he and Mom liked the name.

No offense, Dad, I'd said, I'm just glad you didn't name me Edna, after Mom.

We laughed and he said, A perfectly good name, and maybe he meant mine, maybe Mom's. He proceeded with his birth date, and hers, and said, Catherine, this isn't much, I know. More like sweeping bits of straw out of the truck after we've unloaded the bales.

I liked that, and we laughed again.

Then Uncle Must poked his head into the room. Supper done, he was leaving for his little house, but Dad called, Gerhard! Ardently, like he needed to be saved. And in came my uncle and Dad moved over and Uncle Must sat down on my other side. He smelled of farm soap and Sen-Sen—he must have just stuck a piece in his mouth. Licorice scent on my right, Old Spice on my left. Uncle Must touched the paper with his finger and dictated the names of his siblings who'd died—the ones between him and Dad. He knew every name, date, and the causes of their deaths. Childhood diseases or problems at birth. I wrote them down in the margin of the page, each one a duty (though a kind of sadness too) on account of me being squished between the two men and Uncle's insistence on their significance. And then he was telling me that Katharina Riediger, the great-grandmother for whom I was named, except for the difference in spelling (for no special reason either, Dad inserted), was *sorely displeased* when Gerhard, her third son, who would become his father—*his* namesake— and Dad's father too, of course, married Elizabeth Penner, who became their mother. Katharina Riediger was sorely displeased— he repeated the phrase—because Elizabeth had been an orphan of sorts and a housemaid for the Riedigers. They'd taken her in and treated her well for a servant and then she repaid their kindness by falling in love with their son. Who'd fallen in love with her. I sniffed romance and drew a tiny heart on the paper beside their names, this in spite of the Abraham-Lincoln-like seriousness of my uncle beside me, and my father smiled, though it wasn't much of a smile, more regretful than anything, and he said there may have been other explanations for why Katharina didn't approve of their mother, Elizabeth, besides her being the maid. He reached over me and touched Uncle Must's knee as if to warn him not to elaborate.

But you shouldn't feel badly about your name, he said, just

because your great-grandmother objected to her prospective daughter-in-law.

Why *would* I? I asked.

Personally, Dad sped on, I have no recollection of my grandmother. Being too young when she died. Not even of my own mother, for that matter.

She looked impressive, said Uncle Must. She had some excellent qualities.

Your uncle tries to see the good in people, Dad said. I thought he must be joking, but he wasn't so I kept quiet. To me, Uncle seemed generally disregarding of others, but there was something inviolate about him as far as Dad was concerned.

We two brothers, Dad said. And sighed. The only ones who survived.

Now, decades later, I held the otherwise unrevealing sheet with my girlish writing and it stared back at me with an air of mute apology, like a damp leaf stuck to pavement.

Catherine Riediger
brother Darrell & sister Lorena
Parents Jacob (Jake) & Edna (Toews) Riediger
& uncle Gerhard Riediger
Jake and Gerhard's parents: Gerhard & Elizabeth (Penner) Riediger
Grandfather Gerhard's parents: Johann & Katharina Riediger

I ran my hand over the words, amused again. But fond of it too. A piece of paper—an artifact as ancient as it got for me. I switched into professional mode and compared the dates of my grandparents' marriage in April 1907 and my uncle's birth in February 1909. Time enough: great-grandmother Katharina's unhappiness couldn't have been over the scandal of early pregnancy.

Uncle Must said their parents moved east to a settlement in

Siberia after he was born. Here Elizabeth (Penner) Riediger bore that list of babies at the margin. Five more children—four Elizabeths and one Maria—who died, a second son, Jacob (my father), followed by another daughter, the eighth child, who lived less than an hour. Elizabeth died in childbirth.

Our mother may have suffered from malnutrition, Uncle Must told Dad over my head.

Yes, that's what our father used to say. Worn right down.

In 1924, a year after Elizabeth's death, the widower Gerhard Riediger immigrated to Canada with his two surviving sons. His namesake Gerhard was fifteen while my father was five. The elder Gerhard wondered if he should leave Russia at all, not having a wife, but they'd been planning the emigration when Elizabeth was alive and Mennonites of his acquaintance in Canada wrote to say they'd picked another wife for him. So he went. For the sake of his boys.

In Canada, Gerhard turned into George and Jacob turned into Jake and Jake grew up and married my mother. The End, I'd written at the bottom of the page, drawing a daisy beside it.

A pathetic family tree. More like a shrub. One of those impulsive projects of my youth that I quit soon after. I could probably find names to fill out the branches, high and wide; I knew the genealogy sites for this. The research had never interested me for my own use, however. Who needed a visual reminder that no lines led beyond me and Jim?

Growing up, it was my grandmother Elizabeth who intrigued me most. Unsettled me. She and her husband gazed solemnly out of their wedding portrait on the Big House piano all those years and sometimes, practicing my scales or arpeggios, I gazed back. The maid and master's son. All those babies who died on her. Dying herself in the midst of giving birth.

One day while I did piano exercises, Dad appeared beside me, muttering, Yes, I can see it, there *is* a resemblance. He squinted back and forth from me to the photograph, like he was trying to fasten a string between our noses. I stopped playing.

Uncle mentioned it today, he explained. Your uncle said, Catherine resembles our mother. So I wanted to see. I don't remember her in real life. Just this photo. She's nice-looking, just like you.

I didn't mind him saying so, but the fact that Uncle Must noticed the resemblance seemed creepy. Was that why I'd felt his scrutiny now and then?

They're wearing their wedding clothes, Dad went on, but the photograph wasn't made the day of their wedding. It was taken later.

They don't look that happy, I said.

No one smiled for the camera then. People had to hold still. But I'm sure they were happy at the time. He peered at his young mother. Your grandmother had her trials though, he said. Her frights. Yes, she had a very hard life. He patted my shoulder and left for the kitchen. I placed my fingers on the keys, ran up another scale, heard Darrell react with glee because Mom had made bread pudding for our suppertime dessert. He loved bread pudding, but I did not. I ran up and down the scale five times through, eight notes one way, eight back, more loudly than necessary, then stopped again and reached for the framed picture to closely examine Grandmother Elizabeth. A slender face, round eyes capped with high, curved brows, but looking timid, uncertain, somehow—probably the frights, as my father had said—and her mouth, while full, hinting at a slump. The more I examined her, the gloomier she looked.

I laid the framed photo on its face, went at another round of scales, two octaves each this time, five times over, fingers nimble, manic. It must have been a trial for the family for when I was nearly done I noticed the living room door had been closed. *Resemble!* Why did my father suppose it a compliment to compare me and this tall, fraught, early-to-die mother of his? *Resemble* seemed an annihilating fate, even if Grandmother's features were acceptable enough. I knew that I was shorter than Elizabeth Penner Riediger, I had that difference at least, a pass-down from my mother Edna. I determined to be one of those small, friendly, quick-moving women others describe as perky, pixie, cute. Nothing like this frowning forebear.

After that, I always turned the grim black-and-white framed photograph on its face, where it would stay until Mom dusted or noticed and set it upright again. If she wondered why it continued to fall forward, she never mentioned it. And I'd cultivated my perky persona just as decided; in college, I wore my hair long and rippling, then short and impish, and outwardly I was always sociable, cheerful, well-disposed to everyone. Well-liked. The very words used to describe me as recently as my retirement supper.

When I was ten, there was a big fire in Tilia one night and Darrell and I witnessed it. It was a sweet time with my brother, the havoc of fire notwithstanding, and I'd kept the memory close and unexamined, the smooth feel of it like sea glass in my pocket. But now that I aimed to be open and receptive, I thought of it again and my uncle's role within the memory was amplified. It was like he'd become its real protagonist.

The telephone's jangling had woken us. It was the emergency ring on the party line. Dad's voice in the kitchen then, and Mom's, the sounds of morning except that it was night. Darrell and I scrambled into the kitchen too, tousled, rubbing eyes, hearing our father say it was a fire at the manufacturing plant where the parts for plows and combines and other equipment were made. (Lorena was the only one who slept through the excitement.) All hands on deck, that sort of thing, Dad said, rushing into the bedroom to get his day clothes on, Uncle Must waiting outside already, truck motor purring restlessly in the darkness. We could see a pale orange glow on the horizon in Tilia's direction.

53

Darrell begged to go along, and I begged too. Dad hesitated, then said yes, if we got a move on, if we promised to stick together, stand back, keep out of the way.

There was no time to dress properly. It was winter so Mom pulled snow pants and a jacket over my flannel pajamas and wrapped a wool scarf around my head. I felt bulky, uncomfortable—like a contraption, I thought—and I feared I would be hot—we were off to a fire, weren't we?—and that I wouldn't be able to shed layers because I was in pajamas. But anything to go. I'd never known the elation and calamity of a fire. Outside, Uncle Must was honking the horn.

Did they say what started it? Mom asked.

It was a call for assistance, not a report! Dad snapped, uncharacteristically brusque.

I just wondered. Mom's voice was mild but she pushed me forward.

Uncle Must seemed upset when Darrell and I climbed into the truck. They don't need children to help, he said, but behind us our father answered that we'd promised to behave.

But Catherine! Uncle Must said. He singled me out, protested me specifically. Dad said it was fine and the truck door slammed and we rattled down the lane and along the road to Tilia at a speed I hadn't known my uncle capable of driving. I anchored myself on my father's knee. Stick together, stand back, keep out of the way, Dad warned again when we parked at the end of a line of vehicles on the gravel road near the scene. Uncle Must stalked off ahead of us.

Flames were visible now, and the language I'd read about fire-as-disaster was coming true in front of me: flame like tongues fighting skyward, smoke in billows, the roar of it. Sizzling too, like a giant cloth being torn, the way Mom tore cloth once she got it started with a snip of the scissors. Behind the noise and colour, night as black as coal. Our teacher brought a lump of coal to school one day because some of us, she said, knew nothing of coal.

Dad called, Did you hear me, Darrell? Stay with your sister. Take her hand now; I'm putting you in charge of her. And then he was gone and we trundled after him as best as we could, Darrell holding my hand, half dragging, then dropping it and rushing ahead, only to stop and wait and grab it again. The closer we got, the bigger the flames and the fiercer their howling.

An inferno! Darrell shouted back at me.

Inferno, I echoed. A word I'd read but never heard spoken or quite grasped. I knew burning garbage in the barrel, burning wood for a wiener roast, the low, ashy creep of burning stubble. I repeated it: *inferno*.

Darrell and I planted ourselves at the front of a crowd gathered on the road. We stood close like orphans, exchanging monosyllabic commentary—Wow! Oh! Look!—and then some school friends, both mine and Darrell's, arrived and huddled with us, all of us conscious, it seemed, of being underaged at a solemn and adult event. When something suddenly exploded with a sound like drumming on steel, it made us jump and we laughed, but not loudly, and not for long.

The night was colder than I expected. Onlookers were kept on the far side of the road, well back from the burning, and though the fire was large, apparently it gave its heat upward to the stars. Now I was glad for the secret bed-feel of my flannel pajamas against my skin. I liked listening to the people behind us who told each other that nothing would be saved, who speculated on the cause. Paint rags on a heater or—most enticing—deliberately set?

You think arson? someone asked.

Yeah, maybe a disgruntled employee. Starting it on purpose. (So, I thought, *that's* what arson means.)

But whatever the cause, the voices informed me, nothing would be saved. So we'd come to view destruction, not rescue, windows blown, roof and walls devoured to reveal a skeleton of steel, the skeleton twisting and tottering, and strange, dark shapes inside the building. Machines and furniture under attack. All was lost and we were watching it go. The thoroughness and speed of the devastation astonished me and I felt our importance—me and Darrell, Shirley, Maynard, Bobby, Joyce, and Paul—as spectators. I felt the privilege of being awake in the dead of night. Tomorrow at school we would recognize our connection because of this ruin and the respect we'd allowed one another, accepting the others' comments. And Darrell turning to check that I was beside him and me turning to confirm that I was, gratified by his compliance with our father's instructions, by his care of me, by the emotions exchanged in those brief looks, how we shared them equally. How he treated me as his equal and never once mentioned me being a girl.

If you close your eyes, I murmured in his ear, it sounds like water. Like really heavy rain.

He closed his eyes and listened. Then he said, You're right.

Just containment, the people behind us said. That's all they can do.

The men summoned from town and outlying farms had cleared an area around the burning building. They emptied it of everything flammable and then two small fire trucks with tanks of water arrived from neighbouring towns. Tilia had no fire truck but a woman behind me said, Maybe now we'll finally get a fire engine of our own.

The men at the fire took turns handling the hoses and when the water struck, the fire steamed and spit. Sometimes I could isolate my father and uncle among the silhouettes dashing to and fro against the fiery brightness, moving materials away from the building or unwinding the hose, Uncle Must easiest to spot because of his height and his helmet-like cap. And every time my eye singled him out, he was running. Dad was steady, but Uncle Must was fast and jerky.

The rage of the fire gradually subsided, the crowd of watchers began to disperse. I was tired, I wanted to go home. The fire felt old to me by now. The man who acted as foreman gathered the workers, shouted his thanks, said a town crew would stay the night to watch the low smouldering. The rest of the men were dismissed.

Uncle Must walked away from the fire toward the road, toward me and Darrell, and he was making those movements he sometimes made with his right hand—hand to neck, neck to hip, hip to top of his head, neck hip head again. And again. He made them rarely, but I'd definitely observed them before. Two men strolled behind him. As they drew near I could see their faces. One was Tom Derksen from church. A deacon. I knew he was a deacon because deacons passed the bread and grape juice around at communion. Mr. Derksen and his friend must have noticed Uncle's arm, his jerking like a marionette. I saw them exchange glances and grin, and Mr. Derksen took off a glove and lifted his hand to his temple and made a circling motion with his finger. The sign for loose screw in the head.

I hated that Uncle Must didn't know how he looked when he made those funny movements with his arms sometimes—tics we called them many years later. Hated that he didn't stop. Hush, Catherine, my mother had said when I'd once asked what he was doing with his arm. He's steadying himself, she'd said. I hated those two men. Hadn't I seen them, Tom Derksen and his friend, standing and yakking while my father and uncle chased falling debris to be sure it was extinguished? Standing and yakking and laughing in the foreground while others rushed around making the danger go away.

Riding home, I leaned against my father. He smelled of smoke and sweat. He smelled invincible. It must have given me some kind of nerve because I told him what I was thinking while I watched the fire. I know it was awful, Dad, I said, I know it was bad. But it was kind of wonderful and beautiful too.

I heard a sound like a groan from the other side of the cab and then Uncle Must jumped into the pause after my comment like that tank that exploded in the burning building. Fire isn't beautiful or wonderful! he raged. It's a bad, bad mistake, Catherine, to even think of it that way!

His words felt like a slap. My father pulled me closer. Tears squeezed out of my eyes and I pressed deeper into my father's jacket to dry them.

There was silence the rest of the way home and when Uncle Must dropped us off, Dad was the only one who said, Goodnight. Get to bed now, Catherine, and don't worry, he told me in the kitchen. He doesn't mean it that way. He's got a terrible dread about fire.

Doesn't everyone? I said. Don't you?

Not the way he does.

I crawled back into bed that night and cried some more, because I was over-tired and because of what Tom Derksen had done, his finger forming a coil. And because of Uncle's condemnation. Especially after I'd loyally hated that Derksen deacon and the other man on his behalf.

5.

I took down the albums Jim and I stored for my mother and scoured them for photos from Tilia, anything that pertained to the Big House or Uncle Must.

The voices of my past professors buzzed in my ears:

Every document represents a construction of some kind and creates an impression.

Honour the sources.

You need a tidy, impartial mind to sort and list.

I wrote these sentences into the first page of my Moleskine notebook.

There were no photos of my uncle. Only one photo of the house. I pried it out of its photo corners for a better look, couldn't believe what I saw. As if wilted, this house, as if weary of being large and imposing, as if unwilling to exert for the Riedigers the effort it gave the previous owners who built it—who were rich, it was said, prominent in the community, so much so that they'd moved on to Edmonton to climb even higher in the world. As if the house had known my father came from lesser immigrant stock, not British. Known that Tilia wasn't about to become a major centre and what was the use of pretending it would? That it would turn instead into a small community of mostly Mennonites, modest, pious, sticking together.

I was gripped by the truth or the lie of it. All the years I'd lived there, the house at the end of the lane on that bit of a rise asserted itself on the rolling landscape and the wide, blue sky, superior to every other house I knew. I felt a skip in my chest when I saw it from the road. It was spacious; it was kind. Wasn't it?

The photo was dated 1957. A case of *document trumps memory* then? I knew photographs can fudge the facts but there would have been no reason to tamper with or circumvent reality here, to intentionally position the house at an unbecoming angle. I closed my eyes, opened them to drift over the photo again and there, in black and grey and white, a two-storey house looking smaller than I remembered, a bumbling thing, not crooked as much as out of kilter. Plain. The detritus of play: a wagon, a baseball bat, and—at the edge of the photograph—a doll, which seemed to be missing its head. Weeds crept against the house where there'd always been flowers. Hadn't there always been flowers? Paint bare in spots. A board missing on the wooden walk up to the lean-to porch.

A farm house. A busy operation. Children. Quite understandable that it would have been hard to keep up with it all.

But I'd believed we had.

No photographs of the kitchen. The kitchen had been large and airy too—an alabaster feel about it, light coming in from two sides, pale yellow walls. The Saturday smell of freshly waxed linoleum. The essential meaning of the house, that kitchen, until I reached my mid-teens and preferred to escape to my bedroom. Where we ate, did our homework, hung about. Where Mom spent her life. Where Dad read or did his paperwork. Where, for some years, the television stood so my folks could monitor what we watched. Mom called television the dumb box and Uncle Must considered it evil except for hockey, news, and nature shows. It drew us all, though, like a hearth in winter. The kitchen was big, clean, crowded, everything within it jostling toward some nurturing outcome, the table dominant, covered weekdays by oilcloth and Sundays by a crocheted tablecloth. Mom's sewing machine at a window, facing the lane so she could see who was coming or going. When she spotted the school bus, she draped her work-in-progress over the sleek black Singer. Sometimes, approaching the house, I caught her darting movements through the window and it seemed an apparition of comfort for my mother claimed she loved to sew more than any other work in the world, but she always stopped it when we children came home. She welcomed us as if she'd missed us and sometimes she reached into the cupboard above the sink and brought down the blue cookie tin from which we were allowed two cookies each, but only two, because more would spoil our supper.

There were no photos of Uncle Must or his house, not even the outline of the shack behind the caragana hedge. In my memory of the hedge-planting morning, his house twisted grotesquely out of proportion while he paced among our puny plantings, a mast in the wind. A tall man, a head taller than my father. The hedge must have flourished for in every memory after that it was a high wall of green in summer and in winter, a dense tangle of wood through which the light from his window glowed faintly after dark.

All the district farms had yard lights, giant candles on the landscape that did not dispatch the darkness as much as charm it, a reminder that others were there. Our own light stood on the Big House yard, not Uncle Must's. Most farm houses had porch lights too: more intimate lights that people turned off when they went to bed, like a CLOSED sign on a store. Some mornings I overheard my parents discussing whether they'd seen Uncle Must's porch light on or off when they chanced to get up for the bathroom or one of the children. His nocturnal habits were irregular and it exasperated them when, instead of sleeping, he acted as if he were open for business.

I put the albums back on the shelf but kept the house photo out. I stared at it some more, as if it might revert, if I waited long enough, to the grand dwelling it had been for me.

It refused.

Perhaps my brief foray in appraisal was satisfaction enough. My former boss, Daniel Jute, had pressed appraisal as the first, most significant, archivist task. He said that in rendering professional opinion, we revealed ourselves as the professionals we were. Which seemed circular to me. In any case, the process was rarely as lofty as he made it sound. Archival centres had their criteria, knew what the institutions they served needed to keep. As for unsolicited submissions, an assessment of factors such as content, provenance, reliability, completeness, condition, and costs wasn't usually that complicated. Jute was brilliant but had a repetitive personality, not to mention the air of siege he projected, as if fighting some invisible enemy appraising *him* who might sum him up as a hoarder of dust-bound paper antiques or deem him vaguely ill with archive fever on account of the ancient particles swirling around him, a form of puttering that had nothing to do with life or death issues, except for death's victory in the end. We— his staff—wanted respect for our profession as much as he did; we clung to the tired adage, *He who doesn't learn from the past is doomed to repeat it,* but we kept our pride under wraps, joked that he who's doomed to learn from the past will repeat it in a dozen dreary papers. We let our Man at the Top strut on our behalf.

But how could I use my skills of appraisal for the flotsam of the past now collecting in my head? Matters scant with content, sketchy reliability, uncertain provenance? Me like one of those waste pickers in India or Brazil on their mountain of refuse, squatting on heaps of metal, paper, and plastics day after day, eyes keen, sorting, selecting, evaluating everything, no matter how improbable, in order to survive. Trying to form another person in my mind. You grow older, I thought, you pile up the years, and what's behind you seems clear, but then, like the peepholes Darrell and I used to press into frosted winter windows with our small, warm fingers, our small, warm breath, it ices over again at night.

So I'd cleared a bit of ice.

I decided to take the photo of the Big House to a copy store and have it enlarged and printed on good-quality, heavy paper. Frame it. Or stick it on the fridge at least. A small gesture of archival discernment, an act of reconciliation to its evident bedragglement, to the reality of the gap between memory and truth. I would believe the photo.

I labelled it: George Riediger a.k.a. Uncle Must lived here 1965 to 1968, Tilia, Alberta, and for some years before that, he lived across the road. And then I shook myself, astonished, and added: Home of Jake, Edna, Darrell, Catherine, and Lorena Riediger for much longer than that. I underlined my name.

I remembered now that there'd been something of a tussle between my mother and uncle the day he subscribed us to those books of biography and animals. She'd intercepted him outside, on his way into the meeting with the salesman. Avoid those Uncle Arthur bedtime books, she said. They seem nice enough but they're from the Adventists.

He halted, hand on the door, not looking at her directly. They teach obedience, he said.

Mom's voice in response was low because I was alongside her, trying to listen, and I wasn't supposed to hear. But I was close enough. If it's books for the children, my mother said—and you know I'm grateful, she sighed—I need to have some say in what they're reading. I know the stories are interesting, but they're from the Adventists.

Adventists? I had no idea what the Adventist part of the Uncle Arthur stories could be. Darrell borrowed the volumes from his friend Donald and I'd read them too. And our mother read them, just as she read everything we brought home from friends or the school library. An ongoing puzzle, Mom's interest in our books. If checking for danger, she seemed unable to find it. She didn't raise objections or forbid what we selected so why couldn't she trust our choices by now? Yes, she muttered *gruesome* once, and yes, it was somewhere in the middle of a story from Uncle Arthur, whoever he was. Some of those stories *were* gruesome, so maybe that was the Adventist part of them, and some were sad. But surely they were all about being good little boys and girls. Which we heard about constantly anyway, at home and school and church. I'd learned a thing or two from those books, I thought, tilting to Uncle Must's side in their difference of opinion; Mom ought to be grateful for that. If tempted to skip my piano practice, I remembered the story of the girl who ran off to play with friends instead of practicing as she was told and then a brick fell on her hand during their game and crushed it so badly she could never play piano again.

Never mind the Adventists, Uncle said crossly. I've checked with Jake.

It was confusing, but I couldn't ask. Mom detested eavesdropping for one thing, and for another, what question would articulate my confusion? Without an adequate question, my mother would feel no obligation to reply. It probably wasn't the gruesomeness after all, but something about the distinctions of our church, ours being Mennonite, not Adventist. Something, perhaps, in the proportion of *strict and open,* a phrase I'd heard for our particular version of Mennonite, though it sounded like congratulating ourselves. But maybe it was just an ideal, a hope, this meeting of opposites. Which I couldn't comprehend either. A strain, a pressure, it seemed, sorting out right and wrong, and so much work, keeping the banner of righteousness up and flying. Besides all the other work grownups had to do.

Then I'd found myself tilting back to Mom's side of the matter, my attractive, forceful, intelligent mother, who was surely closer to the open than the strict compared to my uncle, even if he underwrote our extracurricular education. He'd muzzled my mother with her husband's name. Mom wanted to be a good wife—she said as much sometimes. So she opened her mouth but closed it again. She stepped briskly into the house behind Uncle Must and acted as if she'd merely remarked on the weather. She lifted a corner of the white tea towel that covered the rising bread dough and pressed her palm gently onto the smooth, round mound of it. She kept her hand against the soft skin of that dough, pensive it seemed, and lingering as if to listen, and then at last she released it, let the cloth fall back into place and started breaking and beating eggs for a cake.

But just before we went into the house—Uncle Must to the salesman, Mom to her dough, me sneaking in close behind them—the black dog we called Blackie tumbled around us, barking as if on my side or some canine side of her own and Uncle Must turned and silenced her with a single swift and furious Be still!

6.

What an incredible October we had in Winnipeg that year, weather-wise. Leaves mostly down by then, grass browning, lines of geese filling the sky at dusk with their haunting calls and wistful calligraphy, but so unbelievably hot, and everyone in the city, it seemed, nearly tipsy with happiness, as if pumpkins brimming out of supermarket bins were summer watermelons and pots of orange and yellow mums were plantings for spring.

One such glorious day, I wheeled Mom outside. Hard work, it was, pushing the chair, handles too high for comfort, the sidewalk uneven. And my mother's body suddenly repugnant to me as I grew hotter while I pushed: scalp winking pink through tufts of white hair, skin a sag like wet clothes on a line, that awful shape- lessness below the neck. Somewhere under her blue paisley blouse she had breasts, slumping flat now like cucumbers gone rotten. A life-time ago, helping me buy my first bra, she'd seized that very occasion, loudly over a fitting room wall, to tell me she'd nursed me as a baby and it was the *most satisfying thing*.

Her voice seemed a dirge now as it rose to me from the chair. I need to get somewhere, she said, but I'll start to get up and I can't! Then I remember. I can't walk anymore.

It must be distressing, I said.

It's discouraging! It happens every day!

Your awareness of not walking isn't a habit yet, I guess.

I don't know what you mean. The crows sound horrible. Aren't they just horrible, Catherine?

I've heard they're intelligent birds.

Why am I wearing my slippers?

Because you're in your chair.

Three blocks passed like this. We reached a playground and I pushed Mom beside a bench. I dropped into it to recuperate and we lapsed into silence and I tumbled backward into another October. 1963. A humiliation so painfully acute it had seemed physical. The Sunday my uncle went crazy in church. I could pin it by month and year because President John F. Kennedy was assassinated in Texas a few weeks later, and after that, the two events were tied together. I wasn't glad about the assassination but I was glad about the timing because it overshadowed what Uncle Must had done. I thought everyone in Tilia was talking about my uncle, but after the Dallas affair all anybody talked about was JFK and his wife Jacqueline and the new president Lyndon Johnson and Lee Harvey Oswald and Clayton Ruby.

There'd been no warning, nothing unusual that Sunday, no fuss rising in advance like foam when a meat bone simmers in a pot. We picked him up for church. Uncle Must was in charge of the truck, Dad was in charge of the car. He waited on his stoop. Darrell scooted over, Uncle bent himself inside. The three men of the family sat on the bench seat in front in their grey or black suits and crisp white shirts and ties. Even Darrell had a suit. They were a scrubbed and handsome line of complimentary colours, all looking straight ahead as if vigilant against threat, their view full-on through the windshield and unimpeded by heads like my view was. I sat in the back with Mom and Lorena, by the left side window. Sometimes I stared at the scenery and sometimes I stared at my father's neck—his Sunday-clean neck—and his hair trimmed neatly and slicked down in honour of the Day of Rest.

At church, I found my best friend Shirley with Betty. Betty's main friend was June but June went to church elsewhere so on Sundays Betty drew Shirley and me into a special once-a-week triangle of friendship. Every girl in the class was in Betty's thrall. That morning, she informed us with a toss of her gleaming pony-tail that we should call her Betts. She hated the name Betty; she thought she was actually a Veronica, like in the Archie comics, not Betty. She'd already tried Elizabeth and Beth but the varia-tions never lasted. The latest name change always seemed the best, however, and Shirley and I were excited about the idea of Betts. We said we liked it. We huddled outside our Sunday school class-room while she coached us with trial sentences: Oh, Betts, what a pretty dress, and You're the prettiest, Betts. We never resisted saying she was prettiest, because she *was*.

But otherwise it was a typical, interminable Sunday morning. First Sunday school, then church, me and my friends in the girls' section at the front left of the sanctuary, old enough to sit sep-arate from our mothers, but not quite old enough to move into the balcony with the youth. Hymns, readings, a long session of prayer, an emotional flannelgraph story for the children by Maisie Martens. That should have been enough to end on, but no, the adults needed their lesson too so after another song by the choir, the sermon got underway.

Our minister Rudy Klassen sometimes asked other men in the congregation to preach, but he was in the pulpit that morning. When he was preaching, we got long explanations about minute aspects of the text, stuck into an outline of at least three main points and numerous subpoints. He had a teacher-like approach and a monotonous voice. I soon lost track of whatever it was he was droning on about.

He might have been a third of the way through his sermon when I heard a heavy shuffling sound—someone getting clumsily to their feet and bumping a pew in the process—and suddenly a voice flew into the sanctuary, loud and riled up. The change in atmosphere was immediate, palpable.

The getting-up, the voice, was Uncle Must. He wasn't quite shouting, but nearly. Like a protest. I knew the intonation of preaching and the intonation of prayer, neither of which sounded the way people talked on the church steps after the service or at home, but my uncle's pitch and rhythm were none of these. Not churchly speech, not regular either, but pleading. Strangely rhythmical. He seemed to be addressing the minister but his words pelted everyone who was there. He sounded packed-together and it was unbelievable how vastly different all of it was from his usual timbre, his usual grim silent reticence or dogmatic declarations. He'd balled it up into anguish, it seemed, and out of that ball, this gush, this wave of reproach over the lot of us. But why? What? I couldn't gather what he said. I made no effort either; I was too dismayed. It was a mix of German and English, numerous No's but I registered only two words: *Babylon* and *whore*.

I didn't want to look at my uncle but the entire section of girls turned as if one head so I had to be part of the rotation too. I saw my uncle's eyes scrunched shut, his head skewed upward to some point above the platform, his arms waving slowly as if feeling his way through a pitch-dark room. The men around him had ducked out of his range or slid down the pew away from him. Otherwise, no one reacted. The room was tentative.

I felt a hard elbow in my side: the pointy elbow of Betts. That's your uncle! she hissed. I felt heat in my face as if it was I who'd punctured Rudy Klassen's sermon, let the air out of it.

Maybe Betts thought I hadn't heard. That's your uncle! she hissed again.

Redder, thicker warmth, as if I'd been coated in wax. Betty! I whispered, trying to shush her.

Betts! she came back at me.

But Rudy Klassen! Standing motionless, unruffled, and fully paused at the pulpit. He might be the dullest preacher under heaven but in that moment I loved him.

The girls in the pew behind me giggled so I twisted my head again to look at my uncle, still spouting and waving. I saw Dad rise from his seat a few rows back and step forward to stand beside his brother. He put his hand on his shoulder. Uncle Must's rant ended abruptly, he snapped as if out of a dream and his arm flew sideways and struck my father's face. Deliberate, it seemed, not accidental. Now Dad was the one who looked surprised.

Then my uncle's arms dropped to his sides. Dad's hand had remained on his brother's shoulder and he put his other hand on his arm and led him out. Uncle Must let himself be guided like a blind man. Stillness piled up in the sanctuary as the two figures moved down the aisle. Light poured through the narrow windows of the small church, so bright it was hard to look into. The men were blotches traversing that light.

Everyone waited and then, like a period at the end of a convoluted sentence, we heard the click of the outside door and Rudy Klassen resumed his sermon as if nothing had happened. He didn't even clear his throat, he just started talking about something blandly theological. I loved him for that as well.

On the way home, Dad remarked casually that the Rudy Klassens were coming for Sunday dinner. Clearly it was a last-minute invitation for Mom hadn't said anything that morning about company today.

During the meal, Uncle Must was silent and self-absorbed, the same old brown-paper demeanour as always, and Mom was even more spirited than usual with our guests. If the conversation—light and casual—showed any signs of tapering off, she popped in another quick comment about the weather or garden. Mrs. Klassen did her part by offering compliments about the meal. Sunday dinners alternated between roast beef and chicken and this Sunday it was beef. And luckily Mom had a pumpkin pie ready from our own pumpkins and the two women went on for a while about the proportions of cinnamon, nutmeg, and mace in the filling. And the cream, the thick whipped cream—how creamy!

I overheard Dad speaking to Uncle after the meal. No reading today, Brother, he said. Have a rest. Have a sleep. Will you?

Brother didn't reply. Brother with the deep, dark eyes, straight nose, black brows like a warning. The forehead a cliff. Mouth straight too, held together with effort as rigid as a clamp. Long, pendulous ears. Strong, broad jaw. He simply touched the milk separator as he always did when leaving and propelled himself down the lane in his long-legged gait. Amazing how he could jaunt away the same as ever, as if he hadn't made a fool of himself and sunk the rest of us along with him. No warning, and no afterword either.

Dad and pastor Klassen retired to the living room. Mom set Lorena at the table with her paper dolls and then she and Mrs. Klassen followed their husbands instead of doing the dishes. She ordered Darrell and me to look after them; she told us not to argue. She pulled the door decisively shut behind her.

And now my mother was lifting her arms to the heat. She seemed happy to be outdoors. Such a lovely walk, she was saying. A lovely walk so far.

Mom, I said, what in the world was Uncle Must shouting about that day in church? Do you remember?

She swivelled her head slowly in my direction. I remember, she said. But I wouldn't call it shouting.

What was bothering him, that he interrupted like that?

She touched a trembling hand to her neck, said, I guess he hated the Book of Revelation.

The sermon was from Revelation?

What sermon?

The one Uncle Must reacted to.

Oh yes. Yes. I remember that. Chapter 18.

He didn't agree with the pastor's interpretation?

He hated that chapter and something inside him just had to let go.

Oh.

I felt weak. As if humbled. She'd known immediately what I was talking about, she'd not resisted.

I hadn't much liked the biblical Apocalypse myself as a girl, but how was it possible that my uncle would utter objections? Was a hatred of Revelation even allowed in that era when everyone seemed enamoured with John on the Isle of Patmos and his visions of horsemen, plagues, seals, scrolls, trumpet sounds, battles, and blood? There'd been a fair industry around it, linking its symbols to historical or current events, plotting its mysteries in elaborate End Times charts. I couldn't fathom my Bible-fervent uncle adverse to even a word of it.

I remembered, though, that things seemed different for my uncle in the congregation after that, as if he'd lost whatever previous standing he'd had. The *peculiar* of him too blatant now. In my recollection, vague and unreliable as it might be, he was given no further opportunity to preach. Though he continued, it seemed, to attend church conventions as a delegate, because delegates were part of a local group and mutually supervised, I supposed.

I felt unprepared to question Mom further, and besides, two

children, a boy and a girl, maybe three or four years old, twins perhaps, raced each other into the playground. Shrieking.

Little banshees, my mother said.

I laughed. She used to call us that when we got too rambunctious. I wondered if she knew what a banshee was. That it wailed to warn of death.

No, she wouldn't have known and neither had we. She'd heard it somewhere and seized it for our noisiness, the word itself a tiny shriek.

The children's caregiver or mother strolled behind them, backpack over her shoulder, book in hand. The two children bounded up the play structure, slid down the slide, ran between the sandbox and the swings, calling constantly to each other. They were relentless in their play.

Look at them, Mom said, palms raised in their direction as if to scoop them up. And look, she said, pointing at the children's adult on a far bench, now engrossed in her book. Their mother pays no attention whatsoever.

I guess the novelty's worn off, I said. But at least she's reading. Not constantly checking a phone.

She'll look up from that book and they'll be gone.

We're keeping an eye on them.

I mean grown and gone. Mom sighed. You don't know what it's like, Catherine, she continued, having your children small, then turning around and finding them out of your sight.

It was no longer worth the effort to explain to this Edna Riediger of mine that sentences like this could hurt. Not worth parsing the gradations of cruelty they contained. They didn't hurt that much by now anyway, except for the ongoing, fundamental principle of my objection to them. I kept quiet and she was quiet and maybe she'd forgotten what she said or maybe she hadn't forgotten yet and was sorry about it, in which case she would be especially cooperative for a while.

So many horrible crows, she said then. Is the city getting bigger, Catherine, would you say?

I suppose it is.

Incredible, I thought. Revelation, Uncle Must, October heat, my mother's pokes. But I was rested. I was revived, and sorry I'd been spiteful about her current body. How intensely I loved her! As a child, thinking her the best and liveliest, most embracing, person I knew. The hurry of her short, stoutish legs, the way she might shout at us to notice a rainbow or the moon, the slash of her kitchen knife against a gladiola stem because it had to be borne into the house that very moment to stand in a vase and be more constantly admired.

Not the kind of mother, though, to be constantly pulling us onto her lap, holding us tight until we squealed, not the kind of mother, either, who delivered stories about her life with clear beginnings and happy ends. Even then, holding back about the past. A warden personality, always tending us into the future, into what she wished to create in family life. And if we begged for something *not made up* from the long-ago of her life, Mom offered to read to us instead. What I gathered about my mother's childhood was scraps from a heaping bag of them, which I pieced into a narrative myself. Edna Toews Riediger, born 1930 to American Mennonites in Idaho, mother Esther in her mid-forties by then and the pregnancy a shock, though accepted by the older woman in hopes that the child would be a support and companion, like a Ruth for a long-suffering Naomi. The other daughters—Olive and Marie—already grown and married, each with a child of her own. Mother Esther never healthy afterward, having never wholly recovered from the strain of the late pregnancy and birth, but giving her youngest daughter as much attention as she could muster. Edna's father Paul a partner in a butcher shop. Then Mother Esther up and dying of complications related to pneumonia, her darling daughter a mere fifteen. And not even a year later,

Edna's father dying as well, of a heart attack. He'd had problems with his heart for years but no one dreamt it would shut down so soon, so conclusively. There was no need now for Edna to be a prop to elderly parents. But she never forgot how special she was.

She'd been a good mother, yes. But there was very little skill for nurturing left in her by now. It didn't take much and she pitied herself. Did she need or demand more than she was willing to give? She tried not to. But self-pity formed at the intersection of mother and daughter regardless, there where the older woman shrivelled away from me, collapsed into absorption with herself, as if she'd forgotten that I was a person in my own right, not just a supporting player in her longer life. She might ask what I'd been doing but promptly forgot what I said. I knew it was forgetfulness but too often I suspected the reason was not merely forgetfulness but the fact that I'd never been known for who I was.

But enough, I told myself. *Love covers a multitude of sins.* Mom used to quote that a lot. An exculpatory epigraph too, for all of us.

We returned to Maplebend Seniors Home. Back in her room, Mom sighed and said she wanted to rest.

What he did, she said, was nothing, you know. Your uncle in church. Nothing like I had to suffer later.

I know, Mom. I know.

Later was worse. Losing Darrell.

Mom, I know. I could be patient with her now that it was time to leave. I brushed her cheek with my lips. Of course I loved her—how could I not? Even if mothers—mine in particular—never really knew their children. Loved her in spite of her inability to think beyond her own losses, beyond the vinegary conclusion she'd reached that her children had failed to enact the fairy tale she'd desired. Me childless and Darrell dead.

When I returned from my visit with Mom, I lolled in the heat and shelter of the balcony, but it was no beach reading that afternoon. It was the eighteenth chapter of The Revelation to John. A city named Babylon, depicted as a woman renowned for her pride and sensuality. Now desolated but not lamented. *How much she hath glorified herself, and lived deliciously, so much torment and sorrow give her: for she saith in her heart, I sit a queen and am no widow, and shall see no sorrow. Therefore shall her plagues come in one day, death, and mourning, and famine; and she shall be utterly burned with fire... And the kings of the earth, who have committed fornication and lived deliciously with her, shall bewail her, and lament for her, when they shall see the smoke of her burning...*

A figurative text. What had Rudy Klassen extracted here that agitated Uncle so much that *something inside him just had to let go?*

That was *so* embarrassing, I'd told Darrell that Sunday at the sink while our folks and the Klassens sequestered behind the living room door.

Yeah. Darrell picked up a glass, pushed the dish towel into it and twisted. But it added some spice.

Who needs spice?

Pumpkin pie. Let's see, nutmeg and—

Oh quit it, I said.

Diversion, he said. It has its compensations.

Uncle Must? Dad getting hit?

Darrell shrugged. Dad's okay, he said.

Well I thought it was horrible, I said. Humiliating. Though I wasn't about to tell him how Betts had laughed and laughed outside after church. How Betts had said, What a crazy old coot, how Shirley chimed in, Crazy old coot. How I'd chimed in too. Crazy old coot. How afraid I was.

Darrell shrugged again. Yeah, he said, I guess. He dried another glass. Uncle Must is smart, you know. He's actually very smart.

Not today.

I'd washed, he'd dried, we didn't argue, and the door to the living room remained closed. And I couldn't understand why it didn't seem to bother Darrell when it bothered me.

The next day at school, Betts asked me if Uncle talked in his sleep, or had he forgotten his pills? She acted as if the most exciting thing ever had happened and of course the other girls looked at me like question marks and I hurriedly replied Yes, he probably forgot his pills, though it hadn't occurred to me that he might be taking—or should be taking—any kind of medication. Betts filled in the ghastly details of the scene at church for those who hadn't heard. She exaggerated it. And I went along with it. I agreed that Uncle Must was strange and hilarious, yes, precisely, he was *so so so* strange and hilarious. It felt as if all my distress had rushed to my face and was blazing there. And in the hubbub I heard someone asking, Why do you call him Uncle Must? What kind of name is Must?

That evening after supper, after my uncle returned to his place for the night, Dad told Darrell and me that he and Mom and Uncle had gone to Summit, the nearest larger town where there was a clinic and small hospital. They'd taken him to the doctor, he said, and everything would be okay. My parents were standing together by the table while he reported this. Mom stepped closer to Dad and they locked hands and she added that anyone could get worked up and lose track of where they were.

On the Sundays that followed, Dad sat beside Uncle Must near the back of the church, and this relaxed me somewhat, him taking charge of his older brother. But I felt vulnerable and obvious still, my uncle's outburst like a smudge across us that everyone could see. The smudge felt permanent. The news had probably spread from farm to farm and throughout Tilia so that everyone had me distinctly in their sights, would see me and say, That's her! The one with that uncle!

But nothing seemed to change for my father. I'd been proud of him, taking that blow, leading Uncle out. I ached for him too. Every morning, Uncle Must came into the kitchen and Dad said, Good morning, Brother, and my uncle said, Good morning, Jake, with his subtle, bossy inference that it was high time to finish those eggs and get on with their work. And every morning my father smiled and made small talk and hurried with his breakfast.

What should I be doing, Catherine? Mom asked me on another visit at the seniors' residence that fall.

Asked again. Her voice plaintive. What's next for me?

I don't know, Mom.

And don't say heaven either! I'm tired of talking about heaven all the time.

We weren't talking about heaven.

I don't know what to do, that's the trouble. I can't walk anywhere.

I recalled what Joe the chaplain had told me just the other day when he steered me into his small, cluttered office to inquire about Edna Riediger from *the daughter's perspective.* When I said that Edna often asked the daughter what she ought to be doing next, to which said daughter always replied, Nothing Mom, just rest, you've worked all your life and there's nothing more to do, he didn't laugh as I expected him to. He gave me a stern look and said a person's need—and capacity—for purpose rarely disappears. Life is growth, possibility, purpose, to the very end! So questions like my mother's, he said, should be taken seriously.

I figured Joe must have been to a seminar on the subject.

So probe a little, he'd said, easing down bits of his gingery beard with his thumb and forefinger. Follow her thoughts. Go where she's leading you, don't push back. Don't say there's nothing left for her to do. She isn't dead.

I didn't care for correction but I said, That's really helpful, Joe.

So helpful that I recalled it now, just in time, and said, What would you *like* to do, Mom? What is it that feels unfinished?

Unfinished? Everything's finished! That's the trouble.

I took a deep breath in, and out. I felt I might have to leave Mother Edna's final purposes to Joe. All I knew for certain was what I still wanted from her. I wanted my mother to be a source of information. And a confessional too. I longed to say, You know, Mom, I don't think I ever quite lost that feeling, those years in Tilia, of being marked by him. He seemed like that goat symbol in the Old Testament. Remember? Loosed into the wilderness. A scapegoat. As if I'd been banished too, riding on his back.

But the comparison was too sophisticated, far too melodramatic to pursue. I needed to lower my expectations, for they were neither fair nor possible. I patted Mom's arm and changed the subject. I felt depleted.

7.

On November 22, Jim reminded me it was the anniversary of JFK's death. I heard it on the radio, coming home, he said. I would have forgotten otherwise. By now.

When it happened, I said, I never imagined the story would get old, like a classic. The president was dead and that's what mattered—mattered more than anything had mattered for a long time, maybe since John Glenn crawled into a space capsule and circled the earth.

I didn't tell Jim that it also mattered because it had diverted attention from my Uncle Must. I remembered the day, of course I did, everyone my age remembers the day, that slow Friday afternoon at school, and how the principal came to the door and told Miss Siemens, my favourite teacher (though Lester B Pearson and the Suez Canal crisis she was explaining bored me almost beyond endurance), how we were dismissed then to go home or into the spare room where the television stood on a trolley, where Darrell and I and other country students watched the news until the bus arrived. Darrell hunched close, as if he owned the set. He looked stricken. I slipped into the seat beside him and said his name and he said mine, so he knew I was there, but he didn't turn and he wasn't really with me like he'd been at the fire. His absorption in the screen was absolute. Walter Cronkite repeating what he knew and in between, footage of the arrival in Dallas and motorcade to the point of the terrible shots.

My brother had been so intensely involved in the American election. He followed it by radio and newspapers and magazines, every way he could, until the rest of the family was sick of him talking about it, sick of him trying to teach us how the US system worked when none of us cared. Mom, who'd grown up in the States, was the most impatient. Darrell wanted Kennedy to win and wouldn't budge, even when our parents and Uncle Must, who'd worried because Kennedy was Catholic, disagreed with him and insisted he ought to hope for Richard Nixon. One supper my uncle stuck his head out of his usual eating-reverie to announce he prayed every day that Nixon would win. Darrell seemed unconcerned, but I felt anxious on my brother's behalf; I feared Uncle's prayers could doom his candidate.

When John Kennedy triumphed, Darrell was pretty good about it; he didn't gloat too much, and after a while, our parents and uncle seemed to admit the world hadn't fallen to pieces because of it, though once they were used to it, he occasionally went ahead and gloated anyway. I was surprised and relieved to realize my uncle's prayers met the same fate as those of many a prayer, not answered as hoped. Since my brother won the role of family pundit, his next task was convincing us JFK was a good president. He called him astute. Courageous. Darrell was such a keener! He kept us informed about the Bay of Pigs and the blockade and who blinked first, as if he didn't realize we also listened to the news every evening after supper.

The arrival of the bus was announced and the other students shuffled out. Darrell, I said, swatting his arm, we have to go.

Darrell! I boomed in his ear. And then for the first time, he glanced at me. Rats, he said.

The bus dropped us off and we trudged up the lane. I said, I'll bet Mom and Dad don't know about this.

Probably not.

He was pure gloom while I felt excitement about the tragedy. Like a prize we'd won while away. So you'll have to tell them, I said.

Sure. He seemed grateful for the suggestion, my yielding to him as the logical bearer of this news, but then he flared, But we don't have a TV! He bent to grab a pebble, heaved it furiously as if wishing it would explode on the lane.

We've been asking and asking, I agreed. Now *this* happens and we're stuck without one! Darrell and I figured we were the only household left in North America without TV. Sure, a few other church folk were holding out but they were elderly so what did they know? Neither of us could understand our parents' fears and when I tried, asking my mother why why why, she called me a stuck record. Darrell had already threatened to buy a television for himself as soon as he had the money but it would be his alone, he said, and he would keep it in his room for himself.

I figured my parents might be weakening on the matter, though. Better we monitor it from the safety of our home, I'd overheard Mom telling Dad after Darrell and I came home from visiting friends and owned up to the fact that we'd watched television the entire time. Weakening, but dragging their feet. And I knew why. Darrell and I both knew why. It was because of Uncle Must. He'd written a letter into the German Mennonite paper about the evils of television. The letter seemed a barrier now, which our parents couldn't cross. They must have memorized the thing. No—because of the violence, materialism, immorality. No—because it was a time-waster and force of corruption. No—because it divided families.

Because it was a slippery slope.

We reached the house. Mom, who could be skeptical about what we brought from school, believed the assassination news. I stood beside Darrell and nodded like his accomplice while he told her everything we knew and when he was done, Mom said, That's so sad. Don't forget my origins are stateside and I have family there.

President Kennedy never took orders from the pope, Darrell said.

I know that, Darrell, she said.

Mom sent him off to tell Dad and Uncle Must and then she riffled through a pile of *LIFE* magazines until she found an edition with photos of the Kennedy family and she and I sat at the table and looked at the pictures together. Our fingers strayed to the figures in the photographs, slid over them as if to comfort Jackie and the children. Mom reminded me that I'd once kept a scrapbook of the royal family in England and she asked me if I still had it and I said I did.

I guess the Kennedys are like a royal family, she said.

At supper that evening, we talked about the president's death, though it was mostly me and Darrell stumbling over each other with the advantage of what we'd seen, seesawing and repeating just like the commentators on TV. Everyone was tolerant of us that evening; the president's death had affected our elders too. Afterward, they kept the radio tuned to news reports instead of the religious programs they usually had on after the news.

When Uncle Must said, It's no surprise, I was startled because he'd been with us at the table all supper and not once had I thought about what he'd done in church just a few weeks earlier. But then I worried: had he been predicting this catastrophe in his rant?

And now, decades later, Jim and I sat at the table, eating and talking about it again, Jim telling me his memories of how he heard the news and me telling him that the next impossible thing happened the following day, November 23, when Uncle Must, writer of a published letter declaiming the dangers of television, drove to the furniture and appliances store in Summit and purchased a set. Without saying a word, he unloaded that box of evil at the Big House. Then he went off to the barn to work and Darrell and Dad installed it, complete with an antenna on the roof.

We'd started the television off in the basement which was little more than a cellar, as if a clandestine operation, though the antenna could hardly be hidden. Jim laughed when I told him this and I realized once again that reminiscence made my husband happy. Especially when I participated too.

I'd been thrilled with the set, and Darrell as well, nearly enough to pee his pants for joy, he told me. I'd told him to smarten up his mouth. We both affected nonchalance, though, lest a show of enthusiasm land the television back in its box, back to the store. At that time, it was all about the Kennedy event—historical, the pundits said—and thus a completely legitimate reason to have a TV, and neither of us leaked any indication that we knew the names of a whole raft of other programs we intended to watch, and regularly too.

Knock, knock, Darrell said to me that evening during dishes. The television had put him in a silly mood, as if he'd forgotten the assassination.

Forget it, Darrell, I said. My brother had a huge repertoire of Knock-knock jokes but the one he did over and over was the stupid one where he said, Knock, knock, and I asked who was there and he said, Darrell, and to my Darrell who? he would say, Darrell Riediger. He thought it was hilarious to play it straight that way.

Come on, Catherine, he said. It's not the Darrell Riediger one, honest.

No, I said, we're too old for knock-knock. We finally have a TV.

I was just going to make a joke about how I talked Uncle Must into buying it.

I doubt it.

Seriously, he said. It was me. It wasn't even that hard.

He told me he'd cornered our father and uncle by the tractor, first with the news of the shooting in Dallas and then with his declaration—in no uncertain terms, he said—that they had to buy a TV. Immediately. An event of such proportions produced television at its necessary best. News: important and educational. There was no immorality in news, he stated, and no slope was slippery if you looked out for the ice and prepared not to slide. Without actually citing them, he addressed every objection Uncle Must had made in his letter to the German periodical.

He marked on his fingers all the points he'd made, tea towel draped over his shoulder and rinsed dishes mounting in the rack. I was impressed by his achievement and envious because of his influence but grumbled, Would you keep drying, please!

He ignored me and went on, hands tapping and gesturing. You know how Uncle Must can't actually help himself about wanting to know what's happening in the world? How he likes magazines and the news?

Of course I knew. Uncle subscribed to *TIME* and *LIFE*. He passed his copies on to the Big House when he was done with them. Sometimes he tore out pages, probably to prevent us from seeing them. Which only made me think harder about what wasn't there. It couldn't have been naked women, though, because he ordered *National Geographic* too and left intact the photos of bare-breasted females from exotic tribes on other continents. So much inconsistency in him! Even subscribing to *LIFE* didn't quite fit, him being so pious. Scrupulous. But yes, that curiosity, the hungry intelligence he bowed to on the one hand and refused on the other, which must have felt risky, even dangerous, but which, as he finally did with purchasing the television, he somehow managed to align with his dour theology or whatever it was.

I appealed to both of them, Darrell went on, but I was going straight for Uncle. Like an arrow to his bull's eye! I knew Dad would have to pass it through his own head and then through Mom's and then through Uncle's. Way too many heads.

Well, I'd said, maybe Uncle's embarrassed about that Sunday. Trying to make it up to us.

Nah. I don't think that concerns him in the least.

You don't know everything.

I know everything! Darrell laughed maniacally, like a television laugh track, and once again I had to tell him to shut up and get on with drying the dishes.

8.

Showered, naked beneath my robe, mug of coffee at the ready,
Jim long gone to work. I checked my email and there was nothing new besides the notification of a post on Daniel Jute's blog.
I ignored these sometimes, just to prove I could. To prove I was
retired and archival science no longer concerned me. Other times
I read them to prove what I'd been involved with once, which concerned me still: these discussions of new collections, new challenges in the field. And, to be honest, I'd never quite erased from
memory the black sheen of Jute's hair and the electricity between
us that time in his office, the grasping look on his face, though
nothing had happened, neither then nor at the professional events
we attended out of town, because whatever provocation there'd
been, I was determined I would never fail my marriage.

By now there was no spark left, rather chagrin, but like a
near-accident, a livid imprint of him touched my nerves whenever

I read his work. He'd done an interesting series of columns on the world's top archivists and what we could learn from them, another on how archivists were represented in culture and literature, how they appeared as characters or plot devices. Everything from Dan Brown to José Saramago. He wrote brilliantly but always sounded too sure of himself. I could nearly brush his tie through the words on the screen, so great seemed the puff of his chest.

In today's post, he talked about the difficulties with sources around the early Church Fathers and Mothers. I found it interesting. Two clicks later, I was sliding into the story of a monk. Saint Martinian the venerable, the ancient. He of the Caesarean wilderness and then a tiny island in the vast, grey sea. Barren rock his floor, an unreliable hut for his shelter. Years there, weaving his baskets, saying his prayers. He must have been an expert by then, so much practice at weaving, solitude, resisting temptation.

It grabbed me like a shout. *One time, a powerful storm wrecked a ship, and to the island of Saint Martinian, the waves carried on the ship's debris a maiden, by the name of Photinia.* I saw the long fingers paused stiffly over the half-woven container, the heap of soaked reeds at his side, and in that moment, I thought I saw my uncle's face. The hair like dirty straw, not cut closely up his neck or combed straight back like he wore it when I was a kid, but streaming away from his head like yarn. And matted. Because of the salt and humidity. Something like terror—that grey flicker of dilemma—had seized his countenance. Spray thundered against the rock to which the exhausted Photinia clung. She hugged the jagged edges of the rock like a pillow and her arms bled. Ripped garments flounced in the sea. She needed pulling up. Uncle's inky eyes darted from the woman at the island's edge to the wet, black rock at his feet. Back and forth they darted and his hair lifted in the wind and the woman's braid opened and strands of her hair lifted too. The sea pushed in like a cauldron but her hair lifted like wings. Her hair was yellowish. That Sharon Miller who'd burst into my uncle's house on a night as stormy as this one was the face of Photinia.

This vision, if that's what it was, unfolded relentlessly, as any text will, stating the truth with one sentence, hiding it away with the next, my uncle's predicament trembling in him until he shook quite violently. He must have lost his confidence, never mind his competence at prayer. Probably unable to tell who or what the woman was, whether celestial messenger or demon from hell. So Saint Martinian would have thought at least, other Fathers booming in his ears that demons could take on the forms of women. His lips flew apart into an oval, as if for an exuberant Gloria in Excelsis Deo, but he was consumed by further panic, head jerking, hands fisted and beating. It was really something, that drumming, as if the air writhed with shapes of threat or consolation that fought over him as he contended with them. Alone. And all the while Miss Miller hung onto the rock, keening her song of relief and despair, eyes a-flutter as if taking vows of ecstasy or martyrdom.

Remain here, he said to her, for here is bread and water. In two months, a boat will come. And he jumped into the sea ...

I shook myself away from the scene and gulped for air. I was famished for oxygen. But something had been clarified for me. My uncle's strange paralysis about women was hardly original to him; it was the inheritance of an error long and pernicious. Then I noticed my robe was loose—way loose—and I had to laugh, for fear had actually hurtled through my mind in that moment. Fear that I'd been seen! By the uncle or the saint. He had felt that real.

I crossed the robe fiercely over my breasts, knotted the belt, shut down my computer, picked up my coffee, and headed for the sofa to consider it further. To remember, yes, my uncle's strange paralysis.

Uncle Must moved into the Big House in 1965, the night of my first date. It was a double date: my brother Darrell and Shirley, and me and Maynard, who was Shirley's brother. Two sets of best friends, two sets of siblings. We kept it up a couple of months, the four of us, mostly at youth group events, until the Darrell-Shirley pairing fell apart when Darrell took up with Betty, who by that time called herself Liz. She chose Liz because of Elizabeth Taylor and Richard Burton. Aren't those two just smokey? she would say, her mouth a pout and trying to smoulder. After a while, Maynard and I fell apart too.

The trouble was, we'd practically grown up together. Our parents were friends so there were visits back and forth and hours playing games. Hide-and-seek or kick-the-can in every season but winter, when we tobogganed instead. In retrospect, all those Sunday afternoons or evenings seemed autumnal, daylight burning down like a long, slow fire, leaves and dried grasses crackling under us as we hid in the ditch or the garden, the melancholy of overhead geese, our shouts of Gotcha! like bugle notes in tawny air. The house windows turned golden as darkness deepened, our parents conversing amiably behind them.

We knew the rules: stay in the yard. Not even over the road to Uncle's. His single front window might be lit, but it was pale and distant like an uncertain sign of human habitation on a faraway shore. He might be reading the scriptures or his magazines. Writing something, perhaps. He would have been welcome to join my parents and their friends but he wasn't sociable like that most of the time.

Not that the yard wasn't large enough. A couple of acres. Home base was the light pole.

I'd rarely wasted concern on my uncle while we played, though there'd been a worrisome sighting while hiding one evening at the farthest reach of the permissible roaming, by the tree at the end of the lane just across from his tiny house. The hedge was shorn of its foliage and he was visible through it, gesticulating by the window like a light-and-shadow show. He'd opened it to the cool evening air. I heard a man's cry and it sounded like contention. This was before that ghastly scene of his in church and later I wondered if he'd been rehearsing it that night. Fearing Maynard or Shirley would see him and laugh, I abandoned my hiding place, ran up the lane, let myself be caught, dropped against the pole, and said I wanted to do something else.

Sometimes we played inside, around the kitchen table. Monopoly or Careers. We played together so often we knew how the others conducted their game. Darrell bossy, concealing his need to win under a string of commentary. Ver-rry interesting, he would say, rolling the dice and making his move. Just look that up in your *Funk and Wagnalls*. Maynard quick and argumentative, constantly checking the rules, disputing minutiae. As far as he was concerned, we had to get it right, every little bit of it, or the game would stall until he made his point. As for me, they called me sneaky, and when I won, said I'd cheated. Ha, ha, I might be sneaky, I would say, but I never ever cheat. Careful observation, that's what it was, not much talking, making my moves. Buying up Baltic and Mediterranean, the low-priced properties, if I could. Keeping my prospects humble. I just wanted to get enough in a row, own the whole lot of them after GO if there was any possibility. I never revealed or discussed my strategies. And now and then they worked. Shirley needled—for admiration, for alliances.

It could hardly be expected that the transition from this level of familiarity to dating would be smooth, that we could leave behind such intimate knowledge of each other, those hours of fun and fighting. Still, we'd changed. We felt ourselves grown. We wanted to try love instead of friendship. Shirley and I were fifteen, our brothers a year older.

Darrell found me preening in front of the mirror, pushing at the tip of my nose. Yikes! I'd left the door open and he'd seen me and so he said, What in the world?

What does it look like? I said. But no use fibbing. I put on a manner as arch as possible and said I was pretending at Julie Andrews.

Why push it? he said. Your nose curves up already.

It was complicated and so annoying with a brother. So you're saying I look like her?

The ugly version, he said, as I might have expected, but he grinned and I picked up the hairbrush and moved as if to chuck it at him and then he said, No, you silly, you look like yourself, just fine. At least Maynard thinks so, ha ha, and then he got earnest in a vaguely nervous way and hinted at going on a date and wondered, what did I think, would Shirley go out with him? He said that if we doubled, Maynard would want to take me for sure. Mom and Dad would let us go double, wouldn't they?

Shirley will want to, I said, I can tell you that. Every girl in school had a crush on Darrell. I suggested *The Sound of Music*, which Shirley and I had seen already but were dying to see again. We'd ridden along into Calgary with Dad, ate fish and chips in a restaurant for lunch, giggled over to the matinee, then re-lived the fabulous thing with swoons and laughs the whole way home.

Darrell said he wasn't that keen on *The Sound of Music*. Wasn't there something with more action, or no action, something more Ingmar Bergman-ish? I said it was a matter of persuading our parents. Religious, conservative, our parents were on the edge of so many changes, what with television and The Beatles and now movies and dating, and even though we'd all seen films, my parents too—in school, in the community hall, even in church; films with nature or family or Christian themes—for them, the theatre was another horse altogether. Theatres were soft and velvety. Dangerous. They had wine-coloured interiors, everything an evocation of something else, and a darkness much greater than the dark in which films unwound in the church or school auditorium. The story rolled on and on, no matter what happened in the seats. Our being teens seemed to worry my parents and made them unpredictable.

Though it was also true that they were doling out their adjustments, bit by bit. They'd become less supervisory with TV. They'd allowed the matinee. Mom read articles and books about childrearing and was open to new approaches. Just kids, Jake, she would say when she thought he disapproved too quickly. Dad, more traditional than Mom, said he didn't actually care for the word kids—it made him think of baby goats. On the other hand, he was kinder than she was, not as prone to tongue-lashings; if she was a learner she was arbitrary in her reactions too, and our father, while resistant to change, the more forgiving. Our physical nearness seemed enough to soften him. The only spanking I ever got from him hardly rated the name, so feeble it was, so apologetic. Two light swipes, then a short talk about the misdemeanour. My mother, on the other hand, seemed excessively fond of her children when she thought about us, which she claimed she did most of the day at the stove and sewing machine, loving thoughts, she said, yet we were barely in the house some days before we aggravated her.

The point was, our parents were in flux and had to be managed, each of them with their particular style but trying to act as a unit, trying to be a solid, single force in front of their offspring. I told Darrell *The Sound of Music* was our best and probably only option. We wanted to get out of Tilia at least, didn't we?

I insisted Darrell do the asking. He had the gift of the gab and he knew how to charm, our mother especially; he was our ground for ultimate success. And sure enough, we got their permission and the use of the car, the big, robin's-egg-blue Chevrolet, and all that was left was the final drill about the schedule in the hour before leaving: straight to Calgary, directly to the show, just enough time for an ice-cream sundae or maybe a root beer, then home again.

My parents had stumbled over the matter of my age. Fifteen was too young, they said, I ought to be sixteen at least, Mom doing the talking but Dad listening and nodding. It was easier for them, though, she acknowledged, knowing Darrell and I would be together; we could monitor one another. Then, from Mom's fluttering tips on the afternoon of the date—how momentous it seemed, this date!—I gathered that they were relying on me to be the monitor. You know Darrell and how enthusiastic he can get, Mom said, as if enthusiasm were a vice instead of a virtue. She'd treated me like a fellow soldier on an enemy raid and I hadn't liked it but I kept saying yes, just to get it over with.

At the car window before we drove off to pick up Maynard and Shirley, Dad said, I hear it's going to storm tonight, Darrell. Be careful driving in the rain.

The sky was clear but Darrell said, Okay, okay, gotcha, Dad. Careful in the rain.

Okay, okay, okay. He'd been saying that through every instruction our parents gave him lately, never fighting back, though their eyes searched his face when he answered to see if he was listening or just parroting the words. Okay, okay, through all their cautions and fears and hopes. I knew without asking that he'd been to the movies without permission, and who knew what else he'd been up to. A cigarette, or two or three. Smoking wasn't so much a health concern at that time as the most obvious sign to our elders of breaking-in wildness, of rebellion. That coiling aroma, that expense and langour, just the beginning of what would inevitably end as a filthy habit and avoidance of church.

Uncle Must stood on his stoop, watching us leave. He looked upset. Darrell waved but Uncle didn't wave back and Darrell and I chuckled. At the Klassen farm, Maynard and Shirley climbed into the back seat of the car, and their parents stood by the door and waved goodbye too until the four of us were out of sight. You'd think we're going somewhere important, Maynard grumbled, and Darrell said, It's like we're heading to the mission field for seven years, and we all laughed and then he stopped the car. He said, It's a date, for Pete's sake.

Shirley and I got out and traded places to sit next to our fellows. We stayed properly apart going into Calgary but on the way home we inched closer and closer on the bench seat until each couple was touching shoulders and more. By that time, after the movie and the root beer—even Darrell admitted he liked the movie, though Shirley kept pushing him on it like a ditz—the clouds ahead of us got blacker and twisted into knots, and Darrell got silly and singing. Not off key—he had a good ear for music—but roughly, it seemed, in spite of the darlings scattered in the lines.

Shirley tried to sing along, her mood in full beam, but he was making the song up and the duet became nonsensical. I couldn't quite relax into the merriment because Darrell was driving too fast and I was thinking of Mom's warning, how she'd called him enthusiastic. And I watched the sky because we were driving homeward into the threat of a storm, thunder rumble advancing to meet us, my anxiety pushing upward as if it might qualify as prayer. But we were fortunate: we got only spatters of rain during the drive. The fiercest thunder-crack of them all and a flare of lightning as bright as noon occurred just as we turned onto the lane to our house, and then the storm broke open and the rain fell as if released from a cage and beside itself with rage. Missed it by a hair, said Darrell. It seemed an accomplishment.

Dad was up, waiting for us I assumed, but there was nothing to talk about; we'd kept our curfew and when he asked, we said the movie was good. He didn't interrogate us further as Mom would have. He was intent on the strength of the rain. Darrell said, Good night and God bless, Red Skelton-style, still acting extreme, and

Dad said, No fooling around now, Darrell, it's late, but he sounded weary, not upset.

I had trouble falling asleep. I kept going through the movie and remembering Maynard's arm on the back of my seat during the last tense minutes when the von Trapps were hiding in the cemetery, not touching me as much as poised at the ready in case the movie turned unbearably frightening. Remembering how his lips brushed mine, the briefest of brush-bys as he exited the car, as slight as a feather but no feather either—it was the temptation and tingle of other skin. He'd said something too, but I hadn't caught it. Wondering if I should ask him when I saw him next. Remembering the scent of his breath, the slice of Spearmint gum he'd folded between his teeth before he brushed by my face.

When I finally drifted off, the unrelenting rain seemed rain that poured outside the gazebo while Liesl and Rolf danced and sang. A door banging seemed Nazis at the convent gates while nuns hid the von Trapps behind gravestones. Then I snapped out of my half-asleep spell and realized I was in my bed. The curtain had been pulled out of my partially-open window and was flapping and damp and then I knew I'd heard the slur of boots through water and there'd surely been some pounding on the door of our house.

Voices now. I got up and closed the window. My room faced the road. At the end of the lane, in Uncle Must's little domicile, the light was on. It winked at me. The crowns of the trees along the lane bent raggedly, this way and that at every whim of the wind. The thunder and lightning had travelled on, the rain dominant now, gushing. I went down the stairs, slowly, feeling dreamy as if still asleep but drawn toward the stir of sound reaching for me from below. I halted at the bottom, blinked, and there, my parents and uncle in a circle by the kitchen door like a meeting, Mom in her blue chenille robe, Dad in his undershirt and pants, though beltless, and Uncle Must looking horribly thin because he was soaked. He seemed like the trunk of a craggy old tree, rough grey bark in its vertical hills and valleys, and the water he'd accumulated in his run from his house to ours slid down him in rivulets and dripped onto the rug. The kitchen clock showed nearly two o'clock.

My uncle was saying that someone needed shelter at his house. A woman, he said.

He was distressed, but strangely excited. Kind of him, I thought, and generous; I could grant him that much, letting a poor woman in for the night.

My mother was flustered, my father a row of grunts, my uncle trying to explain. She was dumped, he said. They drove off, whoever it was... And nothing he could do about it, apparently, the woman left at the door. Nothing besides let her come in.

What's going on? I asked. Mom turned, frowned, motioned upward with her chin, meaning, get back upstairs. The problem seemed to be my baby doll pajamas. She said, I'll tell you tomorrow, sweetie.

Sweetie? What kind of talk was that, as if I were five instead of fifteen. I hadn't been a sweetie for years. I stayed put and watched my uncle drip and drain onto the braided rug.

Then, Catherine, you're not suitable! Mom's tone was sharp so I obeyed and climbed the stairs. Well awake by now, I lowered myself onto the upper landing, out of sight, to listen. Uncle Must needed to stay the night, I'd gathered that much, and he'd left his house to a woman.

Mom pounced on Uncle with one question after the other. Had he brought anything along? (Nothing.) Had he left everything there and unlocked? (Yes.) Did he, at the least, have his wallet and his keys? (Yes.)

We have our money in the bank, Edna, Dad inserted. Brother Gerhard doesn't keep much at the house.

What was she like? (He didn't know.)

The moist and nervous voice of my uncle: I didn't think of anything to bring, I was in such a hurry. But I know you have everything.

A reply I couldn't decipher, except for an echoed Everything! but Mom's anxiety strong enough to reach me on the landing, all the underwear, clothes, pillows and blankets—and pajamas!—left behind for some stranger. Everything!

Really, it was such a simple, sparse-to-a-fault kind of a place, my uncle's house: a table, two chairs, a tiny, basic kitchen, a wringer washing machine beside the door, an easy chair, a bed, a shelf of books, a roll-down desk with papers. No pictures on the walls. When I delivered fresh baking now and then, or ran some other errand for one of my parents, his house felt like a cocoon to me, small and neat and badly lit. Though peaceful in a way. But nothing of value in it. A pot or two, some dishes, wall pegs with his work clothes hanging over them, his Sunday suit, a wash basin and towel. The house like a cell, everything in place, nothing superfluous.

Mom: Well, why doesn't she come and stay here? You can't leave her there alone with the things.

Uncle Must: She won't come.

Dad: She drove up, in this storm, into the yard?

Uncle Must, vehement: No, no, no. She was outside at the door. She said she'd been dumped.

Dad, as if to himself: Dripping in the rain, I suppose.

Mom: Who left her there?

Uncle Must, dejected but impatient too, as if to remind that he'd related the story already: She didn't say!

Mom, suspicious: You know her?

A pause, then my uncle sounding as wretched as I'd ever heard him: She says so. I've met her, I guess. She knew my name. She was dropped off.

I was getting chilly in my itty-bitty pajamas and wished the tense, investigative threesome at the door would wrap up.

Dad: Should Edna go and stay with her?

Mom, indignant: Jake! In this rain?

Uncle Must, pleading: No, no, just let it be. She'll be all right. The house is nothing, really. Worthless.

As if he considered it lost already.

Mom, her brisk, efficient self at last: Well come in, come in. I'll put you up on the chesterfield tonight and we'll figure it out in the morning. Was she smoking?

Uncle Must, desperately: I don't think so! I don't know!

Well if she smokes, Mom said, let's hope she doesn't burn the place down.

Won't get far in a downpour like this. Dear, droll Dad.

They moved away from the door and I heard Mom muttering, opening the cupboard with the linens. I got up from my perch and returned to bed. Passing my window, I brushed the wet curtain. I looked out. The light was still on at Uncle Must's, flickering and woozy, as if swimming in the rain.

The next day dawned with dazzling sunshine and cloudless skies. Puddles gleamed like mirrors. The green of the garden, grass, and trees was greener, beautifully clean, but out of kilter too, as if heavy with the memory of the storm's assault. The earth seemed bloated, over-ripe. But optimism gleamed in the air, the pride of surviving. All's well, the day seemed to say, and even better, it's Sunday, done for another week, never mind that it took a beating to get there.

Mom, busy in the kitchen, didn't mention Uncle's presence at breakfast. Neither did she give me—her sweetie!—the explanation she'd promised. After breakfast, she donned her rubber gardening boots and tramped down the lane to his house. She was kept waiting at the door a very long time, she told us when she returned with Uncle's Sunday suit draped over her arm. She was kept waiting and knocking until the current occupant of the house finally woke up and let her in. After these tidbits of information, Mom kept her lips together, though they seemed as swollen as buds, eager to burst open at any moment with additional and astonishing news now that she'd seen the intruder herself. Before we left for church, she and Dad and Uncle Must met again, this time behind the closed door of the living room, and perhaps that was her opportunity to let her judgments out. Uncle Must stayed that day with us and at the end of it, he spent a second night on the chesterfield.

It was the summer holidays and Darrell and I had to help around the farm, and both of us worked at other places whenever we got the chance. Monday I was booked to help at the Fehrs's, to babysit and clean. When I returned on my bicycle it was supper time and Uncle Must took his place at the table as always. But he didn't retreat to his house after the meal and radio news were done and he'd parked the truck in our yard instead of his and the chesterfield was still made up into a bed. He mumbled into the living room and closed the door.

Uncle Must will be sleeping here for a while, my mother said.

Lorena asked why and Mom said, There's someone in his house. Her tone was casual, as if the someone were an inconvenience as minor as a sparrow flown by mistake into the lean-to entrance, which would find its way out shortly if we kept the outer door wide open.

Over dishes, Mom told me the woman's name was Sharon Miller. She showed up in the middle of the storm, she said. At night. So of course he couldn't stay; it would have looked wrong.

Seems it's fallen on me to get rid of her, Mom continued, her voice close and complaining, as if my date with Maynard had elevated me to confidante. He won't go over there so I'm the in-between. She claims she has no place to live, and nobody's coming to get her. Uncle says to let her stay. Says something's bound to happen and she'll be gone by tomorrow.

What does she look like? I asked.

Mom lifted the plates out of the steaming rinse and slid them into the drying rack. She's pretty, she said. But shameless.

Uncle Must remained at our house the next day and the next and the stranger remained at his. Mom's expression grew tighter. Thursday, when I returned from my work I discovered that my parents had re-arranged the bedrooms. My things were crammed into one side of my room, Lorena's cot and toys set up beside them. Mom and Dad had re-located themselves and their belongings into Darrell's room, and the small room that was Lorena's would now be Darrell's—cushions and sleeping bags configured into a kind of bed on the floor. His bed had been taken downstairs into my parents' former bedroom for Uncle Must.

Weren't you farming today? I burst out, seeing Dad indoors, grasping that I was about to share a room with my little sister.

Plowing and seeding furniture, he said.

My anger must have showed. There's no other solution for the time being, Dad said. We're doing our best.

Every day of it slouched on to the next. Sharon Miller, who needed shelter from the storm, wasn't going anywhere, and even worse, Uncle Must had turned tail and run. He was simply letting her stay. He refused to even speak with her, never mind force her out. He settled into the main floor bedroom, and after a few days he drove to Summit and came back with a bed for Darrell.

Mom gradually revealed bits and pieces of the mystery woman while her hands were deep in suds, while stirring a pudding to a boil, whenever, that is, she was stationary for a few minutes and in a sharing frame of mind. Sharon Miller—Miss Miller, Mom insisted we call her—originated in Saskatchewan, though she'd most recently resided in Calgary. She seemed to have clothes and other personal things, though whether they came along with her that stormy night or later could not be conclusively determined. No one had seen a car pull onto the yard. Not that we could be watching every minute of every day, she said. The young woman insisted she had no connections, no resources, yet the clothesline outside the small house was merry with bright blouses, skirts, and pants. Miss Miller often wore pants, which to Mom's way of thinking meant she wasn't serious about being as old as she was, which apparently was in her twenties.

Uncle Must was awfully sorry, my mother said, but really, what choice did he have? She seemed to believe this. I learned further that he would compensate my parents for the inconvenience, pay them well, in fact, which must have mollified her, what with all the expenses a family accumulated.

Uncle Must is ten years older than your father, Catherine, she said. He's worked and saved for years. He can afford it.

He'd also given Miss Miller credit for groceries at the Tilia Co-op and asked Mom to invite her along whenever she went into town. Mom considered this too much encouragement for the woman to stay, but it seemed she would comply.

The first time Mom and Miss Miller drove to Tilia together, I spotted my uncle's truck at his house, home from field work in the middle of the day. He darted in and out as if afraid of being caught. I supposed he'd watched until the women disappeared over the hill in order to fetch a few of his things. I was mopping the floor at the far end of the kitchen when he walked in with an armful of books. He stooped with their weight. I asked him if he needed help. This is it, he said, looking past me. Just this pile. The clothes aren't heavy at all. But thank you for the offer.

I resented him in our house, but the constriction he wore aroused my sympathy. I wanted to ask how his house was getting along without him but couldn't bring myself to test his obvious solitude, and besides, I knew the answer already. She's no house-keeper, whatever else she might be, Mom had said, the place was a pigsty. How it's even possible, she said, I'll never know. An absolute mess.

Uncle Must turned and stared out the window at the truck. It's a trial, he said, which I'll have to endure. Future glory, though unseen. It was his pious old foolishness again and my compassion evaporated. He was a headache, that's what he was. A wretched, drab, blob of a headache I wished would just go away.

I actually broke up with Maynard because he said, Your uncle's quite the weirdo, eh, Catherine, letting that bimbo take over his house?

Then I knew Uncle Must was the target of jeering in Tilia again.

He's smart, I rushed back at him, caught off guard and remembering what Darrell had said.

Oh sure, I know, I mean he seems completely normal, but you know, like you look closer, right? I mean— He laughed and the way he looked at me, it was like a puppy assuming he was irresistible.

You're the weirdo, Maynard, I said, feigning casualness, bravado. Then I said, I don't actually want to be boyfriend and girlfriend with you anymore.

Which I could tell had hurt him. The way he blinked, a quick, protective veil over his eyes.

I regretted it a little, knowing I would never experience the full press of his lips, never get beyond that brush-by of his mouth on our first date and me under the pressure of *Sweet sixteen and never been kissed*, and his lips were good-looking, they were definitely appealing, the way they plumped comfortably together, top and bottom, when he wasn't expostulating about something or other, that is. But it was impossible. I might have the same opinion about my uncle as Maynard, but Uncle Must belonged to me, not him, so he had no right to speak of him that way.

And perhaps I longed to reach a better understanding of the man, to overcome my negative thoughts. Perhaps I did, and wished a boyfriend to ennoble me for such a task. I must have known there was no cure for Maynard's attitude, no way it would improve. A dolt, he was, he and his ardent Spearmint breath. I needed someone better-disposed in his heart than I was in mine.

Which Jim has been, I can honestly say that much. Tolerant, carrying others more lightly, more uncritically, than I've ever done. Remembering that break-up exchange, however, I was pleased that I'd managed this subtle defense of my uncle, slender gesture though it was. Not much of a defense—in truth, more self-defense than anything else—but still, I gave up Maynard's lips forever on behalf of my odd Uncle Must.

9.

I'd been excited to retire. I was relatively young and in good health and Jim had planned to do the same, until he leapt for the contract year, that is, and now I was there and had no option but to settle into it. My closest friend Ev was in California that year, caring for her elderly father, and it was lonely without her. I was still a little sorry about the thrift store but would be nothing if not loyal until I found something that might suit me better. Good thing there was plenty of humour in the place; on my thrift store days, I always had stories to share with Jim. I joined a book club. I walked and walked some more. I met other friends for coffee. I read. George Eliot's *Middlemarch*, for the third time. *Possession* by AS Byatt, with its sleuthing poets and scholars and the clues that letters can hide. A good book for an ex-archivist.

And I spent hours gazing out the window. At construction cranes rotating gracefully at the human rights museum being constructed at the Forks, at trains rolling in or out, at people on the street below gripping coats and hurrying through the cold (which had arrived, post-October). The choreography of traffic flow—a stop and go, stop and go. My prospect at sixteen storeys still beguiled me. Sometimes my focus shifted until I no longer saw what was there but entered a realm of alternate sight in which my entire chronology, my entire geography, from Tilia to Winnipeg, seemed compressed and visible on the backdrop of the scene below, and then, for those minutes, I was satisfied and cheered, past and present whole, a single history as insistently precious as an heirloom ring sparkling in a satin-lined box. I felt taller since moving into the sixteenth floor apartment. Enclosed as well. Unimposed upon. A participant in life yet blissfully alone. The paradox of belonging within a bona fide anonymity. I hadn't realized until we were up and in—after living for four decades on the ground in that gingerbread house we refurbished in Kildonan—how desperately I wanted that sense of myself, that perspective. The air different, and also the light, not so much received from above as met head-on.

I bought a packet of Uni-Ball pens to go with my red notebook and began to set down quotes that interested me. Or, now and then, an etymology. *Yearn* from desirous and eager. (Too energetic for the melancholic blend of patience, inevitability, irritation that my yearning for Jim entailed, however.) *Odd* from the Old Norse point of land, with peculiar or eccentric not used until the seventeenth century. *Shame*: links to ruddy cheeks, disgrace, loss of esteem. *Receptive*, from Latin *recipere*, to receive.

My new book club had embarked on a plan to re-read famous Canadian authors. The night before we met for Margaret Atwood's *Cat's Eye*, Jim and I opened the curtains to the moonlight and I told him about the novel, which he'd never read, its wonderful first page, time not a line but a dimension, not looking back along a line, that is, but through it, like water, and about main character Elaine, beseiged by her memories and the betrayals of her childhood friends Carol and Grace and Cordelia. Especially Cordelia, a girl of incredible spite. Elaine peeled skin off her feet because of her.

Though later, I said, Elaine wasn't that pleasant either.

The book had captivated me the first time I read it. Nothing corresponded directly, I told Jim, and as far as mean girls went, I only had Betty, who wasn't *that* mean. No, I said, I wasn't Elaine in the least, yet I'd been given some tale about myself. Maybe the notion of starting life as who you actually are, and then at some point you're a girl, like *girl* takes on another connotation, like a river that divides. At that point, any unkindness is larger than life.

It might have been on account of the moon, beneficent over us, or the way we lay with arms and hands touching, Jim wide awake, listening, the smell of us close and as earthy as mushrooms, that I was suffused with happiness that night. He said, I know what you mean. The book telling you part of yourself. This happens to me with music sometimes. Something expressed that I knew but didn't know I knew.

When Jim says he understands what I mean, it's often his sincerest, best wish, but this time I was sure it was true. I pressed his hand and we moved easily to the topic of him ending his work at contract's end, which he claimed again he really wanted to do and would.

Maybe we could go away next year, he said. Anywhere. For some months at a time.

He seemed quite resolved about this idea, but I said, The school division will ask you to continue, do another contract. It's impossible for you to say No.

No, Catherine, *really.*

Well, where should we go?

We'll put the names of all the countries in the world into a hat and begin with the place we draw.

And if we don't like what comes up, we'll just keep pulling until we do?

Exactly.

All in fun, and we laughed and my happiness increased. Well Jim, I said, I'll see you actually retiring when you do.

So maybe we were done for the night but I swung back to *Cat's Eye*. I consider my childhood reasonably sunny, I said. Not left in a ravine like Elaine. No creepy fingers inside my underpants. Still, a person looks back and feels some damage has been done.

Everyone sustains some damage, he said. Everyone.

And then we were quiet and I felt his hand slacken away from mine, his breath slowing into the rhythm of sleep. Damage, yes. The wounds of growing up. Though he had songs, and his oratorios, to lose his joy and anguish in. Moonlight covered his face, as if he'd been cast in marble, his features steadfast and distinguished.

I got up and mused at the window. I'd probably felt the infamy of my uncle's tirade in church too strongly. Yes, I was sure I had. And of course, I could have refused to go along with Betty and her monikers and her putdowns. I could think of any number of clever rejoinders.

But what was the point of composing alternatives now that were beyond me then? Could I have found the strength to challenge Betty's flashy power as most popular girl? I probably could have; but would I have? The whole apparatus of difference surely challenges a child almost unsurpassably. And then his moving in. Hadn't my distress been perfectly reasonable?

What looking to the past needs most, I thought, was not correction, not even reframing as much as a consoling hand, a hug, the soothing murmur of I know, I know, I know.

One friend I met with regularly post-retirement was Lucy. It was never a surprise when she arrived late—she often did, to anywhere—but when she burst into Starbucks for our November coffee, I gasped. The last time we'd met, her hair flowed beyond her shoulders. Now it was barely there. And downy. Number two on the clippers, Lucy said, but when I remarked that I liked it, that she had the perfect head for it, her hands flew to her skull as if confounded that she had one.

She'd startled me—all of us at the regional archives centre, in fact—just as much when she dashed in on her first day of work. She'd been hired from a program in the east and the words in advance of her were brainy and first-class. She'd been late that morning too and outfitted in purple. Purple dress, stockings, shoes. Purple hair band. When she laughed, she brayed, and it made her seem coarse and less competent than we'd been told she was. But Daniel Jute had warned us that Lucy Benham knew everything he required her to know, and as far as he was concerned, that's what counted. Which, I thought, was rather gallant of him. She rose quickly in the hierarchy, though never beyond assistant director, next to Jute. Turned out she wasn't the least bit arrogant or coarse. She was soft-hearted, actually, and soon we were friends, together with Marilou and Judith, though Lucy and I were the tightest pair within the foursome, probably because neither of us had children. The other two discussed diapers and preschool and other child-related issues at their breaks, as if they needed to oil the hinges to their starkly different after-hours lives.

Lucy's coming out—the most difficult thing I've ever accomplished, she told me later; professionally, I mean—disconcerted the work environment for a while; being openly gay wasn't as common then, and those who'd been trying hard to set her up with men felt betrayed. Afterward, Lucy seemed calmer, though sharpened too, spurred into fearless, steady activism. I'd grown up ignorant about such matters but somehow also keenly aware of how they would be viewed. I wasn't fazed by the revelation, and secretly pleased by this, even proud, which might have seemed supercilious, except that for me, it felt like evidence I'd evolved a little over the years, that I'd managed a workable counterpoint to the conservatism of my childhood church and community.

The point was, I liked her a lot and Lucy hadn't changed, so why should our relationship?

Lucy's own family had rejected her, however, and she used up most of her sick leave in the early months because of it. It rankled her still, and she repeated it now, after settling down across from me. Every meeting, it seemed, required an update on her parents. Doesn't it just boggle the mind, she said, that my folks can't handle it? Both of them the epitome of attainment. Mother's a lawyer, for God's sake. Father's a physician. But now they think they've failed by producing a person like me! Mother keeps asking, Didn't you have a boyfriend in high school? Well, duh, of course I did, Chicken Little me. And now I have a wife!

Nope, she said, it doesn't compute. But I've figured it out.

Her parents, she continued, had rebelled from fundamentalist homes. They probably imagined that the people they'd escaped viewed her as the parents' punishment for leaving.

Lucy tore open two packets of sweetener and emptied them into her tea. And no solace for me with all those relatives either, she went on. A patina of tolerance over disgust. Even Granny, so winsome in her piety, so constantly at me about God and love, has turned away.

I'm sorry, I said.

She recited the latest exchange with her mother. I knew she would need to vent a while, worry her pain like the beads of a rosary. I remembered how Uncle Must touched objects in passing or set them down just so, the cream separator, the engine cover, his cutlery whenever it veered to an angle. I recalled his frequent washing and combing and shaving, some variety of obsessive compulsive disorder, no doubt, though I'd never heard of that either as a girl, and then my mother sputtering, At least he's not one of those … those homosexuals! Hardly able to say the word. And all I could attach to it was innuendo about the two bachelors who shared a farm in the next district over.

I remembered Lucy sputtering too, after some off-the-cuff exposition on appraisal standards by Daniel Jute. Better appraisal standards for people, that's what we should practice! she'd said.

Lucy stirred at her drink. The thing is, she said, I still need spiritual intention regarding myself. With a capital I. Not to believe I was zapped from the sky to be this or that, I don't mean that, or chosen to be misunderstood, or despised, you know. But I couldn't live with randomness either. You absorb the message that you're some kind of freak. Until you realize you aren't. You belong to love that's intentional. Or intentionality that loves. Presence, purpose, all that stuff. Actually, Catherine, I'll bet you and I are mystics!

Good grief Lucy, I said, that's the last word I would ever assign to either one of us.

You've repressed it, that's all. She laughed. And, my good friend, you still don't know me well enough.

We talked and talked, through two teas and a bathroom break each, the comforting hiss of the steamer and music, a female singer, maybe Joan Baez or someone who sounded like her, behind us. We finally got around to Lucy's big news: she had embarked on a story. Not writing necessarily, more in the direction of audio or video. A YouTube kind of thing, she said. Like a little movie, you know what I mean? Adamant as always, but insecure. Where to begin. How to progress.

Quit the flailing already, I said. You used to bring the dullest documents to life. Lucy had spent her last years at the centre doing outreach and her presentations were marvels of creativity.

Well, thank you, Catherine. Lucy clasped her hands as if to trap confidence, but then she asked if she could play me a bit of something, a trial attempt, and her uncharacteristic timidity returned. It's all very tentative, very rough, she said, probably no good. Probably stupid.

Oh Lucy, just start it already!

You have no idea how scary this is. I feel my words will disintegrate as soon as they hit the air.

She handed me two typed pages of script to follow along, as if her voice on the phone recording would be impossible to follow. *She was different,* her voice began. *She comprehended this with no effort at all. It was never new, never unexpected. Every day her difference was plain before her eyes and every day it unfolded more and more plainly.*

But to know she was loved for it: that was the odyssey of her whole long life.

Oh Lucy, that's lovely, I interrupted. She hit Pause.

Honestly, I said. I think it's profound.

Really?

I'm thrilled to say this, I said, and mean it.

Lucy played the rest and I gathered that the protagonist Margaret was on the cusp of an urban pilgrimage of sorts through a fictional city named Surface. When the two-page recording ended, Lucy told me that Margaret's story would be woven through with people and resistances along the way. Surface, she said, doesn't take kindly to Margaret's brand of pilgrimage.

So it's a fable, or parable, then? I asked, thinking to suggest that the name Surface might be too obvious.

I don't know. I don't know if it'll be fiction or parable or mystery. Frankly, I don't know what the heck I'm doing. I'm yanking it in a different direction every week.

She said she'd been attending Winnipeg arts events like a freshly-minted groupie. Signed up for a workshop on point of view, consulted with the writer-in-residence at the library who was most terrifically encouraging and had given her good ideas on the genre. Planned to get a membership to Cinematheque. Was reading and viewing and talking to people. All in all, she was getting excellent feedback.

Feedback, Lucy repeated with a grin. She knew I detested the word.

She wondered, though, about her protagonist's status as retired. Would it be a disadvantage?

Retirement does have an uninteresting ring to it, I mused, artistically I mean, maybe realistically too: people golfing in Phoenix or sailing from one cruise port to another. Not young enough to be ... well, fascinatingly young, but if older, not Hagar Shipley enough either. Wouldn't you agree? No one's looking at people like me and Jim and you and Jill, you know, salt-and-pepper types, or the constant-dye-jobs-to-keep-the-roots-at-bay types, and thinking that we still have lives.

Lucy stared at me, gratified. You don't have to convince me, she said.

Death closer than ever, I said, and a new stage of life with the makings of an opera! That's what we're about!

Brilliant!

So express your character however old she has to be!

Well, thanks, Catherine. Thanks for that. Thanks again. Really. I suppose my Margaret is basically a fictional me. Like that character in the Mavis Gallant story, who says that anything she couldn't figure out she turned into fiction.

Well, good then. Write it. Quit your annoying insecurities.

Believe me, Lucy said, the jealousies and insecurities I've already bumped into, everyone watching each other's work or reviews, secretly glad if someone gets a bad one. Believe me. Not that different from the archivist community. With outstanding exceptions, of course, of course. I'm just honing my insecurities so I'll fit.

She emitted another Lucy-bray and the woman at the table beside us lifted her head and grimaced in our direction.

Lucy's dedication to her project inspired me. Into my notebook I set down statements that I remembered Mom making about my uncle.

Thinks the female side of things isn't worth his bother.

I've never known anyone as shy.

I would have raised him with more manners, but he wasn't mine to raise.

For all I know, he's got a secret vice. (When I'd asked what she meant by secret vice, she declared my question impertinent and wouldn't answer it.)

Well, he's a prayer warrior and we ought to be grateful.

I certainly got the best of the two.

He wouldn't hurt a horse. (You mean wouldn't hurt a mouse, I'd corrected, to which she said, Wouldn't hurt a mouse or a horse!)

Poor soul, misses his mother after all these years!

A list of inconsistent sentiments, negative in tone, like slivers in a field of skin. But if I slipped back into the Big House kitchen and watched her for periods longer than these small flares, I saw a woman of pervasive liveliness who appeared to be at ease with her brother-in-law's comings and goings. She never swerved around him like I did, but took him in stride, it seemed, in her quest for familial perfection. Which required her relentless positivity and a continuous negotiation with her circumstances in order to show respect for Dad and all that pertained to him.

Although my father and uncle bought their clothes in the sale basement of a Calgary department store, one year, for Christmas, Mom sewed them matching shirts in a sand-coloured fabric scattered with red lines and dots. They were holiday shirts with short sleeves and informal collars. The men on the pattern envelope were suave—far more suave than the men in our house. Their hands poised almost irreverently in their pockets and one sported a moustache and blue-green sunglasses. I thought my mother daring to attempt such a pattern for my dad and uncle.

At the gift opening, she was excited. She insisted the two men open their presents at the same time. I was excited too, and nervous for her, because I knew what they were. My eyes flitted between the three of them. For the briefest of moments, both seemed bewildered with their identical shirts and they were suspended in a poignant silence that could easily have gone the wrong direction until Mom announced that she'd sewn the shirts—specially for them, brothers—and the awkwardness disappeared. Dad donned his new shirt over his long-sleeved white one. He praised his industrious Edna. Uncle Must said Thank you and slipped his shirt on as well, though he didn't button it. Mom was thrilled, her eyes on Dad, but I noticed Uncle had fixed on Mom and it was like his pupils got larger and larger, as if he'd never seen a woman as unfettered and triumphant, never a woman as freely joyous as his sister-in-law Edna was at that moment over a pair of shirts.

I drew a blank on comments by my father. He was never one for aphorisms of any kind, and besides, it was entirely atmosphere with him, not specifics: Uncle Must somehow taking the lead but Dad keeping an eye on him. Even while Dad was head of the house. The dynamic was hard to describe. Mom's voice again: You could learn something about brotherly love from Jake and George. I remembered the line of tears shining down my father's cheeks at the memorial service in my parents' living room. A long, rolling line—like the Dnieper River in Russia, I thought, the river Dad and Uncle Must had occasionally referenced with a kind of awe. The other people in that memorial circle weren't choking on lumps in their throats or getting misty-eyed because of my uncle; it was because of Dad. Even the minister, who'd never met the deceased and was thus reduced to general sentiments of comfort, blew his nose noisily in the presence of my father's tears. Dad had no anecdotes or descriptions or plaudits, nothing to inform them of the meaning of his brother's life. Just long, long tears that he didn't bother wiping, tears rolling down his cheeks and dropping onto the lapels of his suit.

10.

Jim informed me his brother Randy and wife Sue were travelling through Winnipeg the next weekend and would come for dinner Friday. Randy suggested going out, Jim said, but I figured you might like to have them here, show them the place. They haven't visited since we moved.

Friday was free, Friday would be great, I would be delighted to show off the apartment, but it irked me a tad, the guys making the arrangements. Why couldn't he check? When I'd complained years ago that he didn't follow the channels—usually I tracked the calendar—Jim said, Channels? What do you mean, channels? As if I was speaking Swahili. I tried to clarify and gave up. Men, I decided, don't get channels, not the Reimer men at any rate.

Now I said, Okay, that's fine. But when he remarked that he was looking forward to seeing his brother, for Randy had always been his favourite, I said, Your siblings seem more or less inter-changeable to me.

Being rather unpleasant today, aren't we Catherine? he said. He was cool to me the rest of the evening.

Honestly, I hated when I got like that. And honestly, we're gen-erally harmonious. And this was far from as unpleasant as I'd been that Saturday afternoon some ten years into our marriage, during that supper on the deck, tuna sandwiches and veggies, a quick meal early and light because there was a concert he was singing in later. The mosquitoes were out, the first of the season, and I'd regretted setting us up to eat outside. But winter had been inter-minable and I was desperate for the rituals of summer. Jim was quiet, withdrawn as he often was before a performance. I enjoyed his events, his fellow choristers were my friends too, but that afternoon I was jealous.

I'd said his name several times to get his attention. Jim, I asked, if you could only have one, your music or me, which would you choose?

It was no whimsical question I'd posed, nothing he could laugh off. I saw him grip his sandwich more tightly and the juice of the tuna mix oozed through the bread where his fingers pressed into it, and then I seemed to see myself as well, my unyielding gaze, my hazel eyes, hard and waiting, a half-eaten sandwich on my plate.

But Catherine, he finally said, they're entirely unalike, each of them. How can you put it that way? What is it you need more of me? Can't we talk about it later?

But he'd begun to say, I could never—

A sky saturated with blue, like sapphire, that day and an air-plane crossing eastward, posting a long, white line of exhaust, the end of it continuously widening, fraying, vanishing into the atmosphere, and I'd known what he very nearly said, which one of the two options he could never give up. Curiously, I wasn't disappointed and I wasn't surprised. Not at all. Music is the solid, unshakeable home of his being and Jim requires it to live.

Then I'd asked, cheerfully, as if to obliterate my previous question and his stumbling half answer, Have you noticed that you don't make sound when you laugh, that you just shake like soda pop and bubble?

Was I laughing? he asked. Now?

No, but it just occurred to me.

Funny, he'd replied, how we keep learning new things.

I wondered whether Jim remembered that day, those exchanges. Maybe I'd gotten better at things. Which meant I ought to get into the den and apologize.

He was paging through scores. Sorry Jim, I said.

No problem. Even if you change as quickly as the weather.

Hey, I said, at work I was always steady-as-she-goes. People considered me *gemessen*, in fact, to use the German. Measured, you know. Even-keeled.

That's good.

It's only with the ones I love that I sometimes—

Jim said he would keep this in mind. At last he grinned at me and I leaned over and kissed his head.

11.

Our family had settled into the new arrangement of rooms at the Big House without further ado, day by day through summer and into the fall, patiently considering it temporary, not knowing then that Uncle Must would live with us for three more years. Not knowing he would never live in his shack across the road again.

School started. The bus picked us up at lane's end in the morning and dropped us back in the afternoon. Lorena entered Grade One and skipped along beside Darrell and me, chattering and swinging her lunch kit. The Tilia school was small, the upper grades housed in one wing, the lower grades in the other.

Most mornings when we left there was no sign of life at Uncle's former house, but afternoons we might see Miss Miller outside, hanging wash or unhooking wash, but more often sitting and reading, a cigarette brought languidly to and from her lips as if for literary emphasis. She sat in a pale green outdoor chair of canvas. If it was hot, she spread Uncle Must's blue patchwork blanket—the one Mom had sewn for him—on a bit of grass near the door, only partially hidden by the hedge. She sunbathed in a white bikini. She lay on her back or stomach, or flopped casually from side to side. Mom observed this from her sewing machine at the Big House and said it was pointless, that woman lazing in the sun when she could get brown just as well—if it was brown she wanted—by coming up to help in the garden or making a garden of her own.

Scanty, she snapped under her breath. Next to the road!

One hot day when the bus unloaded us, Miss Miller was there again, lounging on Uncle Must's blanket. She sat up as the bus moved on and called for Darrell. Called him three times, insistent as a school bell. I headed up the lane with Lorena while Darrell went to see what she wanted. It didn't take him long, but Mom met him at the door when he came inside and demanded to know where he'd been, lagging like that.

The lady of the castle summoned me, he said. Some excuse about a sticky window.

So you fixed it?

Wasn't anything stuck.

Mom's annoyance accelerated and words tumbled out—half-naked, lazy, loose—and in the midst of them, Darrell produced a low, appreciative whistle as if to say he was fine with Sharon Miller just the way she was. He raked his hair away from his forehead like he was Jimmy Dean or something.

You're one bad boy, Darrell Riediger! my mother stormed. Get into the living room and apologize! He went as she ordered and she followed him and slammed the door. They came out shortly and all seemed well. She'd probably threatened his television privileges, the most powerful weapon left in her arsenal.

But the real shocker of that September: Miss Miller was pregnant.

Betty, who'd managed to be Liz for a good while by now, after the Betts moniker flopped, asked me in a voice as smooth as mayonnaise if Uncle Must was the father.

I said, Of course not!

In truth, such a thing had never entered my mind. My brain was in the clouds of my schoolwork, books, piano, a crush or two, and a tizzy of reading, becoming British via the canon that year without being aware that I was, Hardy's *Return of the Native,* which led me to the other wrenching Hardy novels, and *Wuthering Heights, Jane Eyre,* the Jane Austen books, W Somerset Maugham's immersive *Of Human Bondage.* I'd shut my uncle out.

Liz's question annoyed me, troubled me too. I'd generously granted Uncle Must at least a modicum of respect for giving up his house to someone who claimed she needed it more than he did.

Well, everyone's talking, Betty/Liz said. I forced a smile. Though some people, she went on, sure do wonder how he knew what to do.

I widened my smile slightly, enigmatically I hoped, but inside I was a nest of wasps. This so-called friend of mine had raised the doubt and her insinuations were stronger than any ignorance or certainty I could summon of my own. Miss Miller arrived at my uncle's place at night, they were alone, she was attractive. She seemed of persuasive and ambiguous character. And maybe sticking close to him now for a reason.

It seemed utterly impossible, though. I wanted to scream. Because of Liz, because of Miss Miller. Because my family had to drag Uncle Must around with us.

Miss Miller's baby was born in the middle of December and vindicated my assumption of Uncle's innocence. I imagined the click-clacking jaws of Tilia clicking shut while everyone calculated on their fingers or a sheet of paper, checking and re-checking. Impossible for a mid-July rendezvous to have produced the *big bruiser* Miss Miller's baby had been, more than nine pounds at his birth.

Betty-now-Liz hung onto her theories, however. One day, she invited herself over after school. I didn't much like having friends at the house now that Uncle lived with us, but I was flattered too, elated, that Liz had asked. Besides, she'd said her dad would pick her up on his way from town in an hour or so and usually the men didn't come in from their farm work until just before supper.

And who happened to be squawking in a pile of blankets on the kitchen floor that very after-school while his mother, the exuberant Miss Miller, poked away at a rug hooking project? Baby Ricky! Liz kept her mouth shut but I could tell she was pretty fired up to see both mother and child at close range. She knelt over Ricky on the floor, swishing her hair in his face and making cooing noises as if she knew what to do with babies, though she was the youngest in her family and had no experience with children whatsoever.

We went upstairs and Liz flopped onto my bed. Wow, she said, he's the spitting image.

What do you mean? I asked, though I knew.

That baby. The spitting image of your uncle.

Crazy, I said. No way. Clearly, Liz couldn't count. I should have done it for her but instead I said, He's desperately afraid of women. Mom had dropped this to me once and it sounded both inoffensive and accurate. Now, though, out of my mouth and repeated to Liz, it seemed a sacred secret I should never have given away.

Desperately afraid of women? Liz chuckled.

Well, maybe afraid isn't the word.

Liz waited for me to find a better word but none came and I suppose my inability to produce it must have confirmed that she was right. And the name, she said, what's with the George in it?

I sighed. Oh yes, the name. A big bruiser of a baby with a drawn-out name, like he was the king of England. Ricky? Mom had asked Miss Miller when she visited in the hospital after the birth. Short for Richard? No. Ricky, just like that. Ricky Rodney George, last name Miller. No explanations for any of it. What, indeed, was George—my uncle's English name—doing in the middle of it?

I heard that he knew her from before, Liz said.

Maybe she knew him but he didn't know her.

That doesn't make sense.

But Liz didn't want to sit in my bedroom making girl talk. She wanted to go downstairs again. She'd invited herself over to hang around Darrell, not me, that was obvious by now. She'd flirted with him on the bus and all the way up to the house.

Mom was in the process of taking supper out of the oven and sending Miss Miller home. Sending her off with her own miniature hot dish, and one of us—Darrell or me—would have to help her. Carry either the baby or the dish. Dad and Uncle Must would soon be home and Mom had other food to prepare. I sensed her waffling. I had a guest, but Darrell? Mom had red-flag concerns about Darrell and the too-friendly, lipstick-wearing Miss Miller. She may have had her thoughts about Betty/Liz as well, but she'd recently called her Sweet Betty, which showed just how clueless even intuitive mothers could be.

She picked me. Maybe she thought Betty/Liz would tag along, that another walk up and down the lane would be fun for two teenage girls on a late-winter afternoon. Liz pretended weariness and gave me a don't-you-just-hate-it-when-your-mother-makes-you-help-when-you've-got-company look and said she would wait for me to return, and anyway, I was sure to be back in a jiffy. She promptly started talking to Darrell, who was doing his rare bits of homework at the table. He didn't seem to mind the interruption.

I grabbed Ricky. Down the snow-rutted lane we went, Miss Miller holding the hot dish in front of her and exclaiming into the crisp air. She glanced at the peach and rose layers of the winter sunset, said, Pretty, so pretty, but mostly she talked about what a good cook my mother was and what a treat the meal was sure to be. She said, I myself have no skills or reputation as a cook.

My mother had called it a layer dinner and now Miss Miller wondered, was it five layers, six, or how many?

Seven. It's Mom's seven-layer dinner.

Seven. Well, that's good to know.

Was Sharon Miller just guileless instead of conniving, then?

I held the infant child stiffly horizontal, this Ricky Rodney George Miller, examining his face as much as I could without stumbling. He was asleep. He'd been spitting up, yes, and the collar of his shirt behind the blanket was streaked and damp, but he wasn't the spitting image of anyone I knew. He was just an ordinary, fat, round baby, fist damned against his mouth, and bald to boot. He seemed as far from Uncle Must—and Miss Miller, too, for that matter—as it was possible to be. He seemed entirely himself.

My mother had changed her tactics, which accounted for Miss Miller at the Big House hooking a rug. She'd decided to befriend and teach the inexperienced young neighbour, so obviously in need of being taught. The difficulty of it, single and a baby to raise! Yes, she should have given him up for adoption, given the boy a chance, but she hadn't, so they would have to make the best of it. I was busy with music theory homework at the kitchen table on a Saturday afternoon, hearing Mom commiserate with Maisie Martens along these lines. They were in the living room, sipping at tea from our fanciest white and jade-green china cups, a plate of lemon cookies on the coffee table in front of them. Maisie, the best children's storyteller in the church, was also the woman who knew everything about everyone else. Which she might pass on—framed as a prayer request, of course.

And now I was hearing Mom disclose herself. I was convicted, she was saying, I was so convicted! So very convicted!

A patch of silence, the women in the living room taking mutual sips, absorbing the implications of conviction, I supposed.

I've despised that woman, Maisie, for the confusion of everything, Mom went on. For George living here. Then it was like my eyes were opened to how much better his attitude than mine. He may be strange but the impulse of goodness ... Well, it came to me: perhaps she was sent? If he's done his part, what's mine in all this? I've been asking myself.

I didn't want to hear any of this; I definitely didn't want my mother to be complicated and convicted! Shifting into *there's something to be learned in this*. I knew Mom's faults from my perspective, but I had zero desire to know them from hers. Turning herself inside out in comparison to Uncle Must, confessing she struggled! Why not recite to herself the maxims of decent behaviour she recited to Darrell and me and Lorena?

Poor lost soul, Maisie said. That child with a child.

Maisie the storyteller, the woman we all depended on to get important lessons across to children, had quavered her voice and composed another tearjerker in two simple sentences. I'd done enough eavesdropping. I pressed my hands against my ears. All I could hear then was my pulse beating in my head, which was astonishing and a rather good distraction. I pressed harder. Primordial it sounded, like waves in a conch shell. When my teacher Miss Siemens returned from summer holidays last year, she'd brought a conch shell to school. She told us to listen to the ocean at the pink, pearl opening. She said to take our time.

I removed my hands from my ears after what I hoped was a long enough interlude, and just in time. In the other room the two women were saying Amen to a prayer and finally advancing to the reason for tea and lemon cookies on a Saturday afternoon: planning a spring event for the ladies' group. I could safely resume pencilling in musical time values. But I couldn't shake the unkind thought that if we'd all prayed harder from the get-go, maybe Miss Miller would have left by now and Uncle Must would be back in his place.

The Big House was altered after Uncle Must moved in. My bedroom no longer a sanctuary. Lorena had no concept of divided space and snooped into my things. More than once I frightened her with my anger because of it, Mom taking Lorena's side, asking in a whisper, Are you getting your period, Catherine? Upstairs or downstairs, the house as if packed without air and me trapped in the middle, no space to be alone, to be myself apart from family relationships, a kind of solitude I felt desperate for but couldn't articulate.

Some nights I could hear Uncle moan from my parents' former bedroom. A low rumble, like an engine running beneath me. I might fall asleep, then suddenly wake to it—my room above his—and it confused me: what was I hearing, and was it power or weakness?

His presence washed like sepia over the light-filled kitchen. The soft pedal of the piano always depressed while playing, Mom and Dad vigilant, less relaxed. Shush, children, turn the television down. Shush, Uncle may be resting. Shush, Uncle ... Shush, Uncle. Quieter, children. Listen to the radio in your room. Turn the volume down!

Sometimes Uncle Must emerged from his room to watch television too. Maybe he thought since he'd bought it, he was immune to its wiles. He liked *Hockey Night in Canada*; he bent forward and gave himself to the game, eyes on the puck. Sometimes he and my parents joined us for *Bonanza*, the shooting overlooked, the brothers and their father such a handsome, congenial family. As long as there wasn't too much romantic googly-eyes, as Mom called it, shows were okay. If there was no evening church, we watched the Disney show. My uncle even sat through *This Hour Has Seven Days* one evening, scowling, because he'd heard about it and had to see what it was. He didn't laugh even once and for some reason I'd laughed a lot that time at the satiric songs between segments of news, and Darrell laughed too, and I remember our laughter, how shrill and precarious it was.

I had to get my piano practicing done before supper because Uncle Must got headaches from my music. Hymns would be something else, my mother said.

I retorted that my piano teacher didn't assign me hymns.

I understand the repertoire you have.

Her use of *repertoire* appeased me a little. But goodness Mom, I said, it's so illogical of him. Bach was writing for the glory of God. Handel and, and— I was out of composers I was sure of in terms of motivation—so why, I sputtered, don't you tell him that?

Catherine, please. He's trying to make it up to us. Living with us, I mean.

Surely he has the right to take back his house.

Well, it's his—he can do what he wants with it.

And this is yours!

Enough, Catherine! It's complicated, don't you understand?

I didn't understand. I had no idea of the financial arrangements, no idea what belonged to whom. I just didn't want him there. I held on for Sunday afternoons or evenings when my uncle went out walking or drove away for a while, the house returning to us like sun after a month of drizzle, hours in which my siblings and I could run, pound, argue. Goof off. Mom and Dad letting us be. Sometimes he stayed away long enough for us to watch an entire evening of television without it being too loud or frivolous or full of kissing. Sometimes he went away for a day or two or three, on business for the farm or to a church convention. Those were wonderful days when the house seemed to breathe, find its previous proportions, cast off shame.

12.

May, 1967, a hot spring day nearly two years after Sharon Miller took up domicile in Uncle's house and he a room in ours, and there she was again as we stepped off the bus, in that white bikini of hers, drawn out to the sun like a kid to candy and standing next to a dilapidated baby carriage she'd acquired somewhere, wanding her cigarette in one hand and pumping the carriage handle up and down with the other. Trying to bounce toddler Ricky to sleep, from the looks of it.

Darrell snickered, said, The bikini bunnies are out.

Miss Miller shouted my name. I flinched on behalf of the boy in the carriage.

Sharon Miller had a job by then, at the Tilia café, part-time, waitressing or maybe chopping vegetables or washing dishes, but she must have had the afternoon off. I didn't know exactly what she did; our family didn't frequent the café and if my friends and

I wanted a drink or snack in town we went to the counter at the drugstore in the Co-op. Another woman who worked in the café picked her up. I was surprised the owners found her useful but maybe there was something about her that brought in customers.

She's good to her Ricky, Mom had said, you'll have to grant her that. And she's found a good babysitter for when she works.

She still occasionally came up to the Big House, or Mom dropped in at her place—we spoke of it as her place by now—but the intensity of my mother's interest had faded, her efforts at teaching over. She'd had no luck in getting Miss Miller to church. Now we were simply neighbours, to pass, maybe wave at, exchange superficial courtesies with, though a remnant of irritation remained in my mother over her huge investment of kindness without the desired results. She blamed Sharon Miller's mother, about whom she knew nothing, for the younger woman's deficiencies. The way the wash was hung, for example, a towel next to a sock—a single sock!—and the sock next to a blouse. All mixed up like that. And Miss Miller dashing up to the house to borrow some cooking ingredient when she'd been working in town that day and could have shopped for supplies. Some mothers, Mom would say, don't know how to raise their children.

Miss Miller had borne cheerfully, however, Mom's suggestions about raising her baby while the teaching stage lasted, and she'd been game about the rug hooking project, though her craft work was sloppy and never improved. When she filled her latch-hook canvas with a piece of wool from Mom's leftovers pile, she paid no attention to making a pattern but picked up any strand that came to hand. The result was soft, as hooked rugs are, but aesthetically it was a disaster. It looked like mud. Neither she nor Mom ever spoke of her making another. She'd seemed happiest simply to be with us in the Big House, admiring Mom's handiwork instead. Maybe she hoped Mom would give her whatever she praised. Certainly she accepted any gift of homemade food with raptures.

On occasion, Miss Miller went away, maybe for a week or two. The first time she left, I'd suggested to Mom that Uncle Must could go down and claim his house. The locks are changed, she said. She's not really gone.

Sharon Miller was shouting for me again.

Jesus, Cath, Darrell said, now you're in for it!

It made me mad, him talking like that. He was going weird on me. I knew for certain by now that he sometimes smoked and when I'd threatened to report him to our parents he called me a goody-goody (which I feared I was, on the outside at least) and he grabbed my arm and was ready to twist it but then let it go and turned his charm on me instead, made me promise not to tell. I was relieved to be his ally but hated it too.

Darrell held a hand out to Lorena like the good shepherd and set off with her up the lane. Go, fair damsel, he grinned at me, Miss Miller bids thee come.

A third time, my name in the air. Catherine! Almost melodious. It sounded like friends. Perhaps the other woman would urge me to call her Sharon. And I would have to refuse. Mom and Dad were fussy—so fusty!—that way: we had to use Mister, Missus, or Miss to our elders. Not that this neighbour was that much older.

I joined Miss Miller at the carriage but she did nothing along the lines of equality. She dropped the remains of her cigarette, squirming it into the ground with her sandal, took off her sunglasses, said Hi, and asked me a series of questions of no consequence to either of us. Rote questions, they seemed, in whose answers she took no further interest. How my day had been. (Fine.) What grade, and did I like it—school, that is? (Grade Eleven and yes.) How many in my class and did I have a favourite subject? (Maybe twenty or so, and I couldn't decide.)

Miss Miller remarked that she herself had not been much of

a student. She read a lot though, just not the books my mother recommended. I'm more into romances, she said. Harlequins, you know. They really get you turning the pages.

Ricky was asleep but Miss Miller kept her hand on the carriage, gave it an occasional rock. I looked at the boy, at the landscape, at Miss Miller, waiting to learn why I'd been summoned. She was large compared to me, her skin a splotchy field at close range, glistening with tanning lotion, her bikini snagged and jaundiced. She hadn't lost her baby bulge and she was pale from winter but there was an unbecoming rosiness about her nevertheless, from her first forays into her tanning season, I supposed. She smelled of coconut and perspiration. Others had declared her pretty but I critiqued her with more precision: pretty, perhaps, but not beautiful, every part of her slightly excessive, and that unfortunate carelessness about her, as if she knew she was attractive and couldn't be bothered to do anything else about it. Nothing beyond lipstick, that is. She always wore lipstick. She favoured pink and when dark from the sun by summer's end, her pink lips appeared so white in contrast she looked as if she'd been slurping—carelessly, of course—a vanilla milkshake.

Now she rummaged in the carriage at Ricky's feet, pulled up an orange miniskirt dress and tugged it over her head. Sleeveless, it flared away loosely from a stand-up collar. Three cloth-covered buttons formed a smiling line down the upper part of the bodice. It's a glorious day, she said.

I liked *glorious* and said, Yes. Yes, it is. The leaves had practically jumped out of their buds the past few days, the lane trees a tender lime hue like a row of early lettuce. It had rained earlier so they were washed and shiny. It hadn't rained enough, though, not yet, not as much as the seeded crops required. Puffs of clouds that might grow into rain clouds inched across the sky, and all around Tilia, I imagined, farmers like Dad and Uncle were keeping an eye on them. Dust scattered up at a distance on the rim of a hill, some tractor for sure, plowing. I heard the whistle of a meadowlark and the steady, low throttle of insects.

Then Miss Miller asked how things were up at the house—the Big House, she meant—and said she wished she could see us more often. Your mother's very kind, she said. You're lucky with your father too. Such a fine family. Always friendly, inviting me to church and everything. Not that I come, but it's appreciated you know, and I've been thinking …

I felt a twitch of fear, wondering if Miss Miller intended to convert, right now, in front of me. What would I say?

Your mother comes over here now, Miss Miller continued. She hardly invites me to your place anymore. I guess she's nervous because of your men. Your father and uncle and brother. My reputation, I suppose. Work I've done in the past.

Work in the past?

Miss Miller smiled and twisted one of the large, cloth-covered buttons but instead of explaining, carried on to the topic of Uncle Must; how was he doing?

He's doing fine.

She made a pensive face. Quite a miracle, she said, that he would let me stay. And help me so much. But he won't speak to me, won't come around, parcels everything through your mother. Who won't tell me a thing. Is he healthy? Is he okay?

Everything's fine.

Miss Miller pushed the carriage into the shade of the house, then returned to me, dress billowing. I went to Calgary on the weekend, she said.

Oh.

You know, Catherine, I'd love to marry your uncle. Ricky needs a daddy.

I stepped back. What had she said? Incomprehensible, to say the least. Of all the men surely available, men in their dozens, I presumed, Miss Miller would love to marry Uncle Must?

He's an old man, I blurted. He's an old bachelor.

Miss Miller laughed. Old? He's not that old. You just say that because you're young.

How old was he? Mom had recently celebrated her birthday, so was forty-one, and Dad was seven years older, so forty-eight, and Uncle Must was ten years older than my father. Fifty-eight.

He's old, I said.

Maybe I like older men.

How old are you? We weren't supposed to ask people this question but I couldn't stop myself.

Nearly thirty, she said. Sharon Miller fumbled in the large pockets of her dress. Gosh, she said, I could use a cigarette. Her pockets were empty. And has your uncle never married, she asked, never had a girlfriend?

He's not married and I don't know about any girlfriend. Probably not.

This made him sound dreadfully unaccomplished and I wished I had a tragic history of courtship and loss to supply for him. But did Miss Miller think he was … well, did she think, I wondered, that my uncle was an ordinary, easy-type person? I'd just been through months of his leaflets. Yes, he'd relinquished his house, but did she think he was a suddenly-marrying sort of man?

I'm quite busy with my schoolwork, I said, grasping my books more tightly and shifting to leave. I'm not sure what my uncle does or thinks. I know he's old.

Well, you're certainly hammering that theme to the wall, Miss Miller said. Of course you are. You're still so young. She paused and cocked an ear toward the carriage, as if Ricky and I were young in the very same way. One minute she addressed me as a peer, the next as a child. I considered myself grown-up at seventeen, considered myself mature. But next to her, I felt sheltered and prim, unsophisticated, afraid, and all the famous novels in the world or television shows hadn't taken me any further than that.

But, since my neighbour was audacious, I would be audacious too. Doesn't Ricky have a father? I demanded.

Well, of course he does, Miss Miller laughed. Biologically!

Perhaps you could ask him to marry you.

Miss Miller laughed again and grabbed at another button to twist. I'm afraid that's impossible, she said. He may or may not have children of his own already.

May or may not? I echoed.

Married.

Oh.

And instead of leaving, I stood there like an idiot, waiting to be released. Silent, when there was certainly plenty to say. A wonderful spring day, and Dad would return from the fields elated with sightings, maybe of a mule deer in a thicket or a fox on the run, and Mom would have her thrills to speak of, the latest perennials poking up or the early crabapple blossoms, sweet as pink popcorn. I had something special to tell as well. Not tell everyone, not Uncle Must in case he deprecated it, not Darrell either in case he sneered, but Mom and Dad for sure. I'd gotten an A+ on my Social Studies assignment. And not just that, but what Miss Siemens had written at the end of my current events essay on thalidomide babies, which I'd spent hours on. My research was impeccable, she noted, my writing style excellent in every way. The only thing to watch, she said, was my objectivity, meaning I might have veered into passion a little, but in a subject this heartbreaking, it was understandable that one might become somewhat flurried, indignant. With your grades, work habits, and compassion, Catherine, she'd written, you might want to consider becoming a doctor.

I'd already weighed by then the usual options in my community for a woman who got further education: teacher or nurse. But doctor? If I chose medicine—which I wouldn't because I was squeamish—shouldn't it be nurse? But Miss Siemens had written doctor.

I've kept you long enough, Miss Miller was saying, so off to your homework or your piano lessons or whatever you do. She shielded her eyes with her hand and peered at the Big House as if it was too lovely to face without shadow. You might drop a hint to your uncle, she said. I'm grateful, you know, for all he's done. He's done a lot and I'd love to take care of him. A man who's old—since you insist—needs a tremendous amount of care.

My uncle is very particular, I said, recalling Mom's assessment of chaos in this former house of his that Sharon Miller had taken over.

Oh, so am I. Quite particular.

He gets up very early.

I'm certainly capable of that myself.

This was such a ridiculous conversation! I never talk to my uncle about matters of a personal nature, I said. I'd never drop him a hint like that.

You could, Miss Miller persisted. You seem the type that definitely could. Though maybe he'd listen better to your brother. He's a smart type too.

We don't talk about things like that with my uncle, I repeated. I wasn't about to admit I generally disregarded him. Avoided, better said. Lately he'd seemed even more withdrawn so avoidance was a piece of cake.

I'm sure you'll have opportunity for a hint.

How to staunch this loopy woman's unrealistic hopes? How to finally and thoroughly squash them? I would have to be rude. I really don't talk to him, ever! I declared and started—definitively, this time—to walk away.

When it's very warm and you've got the windows open, I can hear you playing your piano and it's very nice, Miss Miller said behind me. It's very nice music. I turn off the radio then, and I listen to you.

I stopped and looked back. Thank you, I said.

It's very nice. Very, very nice. I've often wished I could play the piano. Miss Miller held on to a button with one hand and with the other made a grand sweeping motion as if to shovel me up the lane.

13.

I asked Jim, over lasagna and Caesar salad, if he remembered whether Uncle Must attended our wedding. I'd been recalling his presence in the Big House with gratifying detail and now I drew a blank.

No recollection, he said.

I wasn't anxious, I said, so maybe he wasn't there. It was during his roaming-about-the-prairies period.

Honestly, I can't remember.

It was the day before the Randy and Sue visit and maybe I was feeling I needed to get my uncle sorted so I could move on to other matters—like the lives of my husband's relatives. Maybe I'd just been thinking about him too much.

Do you realize how insular my family was? I said. I could hear the ferment in my voice. No grandparents to speak of, an aunt and uncle in Idaho, another aunt and uncle in the north. Mom's side.

We hardly ever saw them. I'm just beginning to realize what a loss that was. One small family and an uncle. An uncle who was odd.

Every family has an odd uncle.

Oh, Jim, I said, that's what you always say. If love is a muscle, I'm certainly glad you flex it for me.

He grinned. Maybe I'm the odd uncle for the Reimers.

Hardly, Jim. Everyone in your clan adores you. But, did Dad ever talk about him? Uncle Must, I mean. During men-talk times?

Men-talk times?

Yeah, crazy, I know.

Well, he said, holding up a forkful of romaine, maybe once, after your uncle died. He mumbled something about first Darrell, now my brother.

Mom thinks he grieved more for his brother than his son.

Your dad was broken over Darrell. Uncle Must died later. It's newer in her mind, that's all.

Well, you know how often I've told her that.

Jim spread butter thickly on a slice of bread. I glared at the butter. My uncle's getting to be like an earworm, I said. Like some song I don't even like.

Well, you've got the time, I suppose.

That sounds patronizing, Jim.

Sorry. He took a bite, made an appreciative noise. Jim could exist on butter and bread.

I want to drive to Tilia, I said. Maybe early spring. By myself.

Not to patronize, Catherine, but you're retired and you do have time. Why not? He pushed away from the table, did the water, the grind, the whole procedure for coffee. I always thought your uncle a little robotic, he said from the counter. Not that I saw him much. Mostly at your parents'. If I asked a question, he'd answer and that was it. Your dad got him going a couple of times. Seemed to know how. Bits from Russia. Not like he had anything against talking, but as if not talking was his natural state.

Yeah. Yeah. But he had an arsenal of stuff … Oh my goodness, Jim, here's something I'm realizing at this very moment, this exact split-second moment. Whatever I know about the history of our people—the Mennonites, you know, all the stuff in Russia with the civil war and famine and leaving—I hear it in his voice. It's not like we had story hour with Uncle Must, I don't mean that, but it's in his voice! Do you know what I mean?

Then, like a flashback: me and Darrell cozy, maybe on one of Mom's braided rugs or my father's lap, and there were stories as long and sweet as hard candies and Uncle Must was the teller. Not telling them to us children, though; telling them to my parents. At some point when I was very young, he must have talked to my parents a lot. His boyhood village was Fischau, which lodged in my brain because of the name. The train ran by its eastern edge, the nearest station Lichtenau. Settlers planted thousands of trees, more than half of them mulberry trees in hedges for the silkworm industry, which later collapsed in favour of wheat. I remembered as if through tempered glass the coil of my body on my father's lap while Uncle Must told his brother he'd never tasted fruit better than mulberries. And how when he glimpsed a train for the very first time, when he saw and heard it coming out of the distance, he thought it wondrous as a constellation. I'd straightened and asked what a constellation was. The word was explained. I'd seen trains by then, and I'd seen stars, but I was dumbfounded that the one had made my uncle think of the other.

So was it the fact of me and Darrell and Lorena growing up that muzzled him? Who couldn't be allowed to hear what he'd spoken of before? Had I heard Dad saying, We don't need to speak of that, Brother. Children have ears like corn.

Jim served the coffee and said, Sometimes I think you make too much of him. He might have been a little off, not socially adept, for sure, and maybe a bit fanatical, but I don't get why it was such a scandal or whatever it was.

Such a fine supper we'd been having and suddenly it was as unpalatable as a mass-produced snack out of a foil packet. Well, easy for you to say, I said. You and your jolly Reimers.

Dinner with Randy and Sue turned out better than expected, though, even if they complained as usual about the weather, Winnipeg the national winter putdown post, stuck on the plains and lying down for it. At least we have our sense of irony intact, I grouched to myself, not everything straight up and rah-rah. Unbelievable some days, the relentless high spirits that emanated from Jim's family out of those mountains and the vaunted Fraser Valley. But we managed the conversation well, Jim and I, graciously bearing Randy's incredulity about the current cold and Sue's dittoes of amazement. We played it straight ourselves, informing our guests with only slightly inflated dismay that it was only the end of November and look at the snow, nearly record amounts of it, flood forecasters dire about spring already.

But no big deal; our guests praised the apartment and the evening was fun. I'm a capable hostess and my welcome was warm and sincere, and the food was delicious: steaming rice and shrimp and veggie stir fry and key lime pie put together that morning for dessert. I'd braved gusts of pellet snow to purchase fresh brown bread from the Forks Market and Jim had remembered the wine. Sue sidled into the kitchen to ask if she could help, and I said no, the rest was last minute, dumping the prepared veggies and shrimp and stirring. Sue asked if I used the Mennonite Girls Can Cook recipe website and I had to admit I'd heard of it but not ventured there yet, and Sue wrote the website address in the corner of a notepad page—the recipes will make you feel young again, she said—and for some reason it made me grateful. I told her my mother hadn't grown up with the Russian Mennonite culinary traditions, but she'd learned them—for my dad.

Sue returned to the living room to visit with Jim and Randy

and they were laughing and in the kitchen, I enjoyed the sound of it. Red and green peppers, white onions, celery on the diagonal, carrot strips like a kaleidoscope as I lifted and turned, everything changing colour slightly as it sizzled in the wok, salad ready in the fridge, the rice done and plumping in the pot, the entire occasion perfectly animated. I poured the sauce over the works and it bubbled and smelled terrific.

They were noisy, Jim and his brother Randy; they kept laughing, and I could tell that my husband wasn't running any music through his head either, he was completely in the room, in the moment. My dear James Elroy Reimer. One of nine. Born in Abbotsford, BC, six months before me. His name meaning *he who supplants* and he was competitive all right, though in an understated way, possessed of that drive for achievement large families often generate—famous families like the Roosevelts or Kennedys, for instance—especially when the parents are outgoing and entrepreneurial. The Reimer siblings were close and boisterous and creative and every one of the five brothers and four sisters wished to be at the top of the heap, or so it seemed to me as One Who Married In (and was delighted to do so, I could admit when feeling secure, his family larger on so many levels—unscathed, unweighted—compared to mine). Jim in the middle of the pack and the calmest, most moderate—most liberal, his BC connection would probably say—and the most reliably genuine of them too. In my opinion. Growing up, he spent summers picking raspberries, strawberries, and beans on their mixed-produce farm, though all he wanted to do was play baseball and sing. He was a good hitter and a star pitcher at the community level, and then he broke his arm in Grade Twelve, in an accident with a horse, and nothing was ever the same for him in baseball. He could still sing, however, and in college he'd learned to conduct, which snared him, the arm healed well enough for that. His wrists and fingers are supple, his shoulders strong. He let his brothers and brothers-in-law fight over the farm, oldest brother Dave and youngest brother Mike joining forces to win, and all but Jim stayed in the Abbotsford area, farming pigs or chickens or setting up nurseries. And on the side, forming trios and quartets and other kinds of ensembles.

Oh yes, those jolly, musical Reimers, the Reimer family gatherings every other year for the first few decades of our marriage like summer music camp, every meal starting with a song or two, the food cooling while the verses went on and on, and every evening the guitars came out and there was informal music-making around a fire, and then an entire evening specially designated for singing through a long repertoire of favourites, from hymns to contemporary, the chronology of the Reimer family rehashed as they went. No one knew when to quit. As singers are supposed to, everyone listened to the voices around them, but as the evening wore on the original Reimers listened mainly to each other; they seemed to enter some womb-like state in which they were joined, the nine of them singing, and they forgot about their children and spouses and other obligations; they expected the married-in members to slip away and tend to things. Which we did, pitching in for child care and food duties, and only Mike's wife, Sally, resented it, though Geoff, a brother-in-law, usually disappeared from the sing-songs to traipse about the grounds of the resort where the gatherings were held. Geoff had a tin ear and Jim and I figured he consoled himself over his tragic difference within the clan with something small and flat he kept in an inside pocket. Not a mouth organ either, Jim would say.

Jim was the only one of the Reimers for whom music was his living, though. He'd been in the Winnipeg school system more than thirty years. Band and choir and, some years, drama. There's nothing better, he would say, than getting high schoolers hooked on good music. And producing it themselves, with their body's instrument—the voice—or with instruments they could easily learn.

During dinner, Sue asked me what I was doing now that I'd retired and though weary of the question, I realized it was the first time my sister-in-law had inquired so I traipsed down the list— volunteering, visiting my mother, reading, coffees with friends, various events, you know—and Jim put in, as if proud of me, that I was actually tracing backward some, which drifted by harmlessly, thank goodness, but then Randy and Sue, jauntily married and mutually romantic, began to reminisce about how they'd met (roller skating) and Sue was eager to hear our story too. In unison we said, At college. And since we had, like most couples, a cache of shared anecdotes and barbless disputes to rehearse in front of others for their entertainment, we brought out our contrasting versions of The First Kiss.

Jim: It was in one of the practice rooms, when I came in and you'd just finished a scale, E-flat major, I think, and you lifted your head—

Me: Jim, that wasn't a kiss. That was a puff of air on my cheek. I count the first kiss as lips, yours and mine, coming together, touching and holding like puzzle pieces that fit, which happened in the library. We were in carrels side by side and when you leaned over and put the pieces together, the *Strong's Concordance* you were using for some theological paper crashed to the floor, and that Mark guy on the other side of you saw us and whooped or something and we pulled apart and I blushed and you blushed and he laughed and you picked up the book and said, That—meaning the kiss—gives me strength for the Strong. Then Mark boxed your shoulder and said, As long as you don't end up like Samson.

Jim: You'd finished the scale and did such a perfect job of it, I leaned over and kissed you.

We would never resolve this one, so Jim leaned over now to give me a peck, which inspired Sue to jump up and lip-lock with Randy, and they showed off by holding it longer than strictly necessary for a couple wed as long as they were and Jim poured more wine or coffee, whatever each requested, and so it went. A lively evening.

Our two versions were agreeably significant, I thought. My first kiss in the college library, a climate of intelligence and wood, old books, new books, the pale, ethereal light of the clerestory windows. And his in a music room, a windowless cell with a piano, or no instrument at all, just a music stand and a chair. Evening after evening over the course of our marriage wrapped in the latest earphone technology, listening. Listening as study. Leading an invisible choir or band. Mouthing the words. Jim allowed music for ambience if we had guests, but otherwise music as background made him cross and when he shopped with me, he critiqued what was played through the speakers in the store. I don't even hear it, I would say, to which he nearly groaned: How can you not?

Jim, intent on mastery, was obliged to listen.

14.

There was a morning in early December that dawned a solid pink. It seemed a Mary Oliver kind of beginning to the day, a stunning pink like poetry, like summer peonies gifted to the heart of winter. Later I drove to Maplebend Seniors Home through a cityscape sparkling like a Christmas card, fresh snow banked along the road, against houses, curled into every available spot, new lines of it flattering sills, boughs, branches, ecstatic in the sunshine. Bing Crosby crooned carols in a velvety voice from the CD player in the car.

I stepped into my mother's room. Lorena was there too. The visit would go faster.

We sisters hugged.

Don't both of you live in Winnipeg? our mother asked.

Of course we do! Lorena cried. We're nuts about each other! Aren't we, Catherine?

Sure we are.

Which didn't mean we got together much. Not as much as we should, being sisters. We hurried into catch-up mode, Lorena's part-time position at St. Boniface Hospital going splendidly, Roger's window company inching into the American market in spite of the recession, though he travelled too much for her liking, the kids exceptional as always and busy with sports, a volleyball tourney on the weekend and another the next, tussles with time the theme of her entire recitation. Lorena had waited until her late thirties to have her children, which I knew had hurt our mother, what with me not producing grandchildren either. Roger's not ready, Lorena would say, and then one day he was, and Jeffrey and Marcie had arrived in short order. Mid-teens now and keeping me young! Lorena said.

I said it was the usual with us, Jim working and me retired. Nothing new, I said, but my voice had taken on a brighter, quicker tone to match my sister's.

Lorena was in dark jeans and a crisp white blouse topped with a teal scarf. Silver threads wound through the teal. When people saw us together they said it was obvious we were sisters. Besides younger, Lorena was taller and darker, though, and her sense of style, in my opinion, far superior. Lorena's husband Roger, who came from a well-to-do family and seemed to think he'd done our family a favour by marrying into it, appreciated this style one day and dismissed it the next. His origins gave him confidence, no denying that; his businesses were profitable and he had a range of sideline ventures, both local and international, some of them charitable. Confidence, which music supplied to Jim. We two, I thought that morning, daughters of Jake and Edna, nieces of the odd Uncle Must, sisters of dead, wayward Darrell, siphoning family success from our husbands.

Roger reminded me of Darrell. If I stopped, in fact, to consider what my brother would have been like had he lived, the person I landed on was Roger. Except for the monied background, Darrell had had that self-possession too, and the same charm—sometimes manipulative—and intermittent digs.

Lorena always acted as if her husband's remarks—*jello-a-jiggle!* to that stunning, ruffled cherry number of hers, or *plugging in a formula!* to her pencil skirt or jeans and blouse combos—didn't bother her. And maybe they didn't. Maybe she really was waterproof under that rain. Or strategic. We two were warm, even close I'd say, but I'd never asked my sister what it was like to be married to Roger and Lorena had never asked me what it was like to be married to Jim. Perhaps it was a draw, me with the advantage in terms of my partner, Lorena in terms of the children. About whom she was now going on and on.

Oh girls, Mom exclaimed, I love to hear you talk! I have nothing to do here but sit and stare at my hands. Look how they flutter.

The left hand shook the most and her rings—a narrow gold band and a tiny diamond—were loose and shook along. Blue-veined hands, skin thin as a hatched bird's. And birds at that moment passing the room, an aide pulling a cart with the cage and the budgie pair, lime green and blue, side by side on their swing rod, wings touching.

He's taking them upstairs, Mom said. One week here, one week there.

How demur the budgies were, how quiet in their journey along the corridor. I looked at my watch and wondered what class or meeting Jim might be in at this very moment. Years and years ago we used to ask each other, just for conversation, what were you doing at 10:05 this morning, say, or at 2:38, as if we were the only two in the universe and our comparative orbits were of the utmost consequence, and now it was 10:46, and I decided I would ask him that evening what he was doing at 10:46, and I would tell him about the budgies on pilgrimage past my mother's room.

But you'd think the place could afford more than one cage and two birds, I said.

The people upstairs like to see them too, Mom said.

That's my point.

Well they can leave them upstairs for all I care, she grumbled. I never wanted anything like that in the house. Birds, fish, dogs, cats. You live on a farm, you keep the animals outside.

Isn't it lovely to hear them chatter and chirp? Lorena asked.

Mom tsked. Chirping birds are fine if you've lost your rocker, she said.

Lost your marbles or off your rocker, I thought but kept to myself, because like a tattling child with a maddening memory for injustice, my mother had just informed Lorena that I'd been asking too many questions about Uncle Must.

Lorena threw me a quizzical look and I shrugged.

Well, Mom, Lorena said, Catherine's the historian of the family.

Technically archivist, I said.

At least your father had something, Mom went on. At least he had some letters from his brother.

Letters from his brother?

Oh yes, yes, yes, I recalled it now. A slender envelope of Dad's regarding his brother tucked into the box of Mom's personal papers. I'd helped her pack the box when she moved into Maplebend. Every resident had a safety box with lock and key, though hers was never locked and who knew where the key had gone, but perhaps it was fireproof, perhaps that was the point. A couple of sweet notes she and Dad had exchanged, a small bundle of his sermons, clipped newspaper obituaries of friends and relatives, articles pertaining to Tilia and Marble, some early photographs not mounted in the albums. I'd focused then on mitigating her sadness over having nothing significant of Darrell's left, besides a cap of his, somehow never disposed of, a comical brown cap with ear flaps he wore as a child, the woolly inside rim clotted with dirt and perspiration. And a comb. Neither of which consoled her. What was she thinking, she'd wailed that day, not keeping Darrell's letters, his poems? And then she'd answered the question herself. It was his dirty talk, that's why she got rid of those things. Terrible, those words in them, when she and Dad discovered what they meant.

My archivist instincts tingled. I'd forgotten about the letters. My colleagues and I used to debate whether history was possible without documents; it was our version of whether a tree makes a sound if no one's there to hear it fall.

Mom, I said, I'd love to see those letters.

She frowned. Don't you be getting into my box without my permission, she said. She brought her finger tips together, looked at each of us. It wasn't that easy, she said, marrying one of those Mennonites from Russia. I know my family came from there too, but way, way earlier. We didn't have that … that, what do you call it? That shock? I mean your father, your uncle, the immigrants that came later than we who lived in the States. I grew up in Idaho, and we weren't so strict anymore. I didn't think there was any difference when I met my Jake. All you see at first is that you're the same. And you want to be together. My brother-in-law Abe, he warned me. I stayed with Abe and Marie in Tilia. That's where they used to live. He said, He comes with a brother. Well, they farmed together, of course he came with a brother. Later, I got an idea what he meant about the brother. It was always his suffering. Russia. Especially his mother who was dead. As if I never suffered. Or didn't have a dead mother too.

Mom sighed, clasped her hands. Jake didn't like me saying anything about him, she said. I kept my tongue. You need to remember this, girls. You have to keep your tongue!

Lorena and I sat silently a while after our mother's speech, me zigzagging away from tongue to that etching of Maeyken Wens's son searching among ashes for the tongue screw that bound his mother's mouth when she was burned at the stake on a fifteenth century European plaza, one of the scenes in *Martyrs Mirror* that I scrutinized in Aunt Olive's parlour. A safer, more tender picture, to be sure, than some of the illustrations that had nearly hypnotized me during that visit to Idaho. The woman Maeyken was burned and out of sight. Safer, that one, than the picture of a woman being buried alive, only her face still visible, a man with a shovel full of suffocating dirt at the ready for the final deed. Or that decapitated man, blood spurting from his neck in an almost sporty fountain, his open-mouthed head lying on the ground beside him. No shock stuck to American Mennonites, ha!

Lorena stood and shook down her jeans, two slender, dark tubes poised on her boots. I remember him vaguely, she said. But I don't remember much of Tilia. Or that woman down the lane I've heard about.

Your uncle thought himself a saint, Mom said. Saving that woman.

Avoiding her, I said. I stood as well, shook down my jeans as my sister had, wishing I'd worn my white blouse and a scarf instead of my purple zip-up hoodie. I felt stale.

There's nothing important in those letters, Mom said as I left. So don't be getting into my box. They're his, not yours.

Ah yes, keeping her tongue.

15.

I was becoming less afraid of marking up my lovely red notebook. On a fresh page, I wrote:

Dear Uncle Must,

I went along to Calgary with Shirley and her family one day and Shirley and I roamed off by ourselves and I came around a corner, though Shirley was lagging, thank goodness, and I just about fell over. You were preaching there. You had a Bible open in one hand and were waving about with the other. I could have died. I flipped around so fast I bumped into Shirley and said, Let's go the other way. No one was paying the slightest attention. No one was listening. Not even one single, solitary person had stopped to hear what you had to say. Preaching. Though I don't remember you ever preached in church after that time. That time, you know. So you had to do it on the street? Weird, though, I wish I could resurrect it now, that scene, slip into disguise, a costume you know, so you wouldn't recognize me and then I would keep going forward on the sidewalk and stand still for a while in front of you and listen. Just to be nice. Maybe you, under that compunction to wave and speak—your voice ragged, untidy, like a cattail going to seed—maybe you felt like dying too. And no one giving you the time of day.

Cordially,
Catherine.

Cordially? The word ran out of me, right out of my lovely grey and black Uni-Ball pen, but seriously, was that how one signed off on a letter to the dead?

It flowed out just like that, in a conciliation that surprised me. I turned the page, wrote again:

Dear Uncle Must,

The way you patted the hood of the truck when you got out and walked around it, and flicked whatever you'd touched in that spot away from your fingers. The way you set the milk pail down in the very same place every morning, the handle turned just so, perpendicular to some point that mattered only to you. Then double-checked. I'm sorry, I don't know what that's like. I'm feeling compassionate today. There's no right or wrong about obsessive compulsive or depressive or anxious or whatever. I'm sympathetic. But there was always something else. Something awry, it seems to me now, in your view of life and the world, though I dreaded and feared you might be right. The panic of hell and all that. But hey, maybe

I can shift you from your wretched whatevers and get you to laugh. Did you hear the one about the priest, the rabbi, and the Mennonite? No? I didn't think so. Shall I tell it? Oh, never mind, forget about laughing. Did you know I came across a letter you wrote to the Mennonite college, when I worked in their archives? That stint there between my years at the regional centre? You wrote it after I'd been to the college a year, and Darrell too. You blamed the entire faculty for what you imagined was wrong with us, not just the two of us, you said, though you named us, but all young people today. So this and so that, so essentially dissolute. Male and female studying together, imagine! It was a blaming, blinding thing, full of scripture text fragments you'd selected to make your points. And I don't suppose it did an ounce of good. I suppose it was read and filed. It was kept because it arrived as correspondence and that was the rule, file the correspondence. Maybe you got a bland God-bless-you reply, or maybe you didn't. There was no carbon copy of that. You wouldn't have been satisfied, I'm sure, and neither did your letter help them one iota. It was miserable, venomous, and I shuddered to read it, because I'd remembered your generosity. I mean the piano and books and magazines. The television—once you'd been persuaded, that is. Your glimmers of attraction to knowledge. Against the clapperclaw of your attempts to control. It affects a person, you know, that patriarchal control. I actually shook when I discovered and read that letter. I'd been assigned to search for another document when I saw your name. Fearlessly and perfectly handwritten, of course. A fancy old hand. As if you'd never been young. You couldn't believe freedom and beauty were meant for you. Some constraint, some tension, like a blackening square over a window, as if under siege. Was it any wonder we ran, as if chased, from that version of things? Oh, and would you like to know, dear

Uncle, if your three-page missive, filled with quoted line-and-verse denunciations, is still in those archives? Would you like to know, Uncle Must? Well, I'm not going to tell you whether or not I committed a minor crime on your behalf and mine and removed it from that file. It happens, you know, archivists are human, and it could have cost me my job. Do you want to know if I risked it? I'm not going to say.

Actually, I will. I left it but I redacted your name. I couldn't bear the association.

Not cordially,
Catherine.

How covert but swift the process of shame. I wrote this sentence in my notebook too. The high heel breaking at the cocktail schmooze or the inadvertent laugh in a solemn situation, and immediate to that moment the wish—the need—to be erased from it. Yes, erased. Completely removed. The time Jim and I rushed into a movie theatre late because we got stuck in traffic, found seats near the front, endured the looming too-close action, endured an awful odour too, the cloying, foul smell of excrement, me too polite to turn to identify the unwashed perpetrator, perhaps beside me or one over, someone who would be obvious by signs of dishevelment. Inwardly repelled by the unawareness of some people. Jim remarked on the smell as we exited. Back in our vehicle, it hung about us still, and halfway home, I discovered it was me: a fresh slice of dog shit had wedged onto my shoe and then I recalled the bit of soft grass I'd flown over in my hurry from the parking spot, late and not looking down in that dash to catch the start of the movie. I'd been the stink. It arrived with me, people around us must have known. The shame of it rolling over me for days, making me dread a return to the theatre, as if the same people would be there to titter at me behind their hands.

And the time I picked up that teapot in the art gallery shop, an exquisitely unique teapot in a stunning curry-yellow splattered with blue. I'd simply wanted to look by holding it and I lifted the lid and somehow it tumbled, a nightmare of downward motion, a blur of colour from the glass display shelf to the floor. A clattering sound that might have been a cannon firing, so loud did it seem in the sanctimonious hush of the expensive objects around me. Certainly the saleslady heard it; she reached me immediately like the echo that follows a boom. I had picked up the lid but the other woman grabbed it from me. Her hair was bright red. While her head bent to the lid, I saw that the dye job was streaky; there were uneven strips of brown-going-grey. So she wasn't perfect either. Her nails as red as her hair and her pointer finger circling round and round the rim like a raspberry, until she finally said, still peering, It seems to be alright. But reluctantly, as if, in fact, she wanted it chipped, to make everything worse. If anything breaks, she went on, her voice a drumbeat of scorn, consider it sold. Which printed cards on every display shelf had already announced to me. Of course, I said, with as much dignity as I could muster. The flood of humiliation that started in my head had reached my feet but I made myself stay, examining a purple and golden goblet by the same artist. Not touching though. There were three or four others in the shop, all women. I held myself erect but felt myself ricocheting around the room, me of the clumsy fingers. I feigned myself until I sensed my violation to the place had finally subsided and I was able to leave. It took several visits to the art gallery before I could bear to enter the gift shop again.

Examples of no import, I know. But just to say that among the components of all that belongs, there's ample opportunity for *ashamed* to take root.

16.

I was lazing around the apartment, doing bits of housework and reading, but scattershot, it seemed—thoughts ascending and descending like the angels of Jacob's dream ladder—and I heard the clock in the kitchen ticking as if it would tick onward forever and I was unable to stop hearing it tick. Fury rose in me like steam. I yanked the clock from the wall.

Jim's clock. He was beguiled by clocks, by anything clock-like. You're a music teacher, I'd told him once, you have a metronome in your head. When we toured Vienna during his sabbatical, he scrutinized every last item in the watch and clock museum. I walked through quickly and abandoned him. Hours later, after my two rounds of coffee and cake in the next-door café, he finally exited, wary as a mole in sunshine. Jim was no snob, nor unduly acquisitive, but he liked things properly made and substantial, which is why the kitchen clock was an anomaly. Three pressed-plastic clock arms and a cheap mechanism attached to a painted wooden circle, a picture at every number highlighting a tourist attraction in Newfoundland. Signal Hill, Cape St. Mary's, and so on. A souvenir of our Newfoundland holiday four years ago. I'd seen him eyeing the clock in the shop and told him it was tacky. He chuckled and agreed and bought it anyway, on account of the holiday being one of the best ever, he said, giving my waist a squeeze. So the clock came along and launched its tick-tocking in the kitchen. It survived our downsizing in the move from house to apartment. Time ought to be soundless, I complained. Digital clocks on the stove, microwave, radio, computers, and phones. We had watches. Devices that did their duty in reverential silence. If it was one of those keepsake clocks hauled out of Russia by the Mennonites, I could see it. One of those Mandtler or Kroeger clocks. Not that my grandfather had anything but two sons with him, I said. Jim replied that the Kroeger clock brought over by the Reimers had been passed down another branch of the family and there weren't that many of those clocks around anymore, and then he asked me if I had a ticking-clock phobia since a ticking clock is a stand-in for the heart and a fear of it stopping is the fear of death. He broke into "My Grandfather's Clock" to make his point, singing as far as the clock stopping short when the old man died.

You're ridiculous, I said, though you sing it very well.

I got used to the Newfoundland clock, no longer heard it, except that I heard it now and found myself holding it, watching the second hand lurch forward in its desperate staccato. No elegant floor clock, this; no low, resonant tones.

I wanted to shove the clock down the garbage chute. No. No. Just shush it a while. Punish its reminder of time. I forced the clock between the mattress and box spring of our bed. Jim's side.

Jim had the evening free so we went to the supermarket to stock up on groceries. I'd forgotten about the clock. He didn't notice anything amiss in the kitchen either. I was brushing my teeth in the bathroom when I heard a What the hay!— Jim's substitute for swearing. But he might as well have sworn for the disgust in it. I rushed out, brush in hand, mouth foaming. He'd been getting into bed, noticed the mattress lump, had pulled out the clock.

It tick-tocked twice as if revived, then stopped. The arms were bent.

Good grief, Catherine! What's this?

Through foam I said, The clock.

I can see that. What's it doing under the mattress?

Sorry, I frothed. I wanted quiet and it was just too much.

You can take the batteries out if it bothers you, you know. His voice was even but I could tell he was furious. I retreated to the bathroom and rinsed my mouth and when I returned I said, more snippily than I had any right to, considering I smothered his holiday memento, I can't believe how attached you are to that thing—

Though if it was a Kroeger, I suppose you're planning to say!

I suppose.

Kroegers tick too. They may chime. They're noisy. Isn't that what you're grousing about?

We could stop a Kroeger, I said, and it could hang there and be a precious heirloom. In spite of my foolishness, I was hoping to coax him into amusement.

Which is actually what removing the batteries would accomplish.

Jim was usually the most affable of men. He was optimistic. A lot like Dad. Isn't that what they say, that you either become or marry one of your parents? There were women who envied me; my friend Ev had said as much. As far as husbands go, Jim was their ideal. Most days I would agree—and surely, I protested to Ev, as if she'd criticized instead of commended our marriage, it's not a failure of feminism to appreciate your husband, to need him, to love him in spite of his faults, be they his in particular or those of the male species in general. But never mind all that. What I'd done to his clock was a monumental slight. He cradled the thing as if a beloved pet had taken ill, traced a finger along each of the arms, turned it over and carefully popped open the mechanism, peered at the batteries and then removed them with the delicate precision of a heart surgeon.

But then he tossed the clock onto his shoes in the closet.

Our custom was to talk in bed. Sometimes it carried us into sleep, sometimes into sex. There was no conversation that evening. I wanted to say, But doesn't the relentlessness of life's passing—and how unfinished one is—get to you too?

But I didn't. We said formal goodnights. Jim fell asleep and I lay awake. I thought I heard a faint ticking coming from the closet floor. Impossible though. I'd seen him set the batteries on his bedside table. Confused, I kept lifting my head to check by the glow of the electronic numerals on the clock radio. Yes, there they were, two AA batteries like tiny sentinels guarding the time.

In spite of the clock episode, I woke the next morning feeling venturesome and curious, and I dressed immediately, as if a working archivist again, and decided to call the police detachment responsible for the north, for the Gilly Lake area where Uncle Must disappeared and presumably drowned. It took five telephone calls in which I was directed politely from one person to the next to confirm what I remembered Mom telling me about Uncle's death. The fifth and final person, a woman who sounded young, gave me the information. Her manner was professional but her desire to help obvious and touching. Perhaps she was a recent hire trying to prove herself, thus more fulsome in what she revealed than she might be when grown cynical by encounters with the public. Or perhaps she was older and had been there for decades and just happened to care but not care either: I had the impression she might have been breaking protocol by discussing the matter by phone.

At any rate, the police woman located the file, assured me it was clear what had occurred: the canoe washed up, a tattered brown fisher's hat with his name in the rim tucked under the seat, his life jacket in the truck at the shore. There was a squall that day, a sudden, short mid-day storm, and the water would have been choppy. And cold. Very cold. Icy in parts. And, of course, he was old.

There was a Sharon Miller, the woman said, who alerted them to his absence. Suspicion should not be attached to this. He was a loner and the Miller woman about the only person in town who could be said to know him at all. When she didn't find him home, she called the police. Yes, he'd given her money over the years, because she'd helped him with meals and cleaning. Ms. Miller had been perfectly forthcoming; they'd conducted more than one interview with her. She'd been in Winnipeg —the times away were confirmed— and she'd returned to Gilly Lake to find him missing. After that, she moved to Winnipeg for good.

The deceased, the voice from the detachment continued— reading, it seemed—had no longer worked, had lived on govern- ment cheques. Bank account, modest. Modest for years. Sporadic attendance at a local church but kept mostly to himself, poor to passable health, apparently, said odd things if pressed, apropos of nothing. Some of the church people had tried to help him by slipping him food now and then. Phone bills indicated one long distance call a week. Sundays, to Marble, Manitoba.

This Sharon Miller had a key to his place, the woman clarified when I asked—because of cleaning duties already mentioned. I pretended not to know anything about Miss Miller but my moth- er's long-ago doubts rose in me and I was tempted to return the favour of the friendly person at the other end of the line and con- fide the truth of Sharon Miller's domestic chaos, as we'd known it in Tilia at least, and Uncle's neat habits in comparison. But my doubts subsided again in light of the officer's pleasant, logical certainty. When I thanked her for her help, she said she was happy to be of assistance, had related everything she could, was sorry and hoped we were doing as well as could be expected with our loss.

We're all doing fine, I said; it's been fifteen years. I said I hadn't called to re-open the case but simply for review. My father was deceased, my mother in a seniors' home. The woman said she understood. She said a letter would have been sent to my parents at the time and if I wanted anything further in writing, she could certainly provide it. I said that would not be necessary.

It's a need we all have, the woman said. To know more. To know what people were like and what happened.

Was there any suggestion of suicide? I asked.

No note. No threats or hints were reported. You as a family may have your own impressions regarding that.

Just a question, I said. I don't know that we ever thought it was.

Hanging up the phone, I realized the details in the report—what washed up, where the life jacket was, the hat, and the matter of the squall (weren't we told those days were windless?)—varied from my mother's telling of it. My memory, that is, of her telling.

The differences weren't substantive, though. No need to burrow into them.

What struck me as new was this: *After that, she moved to Winnipeg.* Suddenly I was also curious about Sharon Miller, wondering if she still lived in Winnipeg and if we might meet again.

An email from Lucy arrived, loaded with exclamation marks. It was shortly after a coffee date, so too soon to meet again, she said, sticking a smiley face at the end of the sentence, but now she had it—finally!—what the project should be—and she just had to let me know. A memoir film, she called it. An autobiographical documentary, her protagonist no longer the fictional Margaret but Lucy herself, its setting not the metaphorical Surface but places in Ontario and Manitoba where Lucy had lived. She had tons of photos. She would take video of the family home, schools she attended, the cottage. Significant locations. The soundtrack would be songs that had shaped her. And of course, the later stuff—photos of her wedding and current life—was readily available. She'd already dashed down an outline of the scenes.

The email was long, she raved and rhapsodized, she was buoyant with it all. And she was loving *The Archivist's Story*, she said, a novel about an archivist in Moscow's Lubyanka Prison who risks his life to save the last stories of Isaac Babel. She thanked me for suggesting it. What she'd taken away from it, she said, was that everything should be remembered. Morning swims at the lake, conversations under the stars, the fragrance of a lover's perfume. Everything.

Clearly, Lucy was filtering everything she read these days through the lens of her project.

Did I agree? That everything should be remembered? For Lucy, recording her way to *beloved* out of *different*, it was probably true. Out of the mass of her remembrance would emerge the salient particulars needed for her film. I was glad for my friend, but discontented too. I was busy with remembrance as well but she'd discerned her narrative—the patterns, convergences, and agency that represented who she'd been and was. She'd rustled up memories and would sequence them into something persuasive and interesting, something that made sense. Something resolved, something to be proud of.

17.

That year of my preoccupation with the dead hit a low point mid-December. Dusk swallowed the brief hours of daylight with its long blue shadows, street lights were ineffectual puddles of yellow on darkening snow. How scant the sun's daily transport near the apex of winter! But here was Jim, walking through the door with a hibiscus plant. For you, Catherine, he said. For Christmas. Instead of a poinsettia.

The gesture moved me. I loved hibiscus, had had many over the years, each producing lavish blooms until white mites eventually got the best of them. One flower was open, crimson petals like arms thrown apart, showing off pistils, stamens, stigmas, and deep within, a five-sided purple heart. Ardour in an arduous season. It was appreciated more than I could properly express. Thank you, I said, my voice thick. I burrowed my head in his coat collar, tears rising.

This isn't about the clock, he said. It's okay about the clock.

The clock? I glanced at the empty spot on the kitchen wall. What was still bothering him about the clock? I'd apologized several times, and he had too, though I wasn't sure why. We'd made up the very next day, in fact, at dinner, and that evening, reaching for him, he'd seemed the firmest, most indisputable ingredient of my life and the lovemaking that followed was, well, more ravishing than it had been for some time. Sunk into the moment, wholly present tense, both of us. Though the clock stayed gone. The batteries disappeared from the bedside table, the closet floor smelled of leather and shoe polish and held only shoes, and the nail in the kitchen was bare.

I chucked it down the chute, he said. Maybe I've had enough of it too.

Oh Jim, I said. The thought made me sad for him.

But hibiscus! Had he sensed the watering down in me, some uncharacteristic trepidation or clamp as Advent progressed, like stumbling around in a cellar while he strode into lit-up rehearsals for concerts, evening after evening? I'd been staying inside too much, separating myself from the weather, and when I walked it was in the cavernous and echoing main floor of our building with its faux marble. Faux everything. And wiling away too much time over the long white view from our east-facing window, a screen where the past shuffled or played, cranes at the museum-build rotating across it with mechanical ease, their loads dangling and swinging. Tangles of tree branches and snow-covered roofs, the curves and pillars of Union Station a scold to bygone, marvellous days. I'd forced myself to get busy with holiday baking, shopping, decorating. But no matter where I turned, I saw my brother. I'd opened myself to the past and now I had to face him too. As if Uncle Must had stuffed him up his sleeve, only to brandish him for Christmas.

I should have anticipated this. Darrell: a stage trick.

Darrell. Jake and Edna's firstborn, the first big triumph of their lives, his name meaning little dear or beloved one, which he was. Not that our parents picked his name for its meaning, as far as I knew. Perhaps they liked the sound of it or met someone they admired with that name. Even couples of immigrant stock, like my father was, were possessed of postwar enthusiasm—assimilation—and in the 1940s and 50s, they would choose Western names for the future rather than names with family connections. Why pull forward the weighted monikers of grandparents and parents and other relatives they'd worn around their necks for centuries, names from countries they'd left? Mind you, the first thing they did when bending over their newborns was pronounce on whose nose, ears, or chin the child had carried forward in the gene pool suitcase, maybe from some progenitor as far back as Prussia.

Though they went and called me Catherine after that Katharina of theirs, way back. Screw that theory, then.

I arrived thirteen months after my brother. Mom liked to say we grew up like twins, sharing toys, books, and friends. We played well and we squabbled. How many hundreds of times did we do dishes together? Darrell beside me at the kitchen sink was one of Mom's stabs at the modern, more equitable ways of raising children: the boy child acquainted with some domestic tasks. I didn't help with the farming, though, and our folks divided their own roles along traditional lines. Dad supported the semi-equality project. If we didn't have Sunday company that obligated him to retire to the living room for conversation with the men while Mom and the women washed up, if we were alone, that is, just the family—the Sunday meals I loved the best, especially if Uncle Must went away—Dad donned one of Mom's bib-top aprons trimmed with embroidery or ruffles and while she washed, he rinsed and dried. Mom's happiness at these times reminded me of an infant squealing for joy in a bath. Dad rinsed the dishes in a basin of steaming water straight from the kettle and the heat didn't bother him; he lifted them out and set them on the drying rack and they practically dried themselves. He would tell me I was free, that I could read or play piano, and to Darrell he would grin and say, Like this, young man, like this, flourishing the tea towel over plates, cups, and cutlery, and in his son's direction.

Darrell saw something else in it. One late evening when the youth group sang around a fire and we'd just moaned through a long series of "Kumbaya"s which rendered us almost torpid, so little did we want to leave one another and the flame-flicker gilding us all with intermittent radiance, someone suggested we go round the circle and share something for which we were thankful. I offered the affectionate ritual of my parents in their Sunday best doing the Sunday dishes, Dad's jacket over the back of a chair and his tie loosened and Mom's hat and heels off and both of them in aprons, she seeming younger in her glee and stockinged feet than weekdays. Maybe I was dreamy about a someday-marriage of my own. I was probably overly effusive in my gratitude, for parents no less. At the edge of the dark I heard Darrell mutter, Dad's just priming the pump. The guys around him laughed. Maynard thought it hilarious.

How smart Darrell had seemed in comparison to me, as if he knew the world! But a rift opened between us that evening—I felt myself withdraw—and it was deepened by the fact that he'd taken up with Betty-now-Liz, who I believed seductive and designing, and of course he wouldn't see it. Betty's hair was black and waist-long, and it glinted colour like the feathers of a crow, though she wore flower-child clothes for one stretch that made her seem wholesome. The girls of our group tripped through those years with smocks, belts, beads, then miniskirts, barely aware we followed Betty, who followed fashion, powerful Pied Piper of us all, even though she came from a family we considered poor, the whole bunch of them good-looking and easy-going but not ambitious, which marked them as morally suspect too. Betty's father worked seasonally at the feed mill in town and the small farm he also ran was clearly a failure, implements parked helter skelter and the yard overgrown; he might be seen reclining in the shade of the giant linden beside the house any time on any given Saturday, reading the local paper, or maybe the city paper too. And rumours of his fondness for drink, though he and his wife were church members, semi-regular in their attendance, and there was no evidence he was a full-out drunkard.

We girls longed to be thin and doe-eyed like the model Twiggy. I was lucky; I had the slender frame, the slender legs. Though not the height. Betty had full, high breasts and when she complained in front of everyone at youth group one afternoon in the church basement that she should have been a teenager in the fifties because she was closer to Marilyn Monroe than Twiggy I knew she was simpering for attention. But Maynard remarked, as if to console her, that he figured it was better, what she had said about herself. He didn't say Marilyn Monroe but he said, It's better to bounce. If I had any feelings left for Maynard, they fled at that sentence. He had a large white pimple on the far side of his cheek, near his ear, and it was ripe to burst, and he was big-smiling at Betty and Darrell echoed Bounce! like a command and punched Maynard on the arm and yee-hawed and Maynard turned red and his pimple glowed. I couldn't stop looking at it. I wanted to smash it open. Maynard recovered and laughed, and he and Darrell laughed and laughed, and Betty sat there like a queen with a benevolent expression on her face. I crossed my Twiggy-lovely legs and let my short blue skirt ride higher, but I felt truculent and wished to escape. I could have used a good long run through the pasture, down to the creek.

I'd kept my worries to myself, like my suspicion that Darrell and Betty had gone all the way, which is how we talked about sex. Puzzling circumstances, like Betty at Miss Miller's—when had they become friends?—and Darrell absent at the strangest times. Or whistling homeward up the lane. But then he joined the church at the end of Grade Twelve, decided to attend the Mennonite college in the fall, abandoned Betty, and it seemed nearly miraculous, evidence he was with the rest of us again. With me. The fissure between us seemed to close, Darrell suddenly interested in justice, theology, social issues. He was fluent, as all of us were, in the pietistic phraseology of our church but he leapt ahead and talked of theologians—of theological scholars, that is, who saw the complexities, not just the scriptures, which were clear and plain—and none of us knew where he came up with his ideas, though after he went to college it could be assumed they came from his professors. It was exciting and scary, his talking as if theology and history were inseparable, speaking of Bonhoeffer, Barth as well, and then passionately of the need to engage with the Negro situation in the States, which was how Black civil rights were referred to then. He ordered a copy of *Black Like Me* and insisted I read it, and I was stirred by it too and we discussed it.

So the crack healed, though he still affected that cool, contemporary way of speaking which charmed and perplexed our parents, and rallied his friends, borrowing phrases from music we heard on the radio and the records he bought. He followed Bob Dylan and The Beatles with the devotion of an acolyte and never let his idols disappoint him, no matter what they said or did, even when John Lennon made himself anathema in the eyes of our elders by suggesting The Beatles were more popular than Jesus, not to mention the mop hair, screaming female fans, evidence of drugs. Darrell dropped phrases of their lyrics into speech, sang snatches in reply to questions. When I asked him if he'd really split with Betty, he launched into "Dizzy Miss Lizzy" and sometimes he greeted me or Lorena with "Hello Little Girl."

At supper one evening, Dad recounted what he and Uncle Must had done that day; there'd been some trouble with an implement which meant a trip into town to get a part, a costly part, which took its time, and Darrell broke into "A Hard Day's Night." It was impertinent, inappropriate. He'd made farm work look ridiculous. Dad gazed at him while he sang, not comprehending it, and Uncle Must lifted his head too while Darrell squared his shoulders, as if to flick them away like dandruff, and abruptly transitioned to "One Too Many Mornings," and I could see my mother building to retort like a storm. Then Uncle Must turned to our father and said, It's poetry, I think.

The way he turned and said It's poetry, well, it was more than an explanation. It was stronger than that; it was as if he'd slid himself between Darrell and our father like a sheet of plywood. Dad wasn't as easily manipulated by Darrell as the rest of us were. He wouldn't get angry, but frustration simmered in him that season and it seemed to be about Darrell and I could feel it. I feared it would harden into mutual and permanent disdain.

But Darrell had changed; it was obvious. I sensed fresh rigour in him, as if he'd set ambiguity aside. He drew next to me again, like an alter ego. He was the informal leader of our group, and though he still fevered about at poetry, he did so at the kitchen table. As if writing was a family affair or some kind of service to others. He spent hours playing his guitar—also in the kitchen. Sunday after Sunday evening, we friends gathered to sing. We gathered around a fire in someone's yard or in a living room if the weather was inclement. Darrell played well and Maynard played passably, strumming yes to whatever Darrell proposed. They would start with easy, current songs like "Four Strong Winds" and "All You Need Is Love," and sometimes Darrell and Maynard performed or introduced something new, and then we worked our way through spirituals, taking on, we believed, the great sorrow of the American Negro. And the songs of the Jesus freaks. Endless versions of "Kumbaya."

This progression was the arrow-point of our hopes, dreams, plans. Secular to sacred, earth to heaven, the present to the future. Our iteration of the sixties. It seemed a long season, that summer, the best of my life I thought it then, Canada proud in its centenary, the huge success of the world's fair, Expo 67 in Montreal, where man's greatest achievements were on display, *man* still uncontested as speaking for humanity. We breathed the fortunes of our times like bountiful air. There were problems, sure, tons of them. But civil rights, war, political crooks, over-population, and acid rain would be solved—had to be solved, and our generation had come along to sing and do. And Darrell never tiring, it seemed, perched on the black crate he hauled around to our sing-songs as his personal guitar-playing seat, twanging and riffing and strumming, and as he played, his fine, brown hair flopped over his forehead like a cluster of leaves.

One evening the youth group was at our farm, at the fire pit near the end of the lane, and Sharon Miller appeared round the hedge at the house that used to be Uncle's and now seemed to be hers. Wearing white. I couldn't tell if it was a dress or a nightgown. She stood half shielded by the caragana and she stood there for some time, cradling Ricky, facing the music, nothing hostile in her stance. More like attraction. It was close to midnight, still warm, and the moon was nearly full, the sky cloudless, and her garment shone, Ricky's bare limbs and dark hair like burrs against it. Perhaps our singing and talking and laughing had affected his sleep, perhaps she'd picked him up to settle him, and perhaps it helped, for his body seemed at rest. Perhaps she wanted him to absorb the music by osmosis. We sang well, as many of us could harmonize.

No one mentioned, between songs, the woman who listened. I took it as a sign—how naïve I seem in retrospect—that we were having a salvific effect on Miss Miller. So I sang the lyrics toward our neighbour and wished her to be blessed by them.

All That Belongs

That very same evening, Uncle Must detoured toward us through the trees in that clumsy manner of his, on his way from the Big House to the barn. He stopped before he reached us but hung about in the trees, maybe five or ten minutes, a dark figure lurking in the poplars and bush. I was keenly aware of him. Even at a distance his presence made me nervous. What if he began to rant? It was torturous. Darrell seemed not to notice. He and Maynard were singing Dylan: his message to our elders that we were beyond their command. I doubted that Uncle Must would follow the lyrics but, as if he had followed them and taken offence, he galumphed his way back to the lane and on to the barn and my worries evaporated.

Mom was irritable the next morning and barked at me and Darrell, You'll have to wrap up earlier if you're going to be meeting here! Some of us need our sleep! All that carrying on!

Jeepers, Mom—

And don't you start that talk with me, Darrell Riediger!

Jeepers, he said to me out of Mom's earshot, what's got into her?

I know, I said. I know what you mean.

Uncle Must overheard Darrell and came up close and said, Listen to your mother.

Under his breath, Darrell spat, Fuck off!

Had Uncle caught it? Maybe yes, maybe no. Maybe he had no idea what it meant. Whatever the case, on that occasion he abided our presence like a saint. It was me who blanched, who said, as if standing in for my mother, Darrell, watch your mouth! As if the clarity in him was clouding again, some bottom feeder stirring up the mud.

179

Darrell went off to a Mennonite college in Winnipeg that fall and to our family it seemed as prestigious as if he'd gone to Harvard or Oxford. Plus, we were proud of him for saving enough money working Saturdays and summers over the years to pay his own way.

He visited Expo 67 in Montreal before the school semester began. Mom and Dad didn't want him to go, not alone, they thought it too much money for six or seven days of amusement, but he was unshakable and he'd earned it so he took his things to Manitoba by train, then flew to Montreal—his first time on an airplane—and, according to the postcards he sent us—one a day—had a wonderful time.

A postcard of the US pavilion arrived first, the silvery geodesic dome proclaimed in a scrawl to be The Best! Next, a forest of stylized pine trees featuring the Canadian pulp and paper industry. Then, the large white tent of the German pavilion. There was a postcard of Habitat, the Expo housing complex which resembled a haphazard pile of boxes. Fierce! he declared. The future! He always signed, Your son and brother, but not his name.

Why was one so hugely glad—later—for what the dead experienced while alive? I wrapped myself in the hideous cheddar-hued afghan I'd made decades ago when newly married and passionate about crafts, when I sewed my own clothes, knotted macramé plant hangers, wove placemats, knitted afghans and sweaters and scarves (Darling you, Catherine; look at you, so domestic!), and tried to remember as many of Darrell's cards as I could. I pondered them as if they had something to teach me, all these years later. At the very least, I was succoured: he'd been at Expo, there at least, the most successful world's fair of the twentieth century, there among fifty million who attended, part of that jubilant, sprawling celebration; he'd resisted our parents' wishes and he went and he was the only one of us who saw it.

All That Belongs

With Google's help, I finally lined up the week's worth of Expo postcards and could imagine my brother wandering through the various pavilions, buying the cards, scribbling his enthusiasms next to our Tilia address. Licking the stamp. Exclaiming on the back of the USSR pavilion's card how we would have been citizens if Grandfather had stayed instead of emigrated. Soviet accomplishments in the interim were rather impressive, he said, apart from Stalin's paranoid sprees of arrests and exterminations, which weren't broadcasted at Expo, of course. On the card of the United Kingdom pavilion he crowed, Fantastic hostesses in miniskirts!

His presence at the fair seemed a fence to me now against everything he lost. The rest of us got older and Darrell stayed young. Since it was impossible to bring him forward, I had to travel backward—as if through canyons—to find him. I had to pass through every year I'd lived beyond his death before I encountered him again. The injustice of this—that we could only meet at the remove of decades—was overwhelming.

I opened my notebook. So many empty pages available to me!

Darrell,

Right now I'm stunned and angry that you used to exist but now you don't and I've kept on! I suppose it doesn't matter to you but it matters to me, my living this long since then, you not here for even a day of it. That pathetically narrow slice you obtained for yourself. Days and nights and days and nights interminable beyond your stopped-short self, you missing them all. And not just what you've missed for yourself, but what you missed about me! I'm not the same person that I was then. I've been several persons since young, you know. We pile up selves over time. And you haven't seen any of them, Darrell, you don't know me now.

18.

Nearly every winter day yielded dazzling light, the sun's brave arc slung low along the sky, an antidote to sadness, but the temperatures were so brutal, so numbing, that January felt like spite. I ran out of turkey leftovers before I was ready for a flurry of new cooking and was stupidly jealous of Roger and Lorena's holiday to the Dominican Republic, their turquoise-sea-and-white-sand withdrawal, the almond smell of a hot vacation. I offered Roger's mother, who stayed with Jeffrey and Marcie, as many breaks as possible as penance for my pique. I treated my niece and nephew to meals out, drove them to some of their games, and picked them and friends up for swims in the apartment complex pool.

Jim gave me the latest Giller winner, *The Bishop's Man*, for my birthday, and when I told him I'd bought and read it, he was embarrassed. He hadn't seen it lying about. I assured him it was fine, an easy mistake, and if it wasn't written in, could surely be exchanged. But he'd written in it, birthday greetings and love. I folded the gift bag and smoothed the white tissue he'd fluffed inside, said I'd pass on the other copy; someone in the book club would be delighted. It's a good book, I said. Good but hard. Painful. So much hurt in the world, so much cover-up. After this, he bore me off in high spirits to his favourite restaurant for dinner, because I couldn't decide where I wanted to go and begged him to choose the place. We had great steaks, though less-than-stellar desserts, then took in the movie *Black Swan*, which we agreed was very well done. It was a lovely celebration, really, on balance, but I felt Jim's sniffing vigilance the entire time. For some days, in fact, I'd felt his hand touching down upon or slipping lightly across my upper back or shoulders as he passed me in the apartment, unexpected touch so fleeting, so nearly weightless, I couldn't be sure it was there or if I'd imagined or wished for it.

The next evening, he pushed his chair away from the dinner table with more scrape than necessary and got up for the salt and pepper which we'd neglected to set, then towered beside me with the shakers in his hand as if to emphasize I was short and asked me if I was depressed.

I said, I'm grieving.

I regretted and hated this sentence immediately, not because there was anything wrong with grief, but the declaration of it, the nebulous space that an admission demanded. Like wrapping fog around myself.

He sat down, chastened it seemed. Was it a re-run, he asked, about ... well, about children? Referring, I knew, to the fact we didn't have any.

Lands, Jim. Do you really think I'm still lugging that bag of sorrows around?

Didn't you wonder aloud just the other day about who would look after us in our senility?

It was a joke.

That's what I thought too. What then?

A staggering work of heartbreaking genius. Or a heartbreaking work of genius staggering. Take your pick.

It was dumb, it was cruel, and I hated this too, playing with the title of the Dave Eggers book on Jim's nightstand. What was the matter with me? I'd offended him. He heaped a second helping of macaroni and cheese onto his plate.

This would not be the time to remind him of his doctrine concerning weight, that everything rises or falls on second helpings. I made the dish from scratch and he preferred it to anything made from a box. He was being excessively deliberate about maneuvering his fork, about his chewing. A soft dish, macaroni and cheese, comfort food, creamy and cheesy, and he was working it too hard. In long marriages, one grew weary, I thought, of listening to the other person chew.

Darrell, I said, my tone softer. Darrell.

Oh. He said he was sorry about this.

But we ended up testy with each other anyway, whiffs of sarcasm like impolite farts, both of us tired. I said it wasn't like I was a great big dishrag or something, and he said I seemed exactly like a dishrag lately, and so it went, an exchange as petty as lobs of balled paper.

I don't think I'm depressed, I finally said. I can't actually remember if I ever cried over Darrell. (I didn't know how to articulate that shame had been a wall against tears.)

He said to go ahead and cry, the tone more conciliatory than expected but not stable enough. I couldn't relax against it yet.

Well, speaking of dishrag, I said, supper's done and I haven't planned for dessert. Please help yourself to ice cream.

We cleared the table, containered the leftovers, loaded the dishwasher, moved delicately around our compact apartment kitchen, barely three steps to anywhere, like gangly teenagers overly aware of our bodies. The effort not to collide, not to touch, was a rod of tension down my back.

I do hate arguments, I said when we finished.

It wasn't much of one, he said. Not rousing at all.

So we're done then.

Done.

Jim went to the den, I took my place on the sofa and started in on the newspaper I'd bought that morning but hadn't opened yet. I flipped through, glanced at headlines. Names and places trailed after me. Pakistan, Tunisia, Egypt. An attack on a Moscow airport, an update about the Giffords shooting in Arizona. I remembered how Jim and I backpacked through Europe on the cheap, how we scanned for doors or arches or portals of some kind when tired, columns close enough for us to rest against but also reach and rub feet together in the middle. Dropping shoes or sandals—we could hardly do it fast enough—stretching toes, the mutual skin polish of soles, tickling the other too, our laughter astringent and reviving. Now I felt a rash ache in my feet to rub toes, soles, heels with him. I nearly called to suggest we sit on the floor and do it but he was digging in our tiny freezer with one hand, holding his earphones with the other. Looking for ice-cream. As if he'd departed for the next tourist site on our itinerary and left me stranded on the threshold between two pillars, stuck with my aching feet and my swelling disinterest in monuments, cathedrals, famous plazas, history, or anything older than coffee and pastry at an outdoor café. Striding off while I—probably!—remained with some lone traveller who'd become attached to us. Which had happened too often. Nearly every day, in fact, we'd had someone in our shadow. It was our friendliness, that obligation regarding others we'd both been raised with and then layered on at college. To consider everyone who crossed our path as crossing for a reason. Biblical hospitality writ large, welcoming guests with plenteous honour—fatted calves and cakes—but *the honour all mine, my lord,* the potential of entertaining angels unawares.

Until camels barged into the tent opening, that is, dripping saliva over the rugs. The immoderate uncle. The dead brother. Yes, Darrell, who'd always hogged the spotlight. Once he sent me a poem, folded into a letter. He said to pay attention to how he'd used collusion, collision, illusion. I was duly impressed. Hardly subtle, though, these words marching through my head in that British accent he sometimes affected as if wearing a top hat and swinging a cane, elbowing our uncle aside. *Sorry old chap, but I'll take it from here.*

Still, what I wouldn't give to have him sprawled beside me on the sofa, not as reminiscence but in flesh! I wanted something solid against my inability to comprehend that he'd existed once but hadn't since—was it thirty-five, thirty-six, years by now? I figured I'd long swallowed the truth of his absence but now he'd show-stepped in and my throat was raw with the lump of watching him perform. And the fact that it wasn't him at all, but collusion, collision, illusion.

Was I turning into a Mr. Casaubon of *Middlemarch*? Elderly, self-absorbed, living too much with the dead? Jim in the recliner in the other room, nearly horizontal, a bowl of ice-cream balanced on his chest, ear phones on, a grin of musical Elsewhere on his face. And me on the sofa as if flopped in a tourist doorway, looking back.

I fingered for the newspaper, told myself to burrow into one article per section at least. Keep up with what was happening in the world. Keep up, keep on.

Jim raised his head, saw me looking over the rims of my reading glasses. He waved at me and I waved back.

It was so bizarre, Jim and I waving at each other across our small apartment.

I needed my brother Darrell to explain some things, that's what it was. Explain Uncle Must, for example. Settle the man for me, his stories of the Mennonites in Russia, his fervent but selective assimilation into Canada, his ideas of holiness, his tics when stressed. How he could declaim at a street corner and not say a single word at meals. Darrell always acted as if he knew more about him than I did. Now I felt he was right; he'd known more.

Settle *himself* for me while he was at it.

I remembered spring in Tilia, cool molting Alberta days, the wind a coax, green wiggling to the surface, a season when walking became urgent for our uncle. Usually it was Sunday afternoons when it itched at him. He always set off in the same direction, southward from the yard toward the creek. And sometimes Darrell walked beside him, occasions congealed into a single recollection, a single Sunday. Uncle Must stepping out of his room, coat and hat flung on, pressing tightly against his chest the walking stick he'd found and sanded and varnished, as if to get it safely through the kitchen. I was busy with homework at the table. Normally we weren't allowed to leave our homework for Sundays, but the family had been in Calgary the day before, shopping, and the circumstances allowed the exception. And Darrell, who rarely had homework anyway because he sailed through, as Mom would say, perched on the edge of the chair, strumming his guitar, a pencil and notebook on his crate in front of him, stopping now and then to make a notation about a chord. Uncle Must stepped out and Darrell jumped up, thrust the instrument into the chair behind him, and nearly tripped in his hurry. I'm coming too! he called to our uncle and Leave my stuff alone! to the rest of us, which consisted of me and Lorena, colouring at the table next to me. Mom and Dad were having their Sunday nap.

That's when they have sex, you know, Sunday afternoons, Darrell informed me some weeks after his priming the pump remark.

Haven't you noticed the bed squeaking a whole bunch and then it's quiet and they're off to sleep?

I hadn't noticed but I looked at him as if to say, Of course.

Well, now you know, he said.

So we'd been three children in the room, then Darrell abandoned us and we were two. No asking, just announcing and rushing after. What would we want with your stuff? I yelled behind him. The door slammed on the middle of my sentence.

He had the sense to grab his cap and jacket. The day was pale and chilly. Uncle Must wasn't a walker who waited, hands laid patiently one over the other on the knob of the walking stick, but neither, it seemed, did he mind Darrell catching up to him. I followed them out of sight through the window, the swing of my uncle's arms less monstrous, it seemed, once Darrell reached him and they were side by side. As if he was tamed by the uneven, large-stroke eagerness of my brother, nearly as tall as the older man by then, and jabbering I guessed, for his head was turned and he gestured. And then they'd been lost to the swell of the hills, that strange, incompatible pair.

But it was compatible they'd seemed rather than incompatible, disappearing behind the crest and me at my station at the table with an unaccounted-for hurt and loneliness. A hole of silence without my brother's thrumming and humming; just me and the castoff guitar and the little one, as we often called Lorena. A choice he'd made to single out the world of men from the wider humanity we shared, some difference I was beginning to perceive that put me at a disadvantage. A vague sense of—what? Opposition, diverging expectations, assumptions? I couldn't have named its facets, though they were named for me later, in the so-called women's liberation movement. The web of it, which I'd known and accepted for my mother, now becoming visible and spinning into a snare. The fingers of home and school and church underlining relevant texts, proof for how it had always been. Not just farm-browned fingers, either, but the softer, nails-clean, clipped fingers of seminarians. *Woman, know your place.*

But the way they came back, the timing of their return, it was the craziest thing! My English homework that day was Edgar Allan Poe's short story, "The Cask of Amontillado." I answered the questions, was done. And bored. I read ahead to the textbook's next story: "The Open Window" by the writer known as Saki. The story of a young man who'd moved to the country for his nerves, who called on a neighbouring family to make their acquaintance. The family's niece invited him in and while he waited for the woman of the house, the girl explained why the garden door was open that autumn afternoon. It was the anniversary of the tragic disappearance of the lady's husband and brothers, she said. They'd been buried in the bog while hunting for snipe. Her poor aunt had refused to accept this fate, however, and kept the windows open until dusk in hopes of the men and their spaniel returning, in hopes of hearing them sing Bertie, why do you bound? which they'd been singing when they left. Then the aunt came in and greeted the visitor, talking cheerfully of the men whom, she said, she was expecting at any moment. He listened with mounting horror, and even greater horror as he saw three figures approaching in the twilight, guns on their shoulders, a weary dog beside them, and one of them singing, Bertie, why do you bound? The terrified young man flew out the door as if he'd seen a ghost. His behaviour astonished the woman of the house as well as the hunters stepping through the garden door. Probably his fear of dogs, the young niece with the penchant for stories told them blithely, for he'd been chased into a cemetery once by a pack of dogs.

The story unsettled and thrilled me in turn. I'd been taken in by it just as the addled young man had been—those ghostly figures emerging through the dusk, that song. I lifted my eyes from the last sentence and there, advancing over the yard at that very moment, were my uncle and brother. The start this gave me was ferocious, for though not dusk, there was an ashy texture to the day and the weariness and happiness of their return was palpable, their gait strong but the intensity of their earlier departure muted and fulfilled, both heads bowed slightly, Uncle long and thin as a scarecrow, Darrell solid and young and erect beside his stooped-shouldered elder, Uncle Must crowned by his hat and Darrell's cap off and in his hand, his thick, fine hair flopping every which way. Their strides and the swing of their arms were equal and in rhythm now, as if they'd become fast friends while away. As if they might burst into the Bertie song, not that any of us had ever heard or sung it.

This was the most grievous aspect of remembering, the place where forgetting, or ignoring, was the better gift: two men nearing in a pearl-grey afternoon and the utter impossibility of bringing them close enough to determine the meaning or content of their relationship. They neared but never arrived. Weren't around now to think back on it themselves, or decipher it for me. If only I'd asked Darrell during one of our confiding moments over the dishes, So where do you walk? What do you talk about? I might have wrung from him the who and the what and the why of my uncle.

He's smarter than he looks. Darrell offered this more than once. He's got lots of stuff in him, he'd said.

I could have asked, What kind of stuff, exactly? But I didn't. I didn't give a hoot back then.

Better said, I steeled myself against him.

19.

Mom had the stomach flu, something intestinal going around Maplebend, but I visited her anyway. She was a line of humps on the bed, duvet loose over her, wide eyes fixed on the ceiling, not blinking. The room's beige indifference overwhelmed me and I knew that my mother was dead. Adrenaline surged for the unexpected privilege—it was a privilege, wasn't it?—to pull her blanket up and over her head in one smooth motion the way they did in TV shows and movies, like a first layer of earth over a corpse. And even before that, the privilege of closing her eyes. I was excited and afraid and lunged to the bed.

Mom?

Louder. Mom?

Her eyelids moved. Ah-h, still here. I leaned and placed my hand on the blanket.

Catherine. My mother formed the name but made no sound.

You've got the flu, I said. I lifted a corner of the blanket. Her arms were rod-straight alongside her body. You don't look comfortable, I said.

I'm fine, she managed.

I tucked the cover around her body and pulled up a chair. The bed was set low to prevent my mother from trying to rise on her own and I felt I was looking down from a great distance onto the puddle of her blanket, the hills and valleys of her, the lined grey face like jagged rock. Looking down as mother to child. I could never have been a nurse, but—surely!—I would have made a good mother. I touched her forehead. Cool instead of warm. Well, of course, they said it was intestinal.

I'm not afraid of being dead, she puffed, as if she'd guessed what I'd thought when I stepped into the room. Afraid to die, but not of being dead, you know.

A pat on her cheek by way of an answer. A phone rang in the room across the hall. I'll get myself a telephone, my mother gasped. But not today.

You have a phone.

I can't do everything at once, she said. Her eyelids lowered but she jerked them open. They have strict instructions about that. Her voice was a scratch.

What do you mean?

Everything.

I wiggled my hand to hers under the blanket, stroked it when I found it.

Talk, my mother whispered. Tell me what you're doing.

Doing? I spent yesterday at the library. Nearly froze walking over there. Looked at magazines from the sixties. Magazines like *LIFE*. In Tilia, we piled them up. Remember? Until you moved to Marble. Then I burned them in the barrel.

You did?

The woman at the library reference desk had asked if I was

194

writing a book. I old her no. I could tell she was trying to place
me. We'd probably been at some professional development seminar together. The stuff that comes back to you, I went on to Mom,
when you look at old magazines. Netted stockings. Richard Nixon.
Rumours of Paul McCartney's death. Charles Manson.

My mother smiled weakly as encouragement and I plumped
more tidbits from the magazines around her like pillows. The
more I tucked and talked, the smaller she seemed, as if she'd
reverted to infancy and needed stories and songs to sleep. Her
eyes closed. I stopped speaking and listened to her breathe. Breath
like a mossy trail through parted lips in a room otherwise quiet.
Green, it seemed, like the room in *Goodnight Moon*, my mother
Edna the bunny in the bed, me the Mama Rabbit in a rocking
chair. For years I'd collected children's books in anticipation of
reading to my children and when it was obvious I wouldn't have
any, I gave them away, to Lorena's children or as gifts to young
friends. Gave all of them away but *Goodnight Moon*, which I kept
another decade or so because it made me cry. Sometimes crying
about the children that hadn't happened had been a help to me.
Goodnight to all those objects in the room. Comb, brush, and
mush. Even to *nobody*.

My tears would release at the nobody.

But paging around in those archived magazines at the library
had been a swim upstream, my own generation described as
*bearded, promiscuous, high on pot and low of speech ... resentful
... ready to bring down everything.* A generation, one article said,
of *young Oedipuses* whose rebellion was *murderous.* And all this
time I figured we'd been something special. I wanted to defend
myself and my peers, but to whom? The woman at the library
counter? The young man in a toque reading at the library table
beside me? Mom, now in her ill and dozing vulnerability, who
required vindication as much as I did? In one of the magazines I'd
come upon, a Dr. Lendon Smith dispensed advice: *I think that the*

mother with average intelligence is the happiest in her motherhood role. The demands and the rewards are just about right. If she is too smart she gets bored. If she is stupid she can't cope. Had my mother read those lines back in the sixties? Believed them? I'd come a fly's leg away, yesterday, from scribbling a *Damn* over his patronizing words. Or, *My mom was happy and she was smart, so go average intelligence yourself!*

I'd forced myself to turn the page. An archivist knew better than to deface the saved materials of the past.

My mother clasped her lips against her breath and her eyes wobbled open. You can keep going, Catherine, she said. It's interesting.

Goodness, where was I when I stopped? The long-ago fashions?

Any old time will do, she said.

A nurse marched in to take her temperature and pulse. The nurse was smooth and efficient, my mother limp and submissive. Mom gazed at the other woman's face while she peered at and wrote down the numbers. My daughter is telling the story of her life, she rasped.

Isn't that lovely! said the nurse. How fortunate you are.

Not fortunate, my mother chided. Catherine here has had a really hard time of it.

Not only a swim upstream but like a haunting, those magazines of yesteryear. Coming upon My Lai as if massacred yesterday. Knowing full well it was over, was news by now. Old news. Very old news. History. The heartbreak of archival work, saving the present into the future, so it could wrench you again. The end of Camelot. Bombs exploding in a Birmingham church. Me and Darrell and Mom and Dad and Uncle Must alive in the midst of those things. Not literally in the midst, but alive at the time. And nothing we could do about it then, or now. The next news would arrive by radio or in the mail.

This kind of re-reading, even with the outcome known, was like entering a story in which the author cleverly and steadily scattered seeds of dread and the seeds took root. One became afraid of the plot, how it would turn. The story of a child, say, about to discover how dangerous grown-ups can be. And hoping against hope—as a reader—that the words racing onward would take one somewhere good, that the innocent little girl or boy would be spared the devastation about to be enacted by the sicko three houses down who said his puppy had run away, and wouldn't the child like to help him find it? Or by the parents' drinking or thumping in the bedroom above, the words they tossed at one another like grenades in the stillness of the night. What the child would see when doors were ajar. Even if you reached the end with evil averted, the jitters aroused by the narrative could take a long time to abate, the story's thread of apprehension wound so tightly that it cut you inside every time you moved.

Stories could go either way. Miracles came for some and they certainly didn't come for others.

I remembered his name: Mr. Mal. Owner of the café where Darrell did odd jobs during his college year and where I worked occasional shifts the next year, hired on the basis of my brother's work ethic, the man said, except that his eyes took a thorough survey of me first, up and down, then and every subsequent shift. And goodness he was clumsy, the number of times he bumped against me in a day—Sorry, sorry, as if accidental—and, Excuse me please, needing some item just beyond me and then a brush— no, a press—of my breasts while reaching. I don't know why I put up with it or kept going to work whenever he called.

I quit the day I was on the step stool to fetch pancake powder from the top shelf of the supply cupboard and felt his hands under my skirt, cupping my buttocks, giant hands they suddenly seemed and cupping completely and his thumbs—what? Where were they going? A terrified whirl round, and, What're you doing?! Some excuse again, a slight stepping back and a chuckle. But even so, I worked to the end of my shift, tremulous and flushed, and I quit politely, saying I was too busy with my studies to work for him any longer, which was a lie—I could manage the hours and needed the money—and he paid me out and that was that, both of us thanking the other. But not quite enough for him. He seized me in a final steely hug, hard against me and hurting until I could push him away.

I kept it to myself.

I lied to Mr. Mal again, at Assiniboine Park. It must have been ten years or more after Darrell's death. He spotted me at some outdoor musical gathering. Maybe it was the fireworks. Looking vastly older now, he sidled close once again, his breath coffee-stale and rampant, said he'd sold his café, asked about Darrell. I said he'd died. The man was speechless, it took him aback, but then he wanted specifics. I muttered generalities. I said Darrell wasn't with us anymore, and yes, he was definitely too young *to go*. Mr. Mal persisted. He stepped forward while I stepped back. So I told him Darrell had gone to Vietnam and been killed by a commie attack. Dropped like a torpedo in the jungle, I said, and they never got him back.

It was pure fiction—maybe I was wishing something heroic for his death—but at any rate, it roused the elderly fellow to raptures. He saved us from tyranny, he said. That battle of Dieppe was really something. You can be proud of him for that. Yes, you can certainly be proud of him. He kept edging forward, groping toward me as if to pin a medal on my chest for my brother's bravery. You're thinking of the Second World War, Mr. Mal, I said, but we're definitely proud of him. Then I bolted.

20.

I dreamed vividly in a Paris youth hostel while Jim and I travelled through Europe after we married, a long honeymoon accomplished on the cheap with Eurorail passes, two meals a day, sleeping in hostels, walking everywhere. The hostels were communal, often dormitory-style, so we had to get creative for sex. One morning, we toured the Notre Dame Cathedral, then impulsively retraced several kilometres to our lodgings. We shared a warm baguette on the way. The place was open but the front desk was deserted, the room we'd slept in the previous night empty as well. We pushed one of the bunks against the door and did what we'd come to do. Fervently, quickly. The noon bells of a nearby church began to ring as we finished. This made us laugh.

Jim dressed and put the place to order but I fell asleep. I was walking along a beach when I came upon a tiny inlet congested with piled-up stuff, as if the entire cargo of a capsized ship had funneled into this one spot. A large open cupboard with shallow shelves stood upright on the sand. The shelves were lined with dolls—floppy baby dolls with hairless rubber heads, each wearing only a diaper. A teddy bear with shaggy pink fur, considerably bigger than the dolls, perched in the centre of the middle row. She wore a wide black ribbon and bow. The bear and the dolls seemed my responsibility so I watched their faces intently for any expression of need. The dolls' faces were identical: egg-shaped eyes, smiles like bowls. Some of them cooed. I paid constant attention but they required nothing. The bear's expression, however, was blocked by the pink fur and black bow, which concerned me. I took the bear off the shelf and murmured Yes to her again and again, like a christening, and hugged her tightly, and the hiss of Yes was wind in the sea and a wall of water surged in and lifted me off my feet. I held the pink bear like a life raft and the bear ballooned and supported me as we rose and dipped in the swirl. The water was balmy and buoyant, as if drafts of air tumbled inside it. The bear's fluff flattened, grew sleek, and I could tell she was enjoying the adventure.

The wave knocked over the cupboard of dolls. They tumbled about in the deluge too. They weren't afraid but they weren't smiling either. Their mouths were set in a stiff straight line and they stared at me reproachfully as they bobbed off. Then I woke and saw Jim's head tilted toward me and for a moment I thought him part of my dream. He was sitting on the floor beside the bed. I'd been making noises, he said; I'd been gasping, crying out, giggling. I recounted the dream and he said it was interesting but we didn't talk about it further. We left the hostel and resumed our tour of Paris.

The dream stayed in the foreground of my mind all day. It felt like a school poem you're told is famous or important but you don't understand it—you just don't *get* it! I kept glancing at Jim as if I'd forgotten how he looked, the fine, curly blond hair, his round features, brown eyes, the astonishing energy that seemed to quiver just beneath his skin. He constantly studied the guidebook to be sure we wouldn't miss a thing. At every turn, I saw him with fresh surprise and remembered how he'd been there beside me at the end of my dream, as if he'd paddled up from below to solve it.

21.

Uncle Must left us for several weeks—perhaps it was months—
the winter Darrell went away to college and I was in Grade Twelve.
He finished his oatmeal and raisins one morning, got up, carried
two paper bags of clothes to the truck, and drove off.

He's heading south a ways, Mom said. For a rest.

We don't need the truck in winter anyway, Dad added. Since
we no longer have cows, I'm sure I can manage.

A sense of sunlight then, pouring through the kitchen windows, short winter days notwithstanding, some unusual peace
and generosity around me with both my uncle and brother gone.
Mom and I cleaned Uncle's room. We scrubbed the walls, ceiling,
and floor, and washed the curtains and bedcovers. It was the kind
of inch-by-inch cleaning that seems to dispel not only built-up
grime but everything previously transacted in that room. Mom
even wiped out his drawers, though she was careful to remove

only one pile of his things at a time and to replace everything exactly as she found it. Uncle wouldn't approve of her getting that personal with his possessions.

Not that he owns anything of any consequence, she huffed. Not anymore.

We left the door to his room wide open then so the colourful patchwork quilt on his bed was visible from the kitchen, smooth and untouched day after day, and the air wafted gently between the rooms in the blue, green, and yellow hues of that quilt, which Mom had assembled and knotted as a gift the previous Christmas, his earlier blanket long hostage to Miss Miller, beyond rescue and, it could be assumed, basically *kaput*. She'd grieved that quilt every time she saw Miss Miller splayed on it to tan or Ricky crawling over it as if it was some discard instead of something she'd taken real trouble over, those variegated shades of blue. Even if made from leftovers.

It must have been while Uncle Must was away that Dad's heart condition worsened. My parents had been monitoring his health for years, but told me only after my uncle came back. Now they and Uncle spent hours behind the closed door of the living room, talking. I'd supposed they were getting re-acquainted, which was no concern of mine, but on the first day of April, Dad informed me they'd decided to sell the farm and move to Marble, Manitoba, where he'd grown up after arriving in Canada. Where the new wife had awaited his widowed father.

One of Dad's step-cousins offered him a job, he said. In his hardware store. It would be easier for him, working indoors. With regular hours.

I asked if this was an April Fool's joke.

Dad hadn't been aware of the day. No joke, he said.

Mom appeared at his side, said, Dad loves that area of Manitoba. It's rolling hills around those parts, just like here. Though we'll live in town.

Keep it to yourself for a while, my father said. There are things to work out and it may take some time.

When I asked if Uncle Must was moving to Marble with us, Dad looked like there was concrete on his chest. I hope so, he said, but nothing is sure.

I wish he would, he went on, his words dragging. He's in favour of our plan, he said. But he doesn't want it for himself.

He'll come to visit, Mom soothed her husband. She put an arm around him and touched her forehead to his chin.

I panicked about the move at first, until it sank in that I was graduating high school and leaving home anyway. When I settled into that fact, Darrell's assessment of Tilia as claustrophobic became apparent to me: our community was small, ingrown, disposable. I had four months to get my final fill of the place and say goodbye. That should be enough. Besides, Shirley and I would be at the same college, Betty/Liz had found other friends and was no longer part of our group, and in the meanwhile, I was busy: vice-president of student council, on the yearbook committee, a piano recital to prepare for, upcoming departmental exams.

The farm was divided and sold in two pieces, and the piece with Uncle Must's little house went first. The new owner didn't want a tenant, never mind a freeloading one like Sharon Miller. She had no choice now but to get out.

She can be a problem for somebody else, my mother remarked cheerfully.

Mid-July, Dad and Darrell, who was home again for the summer, loaded Miss Miller's boxes onto the pick-up truck and Darrell drove off with her and Ricky to her cousin's place in Calgary. It was an evening uncannily similar to the one that heralded her arrival three years earlier, the sky cardboard-brown and ponderous and the day's heat intensifying as if to boil into storm. No sooner had the truck crested the hill than Mom was bustling down the lane to the vacated shack. She bustled back. The place was a disaster, she reported, everything Miss Miller couldn't be bothered to pack left where it dropped, though nothing had prevented her from taking whatever she wanted, whatever might be useful, that is, whether it belonged to her or not. Plates, pots, cutlery, towels, linens that had once been Uncle Must's were riding away with her to Calgary. Though probably in terrible condition by now, so let her have it.

Mom told me to go down to the house to clean up the mess. I worked at any babysitting and housekeeping jobs I could get those days, freelancing like my brother, and I'd spent that day minding three preschoolers while their mother helped her husband with field work, and the children had whined and fussed from beginning to end. I was exhausted. But Mom said Uncle Must had promised to pay me—he doesn't want to touch a thing, she said, not even see it again—so I said I'd do it.

No one's moving in, Mom said. It doesn't have to be washed or anything. Just get rid of the stuff. Sweep and burn. So they aren't picking through it for evidence.

Evidence?

For the Tilia gossips.

I asked if Uncle Must had made a decision about moving to Marble yet and Mom said yes, he had. He wasn't coming. Relations had never been smooth with his late stepmother, which had coloured Marble black for him forever. I thought of the pretty white house on the farm we'd visited when my step-grandmother was still alive, thought of her puckered, sunken mouth, the stern impression it made. Of her intimidating cedar-chest smell. Well, she was long dead but I supposed my uncle was right: she wasn't the kind of person you would warm up to quickly. Though Dad and his stepmother had gotten along alright. But then Dad was easy to get along with.

Tired or not, I practically skipped down the lane, venting the truth: I was thrilled about my uncle's decision. Broom, dustpan, matches were wings. He was resourceful enough, no need to waste sympathy on him. Money grows quickly in the bank, I remembered him saying. And our family would be itself. A holding-hands row of a family like I used to cut out of folded paper. Sure, I was heading to college but that didn't mean I was leaving the lineup. But Uncle was, and it was a lift more powerful than I'd ever imagined it could be.

I stepped into his former place and saw what Mom meant about the mess. Paper everywhere—newspapers and magazines and books and advertisements and Ricky's ripped colouring books. The single metal frame bed, its dirty, sagging mattress spattered with clothing and two lopsided pillows. Clothes under the bed and behind the tattered brown chair, things Miss Miller or Ricky had worn, none worth keeping. A stained pair of panties and a grimy bra, sprawled on the floor like a provocative grin. That wool rug she hooked, also grimy and matted. A perversely sweet odour in the place, as if a bottle of perfume had spilled into cracks in the linoleum. Besides the sordid reek of cigarettes, that is. I swept everything together and piled as much of it as I could into the child's wagon we'd loaned Miss Miller for Ricky, which I found tipped on its side by the hedge. I made a fire in the barrel behind the house and began to feed the pile into the flames, one item at a time. I kept the fire small.

I was on my second load when our truck came over the hill, slowed, and pulled onto the yard. Darrell jumped out of the cab and sauntered to the refuse barrel to join me. I still had a pile to burn: dusty newspapers, Harlequin romances, bags and broken containers, a limp cloth dog with a gash in its stomach and most of its innards gone, and the rest of the clothing. Darrell bent to the wagon and started shuffling through the books.

Leave it, I said.

Just looking. It's garbage, isn't it?

Leave it. I'm burning it.

Don't you want help? Usually I burn the garbage.

I know how to burn garbage. Fire isn't just for boys, you know.

No need to get touchy.

I didn't know why I was irritated except that I hadn't wanted the job, even if paid, and the panties and brassiere were under the books and I didn't want him finding them and cracking a joke, some mockery or stupid admiration of Miss Miller's figure. He'd come down from the truck with a swagger, stood beside me with a swagger. Ever since he'd returned from college, he swaggered. When he wasn't brooding, that is. I couldn't put my finger on either the swagger or the brooding, not enough to say, This is what I mean, but I felt our closeness was over, permanently this time. I thought of his distance the day of the president's assassination and how it seemed my brother had opened a jar into which he stuffed his treasures, not sharing or making room for mine. Keeping the lid on, keeping it tight.

Brooding was too common in our family as it was, what with Uncle Must and his spells of detachment, and Mom pulsing with worry that the other half of the farm wouldn't sell. The currents of adult emotion winding through the house affected me. I felt obscurely guilty about them—as if I had to catch, gauge, or alter them. Maybe the same thing was happening to my father. Dad seemed to whistle more than before, not mindlessly as if from habit, but deliberately, the way birds will cry incessantly to warn of danger. Feeling accountable, I supposed, because of his heart. And me feeling accountable for my brother. Smiling, watching, trying to be good for both of us, fighting the undertow until we moved, after which—I hoped—we would be happy all the way through.

Hey sis, he said now, his tone light but confidential, I stopped to tell you something. To tell you first.

Okay, I said.

I'm not going back to college. Not this fall.

I felt my mouth contort. I'd looked forward to going there together; did he think I'd be a burden?

Hey, hey, hey! he said. What's the matter?

Because of me?

His surprise was genuine, the swagger in him gone. How could you even think such a thing? Catherine!

Darrell had been the first to leave, the family empty without him. But having him back again hadn't been comfortable either, what with all the attention he got and the longish hair Mom nagged him about—though it wasn't *that* long, and besides, it suited him—and how he acted, deferential enough on the surface but outlandish opinions popping up constantly like weeds, his enthusiasm for the Canadian prime minister, Pierre Elliott Trudeau, whom people in Tilia thought scandalous, and his endless remarks about the war, by which he meant the war in Vietnam, to which none of us had paid much attention beyond what we read in *TIME* or *LIFE* until he'd come home thoroughly aroused by the Vietnamese people. He spotted Mom's stretchy plastic wrap which she considered the latest and greatest for covering food and he nearly had a fit. Don't you know Dow Chemical produces napalm for bombs? You ought to be boycotting everything they make!

And while my parents supposed he'd been doing street evangelism at college, doing something religious when his letters mentioned demonstrations, now he said he left the witnessing to others and hung around with new friends at the downtown university. Keeping abreast of political concerns, he said. Anti-war pamphlets, sit-ins, that kind of thing. Protesting Americans dropping napalm, he said. Protesting that, and other stuff.

Mom and Dad were bewildered. Honestly, they didn't have a clue. Who? What?

Darrell rarely bothered to elaborate.

All I want to do is take a year off books, he told me now. Do something different. California, I think, maybe half a year, maybe a year. However long I can get permission to stay. Probably get involved in the civil rights movement or something, maybe anti-war. He paused, then said, It doesn't mean I won't be back. And, hey, you'll have caught up with me then, both of us in second year, in classes together!

It was a fantasy, this vision of our second year and I knew it. For all my shock about his change of plans, I grasped immediately—with certainty—that he wouldn't return. Like a book clapped shut, and nothing to do with me. What did he have to do with any of us anymore?

I wanted to tell you first, he said. I know Mom and Dad won't like it. I thought you'd understand and it would help.

Sure.

Maybe you want to tag along, he said. To California.

I let out a skeptical laugh, more like a bark. Inconceivable. Then he said he planned to transfer some of his summer earnings to our parents so they could help me with my college education, since I'd only had July and August to work. He would find a job down there. He wouldn't need as much as he'd saved.

I was surprised by the offer and it calmed me, like salve on a cut. Thank you, I said.

The sun was setting in a flushed bouquet of canary yellow, pink, and purple but the rest of the sky was pale and clear, the dustiness gone, the sense of pressure released; there wouldn't be a storm after all. I picked up the rod I'd found on the ground near the barrel and stirred the flames, jabbed at the book that was burning, tried to break it apart, help and hurry it, prevent some smouldering page from floating up to start a fire somewhere else. I knew the drill.

Well, he said, looks like you've got it under control.

I was nearly done with the paper items and had only the clothes, the underwear, the half-empty dog to burn. Tell Mom I'll be up shortly, I said.

But I took my time over the fire while darkness deepened and the drama of sunset faded. Regret seemed useless. These pathetic symbols of Miss Miller's existence and the anticipation of a year at college with my talented, extroverted brother, the hopes of having his sibling companionship again, all crumbling into ash. Flames one minute, smoke the next. And only wisps of mauve, tender as violets, remaining on the western horizon. But crickets chirring, frogs harrumphing in the gully, the warm air a caress, the lap of this gentle landscape, my founding place, and me keenly aware of it all. Aware of my sensations, of my mind and its capacity for thought. I knew I was solid, more fearless, more complex in a positive direction than I'd realized. Everything around me had thinned to its purest, most elemental magnificence, but I'd enlarged, was full. Alive and joyful. Darrell's news had as good as disappeared.

When I entered the Big House kitchen, they were smack in the middle of it, my folks looking uncertain and Mom setting out jam drop cookies and fruit slices as well as milk and juice and instant coffee to drink, which was her way of addressing the anxiety she perceived in the room, anxiety she needed to tend to, triage-like, though she was often the most anxious of us all, and Darrell spinning a story toward their leaning-in bodies, a story of adventure, of seeing the world and, as if another branch of that tree, a story of the degradation and desperation of the inner city, any city perhaps, where he might be a shining ray of hope. Goodness that brother of mine could spin a persuasive, warmhearted web of need out of those places in California where he'd never yet set foot, weaving in pious words—God's heart for the poor, the disadvantaged, and a purpose for him, now on an alternative path.

I pulled out a chair, slid into the circle without my parents noticing. Darrell flashed me a glance, whether to admonish or beg for support, I couldn't tell. I was impressed by how plausible he sounded. I sank into his words, wished I'd be led out of school for a year, for adventure, service, study, something bigger than books. To hear Darrell talk of it, learning with your nose in a book was like taking a walk along a corridor of brick. You couldn't see the scene.

Uncle Must's bedroom door opened and he joined us at the table. Dad apprised him of Darrell's change of mind about college. Uncle Must fixed his eyes on my brother and began to tap his fingers on the table. They clicked; his nails needed a trim. It's not as if I won't have connections, Darrell said, addressing our uncle. My college roommate's cousin lives in California. I could stop in Idaho, visit Mom's relatives. I'll hitchhike to save money.

Actually, he added, Fresno, California is swarming with Mennonites. Reedley too.

Swarming? Mom's voice lingered dubiously over the word.

Sometimes we change our minds, said Uncle Must. He stopped tapping and clenched his hands in his lap.

Dad stared at Uncle Must and then he nodded. Yes, he said. Sometimes we change our minds. Yes.

And so the change of mind was fully accomplished. We helped ourselves to a snack and for the rest of the summer, my brother's brooding disappeared and he worked harder than ever and was reassuring and kind, complimentary to me and our parents and he spoke less often about the suffering, beleaguered Vietnamese and the imperialistic American juggernaut or the segregated South. His detour to California took on the aura of something gripping and inevitable. It turned into something so novel, so right, we couldn't help admiring him for coming up with it. Years earlier, Mom had formed the idea that Darrell would make a good minister and she'd naturally assumed his being at a Mennonite college would bring this vocation to pass. Now she spoke of the practical dimension of a pastor's formation, of experience that only experience could give. Darrell received without contradiction her hints for how a year in

California might build into his future. There are also blessings, he would murmur after her, in postponement.

But Darrell never went to Fresno where the Mennonites swarmed, or to Reedley. He went to Los Angeles.

Like my mother about his poems, I now wished I'd saved my brother's letters. But who, growing up, saves the right things? You don't expect the scribblings of a brother to be important. You don't think that people die young. People you're personally acquainted with, that is. People you love. You can't imagine forgetting them if they do. You assume you'll have plenty of time later to gather and box mementoes.

He wrote me maybe seven or eight letters, most of them during his first year of college and the rest from the US. He wrote on loose-leaf paper, one side only, in large, convoluted script that could be difficult to read. He minded the left margin, however, and in one letter he'd scattered words in it. *Badinage*, I remembered, because I looked it up—*playful or frivolous repartee or banter*—and I'd practiced saying it and waited for an opportunity to use it where it wouldn't sound pretentious, though I never found one. Below badinage, *wick, wicker, wicked* and *six, sax, sex* clung together like two sets of triplets in matching outfits. When I opened the letter, I wondered if the loose words in the margin were some kind of code, but then he said he was always working on a poem, and even while writing letters, his mind reeled with ideas. He had to jot them down, at their barest, since they sprang at him so fast. The words he'd set aside seemed frivolous to me, in terms of their coming at him like oracles. Except for badinage, which intrigued me.

His letters were bridges he crossed on the road away from us. He wrote our parents out of the filial respect he'd been raised to show and honoured it carefully at first, understanding what they needed to hear from him, his handwriting high-spirited but readable. In his letters to me, he was bolder with his thoughts, as if to try on a stream of consciousness in which to scatter his doubts. For our parents, he quoted Dietrich Bonhoeffer writing about the compelling call of Christ and for me he quoted imprisoned Bonhoeffer who was weary of prayer, and despondent.

When the German theologian made his first appearance in a letter, Dad had stopped reading and said, Who's this Bonhoeffer?

Mom cleared her throat. She said, I wondered too, so I checked the encyclopedia, and sure enough, he was there. She gave my father a summary of the young pastor's life and work. Quietly, as if she didn't want to overshadow him in front of Lorena and me by informing him about something outside the realm of her cookery and sewing. But Dad seemed proud of Darrell the letter-writer for finding a man like Bonhoeffer to emulate and he thanked her; Mom's initiative didn't seem to bother him in the least. All of us were caught up with Darrell, our prince out in the world swashbuckling at spiritual dragons.

But those were the earlier letters, breezy and enigmatic—*Hey, Sis! Sis! Sis!* Informing me of his current tastes in music and books, of his ongoing success at debating. During high school, he was best in the club, but at college, he told me, they debated important issues like the space race, nuclear disarmament, the end of the world, not minor things like the role of the student council or the existence of unicorns. His later letters were simply confusing and I refused to let Mom read them, even when she asked. I couldn't risk trying to excuse what I didn't comprehend, which is why I hid them, re-read them once, then burned them in the barrel. On second readings, they seemed even less coherent than the first time, a mishmash of references, theologians, and poets appearing between sentences about pranks he and his friends had played on the girls in the women's dorm, simultaneously descriptive, melancholic, cheerful, and angry, a trail of unique and disconnected thoughts, like a horse clip-clopping on pavement. They made me peevish.

Many years later, when I took a catch-up course in twentieth-century English literature, I came upon phrases he'd used, clearly without attribution. I read the lines in a daze. Ah, William Carlos Williams. Leonard Cohen. Ginsberg. Ah yes, he'd raved about Ginsberg, and this I'd remembered after it was too late to ask him why. I recognized some allusions now and felt he'd let me down, for by the time I took the course, Ginsberg and the Beats seemed tired and old, the fifties ancient history, their poetry like literary dinosaurs. Still, when I encountered a phrase Darrell had borrowed and repeated in his loping scrawl, I underlined it. I used a ruler. When I saw how it stepped out on the page because of my neat underlining, I felt as if I'd reached back and given my brother both order and some context, some justification. As if I'd finally glimpsed the splendor and strain of his youth. His power and despair, whether real or the art of performance. A lifeline of sorts through the confusion I'd felt in him—and growing in me— with each successive letter.

By the time I was in that literature class, of course, I knew he'd been lost to us. Knew he was a prodigal who never came to his senses.

From California, Darrell wrote that he was searching for a new kind of sensibility. I envied him. But it seemed reckless, too, what he wanted. His letters to our parents had dropped off and those he did send could be crude. Or cruel. One arrived while I was home for a weekend visit in Marble. I strolled with Mom to the post office on Saturday morning, neither of us expecting anything as it was just a destination for our walk, and then Mom checked anyway, and spotted his letter among some bills. Her mood unfurled like a sail the whole walk home. By the time she sat down with it at the table, she was euphoric. She'd been waiting so long for a letter, she said. It was painful to watch, then, how abruptly she lost her joy, how she shrank. Oh, he's fine, he's fine, she said at the end, but she was clearly troubled and didn't offer the pages or share excerpts aloud. She folded the letter, stumbled it into the pocket of her sweater. She got busy watering the house plants while I curled up in a chair to read. I was half-way through *A Bird in the House* by Margaret Laurence that weekend, my new hero-writer. Forget the dead Brits; I was all about the Canadian authors now.

After tending to her ferns, Mom turned and said, When Hezekiah got that terrible letter from Sennacherib, he went to the temple and spread it before the Lord.

I lifted my head and my face must have looked blank because she said, with a kind of contempt in her tone, You know that story from the Bible. The threatening letter from Sennacherib. She turned and bolted out of the room to her bedroom and closed the door.

Dad had taken Lorena to her music lesson. I read on and the house was still. Mom stayed in the bedroom a good hour or more. I felt certain she wasn't napping and when I paused between the Laurence stories, between episodes of Vanessa's small town life, there was anguish within me like a burn and I didn't know if it was because Laurence was an effective and affecting writer or because the door at hallway's end was shut so long, the stillness growing heavier, my mother following Hezekiah's example, I supposed, while leaving me completely alone.

22.

I got through the Winnipeg winter, reached March. Intermittent days of warmth turned streets and sidewalks to slush; snow piles sagged, grey with grit. Fresh snowfall covered their collapse, then melted again. I now drove my familiar route to Maplebend twice a week to visit Mom through the shifting hope and ruin of a long transition between seasons.

One morning, she said it again. I wish I knew what I ought to do next.

What would you like to do next?

My mother seemed disoriented.

What do you still want to accomplish? I asked. (Was this what chaplain Joe meant by *probe*?)

She peered into her crocheted bag as if the answer would be there. Well, she said, I wish I could learn how to pray.

Pray? (If there's one person who knows how to pray, I thought, it's Edna Riediger.)

Yes, I think so.

Okay, I said, recalling Joe's advice to simply go with the flow of my mother's mind. That's a good idea, I guess.

Yes, it is.

I think you just have to do it, I said, and that's how you learn.

I've tried and it doesn't help.

Should I find you a book on learning to pray?

Oh, don't get me a book! I've read enough improving books in my life. What good did they ever do?

Well, I guess you're back to the practice method then.

Oh, Catherine, what a good daughter you are! Mom smiled her largest, best-feature smile and trembled her hand back to her lap. And now that you're here, she said, I was wondering if we could talk about what I should do.

Mom—

It's so difficult to—

Mom, what would you *really* like to do next? (One more round of this, I thought, raising my voice to Joe in my head, and it's definitely back to saying she doesn't have to do anything besides twiddle her thumbs or rest.)

Well, I want to visit Darrell's grave. That's what I really want to do.

Surprise and relief, then. Mom, I said, I can certainly organize that. When the weather's even a little bit nicer, I promise we'll do it. We'll figure it out somehow. We'll get you back to see the grave.

Do you think so, Catherine?

Easy, Mom. We'll do it.

I think it would be lovely.

Yes, it would.

I remembered how Mom used to phone me at college, interrupting my adult life. I suffered from homesickness at times so it was good to hear that voice, a catch of gladness in my chest, but it was terrible too. I felt myself badgered over Darrell, the calls a slow climb to the same point, the reason for her spending the money on long distance, reaching out as if I possessed some power of connection with my brother that she, as mother, needed to get her hands on. I was jealous of the attention she gave to Darrell in this indirect way. I wanted voluptuous expressions of affection and affirmation for myself.

Oh, Catherine, just wondering, she would say, have you heard from Darrell by any chance?

And then she began saying, in every call, There's something terribly wrong with your brother.

The first time Mom said those words, I bent my head into the wall by the dormitory telephone, long hair tumbling over my face, lurching for a moment into the terror I heard in them and thinking, so this is the burden of a mother. A mother's ultimate, difficult work. For those few seconds, I had that clear understanding of the role, though it was like an object I'd picked up and knew I could set down again.

I'd rested my forehead on the wall and the paint felt cool and there was a sob in my throat as big as a walnut, but I wouldn't let it out and then it disappeared.

But how did she know? Flimsy, her evidence, nothing more than worry and Darrell's distance, the increasing infrequency of his correspondence. And their first visit south—they'd gone the spring after moving to Marble—which my parents called a holiday before they left but not after they were back, Mom reporting that he lived with *a bunch of shaggy young people* who slept on mattresses on the floor, and his hair as long as a girl's. And *crusted!* They'd begged him to return to Canada with them but he said he'd barely arrived; he had to give it a chance. Whatever *it* was. Dad said that Darrell still played his guitar and sang and had certainly advanced. Maybe because, he said ruefully, that's what he does the whole day long. He has a girlfriend who's rich. I guess she's supporting him.

On the last day of their short visit, Darrell handed them a sheet of paper with his writing on it; he'd just written it, he said. They were already out the door and down the steps and wilting on the sidewalk. It was hot and Mom had a headache. But she was pleased. She thought it a gift, a loving goodbye he could only express in writing. But it wasn't that. It was a poem of some sort.

His poems don't rhyme, Dad inserted into the tale Mom told of it later.

They're dirty too, she said.

Dad had read it first, then Mom, and when she was done, she tore it up. She let the pieces scatter to the ground.

I'm not going to repeat it, she told me. You'll have to believe me that it was dirty.

The worst of it was that Darrell had smiled and said it wouldn't be hard to write again, he still had it in his head. So she'd ripped it up for nothing.

Mom complained that he never answered the phone when it rang and his roommates would say, Oh, yes, yes, he lives here, and they promised to pass on the message but they didn't seem the kind of people you could have a definitive conversation with, never mind rely on, and he never called back.

She wanted me to talk some sense into him.

I declared he had sense in him already. In those conversations, I would defend my brother's notions of justice and peace. As if the situation were merely generational, I informed my mother that I doodled too, not poems exactly, but certainly things welling up. There was nothing, I said, to worry about.

But I resented the need to defend and assure. Was I an angel at my mother's bidding? Mom, I said it's not wrong to want a better world!

Then Mom apologized for fretting but asked what was wrong with the world as it was.

How to even begin to answer? Or explain what it was like to be our kind of young? The world not airtight as our parents supposed. Her generation survived the Depression and the War, worked without stopping, founded camps, youth programs, and schools to inculcate their traditions, sacrificed to sustain them, and now expected gratitude but their children weren't grateful enough. They still remembered what the communists had done to our people in Russia; they thought disillusionment with the West was willful and extravagant, this focus on bombs, overpopulation, acid rain, nuclear destruction, segregation.

No, I could never explain. I wasn't even involved in those pressing issues myself but they were the backdrop to rambling, earnest discussions in the college lounge or outside on the grass when the weather allowed, me mostly listening, thinking *Yes, yes,* thinking of the gorgeous impact of my wavy hair or some fabulous book I was reading at the time. Sometimes I wished not to be listening, not weighted by talk, just reading, but I couldn't easily leave those huddles of conversation. I belonged in them too.

I'm not in Tilia anymore, I told my mother. Neither is Darrell. I'm not there either.

It's a figure of speech.

Catherine, she'd sputtered, don't you start worrying me too!

His heart's in the right place, I said, curling my hand around my mouth at the phone to hide the cliché from my dormmates and wishing Mom would listen to *my* life instead of drawing me into the agonies of hers. It was entirely too much intimacy of the wrong kind, me party to the relationship of mother and son.

Then she startled me. She said, I just hope he won't be troubled like your uncle.

All I could think to do was ask where Uncle Must was living now. Mom mentioned some town, then said with a sigh, Your father really misses his brother.

Mom and I were sitting side by side in Maplebend's blue and rose lounge—it was another visit in March—and she was in good spirits and her mind seemed relatively clear so I said, When you sold the farm in Tilia, which was a dream for Uncle—to farm with Dad, I mean—he wasn't happy, it was a huge disappointment for him, right? He wanted to work with Dad for the rest of his life, and then Dad felt he'd let him down, so he blamed himself because he had the heart problem, right? And he really wanted his brother to follow him to Marble, but Uncle Must wouldn't do it. A type of punishment, really, which hurt Dad a lot and he never got over it … right?

She watched me quizzically through my string of statements-cum-questions and then she looked away.

So how does that sound, I pushed, in terms of what happened?

Catherine, she said, you've always been far too bossy. She reached a shaking hand in my direction as if to comfort me for my faults.

There was no option but to reciprocate. I placed my hand over the older, blue-lined one on the tray and Mom's hand squirmed against my palm as if to get away but this was not intentional, it moved of its own accord. She put her other hand over mine, and I did the same. We were a mound of hands.

A speculative narrative, perhaps, what I'd outlined, but I was sure of it. The important thing was that Dad had enjoyed his job at the hardware store and never regretted leaving the farm. And it wasn't long after they moved that his step-cousin, who owned an implement and repair shop as well, transferred him from the store to the shop because Dad was good with motors and machines and he'd enjoyed that work even better. It's like he sees through a motor to what's wrong with it, Mom had marvelled. And he doesn't have to wonder if we'll get a decent crop this year.

They'd purchased a modest bungalow, Lorena adjusted to a new school, Mom made friends. She was happy that she could live in town and walk to the shops. And Uncle Must took up his *choring around*, first in the Grand Prairie area, then Edmonton. He worked at farms in Saskatchewan, near Swift Current, for a while, and at Herbert. At some point, he ended up in the north, in Gilly Lake, Manitoba, where he found employment connected with mining, until he was too old and ceased to work. All this time, I was doing an undergraduate degree in literature, finishing my Royal Conservatory credentials in piano, working summers to earn money for school, falling in love. I tossed letters, class notes, and textbooks when I was done with them. You never know when you'll move into a smaller place in town, Mom had said, speaking of herself and the Big House, so don't clutter up. I heeded her experience as a universal truth.

I tugged my hands out from under my mother's. I think I know why I became an archivist, I said. It's because we never saved anything.

That's what I mean, Mom said. You're far too bossy.

What bothered Dad the most, she said, reaching for me again, was that he wasn't close enough to hold his brother together.

Six months after their disheartening holiday to California, my parents hurried to Los Angeles again, flying this time, to bring Darrell home. He's ruined, Mom keened over the phone. And it cost an awful chunk of money. A week later, Dad drove into Winnipeg and treated me to supper at a downtown café, a hole in the wall somewhere on Portage Avenue that no longer exists. We both had a hamburger and fries and a cherry milkshake.

I slid into the red vinyl-covered booth across from him, and it felt cozy, as if it was my father's lair in particular. He seemed shy at first, uncertain, his oil-stained fingers clumsy with the menu. When the waitress asked what we wanted, he looked up at her like a boy who'd been granted a wish and it made me feel that anything might be possible, though the menu itself was strictly fast food and snacks. I spoke my order and Dad said, I'll have the same thing, what my daughter said. I loved the sound of *daughter* in his sentence and the expression on the waitress's face. She seemed proud of us.

I figured Mom had sent him to report on Darrell but he started with Uncle Must. I'm sure you remember that we had a bit of trouble with your uncle, he said.

Yeah.

He was too much on his own. People thought him ... unusual. Still do, I guess.

Yeah.

You know how he was ... is, I mean ... but otherwise ... As far as we know ...

The food arrived and we busied ourselves with adding condiments, taking first bites. Then Dad said, Your mother thinks it's not the same, what Darrell has. I mean, it's those drugs—they're such a terrible thing.

Yeah.

Dad stared at the empty booth across from us. Maybe, he said to the booth, he's fried his brains.

He turned his head quickly, met my gaze, said, I mean, that's what we've heard. I mean, it's not the same. Not passed down. She asked me to tell you that.

Okay.

Both of us looked down and for a while we ate without speaking.

The café was almost empty that evening. The waitress was older and she cooked as well as served, and after she was done with us, she collected the chrome napkin holders and salt and pepper containers from other tables and got busy wiping and polishing them. She left us alone.

We were nearly done eating before Dad gave me the full story on Darrell. He said he and Mom had decided I was old enough to know where the matter stood and so he laid it out, one calm, dismal sentence after the other. How at Darrell's California house there was a girl named Happiness—she'd chosen the name on her own—and how she met them at the airport and they rented a car, what she explained on the way. This Happiness was the person who'd called them in Marble and urged them to come. She said everyone in the house was concerned about Darrell and felt it was time he be taken away.

Happiness used a lot of words they couldn't understand, though they soon got the gist of them. When my father used them now—*trip, acid, pot*—he paused slightly, as if to rehearse their pronunciation or perhaps their particular meaning. Anyway, he said, this Happiness had explained that a few of them, including Darrell, were doing acid and he'd had a good trip or two and then he'd had a bad one. A really bad one. His state of mind going into it must have been off. It was the person, not the drugs, she said. Actually, he'd been acting unpredictable for a while. He broke up with his girlfriend, or she broke up with him and took up with someone else in the house, so it was happening under his nose and he was pretty down about that. I guess they couldn't talk him out of going ahead with it. When the drugs took, he got scared. Since she was clear, she stayed with him. But … well, he was worse than before.

Happiness had had his things packed and ready. Mom noticed it wasn't the charcoal suitcase Darrell brought from home. Happiness said she had no idea where that suitcase was. Then Darrell stepped out of the house and greeted them casually, as if they were neighbours he greeted every day across the fence, and he lowered himself into the rental car, into the front passenger seat, and Happiness leaned down to him and said goodbye. She closed his door and she shook Mom's hand and Mom got in the back and

Happiness came round to the other side to say a few more things to Dad. She said Darrell had told her once that he came from an excellent and loving family. She thought this was something they would want to know.

Now Dad's account slowed; he left more space between his sentences. I felt no worry in him, though, like I often felt in my mother. And the exasperation over Darrell I'd sensed in him several summers ago in Tilia was gone.

Darrell grabbed my hand so tight on the plane, Dad said, it hurt. Then I thought he'd fallen asleep and when I took it away his eyes flew open and he begged me not to take my hand away. So I put it back and I said it would stay.

My father stared at his plate. Imagine, he said, your grown son holding your hand.

Darrell's not well in the head right now, he went on. Happiness said he got stuck and it freaked him. He's told us things. His veins fizzing like steam, his skin starting to melt. He's told us about some good … good trips too. He says the regular rainbow we see after a rain isn't the half of it.

Now my parents were taking turns sitting beside Darrell until he fell asleep and Mom made him eat because he'd lost a lot of weight in California.

Dad put his elbows on the table and interlocked his fingers. Thick fingers, marked by his work. He unlocked them and rubbed them over his face. Compared to his fingers, his face seemed fragile. It's the fault of the drugs, he said. Those terrible drugs. They're just trash. It's way too hard on your mother.

I'm not the least bit interested in drugs, I said. It must have sounded self-righteous but I wanted to make things easier for him.

He smiled, just a little. I didn't think so, he said. But don't worry about your brother, Catherine. You shouldn't think about it too much. You shouldn't let it stop you from being as happy—and useful—as you can. He'll get better. We'll get him help.

He stood to pay for our meal and got chatting with the wait-ress. Maybe he discovered she was Mennonite and they were try-ing to figure out if they were related. I waited in the booth like a child. I stayed there as if my father would return and we would order another meal and he would tell me another story with a happier ending.

While I waited, two teen girls came into the café and launched into a giggling argument at the jukebox. When they finally agreed what to spend their money on, I could have cried. It was that song I liked by Bread: "He's a Good Lad." It seemed a message for me about my brother. About the wonderful person he was inside. A song with beat and sway so you wanted to dance, lyrics so sad and yet sweet you wanted to hug someone.

I slipped out of the booth. Hey Dad, hear that?

He didn't know what I meant, and when I said I meant the song playing around us, he said he couldn't understand the words.

He's a good lad, Dad, I said. That's what they're singing.

He listened for a moment, then told me Darrell couldn't find his guitar at the house and Happiness had had no idea either. So it didn't come along. We'll get him another one, he said. I guess. If he wants a guitar. But he hasn't asked.

He's a good lad, Dad. I sang along so he would catch the words.

A good lad, he said. He was unenthusiastic but I waltzed to the door. The girls had dropped another coin in the jukebox to spin the song again and it was playing as we left. Soon I would have a good long conversation—*chin-wag* we called it—with my brother, tell him about my boyfriend Jim. The guys would be friends. Jim said they'd already met, the winter before, when he'd gone to the college to visit a friend. He said he'd had a good impression of him.

Decades later, I knew the statistics. Roughly. How few—the one in how many thousands—had *a bad trip* that was permanent. Tons of people do or have done acid, I heard some expert say in a radio interview, and all of them were fine. LSD was astonishingly safe. Well, whatever, I retorted, punching the radio off, the Astonishingly Safe missed Darrell and our family was stuck with the Rare Bad Luck instead. The exception. Rare was a moot, miserable point when personal, when a loved one suffered the odds, the damage. When he'd played Russian roulette with his brain, and bang!

Whatever had happened, Darrell seemed undone. Instead of better, he got worse. Eventually, labels besides a bad trip were proposed. Broad labels in passing like LSD psychosis or schizophrenia. With a catatonic subset. I kept the names at a distance. I didn't want to know—still don't know—his changed state with any precision. *Maybe he fried his brains.* If I absolutely had to refer to it, the common, vulgar expression Dad used had seemed good enough. Though I couldn't stand the ad that ran for a while in the eighties—that this-is-your-brain-on-drugs ad with the egg sizzling in the frying pan. Egg producers hadn't liked it either.

When I asked Lorena about our parents in the Marble years, she protested, Oh, Catherine, I don't remember, not the way you archivists do.

My memory's no better than yours, I said. We stack up documents because memory is lousy. All of us hang on to some things internally, though. Which reminds me that I should apologize for how mean I used to be. When we shared a room.

I was a nuisance, Lorena said, but her voice was high and I knew she recalled the incidents too. I was so in awe of you, she said. And your stuff.

Seriously, I'm sorry.

Seriously, it's okay. Lorena laughed. She has the nicest laugh.

Pure and forgiving, even of her practiced perfection. Like the African violets thriving in pretty pots throughout her house.

But Marble, Lorena said. In Marble, Mom and Dad were preoccupied with Darrell. Trying to make him better with good meals and heaps of attention. I guess it was four or five months. Like a dripping faucet no one mentioned or fixed.

More than they could manage, I suppose.

You're not kidding. He'd cry, get into rages. Even Dad was terrified at times. And then it's like he collapsed and hardly ever reacted again.

We both knew the next chapter: admission to the institution in Brandon. Where he spent the remaining six years of his life. If things were easier at home after that, Mom and Dad's routine now included regular trips to visit him. They rarely took Lorena along.

Like haze, she told me. You don't really see it after a while, the tiredness, but you know it's there. Like looking through a dusty window.

Dad too? Wasn't he always encouraging? Whistling?

Whistling? No. I don't recall Dad whistling. Ever. He was just the saddest sack all those years.

23.

What remained of my dream on waking was a massive brick
building in which I scrambled for but couldn't find the exit.
My mind focussed and I recalled that it was Saturday. Jim was
home and the building I'd been trying to escape was the Brandon Mental Health Centre. I sat up abruptly. Jim opened his eyes.
He stretched. I had no idea what came over me but I had his
face between my hands and I was kissing him, overlooking the
night-mouth staleness of both of us, concentrating my mind on a
younger Jim I used to seize the same way. We'd kissed more than
once on the grounds of that hospital—maybe that was the link.
How young we'd been! Jim pulled me down, delighted, though
not before I posed my fabulous idea: Let's drive to Brandon today.
Take Mom. It's what she said she wanted to do. We don't have anything planned, do we? We'll call Maplebend, tell them, and if you
assist with bathroom duty, lifting her in and out of her wheelchair,

I mean, it'll work; she has no pride left in that department anyway. I'll do the up-close. Drive to Brandon, around The Mental, have lunch, head south and around to Marble. I promised her we'd visit Darrell's grave.

Jim was game and by mid-morning we were on our way, Jim driving, Mom beside him, me in the back. Amazing how quickly arrangements could be made. I felt a little foolish now, for surely my brother's stone would still be buried in snow. But we were Manitobans and had a shovel in the trunk; we could dig it out. My mother wore a stiff and satisfied air, as if she were some grande dame enroute with servant and chauffeur, unbeholden to anyone. She concentrated forward, though there wasn't much to see. Just road and snow. Dunes, bolsters, riffs. A lot of snow this year. A fresh, clean layer recently, keeping it decent. The sky clouded over as we advanced and the sheen of the sun over the snow quieted, grew somber. As if it recognized the significance of our mission. Jim turned to Mom occasionally to remark on the cityscape, then countryside, and she smiled at him formally, murmured back. He asked if she'd like to listen to music and she said, yes, she would. He passed her a handful of CDs from the storage compartment between their seats. She picked Bach.

Good choice, he said.

Glenn Gould performing Bach. Jim would have a heavenly time on this drive.

I worked two summers at the Brandon Hospital for Mental Diseases, as it was called at the time, though to locals it was simply The Mental—one summer before Darrell's admission, and one summer after. It was a large building of reddish-orange brick, silvery roof, high central tower with wing towers and cupolas to match, standing grandly on the north slope of the Assiniboine River valley. Climbing those three sets of wide steps to the columned entrance, you felt you'd really arrived somewhere for your effort. The grounds were a park, vast lawns dotted with evergreens, elms, maples, and poplars. By the time I worked there, the main building seemed gloomy and inefficient with age, but even then, its original glory glimmered from terrazzo floors and an abundance of wood.

I got the job because Jim's cousin Joyce had some clout in the housekeeping department and put in a word for me to the kitchen. Several college friends had also been hired for various positions at the hospital so we rented rooms together in a crumbling Victorian-era house near the city centre. Jim and friends found construction jobs and took over the basement of a house six blocks away. Jim and I were sort of a couple that first summer, but since nothing was firmly decided between us, we spent most of our free time in the group, miniature golfing, playing baseball, or, as the guys would say, shooting the breeze.

The hospital kitchen had been fully modernized; it was a field of tile and stainless steel, cooking pots and vats the size of barrels. The dirtiest, most boring jobs devolved to summer relief. We spent mornings in the vegetable room washing, peeling, chopping. Potatoes, carrots, mountains of Swiss chard. Ward staff told us that residents hated Swiss chard and wouldn't eat it, no matter how often it was foisted on them, but it kept arriving at the delivery entrance and we kept washing and cooking it. After preps were done, we bent over tub-like sinks for interminable hours of scrubbing pots and utensils and bins. The cooks didn't have to wash what they used; they never doubled up on anything. My back hurt but it was a job, and I needed to earn my next year at school. I got used to the backache, to the *cripes, damns,* and *hecks* blacking the atmosphere like crows, to the regulars' constant griping about every missive that came down to them from the head dietician or hospital administration. My summer co-workers and I dubbed ourselves the Dizzies and survived on private asides.

Several hospital residents helped us in Vegetables. Hank was diligent and morose. He'd killed his wife, it was said, though ruled not criminally responsible. Mike was talkative and twitchy. Every summer, I was told, he selected a target for his running attempts at conversation. The first summer I was there, it was me. Jim, my sort-of boyfriend then, said it was probably because I was short.

You make it sound like an impediment, I grumbled.

I mean you're shorter and don't seem a threat. People feel they tower in comparison. But a cute type of short. You sparkle and people are attracted. Being shorter, people figure you'll listen.

Jim, I said, you're really digging yourself in.

Well, I'm no giant myself, he said. Which was true; for a man, Jim's height was average.

I hate to hurt his feelings, I said. That's all.

You're empathetic, he said. He was trying to help. We were dating, discovering one another. We blathered. Tested ideals. But a decade into marriage and Jim would be saying, I never imagined you'd be so hard to get to know.

And it wasn't even a decade before I got snippy if anyone called me cute.

But Mike: a one-track mind about his breath, rushing at me, mouth agape. Did the sewer smell he smelled come from him? I refused to look in the cavern of bad teeth and dragon tongue. I told him all I could smell was cigarettes. That was foul smelling enough, though I didn't tell him that. Patients rolled their own cigarettes with cheap tobacco the hospital provided. No sewer smell, I repeated until I finally convinced him for the day.

Hey Jim, I said now, leaning forward in the back seat of the car, remember that guy, Steve, who we got to know in Brandon, who worked as a staffer with the geriatric men?

Jim paused the Gould–Bach CD. Yeah?

He claimed he performed a ritual when he left after work every day. Did he ever say what it was?

Some kind of cleansing, he said.

He was petrified of insanity. Remember how we used to laugh

234

at him for that? I told him it wasn't contagious. I kept telling him that if he had to have a ritual, he was halfway there already.

My mother turned slightly, listening but calm and uninvolved.

I was so arrogant then, I said. So insensitive. Optimistic. Or ignorant. What did any of us know about mental illness?

I guess we all were, Catherine, he said.

I leaned back and Jim started up the Bach again.

The second summer, Darrell now among the resident *loonies*, I still laughed at jibes staff made about our place of work, but I didn't like myself when I did. I told no one, not even the friends I hung around with, that my brother was there. No one but Jim, and I made him promise to keep it to himself.

When Mom would ask if I'd seen Darrell, I responded with impatience—how could my mother not get it into her head that I worked in the kitchen, not on the wards, and since wards and staff were segregated within the system, I wouldn't have been on a ward with male patients anyway! And Mom would say, I know. Sadly, as if it was my fault I couldn't interact with my brother. I took to saying yes, that I saw him occasionally. Though I never saw him the way my mother hoped; I merely spotted him now and then while running errands for Sam or other staff between buildings or the wards.

One evening when my parents stopped by my summer quarters, Mom asked about Darrell again, this time in front of my housemates. I deflected the question but later hissed at her that my friends didn't know he lived in The Mental.

I'm sorry, Catherine, she said. I'm ashamed of it too.

I'm not ashamed of it.

Of course you are.

I can't help it though, she'd continued. Bringing him up. He's my son. I love him even if ... The *if* faded away from her sentence and she didn't go after it.

My mother had started using *vegetable* in reference to Darrell, though strictly speaking, he wasn't in a vegetative state; she used it as shorthand for his passivity. I wanted to ask her what kind of vegetable exactly? Artichoke, asparagus, radish, or pea? Maybe a turnip or carrot? A Brussels sprout? I was so mingy inside those days, twisting what I felt about Darrell against my mother. I forced myself to inquire about their current visit. Mostly he sat there, Mom would say—*like a vegetable*—while they sat on either side of him. They drug him way too much, Dad said. To which Mom said, beaming, He let me give him a hug.

If people who didn't know what had happened to Darrell asked me about him, I would say he went to California after his first year of college and I let the sentence fade away too, as if to say, Does anyone ever return from California? For me it was a case of disbelief. Accidents happened, I could work through that. But disbelief over what he'd become, in the flesh, like a plant deprived of water, a head-sunk shuffler. Just the thought of him and I flushed. Mom was right—I *was* ashamed. Infamy piled on infamy after a childhood with an eccentric, gaunt relative in our house, and the kind of family I felt we were now because of both of them, the failure of them like a thorn settling deeper and deeper within me, where it festered. Rotten as dung.

But there—a group of patients in the sun, lounging as if on holiday, some in chairs, some sprawled on the grass, their attendants standing by idly, maybe chatting, but each inmate as if to himself, a sloppy dollop of humanity on a green grass tray. And there—my brother. Darrell. He lifted his head as if he'd overheard something interesting and wanted to reach for it and his face was pearl in the sunshine and he seemed who he'd been before. Always been. Not that I thought him healed; there was no time for a leap like that. It was just a swift, stabbing recognition of a figure who belonged to me and then a sudden memory, skin-close, a school exercise book with a shiny, almost luminescent black cover, the name *Darrell Jacob Riediger* in his best elementary school writing on the inside and page after page of words he'd added to every school assignment. Me, one grade below him, turning those pages with reverence because of the words, because of him, because of what awaited me too. All I'd wanted then was to catch up to my brother.

And there—a cluster of men on a stroll, me and co-worker Ruth moving briskly past them on the roadway by the main building because we were done for the day and were walking home to save the bus fare. No, not a stroll, a stroll was too relaxed and pretty a word for what those men were on. A group trudge, really, a foot-dragging shamble, and Darrell among them. Bowed. Like a prisoner on a chain gang. I felt I couldn't make out who he was, what our relationship might be. I looked away. And Ruth with her tiresome chatter, gesturing back at them and their minders. Sad, isn't it, she said. Sometimes I have to stop and remind myself that that one, or that one, or that one, is somebody's child, somebody's brother, you know. Somebody's son. Maybe somebody's father. She'd been reading about Bedlam, Ruth said, how in the eighteenth century they let the general public come inside the asylum for the price of admission to view the inmates. Baiting was sometimes allowed, anything to aggravate the patients, make it more entertaining. People wanted their money's worth. Isn't that awful? she said. I agreed and changed the subject.

We'd reached the city of Brandon, the Gould CD ending just in time. We circled the former hospital grounds. We saw several vehicles and some buildings seemed occupied, smoke lifting smoothly from chimneys, but overall the place appeared deserted. Twice Mom ordered, Stop, and Jim did. Not at spots I would have expected, though. Once at the edge of the grounds where she searched across a stubbled field beyond the barren trees, and once by the elegant building that had been the house of the head physician and later the nurses' residence. Go, Mom said then, and Jim drove on. He drove slowly, gave us adequate opportunity to look right and left.

Mom said, It seems bigger.

Maybe because it's winter, Jim said. There's no green.

We ate lunch at a chicken place in a Brandon mall. Then Jim lowered the front passenger seat as far as it would go and I tucked Mom in with a pillow and blanket. She giggled. We set off driving again and she slept, snoring lightly, and for the next hour, south and eastward, I heard it, the drawing in of her breath, whispery though, as if she meant to be dignified about sleeping in front of us. Jim slid Beethoven in the CD player; some violin concerto.

Mom slept, Jim drove, and I felt myself at The Mental again, on a summer afternoon. Heat that day like a smash of metal. I'd promised Sam to run some instructions to the Pavilion on my way home, so I turned left out the front doors instead of right. It hit me, the kind of heat you call blistering. A woman passed me, white-haired but otherwise red from top to bottom—red bandana, red sleeveless shirt, red pants, red shoes, her skin red, too. Walking a dog, one of those small mop-like breeds. It was a lovely loop around the hospital grounds and there was ample shade but not even shade could beat a day like that. Both woman and dog were panting. She must live in the neighbourhood, must have absorbed confusion by sheer proximity, I thought, walking in a scorcher. But I hadn't thought to ask if she was okay.

In the slight shadow of pines around a curve of the walk, through the glaze of sun, I saw two figures, one clearly a resident, the other a visitor. An attendant was there to chaperone but he'd moved apart, facing the river valley and smoking. The patient was Darrell. The visitor was Uncle Must. Darrell sat in a white park chair and my uncle knelt, one knee on the ground, the other raised in front of him. His arms were crossed over the raised knee, his hands drooped along his leg. There was no one else in the vicinity besides the disinterested staffer—someone I didn't know. I stepped off the walkway, stepped closer. Darrell's hair long shorn of its hippie length, combed into a jaunty wave.

But for the lazy jaw, the dull eyes—dull even at a distance—he could have been a kid. Younger than me. Good-looking. The ruin of him concentrated in his eyes like blindness. But they were a picture in that pose, Uncle kneeling as if in solicitude, speaking, and Darrell opposite and fixed on him, head poised like a flower grateful to the sun. But Uncle Must! I stepped closer, saw his face, his narrow, dark-tanned features, and his was torment. The face of a Pietà.

Brother and uncle: sunflower and Madonna.

I interrupted, said, Hello, Darrell. Hello, Uncle Must.

My uncle jolted and scrambled to his feet. He gazed at me briefly in stupefaction, then said, Catherine. He shone with perspiration. I caught another movement, Darrell's head jerking sideways, a spark of recognition or joy it seemed, a motion that may have been involuntary, barren of meaning, but one I would cling to, claim as significant, believing he'd snapped my way because of my voice or my name. I tried to catch the whole of his turning but already he'd slipped away, his countenance closing as if underwater.

The rest of our brief conversation that hot afternoon was conducted with Uncle Must focussed on my ears or the building behind me and Darrell staring straight ahead, smiling his bland jester's smile, unconnected to anything we said. I told my uncle I worked at the hospital and he said he knew this and I asked if he'd come to visit my parents and he said yes, he'd come to visit my parents, and I said I was sorry but I'd forgotten where he was living now and he said he'd been here and there.

Do you think he understands you? I asked, meaning Darrell.

I think he does.

Of course, I'd wanted to know what he'd been saying to him and how in the world they managed to get outside together, with an attendant assigned for the visit, but all of that would have been quite beyond the sort of conversation we'd ever had with one another. We stood there a while, not speaking, both of us with our hands clasped, Uncle Must's eyes now seeking the ground, mine lowering too, until I realized how it must look, the two of us standing as if Darrell were lying in a coffin between us and we respectful at his interment. My hands flew apart, which reminded me of the papers I had to deliver.

He boils over, my uncle said, addressing the grass.

Yes. Dad says that too.

But they keep him very quiet. Perhaps it's good he's here.

Yes.

He can't do anything wicked here, he said.

Hmm.

A place like this is nothing but suffering. It's a corral. Suffering all chased down and rounded into it.

It surprised me, how much he'd said. And that figure of speech. Yes, I said, I know.

Then I told him, probably too cheerfully, that it was hot and I had to get going. A compassionate wish had surged within me like the heat, however, to throw myself on the grass and wail beside the men, to hold my brother's feet, to comfort my awkward Uncle Must, to comfort myself, but I couldn't separate that hot wish from the drenching heat and humidity around me and my obligation to deliver the cook's instructions. Back on the pathway, I felt vaguely guilty and then I recalled the woman in red and her flaming face. Heat rash for sure. I couldn't see her anywhere and no one had collapsed along the driveway so I concluded the woman and her tiny dog had made it safely home.

In 1975, when Jim and I had been married a year, Darrell *sickened and took his leave.* That's how my father put it when he called to tell us Darrell had died. It sounded old-fashioned, literary some-how, as if we'd formed a circle around my brother's bed while he bid farewell. Like a biblical patriarch blessing his sons or a

Shakespearean character breaking into speech just before departing life.

But there's a fact I kept to myself: I'd had a dream two weeks earlier with exactly such a scenario, Darrell sitting up in his bed—a hospital bed, linens stiffly starched—and nurses and orderlies rushing about in streams of white, which meant he was still at The Mental. He was as healthy-looking as could be, though we'd been summoned and told he was about to die. His hair had grown back to his shoulders and he was smiling and talking, the way dreams fill up with talk, though seldom words you can recover when you wake. In the midst of this, Mom hauled a guitar out of her purse and it shocked us, for her purse was hard and small and tidy and we kept fussing excitedly about how she got that guitar into and out of it. She begged him to play but Darrell wouldn't even look at her, never mind take the instrument. When she finally got his attention, Mom asked if he had his sheet music or his written-out notes, and he said, no, he didn't, and then he said, which I *did* recall from the dream, that he couldn't play now, he was sick and ready to expire. He said *expire*. He promised he would play her something later.

So it seemed to me that this was how he died, something memorable along the lines of Dad's sentence, though in fact my brother died alone and unexpectedly, in the middle of the night. He'd been ill; he choked on his vomit. Dad said the hospital provided a thorough accounting of Darrell's death and he and Mom had no further questions. They were good Mennonites that way; they didn't want to come across as suspicious or demanding. They may have been relieved. I remember that I was; you don't have to consciously wish for someone to die, I thought, to be glad when they do.

But my mother was in a bad way the morning of the funeral. We were all there, Jim and I, Lorena, our parents. Uncle Must was there too. She started out chipper enough, smiling and chattering while she set the table for breakfast. Then, over our oatmeal and toast, Dad said, He was as good as dead anyway. His tone was doleful and he meant to comfort us but it knocked Mom into hysterical weeping, which horrified my father. He shot up and took her in his arms until she settled, until she finally said, as if all she'd been struggling with was wifely submission, You're right, Jake, I know you're right.

The service was in Marble and that's where they buried him, in the tree-ringed cemetery on the edge of town. Uncle Must wasn't in a suit like Dad but in work-type clothes, though clean and pressed. He was pinched and silent, eyes pink at the rims. He stuck constantly close to my father, as if their years apart had defeated him, crushed him into dependency. At the graveside, he started some hand to head to shoulder to waist and up again movements but Dad nudged against him so their arms overlapped and Uncle calmed and stood still.

I hadn't cried yet and I wasn't crying then though the need to cry was immense inside me. I seemed a bolted dam sluice that wouldn't budge.

But yes, a relief: Darrell not at The Mental but *laid to rest* in Marble's charming rural cemetery. At Peace, his stone would say, near the consoling blue hills of the Pembina Valley.

When he was dead, I felt the stigma of my brother had lifted somewhat.

In Marble now, Mom waking as we turned off the highway into the cemetery. And sure enough, Darrell's gravestone was mounded with snow. But it was next to the cemetery lane which was cleared. We could park close. Jim got out and righted my mother's seat and then, while she and I watched, he shovelled the snow away from the black granite square. I asked her if she wanted to get out, said we could probably manage her into the chair to push her a few feet closer, but she said no, she could see it. Darrell Jacob Riediger, she read. At Peace.

I stepped out of the car. The wind was cold. I moved to the side of the stone, careful not to block my mother's view. Jim put the shovel into the trunk and returned to stand beside me.

I wish you'd known him, I said. I mean, before.

Well, I met him once. Before. I have an idea of him.

An idea isn't much.

We stayed outside in the cold longer than I felt we needed to, but I didn't want to rush Mom or break into her thoughts too soon. Then she knocked on the window and signalled us back. I volunteered to drive.

I've had enough, she said. Isn't it nearly time for supper? At home?

We won't make it to Maplebend in time for supper, I said, we've got a couple hours driving back. We'll pick up a sandwich or something.

Well, sitting beside you is beautiful too.

We drove for a while and then, pulling apart the details of Darrell's funeral on account of this trip, I said, Uncle Must wasn't in a suit.

He didn't have a suit along, she said. How should he know that Darrell would die?

Of course.

I felt sheepish. Where in the world was I going with this?

But I remembered that Uncle Must had arrived the day of Darrell's death and that he'd stopped in at The Mental on his way to Marble. He was the last person in our family to see my brother alive. He'd told us Darrell had seemed the same as the last time he visited him. But we'd glossed over that final encounter. There's a certain distinction in being the last one to see someone alive and I think we wished it for Mom instead of Uncle. I remembered, in fact, that I'd sensed the seed of her resentment or jealousy about it and none of us wanted it to grow.

Now, in the mindfulness provoked by driving, with Mom

beside me, I felt jealous of Uncle too. On her behalf, *and* mine! His the final sighting! This was the problem with nosing around in the past: new shards of emotion worked themselves to the surface. Like nails or glass or pottery heaved up through winter's freeze and thaw.

Of course, I repeated. How should he know?

The birds were singing, Mom said, and everyone was kind. Your father never left me alone.

Good old Dad.

It was such a nice day. Everything was green.

Yes. I glanced in the rearview mirror. Jim was asleep.

Don't you miss your house? she asked.

No.

Really?

Not at all.

I'm glad to hear it. I would miss it if I were you.

I'd adored it, I thought, but that was then. *Then.* A word of such power, for good or ill. My sweet little house with its window box of annual pansies, its crabapple trees and tiger lilies, morning light over our table for two. We married, we did Europe, and when we were done with that, Jim got his teaching job. We lived in an apartment on Talbot, in a three-level block, and I finished my English degree and the next stage had been the small, white house with its white picket fence, and we felt grown-up and successful, dreams unfolding as they should, the Age of Aquarius and all that. That cozy storey-and-a-half, a side gate with the loveliest arch—well, I felt I'd arrived where I'd been heading all along. We called it our starter home, but we liked the neighbourhood and had enough room and eventually we renovated it inside and out and added a garage, and stayed. The only house we've ever owned.

I was on the pill when we moved in. We planned two children, to replace ourselves. I snagged a position at the regional archives, in reception, monitoring visitors, assisting people with a research pass. I longed to work further in, near the catalogues, and even deeper, near the stacks. A position came up and I applied for and got it. I went off the pill and we tried—for years—to get pregnant. One month of hopes collapsing after the next. We took another, more luxurious, trip to Europe—not hostels but hotels and meals in restaurants instead of cheese and bread on a curb—and considered the implications, decided infertility was the card we'd been dealt, decided not to adopt or invest in other measures. At work, my responsibilities grew. I liked history, liked helping others sleuth. I returned to university for a history degree and when the university inaugurated the archival studies program, I enrolled in courses specific to my work. I liked theoretical matters, research, writing. I liked what archives could hide and announce, what ostensibly boring records could reveal—inadvertently, at times. I missed it more than I wanted to admit.

But I didn't miss the house.

Houses run their course, I said. We really like the apartment we're in now. Every time I come to visit you, I drive past our former neighbourhood, past the Safeway where I used to shop, past the bank where I used to bank. Past those small, pretty houses on those long, pretty streets west of Henderson, younger couples moving in now. Life there like a book you keep on your shelf but don't need to read again.

That's pretty too, she said. How you put it.

In the back seat, Jim shifted and turned. Dear Jim, in a frenzy of parting shots in music education. Last influences to scatter like a Santa, last students to inspire, last young teachers to guide. No use telling him he'd done enough. I upped the speed on the cruise control. The sun lowered westward but seemed brighter, a consoling amber in the air in spite of the keen white wind. I wanted to start again. Not *over* exactly, just *again*. Grab my partner and fly into the space of hope and possibility we lived in when we wed, when we travelled on the cheap. When we began with little more than prospects. Confronting even my brother's death with the belief there would be space enough to absorb it, and if tears weren't releasing as they should, they were bound to release in their own good time.

My mother reached for me and I took her hand in mine up to the steering wheel. It felt both malleable and bony but it wasn't shaking. Tranquil today, Mother Edna and her hand. As a girl, I thought her continuously available, conscious of being mother, but it probably wasn't true. Not then, and certainly not now. It was her age, but not only that. As if, at some point, she took her distance, separated herself to be more than maternal. While I was busy untangling myself from her, too.

Tell me something, she said. What you're doing.

I put her hand back in her lap. At this precise moment, I said, I'm on a field trip with my wonderful mother. I chuckled. Otherwise my life is as dull as unbuttered toast.

That's all right, she said. We'll watch the field trip.

Several kilometres later, she said, I always liked to iron. Do you like to iron?

Interesting, Mom! I actually like to iron. We may be the only two people in the world.

No. Maisie Martens—remember Maisie Martens?—she told me she liked to iron.

Three of us, then.

Another long stretch of silence, and then we reached the city and there was plenty for Mom to see and comment on. The traffic moved well and we got through downtown and over the Disraeli Bridge into Elmwood. We stopped to get a sandwich she could eat in her room. You're nearly home, I said.

It's always nice to come home.

Yes, it is.

Darrel's grave, my mother said as we pulled into the Maple-bend driveway. That's what I wanted to do. That's what I did today.

24.

On the Monday after our trip to Brandon and Marble, Mom called, agitated. When was I coming?

I said I wasn't, we were together Saturday, together all day, in Brandon and Marble—remember?—and I didn't usually visit Mondays anyway. She said I had to come.

I sighed and said I would be there as soon as I could.

She sat ramrod straight in her wheelchair, hands flat on her tray, face beaming with some kind of good news, so strangely alight, in fact, I worried she'd gone and fallen in love with a gentleman resident. Which would complicate everything.

It was nothing like that. It was the manila envelope on her tray. She looked expectant but it wasn't until I read *Von Gerhard*— From Gerhard—in my father's handwriting on the envelope that I realized it was the letters. The letters from Uncle Must.

Here you go, Mom said. I'm tired of your questions. And as long as you bring it back.

· We hadn't talked much about Uncle for months, it seemed, since I'd been mulling over Darrell, but archival excitement spiked in me like a sugar rush. And I could see she wanted a reaction so I picked up the envelope and thanked her.

Whatever it contained, there wasn't much of it; the packet was very thin. But it was the thrill of the chase. Through a couple of papers *Von Gerhard*.

So you went into your lock drawer? I asked.

I can't remember anything these days so I looked. It's some letters, I think. You're the historian—or whatever you are. There's nothing to inherit, you know. Darrell wasn't in Brandon because of that. It was because of the drugs. But you don't have children anyway.

Inherit?

Blood, Mom said. What people inherit. What they pass on to their children.

Oh.

I tucked the packet under my coat, which I'd tossed on the bed, and decided to distract her in case she changed her mind. I was there anyway, so might as well take her for a corridor walk. Funny, though, how pleased I was about the envelope, a stealthy artifact it seemed to me now and surely restive under my black coat, like a horse nudging for oats or an apple, and I wanted to get this visit over with, get my treasure home.

Letters. I knew perfectly well how useless letters could be, how they might be general and rambling. But there was always something—*something*—one could parse between the lines, something hidden in the folds. I'd read intrepid journalist Janet Malcolm on Chekhov. When a person dies, she said, everything essential about them dies as well. She spoke about kernel and husk: the kernel buried, the husk weightless in comparison. Still, I thought,

the entire archival enterprise was premised on a contrary hope—
the hope that something essential, something weighty, *did* in
fact remain. Something true. Every morning, the professionals
showed up at their temperature-and-humidity-controlled, docu-
ment-packed rooms and could not betray their confidence that
the papers they guarded had the fullest capacity to embody the
essential.

And I was a card-carrying member of that school.

The packet rode home on the seat beside me. Stopped at a light,
I ran my hand over it. The miracle of paper, and envelopes like
wombs with their paper surprises!

*I've never had the nerve to consider my past fascinating. I'm not
a rememberer.* My words to Jim. Obviously not true anymore. All
this winter I'd remembered. And now I was galvanized by some
husks from the past.

Settle down, I told myself. Today you need to get groceries and
this evening you and Jim are going to Marcie's basketball game
and tomorrow you're on volunteer duty at the thrift store. Then
it's Ash Wednesday. Look at it then.

Documents, I knew, were owed due diligence; they should not
be rushed.

I slipped into the pew of a nearby church for their morning Ash
Wednesday service.

The attendance was sparse and the service short. We confessed
our humanity, *Dust you are and to dust you return.* We sang *Kyrie
eleison* through a litany of sins. And then I was home, the black
ash cross on my forehead, seated at the table and facing the window. Clouds like rags slung across the sky, cranes swinging at the
human rights museum, square towers rising there thick as bat-
tlements, trains and traffic flowing as usual in both directions.
Jim would be gone until late; he was going to the festival choir

practice directly from work. The *St John Passion* this year, with the symphony.

I lit a candle, a beeswax pillar. The flame guttered wildly. I blew it out again. No fire near archives!

I picked up the envelope. Squash-coloured, 10 x 13, the flap torn on the edges and hanging loosely, neither glued nor folded in. Nothing on it but those two words, *Von Gerhard*, in my father's hand. Here I was, reprising the demeanour—the habits—of an archivist, but I was nervous, as if about to understand my uncle more, or less. Either way, change seemed a strain. I thought of Lucy creating a record of her story, wondering again why anyone bothered. Like accumulating steps on one's knees up to a cathedral, wasn't it? When Jim and I toured Europe, I'd watched pilgrims in precisely such ascents. But after I murmured pity once for their sore joints and limbs, another tourist near me laughed and said, Oh, no, it's enormously satisfying, that self-imposed suffering, and all of us observing to boot.

I scrutinized the two cover words, their neat friendliness. Written in ballpoint, miniscule pools of ink left behind on the *n*, *G* and *a*. A cheap ballpoint pen that leaked. I lifted the envelope flap. Probably nothing more trapped inside than a church bulletin or two, and maybe that article in which he'd railed against television. Mom said letters, but she was no longer reliable.

I slipped on cotton archival gloves. They'd been given to me as a farewell gift—and joke—from my colleagues at my retirement party. Gloves inhibited the knowledge that touch transmits but protected photos and papers from human oils. Common intimacies weren't permitted in the archives!

I saw my white-cottoned fingers, knew myself a fool. As if these papers were the Dead Sea Scrolls or something rare and valuable like that!

Was it my hope to understand, then love? This seemed an error to me now. Understanding came to the aid of love, but shouldn't be a precondition, should it? Love had to stand on its own.

Love, then. Period. But I wasn't sure I had the capacity to love well enough. I would rather be finished with the man who might be lurking in this envelope.

Though I could try. And truth be told, I was curious. Too curious not to risk its demands.

I stripped off the gloves, put my bare hand in. Seven items. Three photographs, three sheets of paper, a small white envelope with a folded newspaper clipping inside it. Two of the photos small and of uncertain value, content-wise, and the other a copy of the studio portrait of my paternal grandparents in Russia, the same photo that held ground on our piano for so many years. Uncle's copy, I assumed. Taken out of its frame. Not ferried off in Sharon Miller's final boxes, then. The photos in excellent condition, their corners crisp and—oh, thank you, I breathed to no one in particular—none had been written on, front or back, none compromised by a heavy pen. Unfortunately, not lightly in pencil either, the photos neither labelled nor dated. An archivist's pet peeve.

A quick glance told me that two of the papers were letters, as Mom had said, written by Uncle to my father. The third, also in his handwriting—the script leaning forward, stiffening upward, then leaning forward again—had brief notations and dates and seemed to be a short family history. I put the pages in a row in front of me on the table.

I lifted the newspaper clipping out of its small envelope. It was old and fragile. Habit again: I donned a glove and carefully flattened the fold. Initials of the source Mennonite periodical were written in Gothic script at the top. I was acquainted with the early Mennonite newspapers; their archival centres housed them in print or on microfilm. Something for everyone, those newspapers: poems, sermons, uplifting serial stories, farming advice, news from the wider world, advertisements for motors and cream separators. Above all, news about their scattered co-religionists.

This clipping was a single column with three items, set in dense Gothic type—type I could read, but not quickly. The items didn't have headings as such, just the first word or two in bolder ink. Usually, this was the location of the report or something like A Correspondent Writes.

I placed the clipping into an acid-free sleeve. If significant, I could scan, enlarge, make a copy of, perhaps translate it. I spotted the word *Mord*—murder—at the beginning of one item. A calamity report then, which Uncle had hung on to for some reason. I put it in the row with the handwritten pages.

What drew me next was a receipt from the Tilia Co-op which had been tucked inside the newsclipping. Foodstuffs, $6.30. Points of ink on it as if from behind.

I turned the receipt over and ... oh my! Darrell! I recognized his handwriting immediately. A short note. *Sorry, Uncle, but I can't read German! I believe your story anyway. Darrell.* A sense of scrawl but an attempt, it seemed, to scrawl neatly for his uncle's sake. The capitals large and round and confident. The last *l* of his name flying up and back to the *D*.

I'd been prepping myself to encounter my uncle in the pages in front of me. I'd been unaccountably nervous, self-conscious about even opening the packet, though glad to see letters because letters are excellant sources—personal and thus revealing—but feeling slightly guilty too, for these weren't like the strangers' diaries and letters that researchers in archives snoop through. These pertained to people I knew. Then again, thinking of Uncle's letter to the college that I'd once come across, it wasn't as if I hadn't read a letter of his before! At any rate, I'd felt a mix of interest and dread to face this slender stash from my mother, something I'd wished for but nearly regretted, even before knowing what it said, and now the astonishment of meeting my brother on this scrap. I was amazed how a few lines of handwriting could transport him to me. He seemed a gift, a presence, here with these materials all this time!

Perhaps this discovery was as much as I needed. Perhaps I could quit, not go further. I touched the paper with my brother's writing to my cheek like a talisman and it must have helped, for there seemed nothing to fear in moving forward. Surely these pages would be gentle and friendly. Uncle to his brother. Surely not scolding. For no rational reason then, I was emboldened. I would carry on.

I studied the photos. A small picture of Uncle lifting a sheaf of wheat with a pitchfork. Tall and clearly strong. The sheaf as high as his shoulder. A picture of the three Riediger men: Uncle Must, Darrell, Dad. My brother maybe five or six, standing in the middle. Dad's hand on his shoulder, as if to keep him close, my uncle's arm a blur. Possibly reaching for Darrell as well. Their heads bare. Squinting into the sun. Wearing white shirts and ties, as if they'd just come home from church and taken off their suit jackets. The formal photograph of Dad and Uncle's parents, Elizabeth and Gerhard Riediger, taken in a studio in Russia, which I'd practically memorized along with my scales, when it wasn't lying on its face, that is. Lacy draperies swirled behind the couple, Grandfather seated and Grandmother standing, her hand on the back of his chair, neither of them looking at the camera. In the Big House, they'd looked at the brown chesterfield.

Next, the page entitled Our Mother, the paper the same stock as the letter dated 1945, the folds on the two pages a match, and also the ink, so probably written and sent to my father with the letter. I remembered my teenaged attempt at a family tree. This, I thought, seemed to have branches and leaves.

Everything in the packet was written in German. Fortunately I knew it well enough to read and translate.

Our Mother

Our mother, Elizabeth Riediger nee Penner, was born Febru-
ary 17, 1888 to a landless family in Molotschna. She was the
first living child, the oldest. Her brother Nicolai was born six
years later, in 1894, in Neu Samara. Father Penner had taken
his wife and daughter there in 1891. It was a new settlement
and they settled in the village Podolysk.
Our mother was ten when her father murdered her
mother.

Oh.

I read the sentence again, in case I'd misread it. *Our mother was*
ten when her father murdered her mother.
Oh.

That *Oh* plunged into the ground of me. I don't know if I said
it aloud but it thudded like a fence post being pounded deep,
thudded again and again as I clambered on to read what he
meant, to grasp what he'd said, an Oh meaning *So that's what it*
is; that's the fact of it, something solid and incontestable packing
into the knowledge of us—our family—my great-grandmother
murdered by her husband, and simultaneously I became aware
that I heard—or muttered—another range of Ohs within me: the
smaller, soundless, open-mouthed *O* of pain lifting away from the
other, heavier word, repeating like an echo, moaning in the air.

Her mother's name was Maria Penner nee Plett. He
murdered her in 1898. Our mother Elizabeth had to witness
this.

So the mother of my father, the mother of my uncle—my
grandmother Elizabeth Penner Riediger, the woman in the photograph on the piano throughout my Tilia memories, whom I,

Catherine, apparently resembled—had witnessed her father murder her mother. *Sie musste es sehen:* she had to see it.

This rendering of the sentence was probably too timid, however. *She was compelled to witness it* was closer to what it meant.

I made myself read on.

*But she managed to put her brother Nicolai in another
room and fasten the door. He was four. Her father Penner
was taken away by the authorities when the act was discovered. Our mother and her brother were taken to the Bernhard
Friesens in Lugovsk. Mrs. Friesen was a sister to the murdered
woman. She had eight children already and did not wish for
any more, so the child Nicolai was sent to the elderly grandparents in Molotschna. Our mother thought he died in the
early days of the Great War, though she never knew his fate
for certain. He may have run off and enlisted. He may have
been involved in revolutionary activity. She told me she cried
for many days when they were separated as children. In 1900,
when our mother was 12, the Friesens sent her to work for
the Riedigers who lived in Podolysk where the crime had
occurred. Nearly every day, for one reason or another, she had
to pass her former home. She worked hard for the Riedigers.
Their third son, Gerhard, wished to marry her for she was
pretty and pious. He formed this wish the day she arrived at
the house but he waited some years before speaking of it. She
was willing but his parents were opposed. They made the pair
wait and plead for more than a year before they relented. The
Riedigers had treated her sympathetically as a servant but
had not expected her to marry one of their sons. They feared
for the marriage because she suffered from nightmares and
unstable behaviour. They also thought her too tall. She was
taller than our father. Our parents married in 1906 and our
father helped his father farm. Our mother was calm the first*

*years and our father was good to her but she suffered from too
many births and too many deaths. He often hired someone
to stay with her, to watch her. Here is the list of births and
deaths. As you can see, only we two sons, the oldest and second youngest children, remain in the land of the living.*

Uncle Must then listed the children my grandmother had
borne and lost, as he'd once listed them to me. He went on to tell
of Elizabeth's death and the emigration from Russia and arrival in
Canada, where the two brothers acquired their stepmother, also
an Elizabeth.

There was something compelling about my uncle's voice in
these lines. I could hardly hear it though, because of what he
stated so close to the beginning, that my great-grandfather was a
murderer. Who killed his wife. My head dropped into my hands
and my fingers brushed the crust of the black cross on my forehead which I'd forgotten about.

I took a break to make a pot of coffee, moving clumsily, spilling
grounds on the kitchen counter, the *Oh* still a thud and the *O* still
a moan, but the truth of what I'd seen becoming real to me and
slightly softer already, now that I knew. All my parents ever said
was that Grandmother Riediger's early life was difficult. Something about her mother dying when she was ten, her father gone
soon afterward. An orphan, Mom had said, just like me! Something about her living with her aunt and uncle and their house
full of fat children who had no room or heart for her. And this
exchange:

Dad: Fat?

Uncle Must: They were fat. Much better fed than she was.

Sent out at twelve to work as a maid. A hard life for a child.
Though on account of this, she met and fell in love with my
grandfather.

But had anyone ever said this, what I'd read today?

I thought of my uncle and brother knowing all this. Dad too of course, and Mom. Which, in spite of my arriving to it late, comforted me. They'd managed it, hadn't they?

The coffee must have fortified me for when I returned to the table I found myself ready, even impatient, for the letters and the clipping, for whatever elaboration they might contain. Ready for the hard work of taking it in. *I believe your story anyway,* Darrell had said.

I picked up the first letter.

Alberta [Undated]
Dear brother Jacob,

How are you doing in school? How are you doing with your chores? I am sorry that you are not enjoying school, but so it is. Some like their lessons more than others. When our father married again, our stepmother said My son to you and gave you a kiss on your cheek. She did not know what to do with me. Now she had two children attached to her apron when she had never had a child of her own. She did not know what to do with creatures such as we two boys. But she was fond of you. You taught her how to love you and she was willing to be taught. I did not know how to teach or how to make her willing. My head was still carrying the picture of my mother, her white face, and her last words to me. You have forgotten her but I could not. Our stepmother said I was a strange boy and a trouble. I was not really a trouble; I worked hard. But my silences were strange and they seemed a trouble to her. You must be grateful that she is fond of you.

I am helping with the harvest and you should see me, how strong I am, how dark from the daily sun. I move along with a crew and like to work until I am nearly too sore to go on. I sleep well at the end of the day. The fields are kind to me, and the sky is kindness from dawn to dusk. I keep saying, Thank you for the kindness. I read the Bible when I can but when I am busy with spring and harvest work, there is too little time, so I read in winter and think on it later like a cow with her cud. You must read and study, even if you do not care for school. Get help with everything, so you can learn to understand the Bible. But you can leave out Revelation. Our mother could never hear the book of Revelation without a shudder, so she never read it either. She said there are many places in the Bible that are dangerous to interpret on your own and Revelation is the most dangerous of them all.

I am saving my money, as much as I can. Some day you and I will farm together, Jacob, but in the meanwhile, obey your father and also your stepmother. I will be back to see you and Father at Christmas.

Your brother,
Gerhard

Revelation again. What was it about that book? I remembered my uncle's awful reaction to a section of it, but why did he dislike it so much?

I picked up the second letter.

Tilia, Alberta, 1945
Dear brother Jacob,

How I have longed for you, dear brother, longed to know that you are well and safe in every way. You know that your mother saved her brother Nicolai. She put him away in a room. She turned the key so he would not see what she had

*been forced to see. He crept into a corner. What did he hear?
I have often wondered about this. He must have heard something in the corner where he bent over to cry. She said his
cheeks bore the marks of his crying when she opened the door,
when she picked him up and delivered him, running, to the
neighbours. When I was a boy, rumours swooped around me
like swallows and I pleaded with our mother to tell me what
they were saying. I would not let it rest, so she finally told me
as much as I told you on my last visit. Our father was angry
with me that time in Russia, when I was begging her, when I
would not let it rest and then she screamed. After she stopped,
she told me, and I have told you too, so you will know what
she endured, and why.*

    *When she was dying, our father permitted me into the
room. The dead child had already been wrapped. She was
almost out of breath, out of words, but she said, Watch over
your brother Jacob for he is the apple of my eye and you the
keeper of the orchard. And she said, You must be good to
women. Never harm them, but control your passions, which
my own father the murderer was unable to do. Our father was
weeping and could be told nothing. This is why she had to give
these instructions to me. I was fourteen then. It seemed like
months passed before he stopped his weeping. When I told
him of our mother's last words, he said we were his sons and
that he would watch us both. But he is growing older and now
I have a farm of my own, and since our mother said I should
watch over my brother I beseech you to come. I have asked
Father and I believe he will be fine if you join me. I confess
that I need you. Our father was seasick on the journey from
Russia so you and I often sat on the deck and watched the
sea. It seemed a field to me, a field already in furrows, seeds
of tribulation in the rows from end to end. You tried to make*

me laugh. It seemed easy for you to be happy, and soon you were always happy, no matter where you went.

Your brother,
Gerhard.+

+Here they call me George. I was named after our father, but you are named for our murdered grandmother's father. He was a Plett. I was told he was a good man. I was also told that he never liked his son-in-law Penner, but that's how it turned out. The Penner is a part of us now too. At the end of his life, this Plett, our great-grandfather, said he had forgiven his son-in-law, the murderer. What else could he do, he said, but his wife turned bitter and found a way to blame her husband. Our mother's brother Nicolai took on the bitterness too, this is what I heard, but then he disappeared into the forest or the war. We must try to be like the great-grandfather Plett, who forgave, and to always remember our mother, to protect her if we can, and to keep other women from whoredom.

Fourteen when she died, fourteen years already of knowing she wasn't well or safe, as he wished his younger brother to be. Reaching for her burden. Putting it on. Sympathy swelled within me. I didn't know yet if the sympathy would be big enough to swallow the antipathy and embarrassment I'd felt about my uncle for so long, but it swelled as if determined that these emotions must, at the least, co-exist.

Oh how badly I wanted a walk, the pound of my feet on hard hard earth. Soon, I told myself, soon, but just finish first, there is only the newspaper clipping left. When I'd seen *Mord*—just an hour ago, was it?—I'd guessed something randomly sensational that Uncle may have given Darrell to read in connection with a story he'd told him in person. Perhaps on one of those long walks of theirs when I stayed in the house and read horror stories that were fictional. Now, before even studying them, I guessed that each of the three items in their tidy row would pertain to us. And indeed they did.

Wife murder. ____ **Samara.** It was the last Sunday in March, at 2 o'clock in the afternoon when Penner's daughter was suddenly at our house asking me if her father might have a load of straw. I said, But it's Sunday, and she immediately said, I'll tell my father then. She hurried away. Soon after that, two neighbours came to me and said, Come along to the Penners', something has happened. I said to them, What is it then? They said, The Penner's daughter said her mother has died. I was surprised and told them she had just been here but said nothing of that. We came to the Penners'. The door was open. P. was walking around the great room, smoking. We asked, Has your wife died? To that he answered, I slaughtered her this morning. What a shock that was, to hear him say those words. We asked him, How could you do such a thing? He answered us that it was written, She shall be utterly burned up with fire. He opened the Bible and showed us Revelation 18:8. There was blood on the finger he used to show us the verse. It's written here, he said. Oh, what a box of evil he opened. The woman is a Plett by birth. Joh. Peters

The two following reports offered the same grim news from other writers and perspectives, bits of new detail supplied in each one, but the same event, the same undeniable outcome, three grisly rounds of information. I recoiled from their gossipy recitals, from their horrified tsk-tsking—there seemed sadness in what my uncle wrote but too much thrill here in standing at the scene of the crime. Nevertheless, I was glad for the clipping. I didn't doubt the truth of what my uncle set down to his brother, but seeing the published evidence fixed it emphatically in my mind as historical fact.

The newspaper texts tumbled in my head like coins through the air, old gold coins with Tsarist-era markings, scarred with the burden of my Uncle Must, my grandmother Riediger, my great-grandmother Penner. A Plett's daughter. The mother in the bed with a ploughshare coming at her, the daughter at the end of the room, made to be present for their final argument. The mother's cries, the gush of red, my hibiscus in the corner by the window fuller than it had been all winter, four blooms open at once. Blood splattered so far it rained on the girl. Who hoisted herself up and delivered her brother to the neighbours. Who asked for straw. Who walked with her father to the church. Did she hope some undoing, some return to life, might be possible in the marriage bed of her parents if she kept her steps steady and obedient?

No wonder Uncle hated the Book of Revelation. 18:8. *She shall be utterly burned up with fire* ... Did fear leave a smell? Did the man do it quickly at least, silence her with a single hack? But he wasn't sated. It wasn't enough. The text said burning, and burning was next. Demented but composed, smoking, watching the child as she'd had to watch him, as she picked up her brother and rushed him away. Telling her she must hurry and return, there was more to be done. She did what he said. A sop thrown into the chaos around her mother. Soaking up the discharge by following his orders.

Surely if she helped her father get the straw he would finally be satisfied, he would cease his violence. He would be well again.

The ploughshare thrown to the floor because he was confused about the difference between soil and flesh. If they burned the blood and the bed and the body, her brother would be spared the sight of them. And hadn't the boy always clapped his hands at the flames that crackled in the stove? Perhaps she'd been touched with delusions already, thinking that when they returned from the church her mother would be cooking their dinner as usual. Mother, reaching for her Elizabeth's hand, saying, I didn't need a death this awful. It wasn't required but it happened so you have to be brave. You have to mind your father now and be good to your brother.

Then those correspondents, sitting down with their paper and their ink, sending away their important little news items telling all the Mennonites of the world about this scandalous thing! Hadn't they seen the man's sickness before? He'd seized a phrase completely out of the context—out of a dramatic apocalytic scene meant to comfort those oppressed by Roman persecution by promising the destruction of that pleasure-soaked and brutal empire, here called the harlot of Babylon—and made it literal and personal. Had Elizabeth's mother been unfaithful? Obviously the girl had heard such accusations, spoken of what she heard to my uncle, but there was no hint in the reports of this; the most said was that the couple had lived *in discord* for some time. But never mind that, whatever it entailed. Hadn't they explained, while teaching the scriptures, that one must always employ a herme-neutic of love?

25.

Jim returned from his rehearsal that evening stuffed with the *St John Passion* and said he was exhausted. But to me, he seemed rejuvenated, as if he could easily slip on formal wear and face a concert hall with every seat full. He left the bathroom door open while he prepared for bed. I heard him singing. He wasn't a soloist in the *Passion*, they brought in celebrated singers from elsewhere for that, but he couldn't resist; he learned all the choir lines and he learned the solos too—he learned all of them, yes, he really couldn't help it. This was a man who conquered music like it was Everest, *because it's there*; wasn't that what Mallory or Hillary or one of those famous climbers had said?

He was singing *Ach, mein Sinn, Wo willst du endlich hin, Wo soll ich mich erquicken?* Ah, my soul, where is thy goal, where shall I be refreshed? I sat in bed, trying to read but not succeeding. Waiting for him. Jim stretched out beside me then and I told him what I'd found in the envelope. He listened intently. I felt that the scores in his head were evaporating as I spoke. He let his rehearsal lift away for my sake and I noticed and was more grateful than I could say.

I slipped down close to him. This brings some ends together, I said. What the matter was with Uncle. Why my folks were as patient with him as they were. Why he made that scene in church. Why Mom insisted Darrell wasn't sick from something inherited but from the drugs. Which may have been true, or maybe not. Like her fretting about us not having kids and then suddenly saying, It's for the best, you know, because so many things can go wrong with children.

Some of her views might be classified as old wives tales, Jim said. His breath smelled of his mouthwash rinse. It smelled reliable.

Who knows? I said. Who knows anything? It's impossible to really know someone else. It would be some years before I read the news of studies showing that trauma can hide in our genes, get passed along, but that day I put this much together: what happened in Russia had pulsated down our family line and was reverberating still.

Jim held me a while and we didn't talk but his skin was warm and then we arranged the blankets to sleep. I imagined him choosing an aria or chorus from the oratorio for his fall-asleep thoughts, but it would take me longer to do the same. I couldn't find anything besides *who knows, who knows?*

But Darrell knew, I said aloud. There was a note from Darrell.

Jim didn't answer so I supposed he'd dozed off. How easily he fell asleep! Then, his wide-awake voice startled me, like a bump in the dark. There's something else that comes together, he said. When you said that Darrell knew. That evening I met him? Before you and I even met? I heard him say, not to me, but to someone

266

beside him, there'd been murder in his family. Way back, way back, I think he said.

He said that?

Well, it's the kind of thing you forget. I overheard it; it wasn't for me. But the kind of thing you sort of remember too. I thought maybe he was just ... putting it on, you know what I mean? The impression I had ... Honestly, Catherine, I've never deliberately kept this a secret.

Did it sound like a joke?

I'm not sure. I can't really recall. The impression I had was he told the guy beside him as some sort of comfort. Maybe the guy had something bad he was dealing with. Yeah, I think he meant it as some kind of encouragement.

Some encouragement, that's all I can say.

After Jim was asleep, for real this time, I found myself crying. Silently. Not even sure for which aspect of remembering and knowing in particular. The sum of it, I suppose. The groundwater of my soul rising and spilling over.

26.

Several days later, I set the envelope on my mother's wheelchair tray. She showed no recognition of it.

The papers from Uncle Must, I said. You loaned them to me.

Oh, yes. Mom glanced at her wardrobe where the lock drawer with her box of memorabilia was stored and then at the envelope. A flicker of regret? But she brightened, asked, So, what did you learn?

I learned that my great-grandfather murdered my great-grandmother. *Hat ihr totgeschlagen,* as the German puts it. Slaughtered her. With a ploughshare. After which he strolled off to church with my grandmother, who was ten years old at the time. While his wife was dead. There was no information, however, about the songs or sermon in the service that morning.

My viciousness had confused her.

Sorry, Mom, I said, sitting down on the bed. I felt myself close to tears. It's just alarming to realize I've never known this before.

Oh. Oh, yes. We didn't mention it?

I think I'd remember an incident like that.

I'm so forgetful, Catherine. It's like my head is wool.

But Mom, you knew what happened and you never told me!

Mom was working her pale trembling hand diagonally over the black tray that held her in, plucking at it as though she'd spotted crumbs. Yes, she said. That's true. I didn't really want you to know … Maybe he told us not to tell you. Maybe we told him not to—

I sighed. I was teary and bitchy and not enjoying either. I said, I'm a long, long time away from my childhood, Mom.

I didn't know either. Not 'til Jake and I married. But I would have married him anyway. I wouldn't have changed my mind.

This mother of mine, this Edna Riediger, bending lower, still picking at the tray. When she raised her head, her eyes flashed. Blue-green and glowing, those eyes, and then they narrowed. You're not writing about this, are you, Catherine? We're not famous or anything, you know.

I'm *not* writing, Mom.

You've written!

A couple of research pieces for online encyclopedias. At work. I'm retired.

That's what I mean. He's not famous and neither are we. *Are we?*

Celebrity magazines found their way into my mother's room, brought to Maplebend by staff or visitors, magazines she disdained but read. I feel so sorry for them, she would say, meaning the beautiful people featured in their articles. Everyone knowing their business. How humiliating it must be!

We're not famous and I'm not writing. But didn't you think it important for *me* to know, it being my family and all?

You were a sensitive girl. Very sensitive. Mom gazed out the window, kept gazing as if she'd escaped. I couldn't tell if her posture was resistance or reverie.

Then she was back. You had a wonderful childhood, didn't you, Catherine?

I understand that you wanted to protect me, Mom. But it's been decades since I was a girl.

But now you know.

Now I know.

We both know, she said.

This seemed impasse rather than triumph. So, did it bother Dad? I asked.

No. It was all jammed up in your uncle. Like he'd been there himself.

Mom wouldn't stop fidgeting. He was attached to his mother, she said. Something was wrong with her. Jake couldn't even put a face to his mother.

The woman in the photo, Elizabeth Penner Riediger, the maid who won a son of the manor, the woman I was said to resemble. *Something wrong with her.* All that time, my parents' knowledge of that.

Mom pulled the envelope to the middle of her tray. Bad blood, she said, her palm smoothing it as in caress. Though Jake never liked to hear me talk that way.

You didn't want me to know.

If you were a mother you would realize you can't fix everything that's wrong! Whatever it is you need so many papers for. Whatever it is you do.

There was no answer for this except for me to sigh again.

She lifted the flap of the thin packet, but dropped it. I'll take a look at it later, she said. But maybe I'll throw it all away.

Sure.

Sure?

Sure.

Would it have made a difference? she begged.

I think so.

No, she said firmly. You would have been frightened. She directed her attention to the window again, to her vista of parking lot asphalt, cars, trees still bare of leaves.

Then her head darted round. Would you like to curl my hair?

Mom enjoyed fuss over her hair, but I knew she wished to placate me.

What happened to the great-grandfather? I said. The murderer?

Oh Catherine. They took him away. The police I guess, whatever kind of police they had there then, and he was never heard of again. Come, come, Catherine—she tapped her tray—let's curl my hair.

I fetched a curling iron from the hairdresser's room down the hall. It was the back that needed attention. Mom could spend an hour with the hairdresser, get the works—shampoo, cut, and perm—and an hour later she would lie down for a nap and the lovely do, like a cardboard box pushed out of whack, flattened. It seldom recuperated.

I curled it slowly, one small segment at a time. Her hair was still thick silk between my fingers. She humoured me along with instructions in a girlish voice. Not to set her head on fire. Not to poof it out too big. Not to make her so beautiful the others wouldn't know who she was.

When there was nothing left to curl and she was combed and fluffed, I bent from behind her and rubbed my cheek against hers. I wanted to say that I loved her in spite of everything, but my mouth was too cramped with sentiment to speak. I rubbed again and she purred with delight.

Later that week, my mother greeted me with a white garbage bag on her tray. She held it open for me to peer inside. The bag rustled because of her shaking, but she managed to keep it apart long enough for me to glimpse paper squares, a heap of them, each about the size of a stamp. I spotted traces of familiar writing. The contents of the *Von Gerhard* envelope.

I told you I'd get rid of it, she said.

That must have taken you a good long time.

Yes.

She seemed deflated; she must have prepared herself for indignation. But I kept the photos, she hurried on. I want you to put them with my albums … Lorena can't read German. I can barely read it myself.

I took German as my university minor.

Well, you've read all this already, so—

Right.

You were smart. Always good at school.

Mom pushed the bag my way and I knotted and dropped it in the garbage receptacle. Fluffy, light, nimble it landed, when it should have registered like rocks.

Jake won't mind. He's the one who saved the letters and everything. But he's not here anymore to read them.

True.

I don't know why, but he liked to read them … But I don't like the way your uncle talks in there, as if he took care of my Jake. We took care of *him*. In Tilia, we took care of *Uncle*.

True, I repeated. I seated myself on the bed. I'd wouldn't mention the fragment in Darrell's hand, on the back of the receipt. I suspected she didn't know that Uncle revealed the family secret to her son.

But he could make people listen when he put it nicely, she was saying. When he and Jake talked together it was nice and plain.

I'm glad they took care of each other.

If you were a mother, you would know … you can't just change things. Fix things. You can't … well, whatever it is you do with papers. I only kept them for Jake.

Yes, you said that the other day.

I'm sorry, Catherine. Mom lifted a hand and wormed her fingers through her hair as if she wanted it curled again. I'm sorry. I shouldn't have torn ... I promise I won't do it again.

It's done. Just don't go tearing up anything else, okay?

No. No, I won't.

Such tiny pieces, I said. I've got to give you credit.

The hardest part is trying to get anything done around here! All these bitties looking over my shoulder. Did they call you?

Safe this time. No calls.

One or two younger ones, they let you do what you want. One of them brought me scissors. As if I can hold scissors!

It was a project, then.

Always, come and play games, come and pet the animals, come and fold facecloths! I said, No, thank you, please fold the facecloths yourselves.

I laughed. Way to go, Mom.

But what a seesaw the two of us could be! I wouldn't tell her either why I was relaxed about this disposal, wouldn't tell her that what she'd painstakingly torn into bits were copies, that the originals were safe. Inside a protective folder in one of her photo albums at our apartment. Even the photos I returned to her were copies. Technology being what it is, I didn't think my mother would notice the difference and clearly she hadn't. Mom thought she'd finally dispensed with the family's worst story, while I had stored it away.

27.

I asked Jim if it mattered that there was a murderer in my family tree. He said, No, it didn't make an iota of difference. But a few minutes later he said, ever so casually, Perhaps we won't need to go blabbing it though. There's no reason for it to get around to the Reimers.

Are you saying I blabber?

I'm not saying that! His voice a splash of heat.

I asked Lorena if it mattered. I'd called her to see if it suited for me to drop by, and yes, it did, and my sister was pleased. I brought the originals of our uncle's letters, the newspaper clipping, the translations that pertained to him. Lorena set coffee and brownies into the sunny alcove beside the kitchen. Her house had the fresh, smug smell of regular visits from Molly Maid and of course she looked beautiful and perfectly put together. The white blouse and jeans duo again, accessories lavender. I wondered if the past months of retirement and remembering had etched themselves into my face. But I'd taken some care with my makeup that morning, had flung on my well-honed perkiness too, even entertaining Lorena a while before getting to the reason for my visit. I told her that when I was a teen, my friends and I wore girdles. I was girdled probably four or five years, I said.

Lorena had heard of girdles and looked at me with terrified admiration.

Actually, it felt rather good to be tucked in and flattened, I said. And a special kind of thrill to take the thing off.

Which led us to beehive hairdos, how even Mom became a backcombing pro, and to hot pants and bell bottoms, which my sister vaguely recalled, and we drank our coffee and amused and animated ourselves by reciting outfits we'd worn in the past. Lorena, I said, patting brownie crumbs onto my finger, when I'm very old, older than now and in a nursing home like Mom, please, please, *please* tweeze out my chin hairs and clip the ones that sprout from my nose. Promise?

Lorena laughed so hard. She thought it a joke. Catherine, of course! As if you'll be growing chin hairs.

I think every woman does, eventually, I said. It's a reward for not menstruating.

Lorena exclaimed that I was crazy and a lot of fun. So I opened my bag onto the table and explained about the letters and the newspaper clipping, as nonchalantly as I could, as if the papers were nothing more than distant relatives of beehives and backcombing.

But, of course, Lorena heard exactly what I'd said. Are you kidding me, Catherine? Her round eyes tightened, her eye shadow shimmering gold in the light.

Well, it's long gone. Dad had no memory of his mother. I guess he wasn't thinking of it all that much.

I hardly know anything about our family history.

But do you think it matters? This murder?

No.

But a few seconds later she said, I don't think we have to bother Roger with it though.

So much for that, then. It didn't matter, husband and sister said, but let's not tell the Reimers or Roger.

So it mattered.

But, I insisted on insisting to myself, it *doesn't* matter. It would not. I could scarcely believe my own freedom in this turn of events; me, who'd always been so ashamed of things about us like Uncle Must, then Darrell's illness and death. Something even worse known now, but also as if, in spite of grief, I was lighter. I wasn't sure why, except for looking straight on, discovering myself not overpowered. I remembered the Australian couple, the musicality in *scoundrel* and *convict*. Well, why not in *murderer* too? In *odd uncle*? I would have to practice saying my own genealogical truth, just in case. The way Jim practiced his lines. Weave acceptance in, maybe even pride, like that woman did. Or encouragement, like Darrell had, in the conversation Jim claimed he'd overheard.

I insisted it no longer mattered because it mattered too much to my uncle. I understood that now. A skewed view of women, fear, patriarchal pain. His tenderness to his mother, yes, their bond, but females of other kinds with their real-time bodies requiring, it seemed, repudiation or his help. Always guarded, scurrying then like a night bug exposed to the light. Which had, in turn, affected me.

Though maybe even in those years I'd been stronger, less affected than I realized. I remembered another kitchen scene: dishes done, my parents and uncle drinking their weak evening coffee, me busy with homework. My Grade Twelve year. I noticed they were discussing my plans to attend the Mennonite college that fall. As if I wasn't even there. Uncle Must, who bought us books, magazines, a piano, raising a question about the money involved. Whether I needed to go. The table oilcloth was blue and white squares, white maple leaves inside the blue, and I kept my head down but stopped writing, I traced the leaves in a square with the eraser of my pencil. It had to do with me being a girl, something about females and prohibitions and courses in theology. For me, female child of Jake and Edna Riediger. Uncle had connected these dots because it was what the church said, too. Dad said, Well, I think she'll go, we've decided that much. She's an excellent student, you know, and another year of schooling might be nice for her. Uncle grunted as if this wasn't reason enough. I hunched lower, though it seemed to make no difference, me being at the table or not. Apparently, a question like this—the so-called *woman's issue*, referring to a woman's role not only in the home but in congregational life, traditional subordination in both spheres now being challenged by the wider culture's push for equality—could be freely discussed in front of the very people it affected. As if the affected ones were—in their deepest souls—also men, thus able to be drawn objectively to interesting philosophical and restrictive theological considerations about themselves. As if it was a question of how many cherubs could dance on the head of a pin.

They supposed I was concentrating on homework. I was an excellent student, as my father said. Lorena shrieked from upstairs about something, but Mom stayed at the table to offer her opinion. She described the impact of an educated woman in the home: I would be a better mother, wife, that sort of thing. Or maybe a missionary. Which I'd already informed my mother was not where I was headed. But a word that would appeal to Uncle Must. He said, She's a girl. Mom rose and flew impatiently up the stairs because Lorena would not be quiet. Dad said, Brother. Firmly, respectfully as always. I started round the maple leaf again.

What happened next? I can't remember. Scenario One: nothing

happened. Scenario Two: I got up and said, I'm going! What difference does it make, being a girl? I said this to the yellow-lidded
canisters on the kitchen counter, gathered my books, exited. Scenario Three: So I'm a girl! I'm going! Tough beans! And looking at
Uncle Must, daring him to look back, and he did. The first time I'd
really looked at him since he moved in. Playing chicken with my
stare and he looked away first.

28.

Jim's news troubled him, though he would never put it that way. We were celebrating with pizza at Earl's and since it was his news, he got to choose the toppings: Italian sausage, green peppers, onions, a double load of olives. The school division's budget was reduced and priorities had to be adjusted, which meant his contract was finished in June and there wouldn't be another. He was done for good. Brave noises all this term, fortifying himself against their pleas for him to continue, pleas that both of us knew he could not have withstood. He needed his work, needed it absolutely, his work of training younger teachers, stepping in to conduct, inspiring teenagers with a song. A beautiful addiction, perhaps, and he was disinclined to give it up. He thought of himself as indispensable. Though he would never put it that way either.

No pleading, no decision to make.

His colleagues assumed he was glad. He acted glad, so they

envied him. I was certainly glad. I bent toward him with my full attention and my slice of pizza loaded with olives, trying to keep myself between the lines of his stated relief and his unstated disappointment. Trying to say the right things, in the right tone, though a group of party kids had taken over the tables next to us and it was difficult to converse in the high-pitched ambience of the restaurant. We leaned in further.

I said, It's our chance to be retired together.

Yes. Yes. Retired together.

You make that sound as appealing as liver, Jim. You know how many ideas we've had. Travel. Volunteering. Now we can plan.

I mean the *retired together*. Like kids holding hands and skipping through a dandelion patch.

More like you taking my place at the thrift store! Hey, you can write a song about secondhand goods, start a choir! The Thrift Store Troubadours!

This drew a smile and I rattled on, reminding him of the fabulous dinner and toasts when he first retired, before he'd jumped like a man at sea onto the raft of his contract.

I said, You were praised to high heaven.

It was humbling.

You know how often we bump into your former students, I continued. When we're not bumping into relatives of yours, that is. They see you and they make a beeline. The air of the long-lost lover about them. As if all will be set to rights by telling you what you meant to them. To declare once and for all what you ignited and how it still burns. I'm almost bitter, Jim, these grown kids asserting how useful your life has been.

I expected him to laugh but he didn't. He said, The entire meaning of what I did with them was love. It's been rewarding to watch it come around.

Well, I used to get shivers when I heard your students sing.

I've had a fulfilling career, he said. He took an enormous bite and the cheese stretched and dangled behind it. He tore at it with his fingers and tucked it into his mouth, the gesture as elegant as his conducting. Though all I really wanted, he said, wanted at the beginning, at least, was to sing. Myself.

I knew this about Jim. He wasn't regretting his life, but neither did he get what he'd wished for. His father was choir director in their Fraser Valley church and keen on the new ideas coming from the Mennonite college music departments: the splendid chorales and oratorios. His children got the solo parts; they were the best singers—that's all there was to it. And Jim only nineteen when he sang his first one. His father had combined local choirs and instrumentalists to perform Handel's *Messiah* at Christmas. Jim was away at college but arrived home for the holiday break just in time to be tenor soloist. His the first voice after the symphonic introduction, the *Comfort ye, comfort ye my people*. His father had instructed him to enter his lines with a mother's tenderness and a father's strength. Jim had been shaking with nerves and wondered how in the world he would bring those qualities together. Then he landed the first note, dead on and with feeling, and then it was like he was high on a line, and he could have stayed up there forever.

Years later, listening to a tape of that performance, Jim heard his youthfulness, heard the flaws, but was surprised and gratified to hear how good a debut it had been. He'd sung his way smoothly from the recitative to the aria. He'd managed with considerable assurance the long, upward climb of notes in *Ev'ry valley shall be exalted.* And he'd never forgotten being conducted by his father, as close as the tip of the older man's fingers, and how his father met his eye and bowed slightly when he finished. In approval and gratitude.

I touched Jim's arm with my free hand, intending to rest it there but a whoop erupted at the party table, raucous laughter in its wake like a wave crashing; it broke the impulse and I withdrew my hand.

I'll be fine, he said. I know I will.

Of course. I was imagining the disappointment, the fear. Thinking I saw inside him after thirty-six years. He had the school year to finish and the consolation of his various extracurricular choir involvements down the road. He felt at home in the big compositions, the oratorios, operas, requiems. The oratorios, especially. Instead of talking about his feelings, Jim lowered his life into the stories those pieces told and the visceral conduit of the music. Never mind that we've heard them before, he told me once, meaning the texts upon which the works were based; we haven't experienced them like this. When he introduced his new student classes to a love song, he would ask, How many love songs exist in the world? When they guessed, he said he didn't know either but it must be thousands and thousands by now. But had they ever heard love sung *this* particular way?

The party beside us seemed unlikely to subside any time soon. It was good-natured noise, but what was the point of eating out if you couldn't speak without shouting? Let's ask for the rest of this to go, Jim said. Eat it somewhere else.

We walked down York Avenue and he reached for my hand. He held the box with our half-eaten pizza on his other palm like a waiter's tray.

An April evening, still light, the temperature mild. Spring enlarging in the air like lungs functioning well again after congestion. The trees, though bare, seemed a-stir, their barky surfaces luminous. One of these days, mid-May perhaps, I would open the drapes and realize the city below me was green. Hey, I would cry, a city of trees! Just like they say! I'd exclaimed this when we moved into the apartment and I intended to exclaim it again. How astonished I'd been at the sudden solidity of colour, as if green were a ground creature that crept in overnight, lined the riverbanks, filled every available crack and crevice, not tentative at all but bold. Saving us from despair.

A red car, one of those so-called muscle cars, roared past, the entire vehicle wailing and pounding with a song. Something Dylan-esque. Darrell had been a passionate fan, though he made fun of the voice, called him the nasal prophet. And Jim, when we started to date, apologetic—*I can't listen to the man*—but then listening anyway, *selectively*, he'd said, for me, because I followed my brother in matters of music and liked the nasal prophet too. The wheeze of the harmonica, that emotional tug. Jim, I'd informed him, as if it proved musical kinship, you and Dylan have the same woolly hair!

Now I said, You and Darrell would have been good friends.

You've said that before.

I know.

I was repeating myself those days. Repetition seemed the only erudition I had left. Darrell had tried to learn Dylan's "It's All Over Now, Baby Blue," and it drove me nuts, as we used to say. He wasn't getting it right and every line had to be tried over and over, discordant in the room, his efforts reaching me in the intervals of the piano piece I was practicing. I finally yelled from the living room, couldn't he shush already or go learn it in the barn?

You go practice in the barn!

Like I can carry the piano!

Mom heard us arguing and closed the door between us. Closed it on me like a rebuttal, willing to put up with Darrell's plunking and twanging in the kitchen.

Why *not* repeat it, though, the likelihood of a friendship between my husband and my brother? Even if it never existed, even if assertions of probability—Bach meets The Beatles *et al.*, compliments all round, Jim's kindness in considering the tastes of his friends—was the extent of what they'd ever had between them. That, and one meeting in some bar or café. Hearing him confide there'd been a murder in the family and promptly forgetting it because it seemed a supportive or inconsequential fiction.

We turned on Waterfront Drive toward the Forks, past the scrape and clatter of wheels and boards at the skateboard park, the grunts and hollers of the skaters. But Jim met him also at The Mental; we'd visited Darrell a week before our wedding. It seemed a ritual we had to perform, an enacted fact about me that I wanted my soon-to-be partner to be sure of beyond what I'd told him, how my brother had disappeared behind the blank mask of his face. As if to confirm *for better or for worse*. We found ourselves in an empty visitors' room, a windowless space with grey-green walls and firm beige chairs.

More memorable than the visit was the exhilaration I felt when it ended. We exited that brick building into broad sunshine and then we were tripping down the steps and through the grounds to where we'd parked. I'd been thrilled with Jim's ease, how he announced, I'm going to marry your sister, and not flinched when Darrell stuck out his tongue. Nothing to do with us, Jim said later. *Us* was the two of us doing our duty and now our duty was done.

I think he recognized you, Jim had told me as we'd burst into the sunshine. I thought I saw a glimmer of something when you first said Hello. When you said his name.

I doubt it.

It wasn't worth the speculation. Jim wished to console me—I don't think I'll ever get over what he might have been, I'd said earlier, driving to the facility—and he saw what he hoped for. And that was the end of it. He'd wrapped his arm around my waist and I did the same to his, which made for awkward walking, but we got to his car in the hospital parking lot and then we necked a while in the midday heat.

Now we were strolling from Earl's to the Forks in a comfortable long-marriage silence. Our hands slid apart. Still, I was alert to him, thinking my husband more alert than usual as well, not to me but to our surroundings. He turned his head to this, to that; he held the view for more than a passing moment. The human rights museum under construction, the Gandhi statue, the skate park, the car park, the multi-coloured Theatre for Young People. We'd often walked to the Forks but Jim seemed wide-eyed now, as if the drastic termination of his working life finally booted him into an awareness of where he lived.

We sat on a bench at the Forks plaza and finished the pizza. Last bites, fingers licked, box closed. I wanted to grab and kiss him—my balding, so-often-elsewhere Jim. But he would be embarrassed and he was still somewhat watchful of me. Especially after I'd confessed my grief to him, grief I'd not worked through the stages of, whatever the stages were supposed to be. And Uncle coming alive to me in his various guises: the uptight zealot, the hard-working and compulsive sun-browned farmer, or—sometimes, now—the shadowy, stooped figure too much possessed and shattered by the shattering of his mother. Who merited pity. Condolences. Someone with a rather nice way with words. I mean the phrases in his letters to Jake, not the diatribes. *The crops are kind to me.* And, *the sea a field in furrows, seeds of tribulation in all the rows.*

Seeing too how beset with moderation I'd always been, governed by fear. My ancient angers, the self-pity, the sly, ongoing envy of Darrell who shouldered into the world ahead of me, stating he couldn't hang around the ilk of this old man and his compunctions—and yet, oh lands and oh bother, there was something about those two, as if they were joined at the hip. Uncle Must the *Russlander*, the immigrant foreigner. (Forever immigrant, even though he devoured the English language because he believed he should—and maybe because of Mom, who was a generation beyond a comfortable use of German.) While Darrell tootled off to be American, bold and dogmatic, a here-I-am hero for the turbulence of their race relations and wars and worldwide messes. Their consciousness-raising bravado. An Icarus, wanting to fly.

And me? Canadian. Literally and metaphorically. In between the powers, trying to survive.

Jim asked if I wanted an ice-cream for dessert and I said no, but when he bought himself a double maple walnut I was sorry about this decision and he chuckled and let me eat from his. We walked to the former rail bridge, a public walkway now with a view of the merging Red and Assiniboine Rivers. We propped our elbows on the railing and discussed the weeks ahead: the symphony and choir performance, my road trip to Tilia, his chance to attend the U2 concert because a friend's wife was going out of town and her ticket was available. Jim might be devoted to the classical repertoire, but he'd latched onto U2, The Beatles, and Van Morrison as well. He told me he would surprise me with a holiday when his school year was done; the details would be ready when I returned from my excursion to Alberta. A holiday, he said, in which we would sit in our holiday chairs with our holiday drinks and our holiday notebook to holiday brainstorm and dream.

Maybe this no-more-contracts business wasn't as hard on him as I thought. Maybe relief was spreading through him too, the way it spread through me. Like the feeling one got after bending to a garden or computer all day and then lying flat on a bed, every muscle sinking blissfully to rest.

Then he said, Actually, I've got an idea already. I've been thinking about it a lot. I'm petrified to mention it though.

Well, that's not fair. Just out with it.

BC, he said. Moving to the Fraser Valley.

I couldn't speak. Jim gripped the railing with his hands and started rocking backward. He said, All my family's there and I know they're a crowd but it was Randy who brought it up. He really wants me to come. I think I'd like to, you know, give it a try. We could rent, like now. Keep two places if you like.

Objections in me like a scattering of ants when lifting a rock above their trailways. My aging mother. Looking out at mountains instead of down across flats. West Coast brashness and bleached hair and piety I'd never been able to match. Cascadia like another planet altogether. Rivers white and green and wild instead of taciturn and brown. The claustrophobia of damp and pine.

A train pulled into the station on a long note of screeching brakes. Jim winced until it stopped. I pointed to the sky, primrose, delicate, a swath of clouds incongruently dense and dark and piling against it, apprehensive. I pointed as if it was my last big sky, as if already in BC and inscribing what I would miss. But the idea spun. It fascinated and compelled. My objections slunk down patiently as if willing to be overtaken.

That's an interesting idea, I said.

Really?

Well, you brought it up.

But I mean ...

I'd be up for considering it, that's what I'm saying.

That's good. I mean, it's not a decision. It's just something I've... We can take our time, think about it.

Not to be patronizing, Jim, but you'll soon have lots of time to think.

He laughed and made as if to give me a shove.

The Red was covered in dirty ice but at the end of the Assiniboine, beneath us, spring melt had pooled over the docks, well up the steps to the Plaza. Beneath the dirty ice, beneath this clean white pool, the rivers flowed, but the pond that formed seemed stable and serene. It pulled the grey clouds into itself and reflected there, they reclined, unworried and subdued.

29.

Sometimes a possibility presents itself and you remember it's what you wished for earlier. I'd found myself wandering downtown into the mall and other stores on my walks that spring. I seldom shop for recreation but there I was, idly perusing racks of garments, sometimes making a purchase or two. It seemed as if the revelation of my grandmother's story in the brown envelope had changed me enough to require new clothes.

When I stepped up to pay for the cerise and white scarf I still love and often wear, the woman at the desk so resembled Sharon Miller of my Tilia days I nearly burst out with a greeting and her name. No, no, it wasn't her, but then I remembered I'd been told she moved to Winnipeg sometime around Uncle Must's death. Could she still be in the city?

It wasn't hard to find her number as her name was the same, and when I called and explained who I was, there was only the tiniest pause at the other end before she said she remembered me well and told me to call her Sharon, please, none of this Miss Miller business though she still went by Miller, had never given it up though she married several times—married, she laughed, in a manner of speaking. Then she asked how my piano playing was going and I thought of my performances for Mom at the seniors' home and said it was going well. I didn't elaborate because Sharon Miller had taken over the conversation; it was getting away on me already and I had questions to ask.

After all these years, she said, what a remarkable coincidence. She invited me for coffee. The next afternoon found me at her apartment, not far away, in one of the older blocks south of Broadway. Her place was as dim as the hallway, her drapes completely shut. She left me in the doorway while she opened them. The room was cast into light and I walked in as if drawn on a cord. I saw clutter everywhere, and most mystifying, a blender standing between the piles on the coffee table, its cord tangled and mounds of orange peel and strawberry stems around the base.

Sharon cleared a spot for me on the sofa and gestured me into it while sitting down on a hard-backed chair, the coffee table and blender between us. She explained that she whipped up fruit drinks for breakfast every day; she liked to overdose on fruit-based vitamins, she said, and got tired standing at the counter. She had trouble with her knees. I spotted an extension cord for the appliance under a chair.

We were assessing one another, declaring the other looking good, just lovely, unchanged, etc. And in a way it was true. We were merely older, though Sharon's love of the sun, those hours outside Uncle Must's house in a bikini, that squinting toward the road in midday heat, had certainly called in its dues, her fair skin blotchy with age and sun spots. Lines radiated from her eyes and mouth. She'd definitely put on weight and the marshmallowy softness into which her body had progressed distressed me. It wasn't the weight but the confusion of my recollections that I feared, the loss of the woman's earlier, sharper edges as I'd remembered them.

Well, Sharon said, you look terrific. She got up and put into my hand—without asking—a can of cola. As if I was still in high school and would like it. As if the coffee in the invitation was meant for someone else.

I calculated her age. She'd been in her late twenties when she appeared at Uncle Must's, pregnant; I was fifteen. Which meant early seventies now. The years between us had seemed an insurmountable gap at the time but now the gap had closed. I had, in fact, the curious impression of reversal, of being older than Sharon, not in appearance but in our relative positions. I'd been thinking about her these months, thinking of her as she'd been, holding her in my mind like a portrait while replaying my own life from a position long hence. I felt I'd surpassed her. Felt strong enough, at any rate, to interrogate her, even with a cola in my hand.

Sharon Miller updated me on her life. After she left Tilia, she stayed with relatives in Calgary, then moved to Edmonton, then back to Calgary, and then to Gilly Lake, which, she informed me as if I wouldn't know, was a town in northern Manitoba. She'd taken up with a miner. Later, she followed an old boyfriend to Winnipeg, though she didn't mean the miner, who died in an accident. There were no children besides Ricky, who managed a computer store in Hamilton, Ontario and had turned out better than she'd ever dared to hope, considering what he got into for a while. She had grandchildren, she said, though I saw no framed photos of them. I wanted a look but wouldn't ask; I knew how talk was apt to roam and expand when grandchildren were the subject and then, the time wasted, Sharon might find some excuse to get me out of her place before I'd covered what suddenly seemed critical for me, all the questions that had built up while remembering.

I held my drink unopened. At forty, I'd weaned myself off soda pop, to which I was mildly addicted. Since then, I found it nearly impossible to drink the stuff without shuddering. But I didn't want to offend so I lifted the metal tab, pushed it carefully in and back, took a sip. Not bad. And maybe it helped. I felt intrepid.

Did you quit smoking? I asked.

Of course I did, she laughed. Where do you think I got the tonnage? I'd love to say the craving's gone in answer to prayer, which a certain uncle of yours suggested, but no, not so. But yes, I've quit. Doctor's orders.

Sharon, I said, the name alien on my tongue. Sharon, I repeated, speaking of a certain uncle … well, it was peculiar to us, to me at least, how you showed up at his doorstep out of nowhere, without warning, then stayed for years. I never really understood … How did it come about?

Sharon Miller appeared fascinated by the question. She regarded me with the coy self-importance an interviewee might give a researcher and then her round face puckered inward along its lines, her mouth a gleam of still-excellent teeth, and she made a humming sound in her throat as if she'd pulled a lucky card, which she would be honoured to expound. But not until she'd risen to get a cola for herself. Not until she returned, opened the can, drank at length.

My boyfriend Fred and I had a fight on the way from Calgary to Red Deer, she finally said, and I remembered this man I once met, who'd given me his address. I knew he was living off the highway between those places. So we more or less broke up in the car and I told Fred to drop me there. I said I never wanted to see him again. He was tired of me too, I guess, and he wasn't a bad fellow actually, just bull-headed, so he took me there to be rid of me, and that was it. I crashed the poor man—your uncle—but he was so terrified, his conscience and all, so flabbergasted, really, to be alone with me, he rushed off. Up to your place. I felt rather abandoned, me a guest and him running off, but I thought the house was adorable so I made myself at home.

But how did you find the place? It was pouring. It's not like we had house numbers in the country.

I'd gone out driving one time. I took Fred's car, after a different fight. I found where he lived. George Riediger. I know you called him Uncle Must. I knocked and he was home but he told me I couldn't come in. It was summer, warm out, so what excuse could I possibly come up with? I couldn't think of one so I left. But I'd memorized the route.

Sharon Miller gulped at her drink and I drew gingerly at mine. But how did you know him in the first place? I asked

Well, she said, looking girlishly flirtatious for a second, let's just say my cousin was running ... oh, let's call it a brothel of sorts, but very casual, very occasional. She had connections to a few rural folks, a few men, you know, who might like a little recreation on their trips into town. All discreet, you know. Just a few. We used to laugh that we were improving things for their wives, and I don't mean taking the pressure off. We taught them a little tenderness, frankly. A gesture here, a technique there. So I imagine there was a farmer or two from Tilia or thereabouts and I imagine one of them teased your uncle George, pushed the address at him, maybe mentioning the kind of women we were. Not that we really were whatever he probably called us, but I'm sure he used some word that brought up your uncle's sense of obligation. So he came by, and I drew him.

He came by?

Came by *once*, she said tartly. You don't need to do a double take or revise the list of your uncle's virtues. I know as well as you, maybe even better, how rigid and righteous he was. How good. A little drafty but—

Daft, you mean?

Sharon paused to consider this. Well, she said, you were the smart one, so you say daft, I say drafty. Some of the chinks in the wall not closed, if you get my point.

I took another tiny sip of cola, thought Sharon Miller a little drafty herself.

So he drove up in that truck of his, she carried on, that big rattle trap, and the four of us who lived in the house were enjoying a quiet Sunday afternoon and we saw it stop, and him getting out, touching the hood as he came round it, scared, obviously, and my cousin who owned the place said, Looks like a needy one. We were all sputtering. None of us wanted to fiddle with the guy, and then the doorbell rang and she said, I've got a number between one and ten, person closest has to take him. So I picked seven, and wouldn't you know it was seven, though I saw something pass between her and her sister and it dawned on me, clear as a light coming on, it would have been me, no matter what number I picked, so I was in a bad mood toward her and it made me kinder toward him, if you know what I mean. A sort of revenge.

Sharon broke off and got up again. She moved, rather too deliberately it seemed, to the apartment window. She peered out as if expecting someone in a truck, then dawdled back to her chair. Her tortoise motions seemed a subterfuge and I took another tiny-but-impatient sip.

Is it too much? my hostess asked.

Too much answer to my question, you mean? No. Not that it's that important. It wasn't the greatest, though, Uncle Must living with us. Because of you. I didn't much care for it, is what I'm saying.

Can't have been easy, the other woman agreed. She looked pensive. Like she was recalling the benefits of rural life. Anyway, she said, I was telling you how we met. He was at the door and I answered and he wasn't looking at me or saying anything so I said, well come upstairs then and I gave a little signal to my cousin Jane. Sure, I was mad at her but I wanted to be safe, and it was the signal to check in twenty because I figured he might need some warming up.

Sharon tipped back her drink, swallowed, pressed her fingers against her lips while she burped. So, she said, he sat down on the bed. He asked me my name and for some reason I gave him my real one, even though we usually said false names, just in case, and I thought I knew what he'd come for, but absolutely nothing happened. I'll swear that on ten Bibles if you want. He held his hat in his hands and he was really agitated, I could see that, but his hat was in front of him, covering what might have given me some extra information, if you know what I mean, and so I sat down in the chair, and finally he said, Well, there must be something else you could do with yourself. His concern was quite touching, actually. He was as sad and stern as a man of the cloth. He said, Surely this wouldn't make your parents proud now, would it?

Sharon paused, drank again, went on. I finally asked if he'd come for some, you know ... some sexual engagement. I decided to be formal about it, polite, instead of using other words we had, and he said he couldn't, we weren't married and he'd decided he probably wouldn't marry me. He wanted to keep his passions under control and be good to women too. I nearly laughed when he said, Thank you anyway. And he took this big fat wallet out of his jacket and tried to give me, I kid you not, two crisp one-hundred-dollar bills. Which was serious money then. Serious money, I tell you, at least for me, used to minimum wage, which is why we girls did the occasional job like this on the side. You could get a meal for a buck or whatever back then, or a six pack. But I said, There's no charge for nothing so you might as well put that money back. He put the bills on the bed and said, Take it anyway, and do something better with your life, and the entire time he hadn't even looked at me. And he said, If you ever need help, here's the address. He put a square of paper on top of the bills. He'd written down directions. There was even a bit of a sketched-out map. So that's how I had it. He left and I hid the money and told my cousin nothing happened, which was the darn true fact of the matter, but

I didn't say he'd paid me. For the conversation, I guess. Though it was mostly me looking at him and him looking at the wallpaper. I had the feeling he'd decided to do this and I got lucky. So I came down and said, Nothing to it. Since it was her house and she had the contacts, she always got some of the take. She'd decided halves. There was no way I was going to give her half the money he'd put down on the bed. I was getting tired of the business anyway and now I had money to rent a place of my own and find a boyfriend. I remember I bought myself a suit. A creamy white suit. And I bought a pair of red heels and a red purse. I was a looker in that outfit, I tell you.

So he got you out of prostitution.

Prostitution! It was the sixties Calgary, Catherine, the suburbs! Not some bawdy house for sailors! We were poor, dumb broads with a little anonymous service going on, looking for husbands, actually, though I never seemed to find the ones that hadn't been to the altar already. We wanted to be housewives, if you can believe it. I worked at that Tilia café; you must remember that. I waitressed and worked in the kitchen all those years, darn long shifts to keep food on the table and clothes on Ricky's back. Legit-imate, back-breaking, low-paying work!

I remember you telling me you wanted to marry him.

Sharon Miller snorted. Well, he was single! And generous! He'd go in and pay my credit at the Co-op now and then. I have to admit, I envied your family. I was in my little place with Ricky and working at the café and all I wanted was to be a family like you folks up the lane. Kids playing games in the yard, sitting down for meals, piano music out the window. I'm a hopeless romantic, I really am. I loved the countryside out there.

I didn't plan to visit Sharon Miller again so I said, He lived in Gilly Lake so you must have followed him. How much money did you get out of him there?

Correction, Sharon said, it was he who followed me! Stalked

me, in a way, though I was never afraid. I'd see him at the weirdest times, wherever I lived. As if he just happened to be passing by. With that sideways look of his, never really looking, you know. But it wasn't by chance. I had a steady relationship there for a while, maybe the best I've had. The miner. Killed in a freak hunting accident. So I'd see him, maybe in the corner grocery store or on the street. More like a guardian angel than anything malicious. Out of sight but hovering, if you know what I mean. Not hovering like my mom, I have to say, who was always prying and peeking. God, that woman drove me straight out of her life.

He could be malicious with his opinions, I said.

Well, I don't know, I always thought he meant them well. Not that we really talked. I don't think we ever exchanged more than a few dozen words at a time. If that.

How much did he give you?

Sharon held my look and I held hers. You know, Catherine, she said, I never added it up. Let's say maybe five, ten thousand over the years.

He didn't have anything left at the end.

I got nothing at the end, if that's what you're implying! Not more than a couple hundred, at least. And you should ask your father how much he gave *him* over the years.

My father's dead.

I'm sorry. I liked him too. He wasn't drafty at all.

And how would *you* know how much he gave my father?

Sharon Miller smiled. I was irritated. I set the cola down. It was probably three-quarters full but I'd had enough.

He left me these crazy little notes sometimes, Sharon Miller said. Full of admonitions and advice a little stronger than the fact that whatever I was doing wouldn't make my parents proud, even though I'd told him they'd never been proud of me anyway. Plus, I was no longer in touch with them. Sometimes, just for fun, I called him Saint George—if I got within speaking distance of him, that is. But he didn't like to be teased. He was sharper on paper than in person, but he dropped in facts, like how much he'd sent his dearest brother Jake. And Edna. Come to think of it, he said he put you through college.

I nearly sprang from the sofa. I put myself through college! I declared. Though Darrell helped at the start. My uncle didn't even think I should go! Girls—

It's the impression I got, Sharon said calmly, so maddeningly calmly that I reached for my drink and managed another swallow.

There was a long silence between us as vigorous and tense as an argument. Then I remembered my uncle's letters and the news clipping, remembered what he'd absorbed and sustained. How that knowledge overlapped my sense of him now. The compassion I'd won. My brother's toxic overdose and death. The room stilled and the square of brightness from the window seemed to retreat; seemed unperturbed and peaceful. My desire to best the older woman faded.

But I am—was—an archivist so I asked Sharon Miller, hoping my voice, in the chaos of a room with a blender on the coffee table, would sound professional and detached, Do you still have the *crazy little notes*?

Gosh no! Who keeps stuff like that?

Not enough of us, obviously. But did he ever tell you things concerning his mother, or his grandparents?

No. What do you mean?

Nothing. Nothing in particular. Then my professionalism vanished. I asked, And did you play your little service games with Darrell?

Sharon got up and made her deliberate and maddening way to the window a second time. She responded from there, her back to me. You used to be the friendliest, she said. You used to be so awfully, goddamn courteous. Well-bred. She turned and faced me. You've gotten as pointed with your questions as your mother. I may have lied to her now and then, but I'm not lying to you.

He hung around your place at times and it occurred to me then. It occurs to me now.

Okay. Well, the answer is yes.

I'm sorry to hear it. I really am.

Sharon Miller sat down. Well, please don't worry about it, Catherine. And please don't blame me for seducing an innocent, either. He was of age. He was a beggar. He was like a stallion in spring.

This had definitely been enough, the cola, the conversation, the information. I'm sorry, I said again, though I meant the whole works, not just her and Darrell the stallion.

There was no money involved, if that helps, she said. Your uncle told me what happened to Darrell, by the way. Dying so young. Please accept my condolences.

Her sympathy seemed genuine so I thanked her, and for the drink. I stood to leave. Sharon walked me to the entry, said she had to keep moving, the doctor ordered it. You were all good people, she said.

I thanked her for that as well.

It was probably as much of an ending as could be expected, I thought as I walked home via the path along the river. It was a fine, crisp day. In spite of everything I'd learned, my spirit seemed an anchor, lowered and stable. Sharon Miller had illuminated the past, and muddled it, and then she said we were good people and I responded with thanks of my own, as if it was finally decided. I imagined her at the window now, looking out, then closing the drapes and letting her rooms slump peacefully into semi-darkness and an illusion of order.

30.

I left for Tilia close to nine. In Regina, six and a half hours west,
I stopped at a McDonalds. I ordered a Big Mac meal and choco-
late milkshake and debated with myself: should I find a hotel or
drive another hour or two to Moose Jaw, even on to Medicine
Hat? The trip had gone well so far and it felt imperative to make
the right decision.

But I'd forgotten everything I'd done along the way. Like Jim
would say, I entered the zen of the road. Listened to the radio, yes,
but what did I hear? Watched the road, the sky, the dip and rise
of the occasional hill, the flat plain and horizon, but what did I
see? Thinking, constantly thinking, but what were my thoughts?
The drive had been like a silent retreat, its quality of silence even
deeper than the quiet I lived with during solitary days in the
apartment. The consummate silence of motion, like the perfection of sphere and weight a bowling ball reaches when it's released

gently along a varnished hardwood lane, turning—the exquisite beauty of turning!—quietly onward. After we married, Jim and I bowled with friends every Saturday night, five pin, just for fun, and sometimes I released a ball extra slowly to watch it roll. Not trying to score. Jim and our friends would laugh at me, wasting my shot, but I didn't care, I wasn't competitive about the game. It was the marvel of the object itself, moving away from me until it fell at the end of the lane or tumbled into the gutter.

Did people still bowl? Jim and I hadn't gone for ages. Maybe we should take Jeffrey and Marcie bowling one of these days.

I liked driving and I liked eating in fast food restaurants. Jim felt I should be past their common flavours and bad nutrition— it's not as if you can't afford something better, he said—but I parked his judgment outside the doors of the ubiquitous establishments and ate in them anyway. Their inexpensive efficiency was my comfort, the recognizable tastes and calories ideal for the energy I need to keep shopping when I shopped, driving when I drove. I liked their busyness, their appeal to children, their bright, round-edged inner architecture, their mass-produced accessibility and sense of lower-middle-class life. I liked the anonymity they allowed: a meal on a tray, already paid for, and no one coming by to see how it tasted or if I desired to order anything more.

I was eating too quickly. I wanted to be pensive, to write. I thought of my brother the poet, of the absence of his poems. No last girlfriend to contact, no California address to pursue, no one to ask if perchance someone had saved his words. How in the world would one track a person named Happiness? I thought— how absurdly the mind leaps—of my parents' clock, the farewell gift from their Tilia friends. A cuckoo clock. The cockiness of that bird, intimations of dirndls, bulbous oom-pah-pahs, that heartiness, figures buxom or wide of girth. Like a gingerbread house, and the witch out of sight. I'd been home to Marble one weekend when Darrell was there on a pass from The Mental, drugged well enough to come for a visit, though not visiting as much as propelling our mother into a surfeit of affection that she expressed by baking. He had a galloping appetite for sweets. Mom knew they weren't good for him, but it was his only bliss, she would say as she plied him with more cookies, rolls, pieces of cake. Then I noticed his reaction to the cuckoo. He jerked and clutched himself when it popped out from the clock. I mentioned this to Mom, who was skeptical. But the next hour she watched him and it happened again. Then she cried; that's how much it bothered her that her son had been frightened by that silly bird.

Just stop the clock while he's at home, I suggested.

Oh, let's! What a good idea, Catherine. Time doesn't matter for him anyway. Mom stopped the cuckoo clock and it was never set going again.

I took the Moleskine and a pen out of my bag. I hadn't written poetry since composition class in high school but now, here, a blank page and something that seemed to be a poem came to me while I munched on my fries. I swallowed and wrote it down. Nine lines.

let's suppose—let's wish—that when the door opens
on the hour, no tiny wooden cuckoo appears but rather
a tree—let's say an apple tree with rosy red apples that
drop into my hand one at a time until I have enough for
a pie—let's say a gust of wind sighing your essence into
the room, and a sheaf of papers, and the noise of you, or,
best of all, let's say that when the door pops on the hour,
it's actually you—let's say you're twelve years old and
you're telling me a knock-knock joke—let's say that.

What I'd done was an unexpected thrill which I immediately wished to repeat. I sucked on my milkshake, waited for another idea, and it came: a memory of me and Jim travelling to my parents' house on the Labour Day weekend years ago, fields of grain along the highway as harvest-brown as bread, a reminder of my brother.

driving to Marble, we noticed that the wheat was ripe,
so hot-wavy-golden it seemed baked into loaves fresh
from the oven and then I remembered the day you put
your face into the crust piece Mom had sliced for you,
and you said, Crisp on one side, soft on the other, and
you also said, It's fragrant—fragrant, you said, the
word hot-wavy in the kitchen, and you held the piece
of bread and moaned with satisfaction like a bumper
crop you'd slathered with butter and strawberry jam.

I re-read the two poems. In the euphoria of their creation, I was astonished how much I liked them, even if my better wisdom told me they were unpolished and sentimental, kitschy, maybe like that Rod McKuen people quoted back in the seventies. But still, if I'd gained some understanding of my uncle stored on letters and a clipping my father saved, perhaps I could document—store—something of Darrell, too. Two sibling love poems like a memorial.

But wasn't it true that good things cluster in threes? I waited. A third poem—a nine-line hat trick—found its way onto another page.

poet, poet, poet, you declared, as if repeating the word
would make it true and permanent, while Mom and
Dad, proud of you as peacocks—though yours the bold,
bright plumage, the iridescence—murmured preacher,
preacher, preacher, surely you're called, they said, to be
a preacher, but your ears were closed to their wishes, their
hints and hopes, you didn't even listen while you scribbled

at the table, line after line, humming as you wrote the
sacred texts of your ambition, your eventual oblivion.

Poetically, I sensed deterioration but I had my three. My eyes welled with tears, my lips began to quiver. A boy at the table across from mine noticed and he grabbed his mother's arm and pointed and the young woman jumped up, whispered, Ma'am, are you all right? May I help you?

I smiled. Believe me, I was able to say, I'm fine. But thank you. The woman patted my shoulder, said she was glad to hear it and slipped back to her children while I packed my things, my milkshake finished, poems secured in my book.

I left the city. I was revived, energetic. *Westward-ho!* I decided to drive until I was tired, which might be a while because I was wide awake on account of the twenty-seven lines. I had no idea poets were privileged like this. That Darrell had been privileged like this. I could be bearing gold, frankincense, or myrrh as a companion of the Magi for all the secret rapture three poems had given me. Crossing deserts for them, I thought, re-reading and revising them nightly under the lamp of a star.

My mother had begged me to visit Samuel Bergen, the only person alive and still living in Tilia among the folks she and Dad kept up with after they moved. A lot of people left the area, a flood of them, she said, except that she and Dad went east to Manitoba and everyone else went west to British Columbia. The others figured BC was like heaven or something, because of the gorgeous flowers and spring blossoms and raining all the time instead of cold and snow. But the Bergens stayed. He's widowed now, she told me, and residing in Tilia's seniors' home.

By keeping up, she meant an exchange of Christmas cards. She'd stopped sending hers, though, when Samuel's missus died.

She didn't want him to get any ideas, what with Jake dead, too. But she insisted that I look him up. So here I was.

I hadn't noticed when I was young and living in Tilia how small of stature Samuel Bergen was, not that much taller than I. And I'd forgotten his strangely pale but avid eyes. The word *dapper* came to mind, though he certainly wasn't dressed that way. Tan polyester pants and a frayed button-up, V-neck sweater over a shirt. Typical seniors' home garb.

Mr. Bergen claimed he recalled me well—such a promising young woman, he said, and my parents, such good, good friends—though I couldn't picture him ever being in our house. He was talkative and I was favourably impressed by his alertness but downgraded my evaluation shortly after as I struggled to keep him on track in some form of mutual conversation. In the course of a great deal of rambling information about his late wife, his loneliness since her death, his distant children, and his pioneering days in Tilia—to hear him tell it, he more or less opened this part of the West by himself—he informed me that socially, my uncle George Riediger was nothing at all, but in terms of the farm, he was definitely the brains of the operation. He brought the money into it, too. If it hadn't been for my uncle, Samuel Bergen carried on innocently, merrily, as if we were fellow farmers at the grain elevator rehashing the price of oats, my father would have gone under. It was my uncle who had the knack for it, a knack some had and some didn't, and my uncle who'd known when to jump ship, and he'd done good, yes, he had, selling the place when he did. But Uncle never held it against his brother, Samuel Bergen said, *it* being Dad not having the knack, that is, nor the original money.

This comparison of the two, the nuance I wasn't expecting, chafed in me while Samuel Bergen flew off into praise for my father's many virtues—which apparently he possessed in spite of his knacklessness—though slipping these virtues to me through stories of his own successes, his Bergen-inherited flair for farming, getting into chickens at the right time and passing the enterprise on to his son. Unfortunately, the aforementioned son sold the chicken business without asking him first and barely recouped the investment. I was tempted to remark on his son's lack of knack, but I was still thinking about my dad, who always seemed so smart at what he did. I was thinking there must be some deeper intelligence about farming not obvious to children. And if it *was* true that my uncle was the better farmer, it was the reason, I supposed, why Mom had resented her brother-in-law on the one hand and put up with him on the other.

While my father knew *not a fig* about farming, Samuel Bergen pushed on blithely—imagining, perhaps, that once as old as I was, judgments about one's parents no longer affected a person—he was definitely mechanical. So the job in Marble was a much better fit. You could also say, the dapper old man proposed, that my father was a bookish man, though not bookish in the way my mother and we children were—The whole lot of you, he said, always reading something or other—but bookish as in interested in the wider world, and optimistic, too, and a decent preacher when his turn came round, which wasn't that often since he didn't care to be preaching. If a little too timid in the pulpit, he was thoughtful at least. Why, Samuel Bergen had never forgotten how my father brought John Glenn's orbit of earth into a sermon and in a positive way when many figured it foolish, so much money, wasted on a space endeavour, that could have been given to the poor. He remembered this because he held that opinion himself until my father's Glenn-commendation caused him to change his position. He was the kinder, easier man of the two, Samuel Bergen said. Everyone enjoyed your father.

This Samuel was a windbag, a scrambler, much too alert for me to endure much longer. He'd not yet hauled out sane or insane or their colloquial variants for my uncle and now I feared that he would, afraid he would carry on to Darrell, afraid he would say everyone in Tilia knew of the murderer in our family's tree. Yes, afraid, notwithstanding my resolution to be brave and face all that belonged to me.

I had a wonderful childhood here, I was finally able to interject, my voice loud. I'm so grateful to see you again and bring greetings from my mother. I said goodbye rapidly, three times, while backing away, faster backward than he was forward, and thus I exited the door of the Tilia seniors' home and hurried to the car.

I was saving the Big House for the following day so now I had time to drive around Tilia and area before heading to Summit, the nearest town with a motel, where I'd made a reservation for the night. So much for Samuel Bergen. But interesting, wasn't it, that my uncle the excellent farmer never farmed again after his brother was no longer beside him? Maybe I'd perceived something accurate about them after all, about who was strength and smarts for whom. Consider that, I could tell Samuel Bergen, though I wasn't about to go back and argue with him. I was distracted, almost tranquilized, by what surrounded me: orange-tinted light slanting from the west as if to shine a benevolent angle on my childhood here, and under it, the undulating earth, this enormous reality of space mostly absent of woods or other major impediments. Every farmstead had windbreaks, yes, and the sinuous creek bed was lined with bushes, but these were nicks upon the landscape, nothing essential, and the trees were still bare and see-through, spring less advanced here than in Manitoba. Brown and yellow tones, though green palpably close to the surface. Some fields had been ploughed and lay black to the sky. It was wonderful, this relief that my fond memories of the area were not exaggerated.

I halted a number of times to take photos for my mother, who'd been pleased about this trip. She thought it was for her sake and I let her believe it. But when we hugged goodbye, she clung to me and asked, shaking, Will I see you again? As if I was in greater danger of dying on the highway than in weekly trips across the city. I snapped views of aspen clumps in valley nooks, of the creek, now swift with thaw, and one shot after the other at various distances and perspectives of the decades-ago hamlet on the hill, grown in the meanwhile in all directions. I snapped like a hoarder who can't get enough, but when I reviewed the photos on my camera screen, I saw that I hadn't captured the place at all. The subtle shadings of the landscape seemed, via the eye of my camera, the leached tones of insipid old age.

The Summit hotel, dated but clean, soothed me and made me feel important as overnighting in hotels always does, the small rectangles of soap and bottles of shampoo, the very white towels, the slippery machine-quilted bedcovers in gold or wine or jade as passable imitations of brocade. When I paid money to sleep and use the bathroom and nothing was broken or musty and there was a coffee maker and iron, I was grateful to a fault. The restaurant next door was basic but welcoming in atmosphere and I felt charitable with it too, and with all such establishments, ordinary but scrubbed and small-town generous. Perhaps they were grateful also, for me, a guest from Manitoba.

I gave myself time the next morning to enjoy my eggs, hash browns, and toast, prolonging my breakfast as if the day would be momentous. I read during a slow second cup of coffee. I'd brought along Anne Fadiman's *The Spirit Catches You and You Fall Down,* a true story about the clash of the Hmong and American cultures in California. I liked it because it was interesting and well-written but so far removed from my current life that I could slip into another world without it following me into mine.

Mid-morning I set out, dreamy and full of anticipation, taking a roundabout route to the house instead of driving through Tilia. As I neared the old place, my underarms twinged, instantly damp with perspiration. A bright day, this day, not overly warm but beaming with encouragement, and though I loved wind as a child, I'd hoped for calm, and calm it was. The weather was fully amenable. But my body registered trepidation. There in the distance, the Big House, its familiar shape, the siding re-done in blue—*sky blue* I imagined for the name of the colour, though rather more vivid than actual sky.

I hadn't considered carefully enough what I wanted or what I would do when I reached the old place. I needed a long look, but to stop the car on the road and stare or take pictures? Whoever lived there now might think I was casing the joint to rob it, might call some first responder, which Tilia surely had by now, some burly uniformed authority sure to hold me for questioning, if not actual arrest. To drive by slowly might be equally suspicious, but to fly by and churn up dust at normal rural speeds wouldn't do for me either. Then a car descended the Big House lane, turned toward town, disappeared over the hill. I turned in. I would drive up and knock, in case someone had stayed behind, explain myself, ask if I might stand outside a while and look. No, no, I would say, I don't want to come in. If no one was home—the preferred option—I would remain a few minutes looking about, a perky and just-arrived-here pose at the ready.

I proceeded slowly up the lane into a startling sensation of abundance and hospitality, like a glass of cold milk. I stopped the car and got out and the feeling vanished. So here I was, and it was bewildering, me and the house, our relative proportions, the building smaller, me taller, though I hadn't grown since high school. An alien air between us. The Big House was an utter disappointment. Not because of how it looked, for it looked better and newer than ever, but because it gave me absolutely nothing. I'd lived in that sprawling edifice for eighteen years, grew up in it, and that could be a lie for all the recognition that passed between us.

I stepped forward to knock. Something was missing. The lean-to entrance, that bit of a granary or shed we'd hauled up to the house and attached to it to provide a transition from outside to the kitchen. That intense, short fear to overcome when very young, that unavoidable, windowless passage, daylight to kitchen light, but in between, the cloying odour of dirt, sour milk, manure. It had been hung with a lightbulb but I could never spare the time to find the switch and turn it on. I ran through instead. When Lorena told me years later that she'd been frightened by that entrance passage too, I felt for a moment that she and I were as close as a button sewn tighter.

No answer at the door. I returned to stand beside the car. I examined my childhood home in all directions. Eighteen years living there was no thin slice. I waited, wide open again for nostalgia, for the moment's significance, something sweeping or poignant, whatever might—ought to!—come along. Eighteen years, I told myself; I lived here eighteen years.

My giving over was entirely useless. I was doing the work, the yielding; the house did nothing. It refused to mirror, to exude *I remember you, too.* It was impervious, the blue siding not a taunt as much as a grin in another direction, like primping for the current owner's return.

The house appeared in good repair, the structure stabilized, perhaps, cedar planters at aesthetically strategic places near the door and kitchen windows. I visualized them filled with petunias. The window casings and doors were white. Yes, it was pretty, this white and blue Crayola house with its child-like freshness, though there were no signs of children and the froth of white at the windows seemed elegant rather than whimsical. The barn was gone but newer blue outbuildings clustered at a distance. A shed and a garage. Yes, it was all quite pretty and tidy. No machines parked anywhere. Obviously they weren't bothering to farm.

I wondered about the untilled area east of the house, half an acre or so, which we'd called The Field as opposed to The Pasture or The Crops. Butted by the house on one side, it was bordered on the other by a clump of trees growing out of a sharp dip in the land. As a child, I imagined a giant scooping out a hole and throwing tree seeds into it. We mowed The Field occasionally, but the ground wasn't tilled and so it sprouted wildflowers in abundance. Crocuses in spring, buffalo beans later. One spring day, we converged on that field because of some enthusiasm of my mother's regarding Easter. Probably for the flowers, the crocuses unusually abundant that year. We scurried about, eyes on the ground, and cried out to one another at every sighting of a fresh mauve clump, as if they were eggs or newborn chicks. I remember squatting to count the flowers in a cluster and Dad was beside me, indulging my interest by counting along. Uncle Must on the hunt with us, too, but his eyes must have been everywhere but downward for Dad suddenly called to him in German, *Bruder, schau mal runter, die Blumen!* Brother, look down at the flowers!

Did Dad want Uncle Must to see them, or was it a warning about his large feet and slashing tread?

Mom was nearby, bending next to Darrell. Brother's always looking at something different than we are, she muttered.

The field frolic finished, we'd returned to the house, where Mom treated us to hot cocoa. Uncle Must complained, to no one in particular, You'd better go out in the evening again. Then you'll see them closed. Folded together for the night.

Now I wished the car that drove away—a black car, like mine—would come over the hill and up the lane. I needed a witness for the words *I used to live here. Yeah, I lived here, eighteen years,* someone to watch me throw my arms north, south, east, west in symbolic embrace. But maybe she (I assumed a she, because that's how we'd had it, the woman of the house at home) went off to Calgary to shop. For new accessories, perhaps, or curtains for a summer makeover. I dug my phone out of my purse and called Jim.

I'm on the old yard, I said.

How does it feel? His voice was hearty; he was trying to be affirming.

I can't drum anything up.

He laughed. Then he said he was fine, no need to worry, and I said I wasn't worried and I was fine as well, he needn't worry either.

He asked me if I was finding my dad, Darrell, Uncle Must.

We'd been married for decades, we were long-time lovers, but there was something too intimate about the question. I'd never put it that blatantly, had I? Jim's unwitting perception of my need was terrible and I paused, then decided he didn't mean anything underhanded. They stayed with you, I said. And please don't say it.

Say what?

What you were going to say.

You mean, don't take yourself too seriously?

Exactly.

You wrestled it out of me.

Jeepers, Jim.

Can I make it better by saying I've got our holiday picked out and paid for?

Not unless you tell me what it is. I hate surprises, as you know.

A cruise to Alaska. For June. A finally-retired celebration.

I don't know what I'll do with you, retired and underfoot. We'll have to rent two apartments so we're separated during the day.

We'll have seven days on the high seas to discuss it. Well, not the high seas exactly. The Passage. Are you pleased?

I told him I was, really, and we said our goodbyes and *loves yous* and ended the call.

I *was* definitely pleased. An Alaskan cruise, something hoity-toity to hold in front of this refurbished, fixed-up, pretentious old house. And true as well, that none of my dead were here. Uncle's house at the end of the lane had vanished. No caragana hedge either. No scar on the land to mark where he and Miss Miller had lived. No show of ghosts.

· I turned the car in a wide arc and drove down the lane. I went left, drove to the mile marker, turned left again. I drove the whole square. I drove it three times, passing the blue Big House, looking but not desirous of turning in again. I quailed a little, though, recalling the sensation of the lane's slight rise, its spirit of goodwill.

I drove into town and parked at Country Eats Restaurant where a placard in the window announced home cooking. The place was full, locals in a buzz of jolly greetings and conversation. I was ignored, except for perfunctory exchanges involving my order. I picked the special—ham and perogies swaddled in thick cream gravy, and lemon pie for dessert— and it was delicious.

I decided it wasn't fair—not to me or the house—to strain for re-connection. I wasn't sorry I'd come, but I didn't mind admitting the letdown I felt, that the house betrayed no repercussions on account of my family's occupation. I'd read something to that effect once, in a novel. A book by Richard Ford, I think it was. The narrator of the book was a realtor and knew from long experience that places refused to confer on past inhabitants the honour or dishonour of what they'd shared. Repercussions tracked elsewhere.

31.

Homeward, downward, from Alberta's foothills to the flats of the former seabed where Winnipeg sprawls, and once again I found myself in the meditative state of long distance driving. I chose a cross-country route from Alberta into Saskatchewan instead of the Trans-Canada this time. I would stay the night in Regina, rejoin Highway 1 there. For some hours eastward, I mulled over my infertility. Another facet, once, of my shame. Not a sorrow now, as much as a fact to observe like the landscape. Planning, trying, hoping, nothing. Knowledge and acceptance. The task of acceptance a slog until the body's unstoppable chronology came to our aid and it was too late for children anyway. A pull to the story like hand over hand up a rope. If one had the stomach to write it as a book, it would be a tearjerker, every chapter opening with hope and ending with an obstacle, a goad to keep the reader turning pages to its conclusion. Which would have to be happy, right? Some happy-ending children, that is, adopted or cooked up in a test tube, or something bigger, more sacrificial perhaps, like travelling into Kazakhstan or some such country to an orphanage where children were housed but never held or nuzzled. Stroking their tiny backs to reach the hungry bones and soul beneath their skin. Babying them properly into a semblance of humanity.

But mine was not a plot-driven narrative, this fact of infertility with its symptoms and endless rebounding, not a broad line between departure and arrival. It was more like the scattered small stations and hamlets around me on this road trip, each a story of its own on the map of my mind and existing simultaneously. A territory, not a line. The hamlet of this confession, for example: while Jim and I loved our nieces and nephews, and spent a great deal of time with Roger and Lorena's Jeffrey and Marcie, I didn't miss them when they weren't in front of me. Though I was astonished by them often enough when they *were*. Especially when they were small. Jeffrey's *You've made it very sad* when I pulled a weed in the garden, a long root for him to examine. Marcie's insistence on using only red playdough because, she said, red smelled like her favourite animals. The creatures she formed were lambs and horses. Not dogs or cats or anything else. Lambs and horses.

How did children come up with their ideas, their obsessions?

And my awe of mothers. Lorena and Roger back from a quick getaway to Las Vegas, Jim and I successfully tending their two, and Marcie reposed in her mother's lap as if restored while I recited what they'd done and how good the children had been, though I left out my weariness and the minor challenges we'd had. Mother and daughter like matching fabric swatches and Jeffrey on the floor nearby, bent over a toy they brought him, pretending no interest in the conversation but listening, I could tell, Lorena saying, Oh my precious girl, and squeezing Marcie every time I mentioned her name and, Oh my precious boy, whenever I mentioned his. Lorena sounded tired but an ugly pain that felt like envy had possessed me then, though it wasn't envy as much as greed, for the inescapable way my sister was bound to those little ones. Burdened by them. They were like a potion she'd swallowed that changed her forever and I wanted to be drunk with it and changed as well.

Maybe I would have been a lousy mother. Jim would have been the song-singing father and I would have been the story-reading mom; yes, I would have been excellent at that. I loved the physicality of reading to Marcie and Jeffrey when they were small, their selves tucked under my arms as if completely gathered in, nothing of them anywhere else. And the sound of Jeffrey's *Auntie Cat-in* when he ran to me with books. The scent of their post-bath hair, their cheeks like wet clay, their superhero and Winnie-the-Pooh pajamas. My own voice liquid honey, the stories soaking into them. And the priestess role; yes, that too. Conductress of small ceremonies of worship and respect, the over-and-over-again habits of what was vital and important. Like a Jewish matriarch shawled in lace, lighting candles for the Sabbath. The children in my fantasy rituals were curious and attentive, utterly innocent, empty slates upon which I chalked up their daily goodness. They never had tantrums in stores or refused to eat what I'd cooked for them. I knew these imaginings were unrealistic but since they were imaginary, I'd amused myself with them.

Joy, sorrow, questions, and jokes: towns along the way. Did Jim and I need lessons on what to do? Taking over-population rather seriously, weren't we? Women, older women in particular, annoyed by and apprehensive of the label *professional woman*. The words like a plank on their lips. Roundabout queries and hints. My own mother, in a tender attempt that seemed a jab, Are you submitting, Catherine, to, to … Not saying his name, as if *that* was beyond the pale of acceptable intrusion, and I'd flared back, To God? To Jim? So angry that time, I'd shouted and wept, but Mom figured I'd cried on account of my cruel misunderstanding of the question. Another time my mother was wistful: Will you be having children, Catherine dear? And when I finally told her I wouldn't, she dug about for the doctor's exact words and whose fault it might be, a detail Jim and I had decided unanimously was nobody's business but our own and which, to my knowledge, neither of us had ever divulged.

And roundabout inquisition to determine, was this *our* choice or a suffering imposed upon us? As if we were a choose-your-own-adventure story with two possible paths and if readers knew how to plot it, the appropriate judgment or consolation would follow. And, oh lands, the assumptions! About us being undersexed or inadequate *in that department*, our marriage like a supermarket that obviously couldn't keep its shelves fully stocked. I always felt we coupled more, in fact, than fertile pairs, especially in the opening, eager years when we were trying, when we were sure it was just the odds we had to beat, sure we could accomplish it by multiplying our efforts. How lovely, late-thirties, to give up, stop the heroics, enjoy the sex again. Though I never slept with Jim, even then, without the tiniest wish it would give us a child, and the tiniest fright afterward that it might have produced one. A pregnancy would have been an upheaval.

So much advice. The infertility anecdotes of others. Pressure to adopt. (Then, ran the tale, we'd be sure to conceive.) Vitamins, therapies, positions, snake oil remedies we scoffed at but sometimes secretly tried. The twinkling good humour of Jim's mother an exception, asking no questions but telling me she didn't mind, really she didn't. She said she had more than enough grandchildren already. This memory like a railway station stop with potted red and white geraniums on its platform.

Our friends generally spared us the triumphant stories of their offspring as if afraid to remind us of our lack of the same or make us jealous. They poured out their troubles instead: childhood illnesses, bullying, adolescent piercings, meetings with principals, not leaving home when it was high time to go. Was it sympathy they wanted? Or some inverted comfort on display, as if to say that every situation had its compensations and being saved from what they endured with their children was our reward for what we'd suffered.

Over the border into Saskatchewan, I rounded a curve that brought me to the top of a rise and before me, an endless vista of budding green, bashful tufts of trees, the highway through it straight and like a welt, the glint of roofs of houses and barns. The sun was partially blocked by a large, low cloud, casting half the scene in shadow while the other half shone. If prairie artist William Kurelek were alive and travelling with me, with his canvases and paints, he would know exactly how to render this immense and generous world, its deeper concerns snugged into ditches at the corners and almost invisible. And then I was down the hill and crossing the view, remembering the most abiding conundrum of our childlessness, that the very notion of memory required offspring. Didn't it? What was the point of re-visiting, keeping, recording, telling, saving, if the nub on the genealogy tree wouldn't open, branch out? Daniel Jute at the archives centre asking in his ponderous voice, For whom are we saving this? The question was rhetorical. For the children, of course. For the unruly, amorphous mass of the next generation, *those who partook of us.*

Who would, we all hoped, be interested someday.

Me! I shouted into the haven of my car. It was *me!* *My* body! Barren belongs to me! There.

My dear, dear Jim. The loyal way he kept our silence about whose body was the problem.

When I neared Regina, when I felt I was no longer losing elevation but would, tomorrow, be sliding home on the level, I realized again what I'd realized before but kept forgetting or hesitated to trust: children—what one sent downstream, that is—weren't the point. Not the main one at least. There were always people to love, to funnel stories to.

The point was love. Lateral. In the moment. Ephemeral, too. It could never be adequately described or sung or archived. Had to be—constantly—renewed, given, received. Composed into another song. I slowed to slightly less than the speed limit and savoured the timeworn matter of love. Like a bronze saint's toe kissed over and over again and worn to a sheen. Which is not to say I found it entirely easy to cast off my feeling that the profession I practiced for decades was lesser than it would have been if I'd had children who could be proud of my accomplishments. But, whatever.

I neared Regina, began to look for a hotel. It occurred to me, as if new, that Uncle Must never had children either. He bore his traumatized mother inside him. And now, in some crazy, unintended way, I cradled him and his mother Elizabeth and my brother Darrell, too.

32.

Two messages waited on the land-line answering machine when
I got home from my trip. One was from Sharon Miller, who said
she was moving to Ontario to live near Ricky; it came up suddenly and she couldn't explain, but she wanted to see me again.
The other was a call from a hysterical Lucy Benham saying Daniel
Jute collapsed at work and was dead. She tried connecting earlier,
she bawled, but obviously I'd turned off my cell.

I called Lucy, who was quieter now though tremulous still.
She'd *been* there, she said, how impossible was that? She'd just
gone in to look something up. She'd witnessed it. A massive heart
attack. A man from security who knew CPR had worked on him
and then the ambulance people took over but Jute was gone, Lucy
was sure of it the entire time they tried to revive him. Everyone
was upset. He'd seemed healthy, except that the signs were coming back to them now, everyone recalling he'd been a heart attack

waiting to happen. The wheezing, the days taken off, the many medical appointments.

Lucy said she would keep me posted about the funeral; she wanted me and our other archival friends to be with her at the church. She wanted us to go for drinks afterward because Daniel's wife, Sybil, was possessive and probably wouldn't let us in on the family mourning. We would hold a wake of our own.

Catherine, she said, it was just terrible, the blue of his face. And—oh God, I almost hate to say this—he was wearing a pale blue tie. I mean we loosened it. But, I don't know, it just unnerved me, that double blue.

When I returned Sharon Miller's call, I was informed that she was leaving the next day and if I wanted to see her, it would have to be today. The sooner the better, in fact.

It's *you* who asked to see me, I said.

Oh, yes, yes, yes, well, sorry to bother you but could you come right now?

I said I would.

There were no boxes in sight at her apartment, nothing to indicate she was about to vacate. It's all arranged, all arranged, Sharon said, as if reading my mind. Someone's looking after it. But she flicked her eyes warily over her possessions as if caught by them, as if dismayed to see them strewn about. The scrutiny narrowed, turned on me. She didn't invite me to sit or offer me a cola; she'd summoned me, she said, to add a tiny point about my uncle's death.

We'd spoken of his death briefly on the previous visit, allusions to facts I knew: a lake outside the town, his shabby canoe, his enjoyment of the water. Though he shouldn't have been out there alone, not at his age. We'd agreed, however, that he was one of those people who decided for themselves.

Now she told me I was a good-living person and so she wanted to be honest: he came to her place the evening before that trip of hers to Winnipeg.

To give you money? I interrupted. I was tired and distrustful.

No, Sharon said, not rising to the bait. To see if I needed anything. And to leave me a sermon.

A sermon?

One of his single-sentence preaches.

I expected her to continue but she didn't and in the silence I heard voices, faintly. A radio or television on in the bedroom? So what was the sermon? I finally asked.

From the Sermon on the Mount, I guess, which I figured out later because he'd written it down and left it on the chair by the door. *Blessed are the meek, for they shall inherit the earth.* It made no sense and I didn't want to ask, so I didn't. I was frustrated with him, to be honest. I had no time for it. I still don't get what it means. Do you?

Well—

So, I guess I wasn't in the best of moods and I told him to quit acting so high and mighty. Holy-like. I told him that if he figured he was Jesus or something that he should—Well, not that I know that much about the Bible, but I've heard of the miracles and I know a few of the stories—I guess I told him he should get out there and walk on water already.

You guess you told him to walk on water?

Well, not *I guess.* I mean, *I did.* I didn't say it in a mad tone or anything. I was sort of joking, sort of serious, but it just came to me because I could see Gilly Lake from my window.

So—

So, I felt awful! When he was missing, I mean, and it was *that* kind of accident. Death by water. First thing I thought was that he'd done what I said.

I couldn't reply.

He was old, Sharon went on, and not so steady anymore. But still walking, you know. Crazy to be canoeing alone. In that tippy old thing. He was probably exhausted just getting it off his old truck. But—

Probably, I said.

I mentioned this to the RCMP, she said. But I wanted to clear the air. With you.

Was there air to clear?

Sharon hesitated then said, quite decisively, No.

It's alright then. He did what he'd decided to do. You wouldn't have talked him into anything, or talked him out of it either.

I tell myself that, too.

Something uncertain rumbled between us, as if the room had grown sullen, neither of us speaking, until Miss Miller clapped her hands—remembering something!—and dug into the large pocket of her flowery blouse, the same blouse she'd worn the last time we met. I still have it, she said. I came across it. I know you probably don't think I've organized anything, but I have. I found it.

It was a sheet from one of those smaller letter writing tablets, roses at the top. She held it up, and sure enough, in his hand, *Blessed are the meek, for they shall inherit the earth.* He'd written it the long way across the lines in the middle of the page.

Here, she said, folding it. You can have it. It just seemed kind of nice, you know. I mean, to have it afterward. My Saint George. So I kept it. Even though I don't get *meek.* Do you?

Humble, I'm thinking, I said. Maybe humble and unashamed.

Here. Sharon thrust the page at me.

That's alright.

No, really, I want you to have it. There's something written on the back. German, I think. So take it!

I accepted the paper and moved to leave. I guess I won't see you again, I said, if you're moving to Ontario.

It's been a treat, she said. Who'd have thought, meeting up this many years after Tilia?

Since this is the end of it, is there anything else you need to report? I felt myself stuttering but I lurched on. Regarding me, my brother, my uncle … your Saint George?

I think that's all.

I reached for the door handle and then I remembered that Daniel Jute was dead and that my stomach was hurting on that account, because you never know when someone you've been linked to one way or the other will depart your life forever. I lifted my hands, tentative, and Sharon caught my intention. Her eyes flared and she entered and reciprocated my hug at once.

On the other side of that page with its beatitude, the beginning of a letter to my father. The writing unmistakably Uncle Must's, though wobbly with age. Had he started again on another page? In those years, he usually phoned.

My dear brother Jake.

Just that salutation. Evidence of their long, unbreakable bond.

I stuck the paper in my pocket. It seemed a final hello and goodbye. If my uncle were here, I thought, I would hug him like I hugged his Sharon Miller, each of them as dogged as the other. Calm him like my father did. If he would let me, that is. Which he wouldn't. Hush now, hush, I'd say. Let go the weight of the load you bore!

33.

We were back from our cruise to Alaska. Jim went to school to empty his office. I did laundry, carried our emptied suitcases to the storage locker. I would stock up on groceries, visit Mom. I was pleasantly off-balance between Away and Back Home, weary from our Vancouver flight, basking still in all we'd seen, the wild coastline, thin lines of waterfall howling down rocky mountainsides, land to be seen but not infringed upon. Light dancing continuously on the ribs of the sea, that shocking, unearthly green, speckled with ice. The days long, for we were nearly at summer equinox, and the sunsets stunning. Whales that rose for us. Every evening on deck to observe the sun depart, scenes of black and white and shades of subtle blue, sharp and truthful, as if we'd stepped into an Ansel Adams photograph, the brooding mountains wrapped in trees, and higher, snow on their flanks, where the sun—a glowing apricot—sank into the V of two faraway peaks.

I had some time before my mother and the groceries, though. I checked my Inbox. Lucy had forwarded Daniel Jute's latest— last!—post, discussing the role of the early female scribes. I clicked a link and read. Diemut. Also Diemud, Diemudis, or Diemoth. Twelfth-century nun, attached to the Abbey of Wessobrunn. Professional scribe. *Learned and pious. Elusive.* Her name meaning humility.

Meek, I thought.

A period of probation in the nunnery, this Diemut, then permission to live as a recluse. Her cell attached to the church, a small window between them to hear the services. An outside window too, I could only hope as I read, for the sake of the woman. Some view of street and sky.

Diemut had copied, in *a most beautiful and legible hand,* forty-five volumes. At least two volumes of the Bible. Missals and patristic texts. Never signing her name. Doing what she loved. Bent over. I imagined her weary by every day's end but thrilled that words took shape and context with every additional stroke. At night, dreaming the texts. Believing, as other women religious did, that the source of our troubles is the sin of forgetting.

I wanted this scribe to possess some vellum of her own, some sheet spoiled for manuscript use upon which she recorded reflections that were personal, besides the letters she wrote Herluka, her fellow recluse at a neighbouring monastery, letters later destroyed by the Swedes in the Thirty Years' War. To set down the priest's breath perhaps, sliding her the Eucharist, holy that day, or foul. To complain a little of chilblains, to describe—precisely—their itch. To set down her own history, her struggles with herself and others.

I finished the article. I had time for a walk. Such a wonderful city, this, and so good to be home. North along Fort, west along Broadway, boulevard elms perched like bouquets in vases down its length. Clearly introverts, those anchorites, those women scribes.

All That Belongs

Called to be special. North along Garry. Office buildings in blue or brown glass, the sky sunk into their panels, buildings and clouds co-mingled to dwarf Holy Trinity Anglican and St. Mary's Cathedral. Murals of Winnipeg's past. I walked and walked and felt my legs, the sensation of limbs that move and are well, and I was lost in Diemut, diligent woman copyist of forty-five volumes. I ducked into the back alley just ahead of Portage, feeling mischievous, as if I'd given my hermitage the slip. The alley was constricted and shadowed. Garbage, bricks, fire escape staircases pressing close, my beloved city medieval and grey. I thought I smelled horses. Gardenias too. Living alone in a cell was one kind of happiness, leaving it, another. I tried to meet the eyes of everyone I passed, smiled if I succeeded. I perceived the scent of the moon, the colour of air, the sound of cobblestones. Wit and courage filling me up.

I reversed then, headed home, entered the apartment refreshed for the rest of the day. What was this stage but a recognition of all I once knew and all that I didn't? An embrace that released. Aliveness to all that belongs. Diemut still pressed on my brain and it seemed I'd returned to my chamber and crept into bed, then gotten up again and lit a smelly tallow candle, readied my ink and quill, remembered where I'd been. And been before that. Sweet, valiant accounts of those I'd loved or endured for ages and ages. Of children I'd never been given. Of what I'd lost, of what I'd managed to preserve.

Notes & Acknowledgements:

Some of my favourite people are archivists, but this is a novel: its characters—archivists or otherwise—as well as its small town settings and institutions such as archival centre and seniors' home, are fictional. The event discovered in the family's past was drawn from news items I spotted in a Mennonite periodical while doing unrelated research.

My warmest thanks to the Turnstone team for all you've done for this book; to Sarah Klassen and Al Doerksen for reading and responding to an early draft; to Agatha Fast for letting us use her painting on the cover; to the Canada Council for the Arts for financial support; to my writing community and friends across the country, especially in Manitoba, and now B.C., for your companionship; and, as always, to Helmut and our family for your constancy and love.